LYNN VROMAN

I0687415

FRACTURED ENERGY

BOOK 3 OF THE ENERGY SERIES

Untold
Press

⊢RACTURED ENERGY

Published by Untold Press LLC
114 NE Estia Lane
Port St Lucie, FL 34983

ISBN: 978-0692525838

PRODUCED IN THE UNITED STATES OF AMERICA

10 9 8 7 6 5 4 3 2 1

DEDICATION

Victoria, Katherine, Olivia, and Rhys,
always everything is for you.

ACKNOWLEDGMENTS

Thanks so much to Jen and Sean. You both truly are extraordinary people. I really am so fortunate to be part of the Untold team. I'd also like to thank my awesome friends, Angela McPherson and Jadah McCoy. You both inspire and encourage me every day. Thanks for the late-night conversations, the laughter, and support. I'm so lucky to have you!

To my family, Steve, Victoria, Katherine, Olivia, Rhys, Kody, and Mac. I love you all so very much, and thanks for putting up with me while I lock myself inside my writing den.

Of course, I couldn't have done any of this without my readers. Thank you for continuing to follow Lena and Tarek's story. I hope you love them as much as I do.

CHAPTER 1

LENA

Hunting

They thought hiding in plain sight a brilliant idea. Set up camp in large cities where thousands of unassuming witnesses kept them safe from open attacks. Perfect, right? Surely, the rogue army wouldn't think to involve innocent people.

Their first mistake.

No matter how big the city or how many people saw us, we had no problem killing Exemplians.

Why?

We had Winston, the mind-scrubbing champion.

Cheveyo, Earth's Warden, believed this was the last nest. We hoped the Exemplian pricks would give up after tonight and move on to another world, another world my small army would follow them to.

But this last trip to Earth... I wanted to make sure they remembered me. I looked toward the sky before opening the café door and turning off my contego suit so the glow wouldn't show through my sweatshirt. Exemplian satellites no doubt pointed in my direction. Whatever. Wouldn't want them to miss the show, anyway.

I tugged my hood lower to cover more of my face and walked in. After stomping snow from my boots, I trudged between tables, dodging internet addicts hunched over their computers. For show, really. The three Guides, a middle-aged man, woman, and a muscle head, sitting by the window knew what I was as soon as the tinkling bell announced my presence, probably before then.

I felt them, too. Their static crinkled in my head so loud, I had to grit my teeth and force myself to walk to the counter. From the mirrored wall behind the clerk, I watched them scrutinizing me over their TracFones and *café au laits*.

"*Puis-je vous aider*?" The clerk snapped his fingers in my face and asked a second time when I ignored him to keep staring in the mirror.

"Oh, um…*café noir, s'il vous plait.*"

"*Oui.*"

With any luck, the barista wouldn't ask me anything else. Winston only gave me the "Black coffee, please" line to memorize. While waiting for my order, I pretended to admire the pastries in the glass encasement under the counter.

We'd been tracking them in Quebec for the better part of two months. These nesters were craftier, moving from spot to spot, but still easy to find. That it took us under a couple months to get their schedules down made the Exemplian authority look sloppy.

When the guy handed over the coffee, I gave him a coin. He shook his head, saying a few more things I didn't understand. I shrugged, getting the gist when he wagged the money in my face, speaking much slower. Funny. No matter how drawn out his words were, I wouldn't get it.

I handed him a couple more coins then turned from the register, giving the Guide trio a nervous glance. The idiots were already on their phones–more than likely letting their Protectors know they were on the move–and collecting their stuff to follow. Exemplians thought anyone not born on their world a moron. More than likely, they probably figured I was some clueless recycled Guide, living another life, right here in freezing-as-fuck Quebec.

Their second mistake.

The trio had followed me all morning until I gave them the slip fifteen minutes ago. How fortunate were they that I happened to waltz into the very café they were in?

Seriously, total dumbasses.

My heart hurt. Dumbass. Every time I even thought about the word, Wilma's face flashed in my mind. Her little pet name for me when I pissed her off. God, I missed her.

I walked down the busy street at a decent clip, brushing tears away. This wasn't the time. *Now*, I'd make every single person who followed me pay a little more for her death.

Make them pay over and over...

I turned the corner, off Rue Saint-Jean, away from the crowd shopping for Christmas. Slush soaked through my boots, numbing my toes. The late evening drizzle infiltrated my thick hoodie, too, drenching me from hair to skin. I ignored it, used to physical discomfort, and stopped to take a few sips of my steaming drink, giving the Guides a chance to catch up. *Gross.* The rest of the coffee landed in a snowbank. Still hated it.

When the fuzz returned, I got moving. Cheery sounds of shoppers and holiday music wafted after me as I strode farther, careful not to go too fast, lest they lose me again.

The streetlamps broken by yours truly a few hours before helped keep them confused, giving me the edge I'd need. Cell phone lights glowed behind me, though not putting much of a dent in the black. Unfortunately, complete darkness didn't hide the fuzz getting stronger in my head, something I had grown to hate yet tolerate. Hopefully their Protectors were close so we could end this soon.

Arrogance happened to be the main weakness all Synod Exemplians had. No matter how many nests we'd destroyed, every single idiot we encountered believed they were smart enough to take us on—once they figured out who we were.

That would be their third mistake.

Exemplians were a quick study, always predictable. After a while, their stupidity bore me. But killing them never got old. Ever.

I stumbled when I turned around, making sure they noticed. Their chins lifted, and they were close enough for me to see smiles on their faces. I loved this part. When they believed their nervous prey finally figured out people stalked her.

Loved it.

I moved faster toward the one unbroken streetlight in front of an alley crammed with industrial-sized garbage cans. The smell coming from the frozen trash was way more pleasant than the fuzz clogging my head. I pretended to talk on my phone, adding a lot of scared flavor to my voice. Stupid Guides ate it up, my fear giving them the courage to come closer.

As soon as they were a few feet in front of me, I slid back my hood and gave them a smile of my own.

"Oh, no." One sputtered that a few times, stopping while the two others, though not smiling anymore, kept coming at me.

I frowned, tapping my thigh. "Aww, not happy to see me?"

The biggest Guide, a guy who could've been a Protector, came closer, signaling the other two to stay put. "We knew who we followed."

I cracked my knuckles. Definitely my favorite part. "Really?" I nodded to his buddies. "'Cause those two seem kinda surprised."

He took one small step forward. "Well, I'm not." He held up his phone. "And we'll have a surprise in a minute."

"A minute?" I pushed off the lamppost. "Plenty of time."

Before he could get another stupid threat through his thin lips, I rushed to palm him under his nose. Blood spurted everywhere as he whined and doubled over. I clapped him over his ears and slammed an elbow in the middle of his back.

I didn't wait around to see if he got up and chased the other two, who ran down the dark street screaming their fool heads off.

"Now!" I yelled into the garbage alley, not slowing down, already close enough to the cowards to sweep out the legs of one. Winston came charging behind, freezing the other with a wave of his hand.

Using a move I picked up during training, I cupped my guy's chin with one hand and palmed his forehead with the other, torqueing his neck enough for him to scream. His agony carried far enough to cause the distant footsteps down the street to move faster. Three Protectors, two women and a guy, raced in our direction, loud and sloppy. I turned to Winston shaking my head, not moving. He shrugged, keeping his Guide frozen against the side of a brick building.

Another mistake we'd depend on, adding it to a long list.

Farren, Oren, and Erin left the shadows to meet the Protectors coming full-throttle in our direction. They didn't have to do much, the Exemplian Protectors backing off as soon as the trio came into view. What these three did on Empyrean must've carried over the rumor waves because the three assholes turned at least two shades lighter.

Farren moved to stand beside me, deceptively calm. He nudged me before feigning a motion to go after one of the Protectors. The woman actually flinched. "Well, I'll be damned." He crossed his arms, chuckling. "All right, raise your hand if you're first-cycled Protectors."

When they all hesitated, glancing at one another and their Guides, Oren started to swear. Vulgar swearing. He'd have made Wilma proud.

Farren walked over to clap him on the shoulder. "Calm down, brother. It isn't like we're into killing babies. These people aren't innocent."

Oren dragged a hand through all that pretty hair. "Now they're sacrificing new energies? It'll be like slaughtering lambs." *Always the crusader for the so-called innocent, something I figured out when we met while fighting together on Empyrean, when he wanted to kill me. But Oren wouldn't get his way tonight. No mercy. None...unless they wanted to give us some info. At least one always tried when we'd trap a nest. Few ever had anything useful enough to keep them living.*

"They killed, Oren. Don't forget it, no matter how young they are." I wrenched on my Guide's neck a little more.

His screams made the male Protector wince and take a step closer. "Please. Don't hurt him," he said.

Christ, in the faint moonlight he looked no more than sixteen. "*Don't hurt him?* Are you begging?" I kept my hold. He could beg all he wanted.

"Yes. Please, don't."

Were those tears in his eyes?

Still, I wouldn't let it get to me. "How many energies have you collected here?"

The guy took another step, causing Farren to tense. "Far enough." When the Protector stopped to look at him, Farren nodded in my direction. "Answer her."

"Th-three recycled Protectors."

Fractured Energy

I so wanted to pop the Guide's head off like a dandelion. "And of those *th-three*, how many unassuming people begged for their lives?"

He locked gazes with his Guide, his lower lip trembling.

"Answer!"

"Go ahead." The Guide swallowed, his voice calm like a father talking to his toddler. "Answer her, Peter."

Now tears fell. His young face actually had my conscience waking up. "All of them."

"So what makes you think it's gonna work on me?"

Before the boy could answer, the first Guide I knocked down came from behind, snarling like a wounded animal. "Kill them!"

Winston rolled his eyes and lifted his other hand in the raging Guide's direction, flinging him toward the arms of the Protector who pulled her soul-stealer from its holster. She obviously forgot about the little army surrounding her and aimed at me. But the bullet never left her gun. Winston threw the duo against the wall as if they were nothing more than bouncy balls. Not only was he a mind-scrubbing champion, but the strongest Protector in the universe, too. Glad I found him before Exemplar did.

Erin, the deceptive-looking warrior I used to call Soccer Mom, stood next to them, enough of a threat to keep the Protector docile. She snatched the weapon the Protector dropped. "Hey, Lena, another one for the collection."

She tucked it in her waistband, flashing the green-lighted suit we all wore under our clothes. The suits were gifts from Teenesee, Empyrean's Warden. They masked our static, making it harder for Exemplian nests to detect us. We used whatever we had to kill the assholes, whether gifts or weapons we stole from them.

I smirked and stifled the urge to break my Guide's neck. Instead, I bent low so he could hear me. "What's your name?"

He swallowed a few more times, his shaking almost enough to escape my hold. "Denzel."

"Well, Denzel, what would you give to prevent my friends from killing your Protector before I snap your neck?" I twisted to emphasize my question.

"Ah, please…anything, I'd give anything."

Peter staggered forward, the sound of his Guide's agony magnetic.

"Stay back, Pete, or you ain't going to be alive enough to hear the rest of the conversation." Winston, as cool as always, trapped the guy with his words.

These guys were asking to get killed. Not that they needed to ask, but…*damn*.

Winston glanced at me, looking bored, which he probably was. We all knew how this would end; the story hadn't changed since we began hunting all Exemplians a year ago. "Go on, now. Ask your questions so we can go home."

I let go of the Guide's neck to face him, sliding out the soul-stealer we swiped off a Protector in Spain from my hoodie pocket. "All right, you heard the man, time for some questions." I pointed it at his head, not bothering to aim anywhere else on his body. The guy's contego suit glowed at the collar of his fancy winter coat.

Right on cue, a bright blue light zipped down from the sky like a falling star to hover above us.

The pull from Zander in his energy form was a high I'd practiced getting used to. My knees trembled when he came within ten feet of me. A ten-foot radius was a big improvement, something Zander and I spent hours perfecting during training.

I looked up with a wave, trying to play it smooth as sweat beaded across my upper lip. Zander knew not to get too close. I'd melt if he did. "Oh, look, your ride's here."

A gasp reverberated off the brick walls, as if all the Exemplians we cornered inhaled in unison.

Denzel remained calm, covering up his shock expertly. He definitely wasn't first-cycled. "Ask your questions and be done with this."

"Fair enough." I wagged the gun in his face to hide the shaking in my hand. I wanted to kill him, but when he talked...well...that gave him humanity. "How many of you are in Quebec?"

Denzel, even on his knees in the dirty slush, managed to hold his chin up. "There are only the six of us."

I cocked my weapon, the click echoing in the hollow alley. "Liar."

"I'm not." He looked up as Zander floated around his head. "The Synod has given up the search in this dimension."

"So they're moving on, then? To where?" I switched, pointing the soul-stealer from Denzel to Peter. Ah, yes, that calm evaporated from his eyes.

Denzel tamped down the air, his bottom lip trembling. "Please, I do not know, I–"

"Wrong answer." I lifted my weapon to point between Peter's eyes.

"Wait! I don't know, I swear. They...they–Please! He's a child."

"Don't care. Time's up." As I was about to pull the trigger, Denzel came off his knees.

"I have information. *I do*. Don't kill him," Denzel said.

"No, Denzel."

"Shut it, Peter, or I might shoot you for being rude." I clicked the safety on my gun, lowering it, trusting my people had my back if Peter tried to make a move. I walked up to Denzel, whose forehead came to my nose. "You have my attention."

"I have information that may interest...*you*."

"Denzel!" Peter's footfalls shuffled closer, but Farren shadowed me.

"Don't do it, boy." Farren prodded my back so hard he almost pushed me into Denzel. "Hurry up, Lena."

I kept my attention on the Guide, waiting. "Talk. Now."

Denzel's throat bobbed once. Twice. He lifted his trembling chin higher. "Not here. I will share all the information I have if you spare Peter and me. Take us to Arcus; give us asylum."

Ballsy son of a b–

I glanced over Denzel's head to Winston.

He raised a brow. "Your call, Tainted."

These bastards would do anything to stay alive, but...we needed information. If we found him in a lie, we'd kill them both. Quick fix, yet what he said...the information being for me... My curiosity was effectively piqued.

"I'm warning you now." I leaned in, putting the tip of my gun at the edge of his mouth. "If you do anything, *anything*, to screw us over, I'll give you both to the squid."

Fear shined in Denzel's eyes and his shaking grew worse. I didn't blame him. Whatever rumors he might have heard about Arcus's squid population probably wasn't even close to how dangerous they really were. I pulled out a pair of gallium cuffs, another goodie we swiped off a few now-dead Protectors, and slipped them on Denzel's wrists. Farren took out his and did the same to Peter.

I pulled out my remote, which caused Peter to whimper. I ignored him, keeping my eyes on Denzel. "We all have one of these handy-dandy little contraptions." I held the remote right above his nose. "Do one thing that pisses me off—either of you—and you're both instant drooling sloths, got it?"

Denzel nodded so fast he looked like a bobble head. "Y-yes, of course." He tilted his chin toward the rest of his group. "What will you do with them?"

I cocked my head to the side, as if really contemplating that question, while Zander started buzzing around all of our heads like he couldn't wait to do his job. "Tell me something, Peter." I turned to face him, the kid so young I had to clench my fist to avoid reaching out to comfort him. Oren was right. Killing the boy would be like murdering a baby. Thank God, he was the only one too young to be here. "Those recycled Exemplians you all killed, the innocent people who had no clue about anything, did their begging work?"

A tear slipped down Peter's cheek before he said, "No."

"Exactly." I shoved Denzel toward Winston, who also grabbed Peter's elbow. "Take these guys home. I'm gonna go to the states with Farren, meet Zander."

Winston didn't question me. I didn't need to go, seeing as Farren could grab Zander and take him home without my help. But he understood. "See you on the flipside." He yanked our two prisoners into the garbage alley, and a few seconds later, a quick flash of light showed, followed by a swirl of howling wind.

I glanced at Farren, clicking the safety off my gun. "Ready?"

He rolled his shoulders, nodding to Oren and Erin, whose guns were already on their targets, and aimed at his own. "As I'll ever be."

Lynn Vroman

CHAPTER 2

LENA

Oblivion

Our plane descended in pitch black. The pilot's thick French accent came through speakers, asking us to kindly buckle our safety belts. Farren reached over to click mine tight when I didn't bother to break my concentration on the window to obey. I didn't much care one way or the other. Landing in a 747 was safer than portal jumping to find people who wanted us dead. Even if I ended up being an unlucky rare statistic, so what? Cheveyo would get my energy and send it back into the population blissfully ignorant of this life.

Most nights I fantasized about that possibility. Send me to the dirtiest, dankest trailer park; I didn't care. I wanted to get off this ride, forget it ever existed.

Farren grabbed the hand I had on the armrest and squeezed, partly to reassure me, partly to combat his fear of flying–or landing, rather. Who would've thought one of the fiercest people I'd ever met would be afraid of some turbulence.

He hadn't said a word the whole six and a half hour flight. He tried a couple times to start up a conversation before boarding, but I ignored him, not even pretending like I listened to what he had to say. The one time I acknowledged him was when he brought up our goal: closing the lines. Which would require us to hunt in yet another world. I had held up a hand, not bothering to give him my attention. "Not now."

The thought of having to go to another place, seek out the True Warden, kiss his or her ass enough so they didn't kill us and let us in on any new Exemplian nests...no. I wanted to invite in the blankness and let it have its way with me.

When the plane skidded to a stop on the tarmac, we waited another fifteen minutes before the flight attendants gave us the green light to deplane. Farren unstrapped himself and reached overhead to grab our bags. "Let's go, kid."

I stood and stretched my arms and legs, then followed him to the exit. The winter draft coming through the gaps of the jetway was more pleasant in Phoenix than the frigid, bone-chilling cold in Quebec. I actually took the time to enjoy the mild temperature, looking forward to Cheveyo's cave and the nights I planned to stay there without anyone butting in. I'd grown to anticipate a few tokes on that pipe of his over the last year. My mouth even started to water. The Warden had a verbal gift, too: when he spoke, it created the best high imaginable. The combination of his magic and his pipe gave me the perfect prescription to quiet my mind. Another few hours and I'd be too high to think, how I enjoyed my off time lately.

We shuffled out through the exit, no luggage delaying us at the baggage claim. Farren opened the door to the nearest taxi and grumbled our destination to the driver after we piled in. He slouched as the taxi took off, stretching his long legs in the roomy backseat. I didn't waste any energy bitching at him to keep his legs on his own side. That'd accomplish an opening for conversation.

After fifteen minutes he spoke, done with the silent treatment. "He'll be pissed when you're not with me."

Fractured Energy

I shrugged, watching downtown Phoenix race by, my mind completely focused on tonight's planned activities.

Farren was never one who put up with silence, especially when he wanted to talk. With speed I envied, he reached out to pinch the skin on my upper arm.

"Ouch! Christ! What the hell?" I whipped around, rubbing my arm and doing my best to muster up enough anger to scowl at him.

He leaned back and adjusted his big body so he could face me. "I've been pretty accommodating, allowing you to act all crazy sad and broody. Knock it off."

"Well excuse me if I can't bounce back after killing people as fast as you." I moved to return my attention to the window when he held up his fingers. The threat of another pinch was effective in changing my mind.

"We all know that's not true, so don't even try to sing that lie." He rotated his neck, stretching out kinks. "We've been gone two months. Don't you think you've punished Tarek enough?"

Oh, I so wanted to go back to the no-talking game. "I'm not trying to punish anybody."

His voice turned to a whisper, compassion darkening his deep brown eyes. "It's been over a year, Lena. Wilma wouldn't want this."

Tears came, blinding me. I swiped at them, pissed that all it took was a simple reminder. A reminder that she was dead and not somewhere waiting for me. "You don't know anything. Anything! I… It's my fault, Farren. My fault she's dead, and I'm gonna do everything I can to…to…"

He scooted closer and scooped me up, stroking my hair as another floodgate opened. When the black let up to allow emotion, it took forever to seal the cover down again. Seeing Tarek…well, he reminded me I'd put him first–before everything. Before Wilma. I'd never make that mistake again.

After my tears dried up, emptiness thankfully came to the rescue. I went to pull away, but Farren's arms tightened. "Wait, kid." He kissed the top of my head. "I've missed you."

Nothingness always felt good once it reclaimed my mind, but I stayed in his arms. "I'm with you every day."

Scruff on his cheeks scratched my scalp when he shook his head. "No, you aren't."

∞ ∞ ∞

We could have rented some sort of ATV or dirt bike or something for the last leg of the trip to Cheveyo's, but both of us preferred walking. It didn't matter that it took close to an hour to get to the cave. Even though we were still tired from our mission in Quebec, the hike helped ease the weight. Allowed us to stretch our legs without worrying who might be around the next corner ready to kill us. No Exemplian was brave enough to come within five miles of this area. Teenesee had her beauty, which was crippling, but Cheveyo did this thing with minds that would make even the strongest Protector ask for death with one word.

By the time we found the cave, night covered the desert and the mild winter temperatures turned frigid and uncomfortable. No worries, though. As soon as Cheveyo sensed our arrival, he came out to wave us into his warm, inviting sanctuary. "Welcome, both of you."

My body went lax with every word he spoke, and tingling invaded each muscle, satisfying the craving I'd developed over the past year.

I smiled the first genuine smile in a while and patted his back as he hugged me. His hands shoved the tingling in my brain into overdrive. Cheveyo knew I needed what he could give–I'd told him as much at least a hundred times during a night of getting completely wasted off both him and his pipe. "Care if I hang for a few days?"

He pulled away. The same concern shined in his eyes that glared in every other person's who knew me. "You are always welcome here."

I squeezed his shoulder and slinked around his slight body to find Zander sitting at the fire, high and happy. Cheveyo and Farren stayed at the cave entrance, whispering back and forth, talking about stuff I'm sure I wouldn't care about.

Zander glanced up when my shadow rose on the opposite sandstone wall of the fire. "Hey, darlin'."

He always called me that when high, something I secretly loved. The old pet name let me drift back to when life was simpler. "Hey, yourself." I slouched down beside him, grabbing the pipe and lighter from his hands. "You sharing?"

"More the merrier."

Not that I needed his permission, my lips already sucking in the skunky smoke, holding it in my lungs until nature forced me to exhale. I took a few more hits before handing it back to him. Zander wasted no time bringing the bowl to his mouth. The past couple years had been a train wreck on him, too. Probably why I felt better around him. We had pain in common.

I leaned back on my elbows, watching the fire, enjoying the high. "You take the energy back already?"

He huffed in more smoke before answering. On a cough, he said, "Yeah. Holding them in makes my head hurt." Zander handed the pipe back to me.

I accepted his offering, looking forward to when my eyes would slam shut. The buzz always refused to let the nightmares in.

We watched the fire in silence until Farren and Cheveyo came closer. Ginger gave us the disappointed scowl a parent would give when finding their underage kid at a party. Stupid look on him, seeing as how his features made him appear our age. Well, maybe even younger now that I was a few months shy of my twentieth birthday.

Farren planted his hands on his narrow hips, blocking the view of the fire. "I'll be back tomorrow to pick you up. Be ready."

I took another hit. "Don't think so."

Farren squatted in front of me and snatched the pipe, handing it up to Cheveyo. "Tomorrow." He pulled Zander up with him. "And you'll be ready, or I'm dragging you."

"Guess you better get ready to drag, then." I pulled a blanket up to my shoulders, ready for oblivion.

"Always love a challenge. Don't forget it." He pushed Zander toward the exit. "You smell, boy."

Zander laughed, obviously too messed up to care about hygiene, and stumbled out of the cave. Over his shoulder, he said, "Bring some back with you, Lena. We can smoke with the squid."

That wouldn't happen, and Zander knew it. I had strict rules about when I indulged, and he did too, actually. I'm pretty sure he said it to piss off Ginger, which worked brilliantly.

Farren pointed at me, his lips twisting in a sneer. "If I think for a second you're stashing, I'll strip search you before we leave."

I snuggled deeper into the blanket. "That might piss off a couple people back home, don't you think?"

His face reddened and he sputtered a few curses under his breath. He gave Zander another shove, harder this time, causing the smaller guy to stumble and fall. All Zander did was laugh as he tried to crawl back to his feet.

Farren dismissed him to crouch in front of me again. "For the record, I don't like you much right now, not many of us do."

He didn't wait for a reply, not that I had one, and stalked toward the cackling Guide. They turned the corner, and in seconds, the wind kicked up followed by silence.

I wasn't gonna lie, that hurt. Everyone who loved me had taken an emotional beating once or twice in the last year, Tarek being the primary target. But he kept taking it, no matter how hard I hit him. He deserved better. They all did.

Cheveyo watched me from the other side of the fire, smoking. I didn't beg him to start talking, turn on the magic that dulled my brain. He'd take the pain away soon enough.

After one final hit, the Warden slid his pipe into the leather pouch sitting beside him. He tapped his fingers on a knee, giving me his complete attention. "Thank you, for all you've done here."

He didn't turn on the juice. I got nothing from his voice, not even one tingle. "Of course. This is my home, too."

He nodded, still tapping that knee. "Are you worried…about where you may have to go next?"

"No." I pulled the blanket higher, hating that the buzz began to ebb.

Silence wafted between us while he scrutinized me until I fidgeted.

"It is not wise to live with such hate, Lena. It will destroy you, if you let it."

"I don't care." *Give me what I need!*

"Yes, you do, deep down under the pain. I can sense it." He rocked, keeping his intense eyes on me the entire time. "But I will help now."

Ah, there was the escape, flowing over me like rain on a field, flooding me. My eyelids fluttered and my mouth went slack, the power so potent I lost control of my entire body. He gave me more than usual, for which I was grateful. I'd let him know in the morning, when my body was my own again. Through the haze, Cheveyo's voice gave one last punch. "This will be the last meeting between us, my wayward friend. From this time forth, you will face your pain, whether it destroys you or not will be on your shoulders."

I'd be pissed tomorrow. At that moment, the warning filled with brain-numbing elixir gave me more of what I wanted.

Time stood as the tingling erased everything–except the one person I couldn't run away from. He never let me run far.

I love you. Even if you don't want to hear it, I do. When you come home, I'll be here waiting. I'll always wait for you. Always.

Must be midnight. At least, midnight in the Poconos. Tarek always found me then. I slid closer to unconsciousness, hating how his deep voice could make me feel, even under Cheveyo's magic.

My giant would never give up.

Not until I destroyed him.

Again.

CHAPTER 3

TAREK

Wishes

Always. Even if it killed him, he'd wait. Wait until the air left his lungs and refused to return. Longer.

He lay in bed, staring at the dark ceiling, the black sky no match against his eyesight. Perfect senses, another cursed plague that came with being Arcus's Warden. Everything was brighter, smelled more sour or intoxicating, and sounded closer as if the animals lived inside his ears.

Everything.

Yes, Tarek could see better, especially when he chanced a glimpse into Lena's lifeless green eyes. Something he tried not to do often, despite that being near her was like fire and burning flesh and electric currents. Addicting, masochistic pain. She was pain, and after two months without it, his cravings had become more than he could handle.

Wilma's death destroyed Lena's heart, and no amount of words he thrust on her, no amount of promises, would bring it back to life. He had tried, so many times over the past year, whenever she'd let him near her. Nothing ever worked. She'd take what she wanted like a thief and leave again, until she was ready to come back and flay another piece of him, and he'd let her. Because if she was a thief, he was a scavenger. A pathetic scavenger willing to accept scraps.

When the portal opened hours ago, Tarek was more than ready to scavenge again, take whatever she might decide to give. They were prisoners to this Exemplian war. He remained trapped on Arcus, and she, fighting on Earth, risking death. These moments, when she'd finally return, dirty and broken, all he wanted to do was make her whole. Heal a woman who hadn't been the same since the day Wilma was stolen from her. The day she began to lock him out. Slow at first, but then the door slammed and bolted shut on her heart. No entries allowed. Only torture. She loved torture. Loved it more than she loved him.

Only Farren and Zander had dropped into the village, an angry Protector and intoxicated Guide.

She wanted to stay, brother, one more night.

Another piece of him broke off and fell at her feet. He'd give it to her. He'd give her anything.

His body hummed even as he counted the splintered cracks on the ceiling. All that energy, that power, brewing in his chest, and he lay powerless to fix the one person he needed.

Her guilt ate them both. It dug into his brain as if she stabbed him with it, his building power a useless defense. If only…

He raised his hand and closed his eyes. The air sizzled, molten and heavy, around his fingers, but nothing else. No openings. Just the hint of his world seeping into another, a world his body couldn't lift into, no matter how hard he had tried in the past two years. Escape the responsibility. Take Lena far from wars and hate, make her face her demons, destroy them so they'd quit destroying her.

Tarek mended the bleed but kept his hand in the air, fingers splayed. He fantasized a tear, imagined a different history. Then he slept and dreamed about the woman who would forever live in his past, present, and if he were fortunate enough, his future.

CHAPTER 4

LENA

Unexpected Surprises

Drowning dreams sucked.

They always had a way of reminding me to live, even when I swore I didn't want to. Fight or flight came knocking, and though I tried to deny it entry, the feeling won every time. I guess I should've been happy about that, the still-wanting-to-live thing.

I guess.

Water poured onto my face.

I leapt from my makeshift bed of hides, gasping.

Another bucket of ice-cold water dumped over my head. This time, it sloshed into my nose, burning a path up my nostrils. I coughed and moved closer to the dying fire as if it could save me from another attack. When I finally gathered the wherewithal to crack open my eyes, my brain still fuzzy, I found Farren standing next to my bed, a bucket in his right hand and a smirk on his face.

"What the fu–"

"Oh, you're up. Good." His way too chipper voice didn't fool me at all. He tossed the bucket on the ground, the loud thump against the stone jolting my sensitive ears. "Hope you weren't waiting for me long, but you know, traffic and shit."

Not funny at all.

I pushed up to my knees, ready to give the best of all verbal beat downs. "You mother–"

"Language, kid. Not nice." He stalked over and gripped me by the back of my sweatshirt, dragging me over to the natural waterfall in the far right corner.

I screamed and dug my fingers at the big, freckled fist bunching up my clothes. My feet swung in the air and were unfortunately not close enough to get a good kick to his shin. He gave me a shake that rattled my teeth, effectively stopping my attempts at freedom.

"Don't you dare, Farren!"

He dared. Dared all over the place. Flicking his wrist, he dunked me under the cool spring, not letting go while water splashed on my head, my long, shaggy hair now preventing me from being able to breathe.

When I gagged, he pulled me out–for a second. "Here, let me help." He pushed strands away from my face before heaving me back under the water, my curses echoing through the hollow cave. Farren yanked me out of the stream, holding me high enough to look him in the eye.

"You sonofab–"

My head met water again.

Gurgling around the gushing water flooding every single orifice, I managed to sputter a couple words. "Stop, goddammnit!"

His voice, all happy and grating, reached over the din of the splashing water. "You say something?"

"Stop!"

"Apologize."

Even dangling there helpless, I had a hard time doing what he wanted. "For what?"

He immersed me deeper into the spray. When he pulled me out, Farren cocked his head to the side, one red eyebrow raised.

Ugh. "I'm sorry, okay?"

He shrugged, dropping me so fast I couldn't get my footing on the slippery stone ground, falling square on my ass. A few seconds later, my bag landed with a thud on my lap. "Get dressed." He scrunched up his nose. "Burn those clothes, and for the love of everything holy, brush your teeth."

I searched the cave, hoping Cheveyo was around to give me one last dose of who-gives-a-shit before I left. When all my scouting did was land on Farren, who drilled me with about as much impatience as I could stand, I crawled up to my feet, clutching my bag to my soaked sweatshirt.

Farren pointed to the farthest dark corner. "Now, kid."

"All right...hold on." I scanned the entire space, willing the Warden to appear so he could say one more word. Just one.

"He's not here." Farren's deep voice boomed in the cave, aggression barely masked with false politeness. "I'm to remind you that you're cut off–cold turkey, no more happy juice."

Panic turned my legs to rubber. Eyes and ears refused to accept both Cheveyo's absence and Farren's words. "Wait, no. I...no." Then I remembered: *this will be the last time I help you.* I held my bag tighter. "No."

"Yup." Farren's voice was loud, unsympathetic. "And you got five minutes before I take you home as is."

"But–"

"Five minutes. The people we brought back are yours to question. The Guide refuses to speak to anyone else."

I shuffled off to the corner, completely pissed about the prospect of having to stay sober and the headache playing racket ball in my skull. "Guess someone should've killed them, then."

Farren's voice chased after me, finding my corner while I stripped. "Is that what you really want?"

I yanked on my shirt, hands unsteady. "No." I whispered my response, but the hissing sounds of it snuck through the cave. Exhaustion–it never left.

Farren's voice softened and his words carried no more bite. "Thought so. Don't forget to brush your teeth."

∞ ∞ ∞

Never would've believed I'd consider Arcus home. It was, though. After two months of being gone, when the portal released us, all that color, the beauty, lightened my mood.

On the outskirts of the village we all helped to rebuild, Farren stopped, grabbing my elbow. I glanced up at him, but his attention was on the people, so many now, living, laughing, working. Sometimes I compared what we'd done here to an animal shelter, a place where we took in strays and the unwanted, giving them a facsimile of belonging and peace. And like an animal shelter, there was no guarantee of living for long. The price we all paid, jumping to Earth to find nests being the objective lately, was a high one.

"Never gets old, kid, what we got here." Farren finally shifted his gaze to me. "Try not to forget you've more life to live, more people to love who love you."

So many things I should have said but couldn't. One thought shoved into my head, forcing its way out of my mouth. "You know the happiest I've ever been? Ever?"

He shook his head once, his expression so intense I had to look away.

I swallowed. "Two summers ago, before Avery came to ruin our lives."

Avery was the Synod bitch who tricked me into going to Empyrean with lies, and then betrayed us during the final battle. The battle that killed Wilma.

Fractured Energy

Tears flooded my eyes. If only I could turn off the part of my brain that urged me to keep feeling, life would be easier. "I...I wish we could go back, have everything we had. Wilma would sti–" My voice skipped, and I had to stop and let the emotion escape before continuing. "She would still be alive. And Tarek? I would still have the fantasy of what-if, at least. The fantasy...so much better than this."

Farren said nothing and reached for my hand, squeezing it before bringing it to his lips for a soft kiss across my knuckles.

When I found the nerve, I lifted my head to catch his sad smile, my hand still secured in his. "I have this hole...right here." I placed my free hand on my heart. "And no matter how hard I try, there's nothing that can fill it. Not Tarek. This place. You. My family. Nothing."

"You will heal, one day. And Wilma...she'd want you to." He gave my hand another squeeze, his warmth racing up my arm. "You and her? The Pairing was a miracle. Someday, you'll learn to cherish it instead of mourn it."

More tears slid down my cheeks. "I don't think I'll ever be...full again."

He tugged on my hand, gently guiding me down the hill to the village. "You will. I got faith in you." We headed toward the worn path leading from the woods to our pseudo town. "Until then, try not to push everyone out." He shrugged. "Of course, there's no way you're getting rid of me. All those *other* people who love you but are tired of your crap might begin to feel differently, though."

Surprised, I laughed. Laughed until my tears dried and the emptiness actually filled a little. Man, I loved him. I'm glad he reminded me of that now and again. "You're a regular Yeats, Ginger. Seriously."

His grin appeared, melting even more of my sorrow. "Whoever that is."

We walked down the path, hand in hand, until reaching the muddy roadway in between buildings. The cabins all looked alike, built under Tarek's supervision, the master shack builder. Farren's nickname for him. Regardless, Tarek did have skills, each hut weather-tight and comfortable enough.

Winston's stood out amongst the rest at the end of the road, his skills with a can of spray paint rivaling any artist I'd ever heard of. He painted Shaina's hometown, Brooklyn, on the outer walls. The people he created walking on the sidewalks were so lifelike I swore they stared at me every time I walked past his place. Now the uncontended strongest Protector alive, Winston proved to be more than a weapon. A real Renaissance guy, he was–if you dug deep, deep under all the attitude. Only Shaina, the love of his life, ever got to see his gooey, soft center.

The holding cell where we kept captured Exemplians sat beyond Winston's place. We all agreed any potential threats should be closest to the man who could convince anyone to behave with one simple look. There was Tarek, but he insisted on staying in his cabin by the river.

About six months ago, I refused to stay with him, living in a cabin of my own.

We were ten feet in front of the "prison" when my blond giant pushed the door open, meeting my startled gaze head on. Still, even with the emotional distance I put between us, the sight of him created an ache in my chest so acute I had trouble not falling to my knees. I loved him more than breathing.

I wished I could stop loving him.

I wished he would stop loving me.

Fractured Energy

"Um…" Farren let go of my hand, walking backward toward the hut he and Belva shared. "I think I'll skip the interrogation, leave it up to you two."

Winston followed Tarek out the door, having to move around him since Tarek was too busy drilling me with those silver eyes.

Farren smiled, obviously his mind already on the beauty in his house waiting for him. "Ah, you three, I guess. I've got some things to catch up on." He wriggled his brows, his face reddening.

Belva, the bonafide Arcus ancient and my best friend, had Ginger wrapped and tucked. I loved how happy they were. Truly.

But their relationship was the last thing on my mind, my attention glued to Tarek. He didn't come over to sweep me in his arms, like before. He stopped doing that when I refused to allow him to get close. Not to say we never got close. We did. When I used him.

And he let me, knowing my intentions.

"Ah, hey." So lame, but my mind went blank. A normally preferred state, but guilt always curled around the blankness Tarek caused.

Disappointment clouded his eyes, and a part of me desperately wanted to erase all the hurt I caused him. But it was such a small part, buried under a mountain of barrenness.

He took a step closer, leaving a few feet between us. Whatever pain brewed under the surface, Tarek always managed to slam a mask of indifference in place. He had to practice it, though. So many times in the past year, we had to hide in our cabins as tropical storms raged through the forest while pitch black stole all natural light. None of us would go near the castle, the hailstorms deadly. This place depended on him not getting emotional, something he managed to control within the last few months. Something

I refused to help with. Forcing him to shut down was another thing to tally on my guilt board.

He nodded, not bothering with superficial niceties. "The guy is ready to sing." He turned away from me, heading back into the hut. Without looking back, he said, "Come on."

I glanced at Winston after Tarek disappeared into the prison. He shrugged, pulling his dreads into a thick ponytail. "You heard the man."

One thing I always appreciated about Winston: he refused to treat me any different. Unlike most people who walked on eggshells whenever I happened into a room, he was still an ass. I actually depended on it, his assumed apathy. Whether it was genuine or not, I needed it.

I waved a hand in front of me. "After you, chief."

He bobbed his head, a song forever playing inside his brain even sans earbuds and iPod. "You feeling all right?"

I must've really looked like hell for him to ask. Probably killed him to do so. "Sure, fine." Not waiting for a reply, I scooted through the doorway.

Winston followed, shutting the door behind him. The light coming into the one-room hut came from the window too small for even someone like Mom to crawl through. No fire lit up the inside, but with the tropical temperatures here, it wasn't necessary. The place could've been a sauna, sweat soaking my clothes after thirty seconds. The purple glow shooting from the sky to the window added an intimidating layer to the atmosphere. Too dark to really see anything, but bright enough to realize exactly where you sat. If I were on the wrong side of my group, sitting in the middle of the room on the dirt floor, I'd have had a hard time not pissing my pants.

I stood in front of the two Exemplians, switching to breathing through my mouth. The smell in the room made my eyes water. Couldn't hold it against them, trapped in here for the better part of two days would make anyone smell like an overflowing garbage can in summer.

Denzel matched my scowl while Peter searched Tarek's and Winston's faces, twitchy and nervous. I felt bad for the kid, what with feeling the need to protect his Guide from a Warden and someone like Winston. But he was smart to be scared, though the two men in the room weren't the real danger–not this time, anyway. If Denzel had nothing important to say, they'd both be dead, a snack for Belva's cephalopod army. That threat wasn't idle. We'd done it to others.

Never one to drag out the inevitable, I got straight to it. "You'd better start talking."

I didn't bother to ask a bunch of obvious questions, either. If the Guide didn't know what I wanted to hear by now, he'd have to deal with the consequences.

Good thing Denzel understood. He opened his mouth– and gave me something I hadn't expected.

Hope.

"It's about your Protector. Her energy, at least. I-I know where she is."

I didn't want my heart to skip, and I didn't appreciate the pain absorbing my desire to rid us of a few more Exemplians. "I know where she is, too." My voice came out airy, almost invisible.

"Yes, but I can tell *where* it is. It... They have not destroyed her."

Willing tears to stay away took every ounce of energy I had left. I wanted to slump to my knees and beg him to speak, prove his words. "Liar." The quiet accusation screamed inside my brain.

"No, I'm not." Sweat drenched his face. "She has become a symbol of sorts, a warning."

A flash image jumped into my head of me ripping out the Guide's throat. I slapped him across the face, hard.

Blood trickled from Denzel's lip as he righted himself to stare at me again. A spark of respect inched its way past my rage when Peter moved to sit in front of his Guide, the boy's shaking difficult to miss.

"You ain't going to save him that way." Winston, with zero effort, yanked the kid off the ground and plunked him near the door. "Now, you sit tight and let the grownups talk."

Please, don't be lying...please. I tried to focus, tried to act as if he hadn't given me that which would end up crushing me if it were a lie. "If that's all you got, this is gonna be a short conversation."

"O-of course." He used his dirty sleeve to catch the blood dripping off his chin. "She–Cassondra–has Wilma's energy on display, every public screen frozen on the prison that traps your Protector's orb."

Tarek moved behind me when I wobbled, leaning his chest against my back so I could stand. The act was subtle; anyone watching would assume he wanted to get closer to Denzel. I knew better. Even when I treated him badly, my giant was there.

Tarek's deep voice filled the room, asking the question I couldn't shove through my lips. "Where, exactly, is Wilma displayed?"

"In Cassondra's old office. The blue light from such a strong Protector shadows the whole room, making it impossible for anyone to sit in there for any period of time." He glanced down at his lap, shaking his head. "It has turned into a shrine. Everyone has witnessed the Protector's energy struggling against its confinement, wanting release." He looked up at me again. "It is a warning to anyone who might indulge the notion of treason."

"Oh my God." I swayed. Tarek's large palm slid to the small of my back, holding me steady. Wilma, trapped and still fighting, was a spectacle for those bastards, a sideshow. I clenched my fists.

No. Way.

"There's more." Denzel pushed up to his knees, as if praying to me. "A-Avery is now in concert with Cassondra, helping her find rogue Exemplians Avery herself helped to hide. They've been done with Earth for months, sending first-cycled Protectors to distract all of you."

I turned to Peter, who huddled by the door, knees drawn to his chest. "They're sacrificing innocents." Man, Oren was gonna be pissed. Raging, actually.

"Y-yes. They have collected so much more from other worlds while you've chased benign threats there."

Tearing my eyes from Peter, I found Denzel again. Even with the slight purple glow, I could see all color had drained from his face completely. I took a step forward, Tarek following. "What else, Denzel? What aren't you saying?"

His restless eyes kept shifting from me to Tarek. "Cassondra has Synod elders convinced they can win...against your people." Still he held back, biting his upper lip as his throat bobbed, all the bravado he displayed earlier gone.

"Denzel?"

He whipped those crazy eyes from Winston to Peter, who cried, before settling back on Tarek and me. "They are being smarter, more strategic, this time. Much more sophisticated than the fiasco on Empyrean."

When he stopped talking–stopped sharing–I yanked him up by the front of his shirt, shaking him until his head flopped like a ragdoll. "Tell me!"

Tarek pulled me away, Denzel's agonized cry following, and thrust me toward the window. He shook his head, slow and lethal, when I made the move to go at the Guide again. I stopped, reining in the fury. My giant didn't need to yell, prove he was in charge. In this world, he was God.

He pushed Denzel roughly on his ass, giving our prisoner his undivided attention. As pissed as I was, I didn't move from the window, and Tarek's back to me showed he knew I'd listen. "As you can see, patience is running thin."

Denzel answered by sobbing, shaking his head. His crying seemed contagious, Peter's wretched noises growing louder.

Tarek persisted, his outer calm something I'd always envied. "None of us will enjoy killing your Protector, but we will." He squatted, the two men now face to face. "Talk." Denzel swiped the tears from his eyes, his bottom lip trembling, but as usual, Tarek's deep voice had a way of gaining the truth, with or without the threat of death. "Please."

"They are coming here, Warden. There is no talk of collecting your energies or pilfering resources..." He placed his hand on Tarek's forearm, coming closer. "Exemplar is going to burn Arcus to the ground."

CHAPTER 5

LENA

Used

We weren't monsters. Honest. Yeah, we spent a bunch of time killing people lately, but their energy didn't go to waste.

What we had never done was turn a life into an exhibit. Annihilation would've been better. Winston said even in energy form, after a death, Wilma would retain her memories. Know exactly what was going on. A new life would allow her to start over. Forget.

Denzel's confession and Winston's revelation solidified my resolve. Cassondra and the whole Exemplian population may want to destroy our home. To be fair, I had the same sentiment about theirs–after I got Wilma back.

But no, we weren't monsters. As soon as Denzel quit sobbing, we let him and his Protector out. I wasn't about to cater to them. They could've went off to live in the forest for all I cared.

Mom, being the nurturer she was, took one look at Peter's pathetic face and turned into full-on rescuer, babying him, regardless that the kid smelled like ass. She shot me a frown, after hugging me, and ushered him, along with Denzel, toward the river. Grace, Oren's Guide in her past lives, brought up the rear. Zander tagged along with them, not really trusting Peter's innocent act. That's what he called it, anyway.

Belva went to control the animals, the squid specifically, in case her pets decided they were hungry. As she passed by on the way out of the village, Belva stopped to give me a quick kiss on the cheek. "I'm glad you're home."

"Me too." I smiled, not at all feeling it. While they went to take care of our new tenants, we had to figure out what to do about protecting everyone–and find a way to set Wilma free.

She nudged my arm before running to catch up, all of them disappearing into the woods.

I turned to Winston, who was about to sneak off to his cabin. "Hey! Wait a second."

He stopped, his shoulders slumping like I had just told him there wasn't a tooth fairy. "What now?"

"Um, *what now*?" I stepped forward, my hands flailing. "Oh, let's see…I dunno, maybe we should figure out how to not get killed or something?" *Oh, and save my Protector from being an exhibit!*

So he decided *that* question was important enough to turn around to face me? Dude was full of surprises. "They ain't coming *today*."

Seriously?

"Uh, you… That's… What the hell, Winston? We need to do something. Now. Wilma…we have to bring her back." I planted my hands on my hips, ready to go toe to toe. Sure, he'd whoop my ass with a fling of his hand, but I'd risk it.

Always unflappable, he gestured toward the tree line with a slight nod. "Sometimes, you need to stop and remind yourself why you care about life in the first place."

I searched the trees to find Tarek stomping up the hill, getting swallowed by the forest. Whatever. No. "I–"

"Don't be a bitch, Tainted." Winston resumed the path to his place. "You didn't die with her."

My vision went red. "You sonofabitch. What gives you the ri–"

"Save it. That angry, wounded routine won't work on me." He went into his cabin and slammed the door in my face.

Stunned, I stared at his door with a painting of two kids playing hopscotch with lacquered smiles, mocking me. Did everybody go insane? Crazy that I was the only person taking what Denzel said with an ounce of seriousness. Didn't they hear what that woman was doing to Wilma? We had the chance to save her, for Christ's sake! I was the bitch? Right.

I turned back to the forest, the bustle of our tiny village sludge in my ears.

Well, hell.

Right.

"Goddamnit!"

What I wouldn't have given for one hit of Cheveyo's voice…

A few people stopped, glancing my way. Ignoring them wasn't hard. I'd been doing it for as long as they lived here. But when Jake came out of his cabin, a mixture of relief and concern shading his dark eyes, I booked it. That stupid, pathetic concern, not what I felt like dealing with, even from the man who stepped in as my father.

I stormed past Jake, throwing up a hand when he tried to stop me. Guilt for not talking to him after being gone two months would have to sit on my conscience a while longer.

I headed in the same direction as Tarek. The peace in the woods, even with the pink squid giving off tiny mewls, calmed me enough to notice the darker shade of the sky. Ah, that would explain the panicked sounds echoing from the tops of the trees. The poor animals had no weatherproof cabins protecting them from Tarek's moods.

At least the change was proof one other person realized how our situation had become even more screwed up.

When droplets of water dipped below the canvas of leafy treetops, I picked up my speed, the cabin by the river a magnet. By the time the cabin door came into view, a heavy rain drenched the forest floor, the soil turning into almost quicksand. Not that a rainstorm was enough to batten down the hatches, but everyone who had lived here for longer than six months knew this could turn into something worse. A lot worse.

I ripped the door open, throwing it shut against the storm. Completely soaked, I wrung out the bottom of my sweatshirt, the sounds of my effort plopping onto the wooden floor. The only thing I managed to do was stare at Tarek's heaving back while the puddle grew deeper at my feet. He didn't turn around.

So many words wanted to fly out, the pushiest ones being "I'm sorry." For everything. Those words always wanted to smooth the rough edges I'd crinkled between us. But Wilma's face would swim in front of my eyes, along with something she'd said to me, before all of this: *You found a backbone… What good is it when your one goal is to find a way to be with a man?*

Christ, the guilt eating me never got full.

Even though no more water released from my shirt, I kept twisting, the silence between us as wide as the fluorescent river rushing beyond the cabin walls. All the righteous indignation Winston sparked minutes before vanished, replaced with cowardice. The smart thing to do would have been opening the door and bee lining it to my cabin to wait out Tarek's mood. I slid closer to the door, already turning the knob.

"Don't." He turned, his face tortured, eyes bright. "Don't go."

Fractured Energy

I froze, my hand slipping from the latch, shaking too much to open the door, anyway. We stared at each other, my heart breaking. The mad never hung on when Tarek was near, only guilt and shame. The two emotions a way heavier burden.

Say something!

Just...say something.

"We need to figure out the next move." *Not that!* No.

His beautiful face pleaded with me as the storm outside grew louder.

Shaking hard, I had to back up against the wall to stay on my feet. The thought of escape, running–again–flitted through my mind. Instead, I closed my eyes–and finally did what I should've done as soon as the door shut.

I reached for him.

A groan left his lips before he stalked over. He lifted me off the ground and pressed my back tighter against the door as our lips fused together. The wood dug into my skin, pain mixing with the fire he always created inside me. On their own accord, my legs wrapped around his waist and my thighs squeezed him as I held onto his neck, drinking him in. Drowning. His lips were rough, unforgiving, his tongue pushing past my teeth, deepening the kiss until I couldn't breathe. No worries, I didn't want to anymore. I wanted to feel, his heat way more potent than Cheveyo's words. Knowledge I always forgot until I had Tarek close.

The fire turned volcanic when Tarek slid a greedy hand under my shirt, running it over my bra, cupping and squeezing. His touch, like honeyed lava, burned me–I wanted more. Threading my hands through his silky hair, I yanked him closer, biting his lips, sucking on them as his hands kneaded my skin. Almost too painful, pleasure flowed through me, our clothes now the enemy. I tugged on his shirt, not able to pull it off in our position, making me so mad, I screamed into his mouth.

Tarek got the message, stumbling to the narrow bed, dropping me down, stripping bare in seconds before covering my body with his. He wasn't gentle. Good. I didn't want gentle. His lips crushed mine again, his fingers deft and strong, ripping the fabric of my thin, worn jeans until they lay in a shredded pile on the floor. He wrenched my sweatshirt over my head, too thick to tear, and managed to rip my bra in two.

The heat of our bodies touching, a feeling I never grew tired of regardless of the shame, made me cry. Hot tears traced down my cheeks. His lips left mine when the wetness made our kiss salty. Those eyes, full of passion and longing–the same emotions I knew swam in mine– didn't hide the sadness. He brushed long strands of hair away from my face before cupping my cheeks. "I love you, Lena. Do you hear me? I love you."

I wanted to say it, I did. I hated that I loved him. My love was killing us both. I touched his cheek and brought his lips back to mine, hoping it would be enough.

Knowing it never would be.

∞ ∞ ∞

We lay there, not talking. Not moving. The reprieve sex gave never lasted. The emptiness I carried always came back to add another layer to the ever-growing wedge. I missed him. Missed us, and by some miracle, this time the feelings we sparked together fought against the shadows always threatening. But even though this new, and welcomed, sensation hit, the gap didn't close. Who knew if it ever would? Don't know if I'd ever let it.

Sliding his hand from my hip, I crawled off the bed, the violet sky preventing me from finding my clothes easily. I fumbled until my sweatshirt found my hands, though my jeans remained in a denim pile on the floor. They belonged to the old clothes graveyard. I flipped the lid of the trunk where Tarek kept his clothes and pulled on a pair of sweats we'd brought back from one of our scavenger trips. They fell as soon as I pulled them up. Whatever. I just had to make it to my cabin.

"Lena."

Darkness wasn't enough camouflage for me to hide under. I hated this part–when I'd leave. He used to plea with me to stay. Lately he'd stopped, until now.

I cinched the drawstring as tight as it would go and refused to turn around, face him. "Um, I'm gonna go back, talk to Farren."

"What can he do for you that I can't?" The edge returned to his voice, the warning.

I glanced out the window, the sky that returned to its normal violet hours before, turning opaque. "You can't leave here, for one thing." *Why?* Why did I beat him up?

"Please."

"We need to figure out a way to save her. Not to mention, stopping the bastards from destroying everything we built. Maybe you and Winston could–"

"You can't go to her." His deep voice was barely a whisper. The bed creaked and footfalls thumped until his hands were massaging my shoulders. "It's not possible."

I shrugged from his touch, those long fingers that created fire now feeling like spiders. Did he really think I'd leave her there? Wilma would've never left me anywhere. Christ, she followed me to Earth, lived in a trailer park. But I was supposed to forget about her, let her suffer?

Never.

I went to the door, hating myself–hating him a little, too. "I'm getting her." I ripped open the door to the light sounds of a drizzle. "Even if it kills me, I'm gonna bring her home."

He said nothing.

The darkening skies said enough.

CHAPTER 6

AVERY

Prisoners

She followed the arrow holograms marking the wall, though the directional assistance wasn't necessary. Most of her days for the past seven months consisted of walking this hall. She'd reach her destination in exactly four and a half minutes from the time the lift dinged and the doors opened. Three hundred seventy-two steps. Today, she counted out each step, checking her handheld every so often, acting unconcerned.

On the inside she screamed, imagining the deaths of everyone she passed.

Avery waved at a few Protectors who gave her slight nods and false smiles. They hated her. This did not worry her. The feelings she harbored for the Synod elders and their authority were much the same. They could rot for all she cared.

However, they needed her. Her information was what kept them in business. If not for her, Lena would have more than likely gotten to more True Wardens. Sending expendable Exemplians to Earth, a cover so they could keep Lena's army busy was her idea. Her sacrifice to buy more time.

Guilt saturated her, causing her to stumble on the hundredth step. What choice did she have? Either risk death by Arcus's Warden or one of Lena's small army, or barter with Cassondra for her life. One route, the outcome was certain. To beg mercy from Lena, for lying and sabotaging the plan on Empyrean, would spell death for her and Nicolette. An end Avery wasn't ready to meet. Not yet. Not while she could still fight—even if she had to cooperate with the enemy as of late. But they would all pay, with or without her help. Lena would make sure of it...somehow.

She glanced toward the wall, the screens always on one image. The blue orb ricocheted against its prison, so bright it was like staring into the sun.

Wilma.

No matter how Avery would have tried to explain, the death of Lena's Protector would be placed directly on her shoulders if they had attempted to go back to Arcus. She could not blame them—especially Lena. Avery willingly carried with her that burden, a reminder.

A punishment.

Three hundred seventy.

Three hundred seventy-one.

Three hundred seventy-two.

Trepidation mingled with the guilt as soon as she stopped in front of the door. Cassondra knew how to exact atonement. The woman proved that with Wilma's energy. What she did to Avery and Nicolette was minor in comparison, but still a punishment. A punishment that Avery's Protector suffered from the most.

The scanner to the left awaited her hand and eye. Avery placed her shaking palm on the reader pad while leaning in to have her retina scanned. After the lock acknowledged whom she was, the door clicked, sliding to the right.

Examplians were not animals—not of the obvious sort. The room remained at a pleasant temperature, and without her even having to test it, the bed would rival the softness of fresh-spun cotton. The brightness on the screen mounted to the wall was even muted so as not to be disturbing. Though the image–Wilma…always Wilma–crawled and festered under the skin, regardless of the low lighting.

A pasted smile made her lips tremble with the effort. Avery stepped into the room, but her smile evaporated when her eyes landed on the bed. "No. Not again."

She rushed to Nicolette, who sat in her own filth and waste on that cloud-like bed, and knelt before her. Under the sleeve of her Protector's robe, peeked a gallium cuff, circled on Nicolette's thin left wrist. The metal glowed and sizzled as it sank into the delicate skin, half the weapon already absorbed into the bloodstream.

Through tears, she stared at the weapon, not able to touch it. Not able to do anything but watch while the cuff killed more of the person she loved above everything and anyone. Swallowing the sobs took effort. Even if Nicolette had no cognitive inclination she was there, Avery would not crumble. She could not. Nicolette wouldn't have wanted her to.

Avery sat beside her and smoothed tangled, greasy hair from Nicolette's eyes, not giving a damn that she sat in piss and grime. There was no smell. Odor vapors wafted through the vents, eating the stench. One would not want to disturb the comfort of those who worked in the bowels of the authority building.

"I'm so sorry. So very sorry." Avery tucked the matted hair behind Nicolette's ear and began the usual routine, whether her Protector could hear or not. Ever careful with her words lest ears be listening, Avery went on to describe her day, telling of the sins she again committed, her way of confessing. She told of sharing her secrets with the enemy, giving them access to her files they had not already pilfered. Giving them access to life she once promised to keep hidden.

She held so many more secrets. Secrets Cassondra bled from her through punishment to Nicolette. Whatever secret Cassondra wanted now was again costing Nicolette more of her mind.

Her time grew shorter, only a few more moments before Protectors would come to demand she leave. Avery leaned in to kiss Nicolette's sagging cheek, letting her lips linger on her Protector's clammy skin, wishing it were enough to wake the once-stronger woman from her stupor. Knowing otherwise, she brushed another soft kiss across Nicolette's gaping mouth before standing. Anything Cassondra demanded, Avery would give. The cuffs stealing her Protector's mind ensuring compliance.

Like every day, the doors swooshed open after precisely fifteen minutes. To Avery's surprise and dismay, Cassondra waltzed into the room, expressionless. Terrifying.

Rage, deep-seeded and blinding, took over Avery's vision, as well as her better judgment. Before she could rein in the fury, Avery moved, with speed she rarely possessed, to smack the Synod authority commander across the cheek.

Cassondra barely flinched, her colorless eyes igniting with mild exasperation as she flicked a wrist, sending Avery through the air. Cassondra wriggled a couple fingers, stopping Avery before she crashed against the wall. Frozen in midair, all Avery could do was glare down at Cassondra from her position, hate shooting from her eyes, wishing it'd be enough to kill.

"Why have you cuffed her this time? *Why?* Is it not enough she rots away in this room?" Avery kicked her feet, the part of her body able to move. "She does not deserve this." She wanted her words to have fire, but they came out weak and watery, matching the tears flowing from her eyes.

Fractured Energy

"I believe the both of you deserve death. Worse." The doors slid shut behind Cassondra, and she flicked her wrist one last time, bringing Avery to stand on the ground. "Do not strike me again, Guide. You will regret it."

"You're killing her!" Avery got down on her knees, beyond angry. Desperate. "Please, please, take them off. Please. I–" Avery stopped before giving the woman what she wanted. Everything.

"What, Guide? What will you do if I release your Protector?"

"I do not know. What is it you want?"

"We plan to attack them soon, yet by your actions, we do not have the advantage."

Avery and Nicolette had managed to deactivate Arcus's satellite feed during the three months they spent hiding, before getting caught. The one benefit Lena and her army had against Exemplar. Camouflage from the Synod authority, from Cassondra. Without a satellite pointed to Arcus, there were no screens to track any movement in that dimension, leaving Exemplar at a loss. When they attacked, and they would, it would have to be blind. It would hopefully give Lena enough time to fight back.

Cassondra moved closer, squatting as she pulled a remote from her pocket. A remote that could deactivate the cuffs or make them stronger, turn Nicolette's mind to mush. "We know you destroyed the satellite." She nodded toward the bed. "And we know she helped you. A crime that calls for complete annihilation. We have feed of you both infiltrating the satellites' mainframe, and if–"

"You wretched woman!" Through tears, Avery faced Cassondra as she backed up until Nicolette's knees brushed her back. She reached behind her, her hand hovering over the cuff. "Yes, we destroyed it, deactivated the thing for good. The only source of intel you have on Arcus's activity is my knowledge. And let me tell you...it would be a

55

mistake to blow Arcus away. Not with–" *Oh, no!* She almost gave everything. *Everything!* Her chin lifted. No more. "If you do not take this cuff off her, I swear I will touch it. Then you will not have me to leech information from ever again."

Cassondra tilted her head, holding the remote out. "You would sacrifice yourself for this Protector?"

No longer afraid, Avery's body stopped trembling and her voice grew stronger. "Absolutely."

Cassondra smiled. "Very well, Guide."

CHAPTER 7

LENA

Innocent

My legs refused to move faster, shaking knees preventing me from running. I stumbled toward the village, the drizzle breaking through the leafy canopy excellent cover for the tears. He was wrong. I could go to her.

I needed to.

All we had to do was keep Exemplar away from our home long enough for me to think things through. Keep them from the children who lived here. No, more than the kids. We had to protect all the people whose only crime was to love those Exemplians no longer willing to live under the lies their world spewed. The innocent.

Christ, what if they came down as they had on Empyrean? Killing people as soon as the tears ripped open the sky, dropping Protectors to the ground. Logic said there were no nests here. This world was small, and we had plenty of scouts tracking its borders, not to mention warning calls from the squid. But, what if…

My heart thumped too hard, threatening to escape. I glanced up beyond the mewling squid and their homes to the purple sky. Those bastards could drop down any second, taking everyone else I loved, slaughter us and turn this world to ash.

My heartbeat thrummed faster, breathing becoming impossible.

I had to stop... I had to... *I can't breathe.* I yanked at my sweatshirt, the collar so tight I swore it came to life to choke me. My legs decided they didn't want to work anymore, forcing me to my knees, my eyes not leaving the sky.

They could come, and we'd be defenseless. Eighty of us, half being innocent people who only knew life on Earth before this. People we promised to protect. They'd die. Today. This second.

Not again. Not this...

I wheezed, my airway closing. Bending to all fours, I tried to remember what Shaina said: *Breathe in deep and slow. Push out the bad, and bring the good back in...*

Push out the bad.

Bring the good back in.

I fell, rolling to my back. The position made the pressure worse, my lips turning numb.

I struggled to my knees again, trying to concentrate while drowning.

They could come down any second...

My hands dug into the wet soil, my lungs squeezing, withering. Tingling took over my skull, and all I could see were thin pins of white light shooting through the trees.

Okay.

Okay.

Before blackness took over, leaving me vulnerable to Arcus's wildlife, I pushed through the panic and pulled in a deep breath. *Push out the bad... Bring in the good.*

I focused on the wetness soaking through Tarek's sweats, sticky and warm.

Breathe!

Next was the gritty dirt under my fingernails, the scratchy particles irritating the sensitive skin.

Breathe...

The squid became louder as my lungs filled with air.

Fractured Energy

Push out the bad.

Not only did Belva's pets grow louder until their squealing turned to screams, but snapping twigs and branches rushed closer, too. My head shot up.

Peter.

Still not breathing well, I forced my hands off the ground to reach for my bag and gun–no. I left them in the prison. The kid stalked closer, the squid screaming but not attacking. Whatever Belva must have conveyed to them earlier stopped her army from coming off their high perches to squeeze the life out of the Protector. Which meant there went my protection.

Peter moved closer, his face grim, lips in a thin line.

Holy shit, the kid wanted to kill me.

Wheezing, I fell on my ass, holding a hand up. "Don't... Stay..." *Breathe!* "Stay away."

He didn't listen. As soon as he stood above me, I held up my chin. So this was how it'd end? Me on my ass, dealing with a panic attack while a sixteen-year-old kid crushed my skull.

Peter squatted, facing me, his light eyes sad. Before I could bring in enough oxygen to give him another feeble warning, he sat beside me and rubbed my back.

What the...?

I had no strength to shrug away from his hand, too busy relearning how to move air in and out of my lungs. My eyes stayed glued to his, though. If he wanted to kill me, he'd have to do it face to face. As his hand made circles trailing from the base of my spine to my neck, breathing became easier, less forced. When the tingling numbness ebbed, and I could form a coherent sentence...well, I didn't really want to.

His young face, a scattering of pimples on his forehead, soothed me. Concern–not pity–colored his smooth cheeks. The palm on my back became too hot, his sweat soaking through my already drenched sweatshirt. I scooted a couple inches away, the wet ground soaking clean through my pants. As uncomfortable as it was, I couldn't get up. Not yet.

Licking my dry lips, I smoothed back hair with a shaky hand. "Thanks."

Worry still darkened his eyes, his cheeks flush. "A-are you okay now?" Peter's voice pitched from bass to soprano in a millisecond.

I pulled my dirty knees up to my chest and rested my head against them. "How old are you?"

His face reddened more as he switched his attention to the treetops and surprisingly quiet squid. "Fourteen."

The kid was even younger than I thought. "You're kinda tall for a baby."

He fidgeted as if he didn't know where to put his lanky arms. Peter finally settled on brushing his hair from his eyes, his dark blond strands sticking to his cheeks. No matter what he tried, the floppy mess wouldn't obey, landing right back into his eyes.

"My mom can cut that for you." I pointed to his hair. "It might help against the humidity here." I pushed my own mop away from my face. *Maybe I should take my own advice.*

"Yeah, sure. So…you're not going to make us leave?"

Goddamn, his face was innocent. "Nah, we could use another Protector. Seems like now more than ever."

He shrugged, concentrating on his borrowed tennis shoes. "I don't know how much help I'd be." His gaze flashed to mine before resuming the study of his Nikes. "You saw how well I protected Denzel."

Oh, man, was that…? Yeah, it was. My heart melted. *Weird.* Nice…

I slid closer to him and tapped his shoulder with mine. "Not your fault. It doesn't sound like you had much training." I bumped him again. "You're a kid, for Christ's sakes."

He frowned. "Doesn't mean I can't... I can do the job, all right? I can." He took another swipe at his messy hair. "I won't be a burden here. No one will have to–"

"Okay, okay, sorry." So, I was apologizing to him? Wow. A couple days ago, I wanted to kill him. "I'm sure you can help us. We train every day when we're not killing your buddies. You can train with us, learn more."

He bowed his head, those fidgety hands now sifting through the black soil. "They weren't my friends, those you killed. I didn't even know them until Denzel and I were called to serve. But...they weren't bad people."

I pulled a deep breath into my newly cleared lungs, waiting for him to continue. It took a lot of willpower not to pat his back and give him encouragement. This kid... Screw him for making me feel again.

Peter glanced up from his dirt pile. "Denzel's been my Guide since birth. He promised..." His voice quivered, and his attention returned to the ground. "He promised my mother to keep me safe. *Me*. Not the other way around, like it should be. That's why he gave you all the information. Not for his life. He would've gladly died to be done with it. But my mother, she'd be devastated if..." A tear fell into the hole he dug.

Wait, his mother was still alive? Now, that was odd. Tarek told me once, a long time ago, parents usually didn't stick around after a birth. Peter... His mother must've been exceptional.

I placed a hand on his shoulder, battling through the apathy shield I'd constructed over the last year. "Your mother must love you, very much. And...Denzel made the right decision, regardless of his reasons." I switched my hand to hold his and squeezed. "We aren't the enemy, Peter. Your government is. What they do, it isn't right."

He refused to look up, but he did nod. "Denzel believes that, too. He…he always hoped for change. Many Exemplians do, though they can't admit it publicly. It would be a sure way to an arrest and Tainted."

I stayed quiet for a moment, tamping down all the hateful, angry words I knew he didn't deserve to hear. "It's not treason to believe differently than the majority. You know that, right? You're not *Tainted* for having a conscience."

Peter glanced up, his eyes sad and shiny with tears, but he smiled. "You sound like Denzel and my mother."

"Hey!" I swatted him on the shoulder. "And I was beginning to not hate you."

His laugh made him sound so young, innocent. Against my will, strange–and strong–feelings of protectiveness filled my heart. No kid should have to deal with this. Oh, wait…I'd been dealing with it since I was seventeen, almost three years now. I'd never really been a kid, and it looked like Peter hadn't either. No fair. None of it was fair at all.

On shaky legs, I stood and offered him my hand. "Come on. I want you to meet someone." Well, he'd already met Oren, but those prior circumstances sucked.

"Okay?" Uncertainty shadowed his eyes. "Why?"

"Maybe I'm feeling nice." I kept my hand out, not saying anything else.

He stared at it for a solid minute before the tension hanging out on his face finally relaxed. After a sigh, he clasped my hand and pulled himself up. "Are you still mad at me?"

I let go of him and led the way home. "Never cared about you enough to be mad."

"And now?"

Good question.

I ignored him and picked through the forest, pushing wet hair from my face. Sometime during our little heart-to-heart, the drizzle stopped and the tropical stickiness returned.

We walked a while, saying nothing. The kid trampled the ground like an elephant, his footsteps loud enough to ricochet off the trees. I cringed every time he broke a branch. Stealth would be something he'd have to work on if he wanted to live longer than a few weeks.

As we neared the village, Peter's squawky voice interrupted his clopping feet. "What happened to you, back there?"

He surprised me enough to stop. "What do you mean?"

"Well...your lips were blue, and...you were wheezing..." Those loud feet shuffled behind me. "Are you sick or something?"

Sick.

Probably, but only in my head.

The first time I had an episode, about a month after Wilma died, I thought I was dying. But come to find out Shaina had been going to nursing school before getting stuck here. Even though she'd only had a year and a half of school, she had more medical knowledge than any of us. Shaina kindly informed me all I had was a panic attack. Another reason why Cheveyo's word juice topped my favorite things list, it kept the fear away.

It kept everything away.

I sighed and started walking again. "No, I'm not sick."

"Okay...um...good." He didn't say anything else and hurried behind me until we reached Oren's hut.

Oren answered in the middle of the first knock, always alert and always pissed. The only time he ever relaxed was while Grace was around. If he were not such a dick, he'd be close to perfect, seeing as how he was the prettiest person living here. He might have even rivaled Belva in the looks department. "What do you want?"

But like I said...dick. I wouldn't ever admit I liked him, though. Liked him a lot, even when he was being an asshole, maybe more so because of it.

"Oh, the usual, to blacken your eye." I jammed my foot in the entry when he went to slam the door in my face. "*But*, since I'm feeling a bit tired, I thought I'd come by for something else."

"Not interested." The door closed another inch.

Don't think so. I moved my body into the doorway. "Stop being a dick for one second and let me explain."

He quit trying to shove me out of the way when his attention reached over my shoulder. Peter cleared his throat so many times I had to wonder if his voice box could handle it. All the hard and nasty left Oren's eyes, but he did manage to hold the scowl. A secret about the guy not many people knew: his heart was too big for his chest.

Opening the door wide, Oren moved aside. "You have five minutes."

I rolled my eyes and signaled for Peter to follow me in. When I turned to find the kid didn't budge, his cheeks pale as he took in Oren's mean look and big arms, I grabbed the front of his shirt. "Don't worry. He doesn't bite too hard."

The inside of Oren's shack didn't match his pretty face. A bed, trunk, and small table with a few cups on it were the only things in there. The one personal item was a quilt covering his mattress. Grace told me a while ago she'd made it after the first year they met–in her present life. She admitted he'd cried when she gave it to him on the anniversary of the first day he found her again. Of course, she swore me to secrecy. Big, bad Oren didn't cry, and he didn't care at all about innocent people, especially young kids like Peter. *Right.*

Fractured Energy

Oren stood in the middle of the small cabin, his arms crossed over his chest, waiting. When I didn't get right to it, his annoying voice filled the place. "Now you have four and a half minutes."

Peter's swallow was as loud as his walk through the woods.

I chose to ignore Oren's hard surface and focused on his soft center. "I wanted to stop by and officially introduce you to our newest Protector."

"Why?" Oren raised a brow while I pulled Peter over to stand beside me.

Yeah, these two would fit together perfectly.

"Peter, this is Oren." I shoved Peter in front of me. "Oren, Peter. Our newest *fourteen-year-old* Protector."

Shock pushed past Oren's scowl before rage took over. His face grew cold and deadly, causing Peter's body to shake so hard I worried his knees would give. I'm sure Peter thought Oren wanted to kill him, but I knew Oren was feeling the exact opposite. Well, Oren probably wanted to kill somebody, more than likely the person who sent Peter on the suicide mission.

Oren took a step forward. He was about an inch shorter than Peter, but the height difference obviously didn't make the kid feel less intimidated. We'd better not have to find him another pair of pants. Pee stains could be a bitch to wash out.

Keeping his arms crossed, Oren targeted Peter with his blue eyes. "Fourteen? As in first-cycled fourteen?"

When Peter didn't answer, I heaved him closer. "Answer him."

"Y-yes." The poor kid's voice cracked. "But I can fight. I-I won't be in the way. I swear."

Oren couldn't even keep up the faux scowl after the boy spoke. He took another step closer and let his arms fall to his sides. If I didn't know any better, I'd have sworn Oren wanted to pull Peter in for a hug.

As if he realized he was seconds away from coddling, something Peter didn't need, Oren backed up and worked to paste on the scowl again. "How am I supposed to believe you, boy?"

Silence took over after that. While I knew Oren tried to rein in his bleeding heart, Peter didn't–and he wouldn't find out, either.

Peter cleared his throat. "Um...Lena said I could train...with all of you..."

"Yes. And?" Oren crossed his arms once more.

"I'll show you, all of you, I can hold my own."

Oren nodded, his hard face not fooling me. Compassion filled his eyes, brightening up the boring cabin. "You *will* train with us, every day. Do you understand? We need fighters, not children. It'll be a challenge." He gestured to Peter's skinny, lanky arms. "But *I'll* make sure you become a man."

Peter bowed his head. "I won't be a burden."

Oren's hand whipped out, as if to pat him on the shoulder, but he pulled it back, keeping those muscled arms tightly crossed. "Don't worry. I won't let you be." He went to the door. "You'll stay in the cabin next to mine and never go anywhere in this place without me, understand? I even catch you taking a piss in the woods without me, you'll regret it."

Bringing his gaze back up to meet Oren's, his chin trembling but eyes full of determination, Peter nodded. "Yes, sir."

"Good." Oren opened the door. "Lena, out."

I shrugged. Whatever. I didn't want to stick around anyway. I walked out, my good deed for the month done."Fine. But I'm calling a meeting. One hour, the mess hall, be there."

He answered with his door–slamming in my face.

Lynn Vroman

CHAPTER 8

LENA

Reality Check

"Open the door." I pounded against the wood, wishing it were Winston's face.

After leaving Oren's, I headed over there. He always had a plan, no matter the situation. Winston's ideas saved Empyrean, giving Teenesee back her world. If he hadn't helped open the lines, Empyrean wouldn't have survived, the world becoming barren.

Depression always came when I needed it least, like now. I couldn't think of anything without driving the subject around to that day. Shaina said my so-called panic attacks were a symptom brought on by depression. It felt like more than a *symptom* to me. I shook my head, refusing to let the black win.

"Winston! I know you can hear me. I'm calling a meeting. One hour." I pounded until the bound logs rattled. "Come on!"

Shaina finally opened the door with a soft smile and a glow in her cheeks. "Sorry, *mami*. We were busy."

Heat flamed my face as I looked everywhere but her dark, content eyes. Even though I'd been doing the same thing a while ago, others doing it made me squirm. It helped ease the heavy sadness threatening at least. Embarrassment was lighter to carry.

"Crap, no, I'm sorry." I kicked at the dirt. "Um…is he…dressed?"

"Yeah, Tainted. But next time you might not be so lucky." Winston came up behind Shaina and rested his arms on her shoulders. "What's the problem?"

I laughed. *Really?* Before I could get mean, because there was nothing I liked more than explaining the obvious, Shaina interrupted. "You had another attack, didn't you?"

When she gave me that look, the one that drilled right into my skull daring me to lie, I always felt like a five-year-old. It didn't matter that she was eight inches shorter and probably a hundred pounds on a heavy day. No wonder Winston loved her. He needed someone who refused to take his crap.

I held her stare, because looking away and ignoring her would get me an earful of not-so-nice Spanish words, but sweat soaked my armpits. "I thought you were a nurse, not a shrink."

Oh, damn. That might get me a swat to the side of the head. Granted, she'd have to jump up to do it, but I'd bet everything I owned she would have no problem with that. "Don't backtalk me, *chica*. Did you or didn't you?"

"I handled it." I glanced over at Winston. "Could you please tell her to stop? We have stuff to do."

Winston actually cringed. *Cringed.* Badass Protector afraid of a teeny, tiny lady.

"Oh, hell, no! Winston doesn't *tell* me what to do—or say." The fire shooting from her eyes and smacking me in the face made the sweating serious.

"But—"

"But nothing." Her voice remained angry, but her eyes softened, making it easier to look at her without acting like...well, without acting like Winston. "When's the last time you had sleep?"

"I slept at Cheveyo's." I found my hands, not able to maintain eye contact. "I'm fine."

She stomped her tiny foot. "You're nowhere near fine. And did you sleep or pass out?"

"I… What difference does it make?"

"That's it." She grabbed my hand. "You need sleep and calm–the natural way." Shaina turned to a quiet Winston and tapped her temple so hard I thought she might've bruised herself. "You tell everyone with that mind thing you do to meet in four hours, not one–and only for a while, understand?"

Winston smiled, love for his woman shining all over his annoying face. "Yeah, beautiful, I'll tell them." He nodded to me. "You go on now, Tainted. Listen to the boss."

"But…but…we have stuff to do! I don't have time to lay around." I pulled my hand from Shaina's. "Please, I'll sleep when we get shit figured out."

She snatched my hand right back. "Don't you use that language with me, missy. And you'll get things figured out when you spend some time on you for a change."

Weird having to deal with her. I was so used to being the person in control with my own mother, and having someone like Shaina tell me what to do sucked. She was thirty-three, for Christ's sakes. She usually ended up being right, but still…sucked.

"Fine, but make it two hours." When she went to speak, I covered my ears. "Two hours. No matter how bossy you are, I'm faster than you, and I'm not too proud to run and make you chase me while I yell for everyone to get to the mess hall."

She stuck a finger in my face, opened and closed her mouth, and settled on planting her hands on her hips. "Deal. But I'm walking you to your cabin, and *I'm* not too proud to sit in front of your door to make sure you stay in there." She stormed past me. "Two hours, Winston! Two stupid hours."

I grinned at him with a shrug while he winced, and said, "You know Imma pay for not butting in."

That made my smile wider as I went to follow the pissed off, awesome woman to my place. "Good."

My cabin was down at the farthest end from Winston's, away from everyone else. When I decided to stop staying with Tarek, he refused to make me a special cabin away from everybody. He'd said if I didn't want to be with him was one thing, being by myself and isolated was something else. So, I built my own. It wasn't as secluded as I would've liked, but it gave some privacy–and it was the ugliest, leakiest cabin in the whole village. Farren helped. So did Zander. But none of us held the title of master shack builder. Tarek owned that completely.

When we reached my door, Shaina pushed it open and pointed inside. "Two hours, *mami*. Not one, not one and a half. Two."

I sighed, trudging past her. "Yes, ma'am."

After opening the hatch on the back wall to air out the place I hadn't stepped foot in for two months, I lit the few half-burned candles on the small table near my pallet. Oren's place looked like a palace compared to mine. I turned to find Shaina still standing by the door, arms crossed.

"Um…see ya in a couple hours?" I couldn't be mean to her. She wouldn't have let me, anyway.

She didn't budge from the door. "What triggered it this time?"

I fidgeted with the drawstring of Tarek's pants. "I…well, Winston tell you what Denzel said?"

"He did."

"Don't you think that's enough?"

She shrugged. "Could be." Silence sat between us for a few minutes before she continued. "But I would have to take an educated guess and say you were on your way back from Tarek's cabin. Seems like you have one every time…after."

Anger scratching under my skin begged to take a swipe at her. "What're you saying? I should stop…seeing him?"

"That's not what I'm saying at all." She moved to hug me, but I stepped back. She sighed, shaking her head. "What I'm saying is you should forgive yourself, let him back in."

I'd confessed to Shaina all my guilt one night after a particularly bad episode when I swore a heart attack finally came to get me. She'd been gently pushing me ever since.

Like always, she was probably right. But my conscience refused to listen to her. "I…can't." I wrapped my hands around my middle to keep all the ugly terrible from tumbling out. *Does she think I haven't tried?* I had. So many times, but I'd see Wilma's face and hear her words…her accusations.

Shaina reached out to smooth hair away from my eyes. "You will, one day. For now, try to see the good around you."

A tear slipped out before I could stop it. "I do try."

In seconds, she circled her arms around my shoulders. She had to stand on her tiptoes, but I appreciated it. "I didn't know Wilma, but from what I hear, she would've wanted you to go on living…not just exist."

How many people had to tell me that before it finally sank in? I hugged her tight, doing a good job at getting her shirt wet. "I know."

She pulled away, tears shining in her own eyes. "Get some sleep. At least, some rest."

"Okay."

On her way out the door, she turned, compassion filling her eyes. "And, Lena? I don't have to tell you not to see Tarek because you *don't* see him, not really. If you did, you'd not only see the pain in his eyes, but the love, too.

He won't give up on you. Don't give up on him." She shut the door, not waiting for a reply.

I stood in the middle of my little room staring at the door, hoping it would open to reveal the right answers, some way to make the hole in my chest fill up. I wanted to stop feeling, concentrate solely on keeping everyone safe. I wanted it more than anything.

Push out the bad... Bring in the good.

I went to the small trunk at the end of the pallet, sinking to my knees after I kicked up the lid. On top of a small pile of personal possessions were two shirts: one I took from Wilma's closet on Earth, and the other, the shirt I'd had since my second trip to Arcus–Tarek's, soiled and still wrapped around a pillow. Thankfully, it survived the mess after Protectors ransacked my apartment back home.

My clothes landed on the floor, except Tarek's sweats. They went into the chest with no plans to give them back. Wilma's oversized black T-shirt slipped over my head, its light weight a cocoon. With Tarek's dirty shirt-pillow smashed against my chest, I lay back and willed sleep to come.

I missed him.

I missed us.

Most of all, I needed Wilma.

God, I needed her.

CHAPTER 9

TAREK

Shutting the Door

He watched her walk away. She stumbled along the path in the pelting rain...and fell. Damned eyesight, it forced him to see too much.

Tarek wouldn't go to her, even though his feet screamed at him. She didn't want him to follow. She never wanted him to follow.

The boy had almost made him change his mind. The young Protector stalked toward Lena as she lay helpless, suffering from yet another of her attacks. Tarek's fists curled and a foot left the threshold of his doorway. Then the boy knelt beside her and rubbed her heaving back. She didn't demand for Peter to leave. She let him comfort her, something she hadn't let Tarek do since...

I put you first! I always put you first... Wilma died because I was first for her. But she...she was never first for me...

The last thing she'd said to him before she turned off her emotional faucet and shut him out. She didn't bar him from her body, but her mind...her everything else.

The cabin suffocated him, ruined with memories of her, good and bad. The first time they made love, and the mornings, right after that day on Empyrean, when she'd crumbled and sobbed until her thin body had no more energy to purge the wretchedness in her heart. Before she gave in to the emptiness attacking her now.

He yanked on his clothes and raced for the river, the tumultuous storm on the inside reflecting on the outside, the squid mewling and rushing water pleading.

Wilma's energy was whole and suffering. When the Guide told them, hope filled Lena's eyes, real emotion underneath the shock. But the man had given her fool's gold, an unobtainable wish. To go to Wilma, attempt any kind of grand rescue, would lead to the death of whoever stupidly tried. Lena would try, and she'd talk a Protector, probably Farren, into taking her to Exemplar, too. They'd die, and he would lose her. Forever. It'd never be a viable option.

He gave her truth, and she walked away from him. Again. What did she want? Lies? Romantic, foolish notions of rescue? They had people, *living people*, right here who needed protection. If Wilma was alive and his energy was floating in an Exemplian prison, she'd say the same thing. But…Tarek couldn't leave Wilma there. *How could I leave her there?* To be in energy form…to be helpless…he couldn't do that to her.

The river grew louder, piercing his eardrums. The squids' cries drove him to his knees. *Calm down, calm down, calm down…*

Gritting his teeth, he forced his mind to a quieter place, a blank space. The cabin in the meadow, near an apple orchard. His haven, his mental home. The river thrashed less and the squid no longer screamed, but cried softly.

He saw her there in the meadow, young and happy in her first cycle, watching as he built their home.

He saw her two years ago, not as happy, but alive with passion.

He saw her a year and a half ago, when she lifted her shirt over her head, love for him flushing her cheeks.

Fractured Energy

The river returned to its normal docile state, the biting rain grew gentle, and the squid purred. Her happiness was his salvation.

Tarek turned his face to the lightening sky and breathed. Then he lifted his hand to reach the purple and wished.

Nothing.

He lowered his hand and bowed his head.

No more. He couldn't do this anymore. People depended on him, and he couldn't help them if he remained dependent on Lena.

Meeting in a couple hours, big man. Usual spot.

Winston's mellow voice laced through his brain, pushing him onto reality's main platform. Tarek shut his eyes. *I'll be there.*

He had to stop drowning.

Her guilt could no longer be his weight.

He went back to his cabin and shut the door for good.

Lynn Vroman

CHAPTER 10

LENA

Burned Bridges

Knocking, or persistent knocking, annoyed the piss out of me. The cabins weren't huge. One knock would do it, and if I ignored the first bang on my door, chances were I'd ignore the third or fourth. The tenth, though…the tenth irritated me enough to answer.

"What?" Yes, I answered, but I'd be damned if I was gonna get up to open the door. I already had a good idea who it was, anyway, thanks to the fuzz clogging my head.

"Um…Winston told me to get you?" Zander's voice hit my ears, making me groan.

"Well, come in. Don't stand out there, pounding on my door."

Purple light shined a vague path to my pallet after the door creaked open a small gap. Zander looked away as soon as the door opened wider. "Where're your pants?"

"Shredded on Tarek's floor."

"Jesus, Lena, I don't need to hear that." Keeping his eyes averted, he lifted the trunk lid, rifled through until he found another old pair of jeans, and threw them behind his back.

"Thanks. While you're in there, wanna hand me a shirt, too?"

A red T-shirt flew in my face.

"Good aim." I pulled Wilma's shirt over my head, careful to fold it, and wrestled into my clothes, sweat from the tropical temperatures making my skin tacky. The jeans stuck on the ride up to my waist, and the shirt bunched at my boobs. "Ugh! I miss Quebec."

Zander laughed. "Doubt it misses you. Canada's for nice people."

"Ha, funny." I finally got the shirt on and stood. "My virtue's safe now, Zander. You can stop blushing."

He turned with a shrug. "It's not you I'm worried about. Tarek might beat my ass if he caught me staring at your...um... Shit. Why do you got to make things so weird all the time?"

To think he helped try to kill me once. Now, he actually happened to be a friend. A *real* friend. I pushed to my feet. "Because it's fun to make you squirm."

"Fun? You suck." He went to the door. "Let's go. Everyone's waiting on you."

"Is... Did Tarek come?"

"Well, yeah. He's the Warden."

Relief made my knees wobble. The two hours I'd spent hugging his pillow, I thought about Shaina's words. Maybe I should start to force myself to see past the guilt–if Tarek didn't try to block my access to Wilma. If he did... I really hoped he didn't.

I moved past Zander, leading to the mess hall. "Just asking. Did anybody bother to make food?" Not that most things we ate here tasted good. Smaller animals were edible, but tasted like how cow crap smelled. Crazy what you get used to when hunger gnawed at the stomach lining.

Zander caught up, walking to my right. "I think Jake might've grilled up those snake things. But Oren brought back a ton of chips." He nudged my shoulder and wriggled his brows. "I already claimed the BBQ, so...too bad."

Barbeque was a village favorite for some strange reason, and chips were a delicacy here. See? Oren had this huge-ass heart, always doing things the innocent people here appreciated. "Ass."

I didn't know if I directed the curse at Zander for taking the best chips or at Oren for making me like him more.

We breezed through the entry of the mess hall, a building with no doors and big enough for thirty people. A tent made of sticks, but it was where people hung out. The place was a hell of a lot bigger than the cabins, and with the fresh air circulating through more pleasant, too. A tiny window on the back wall could only give so much relief.

Today, the core people sat around some rough tables, the people who had been here from the beginning. Erin gave a wave as she ran past us, sweaty and in skimpy clothes. Likening her to a soccer mom when I first met her was stupid on my part. Lethal, the best way to describe her, and she always ran at least five miles a day, even when we were scouting for Exemplians on Earth. Though she couldn't beat me, something I proved every time I ran with her. One thing I could do better than any Protector here was outrun them, everyone except Tarek.

"Hey, lady. You ever take a day off?" Zander bent to elbow Erin's sweaty side and winked.

"Never. Why don't you come with sometime? Maybe exercise?" Erin came to Zander's shoulder blade and was half his size, but she'd kick his ass if she felt like it. At that moment, she smiled at him while pulling her arms behind her head for a stretch.

Zander's eyes landed on her chest.

Which accomplished a punch in the shoulder by me. "Pervert."

"Hey!" He rubbed his arm…and lifted his eyes to Erin's smirk. "Wanna sit with me?"

She sauntered past him, all sweaty and gorgeous. "No, but you can sit with me."

81

Zander grinned and followed her like a puppy.

What was that?

With a shrug, I moved to follow until I caught Farren and Belva coming my way. "Hey, guys."

Farren unhooked himself from Belva's side to give me one of his bear hugs. "Hey, kid."

I grunted, pushing against his shoulders. The guy could dunk me under freezing water and say things that pissed me off, but after one of his hugs, my temper would always soften. Brothers were like that, and yeah, he filled the brother slot a long time ago. "You're suffocating me, Ginger."

"Don't care." But he finally set me down. "I heard about Wilma, what those bastards are doing to her. You okay?"

I glanced at my sneakers, refusing to get all moody. Now was the time for action, this moment. Self-pity had no room here. "Yeah, but…"

"We're going to find a way to get her back."

My head snapped up to find the excitement of battle shining in his dark eyes. Instantly, my body relaxed and hope filled the bottom of the hole in my chest. If Tarek refused to help, we could still get her. Farren would fight.

Farren would always fight.

"We might be doing it on our own."

He punched my shoulder. "Highly doubt it."

"Um…ouch?" I rubbed my aching arm. The guy hit like a Mack truck. "And we'll see after today, won't we?"

I ducked under his arm, gave Belva a quick hug, and went to sit with Mom and Jake. A plate of the grilled meat–ah, snake-crawlers or whatever–was on the table, the smell a little more pleasant than road kill. I grabbed one off the top and started chomping down. Some salt and pepper and the thing wasn't half bad.

Fractured Energy

Tarek stood in front, his eyes roaming everywhere but in my direction. Typical. He always acted distant after we spent a couple hours together. A part of me, the part I discovered still beat strong two hours ago, wanted to wrap my arms around his waist and promise things. We needed to fight on our home front, and us together would be more beneficial than us apart. Not just for him, but for me, too. Hell, it'd be better for everybody here. Besides, with the news about Wilma, her having a chance...yeah, time to close the gap. I trusted him. He wouldn't let Wilma stay there. Stupid of me to think it. Tarek said *I* couldn't go to her. Someone else could, like Winston. I got up from my seat after squeezing Mom's hand and went to take the spot at his side.

Then Winston and Shaina waltzed in with Oren—and Peter behind them. Oh, and Denzel brought up the rear.

No way.

I threw my lunch on the table and stalked the ten feet to confront Oren instead. "Are you an idiot?"

His eyes hardened, but he kept moving, forcing me to walk backward as he signaled Denzel and Peter to follow.

I shoved him, making him move zero inches, but he did stop to give his famous scowl. Unfortunate for him, it didn't work on me. "They can't be here."

Oren motioned for the two to sit by Winston before acknowledging me. "Wasn't my idea." He pointed to Tarek. "What he says, I do." He pushed past me to sit across from Peter.

Tarek's eyes finally landed on me, in time to see me charge him. Screw the awkward I-hate-myself-after-sex crap. Forget the olive branch, too. Including people who still might be the enemy, while we figured out how to kill their friends, was a bad idea. "Why?"

His gray eyes landed on the decision I questioned. Without looking at me, he said, "Because we need them."

"For what? To, ah, one night maybe leave to tell all their friends what we plan to do?" I waved a hand in front of his face when he still didn't glance my way. "Hello? You still there?"

That probably wasn't the smartest thing to do.

Tarek's silver glare moved from my waving hand to my face, his own hand coming up to pull mine down. His touch was gentle, cold. "Don't do that. Ever."

Sometimes I forgot he was the Warden–and sometimes I neglected to remember what that meant. He ruled here. What he said went, no matter what. If I ever disagreed with him, we were alone when I told him about it. Anyone else were to ever wave a hand in front of his face–disrespect him–they'd be dead. Period. Not even Winston would've done that to him. Damn, the bridge grew wider.

But my chin lifted despite the shame racing to blot my cheeks. "We can't take any chances."

He crossed his arms. An arctic blizzard would've been warmer than his eyes. "Do you think I'm stupid? Rash?"

"I… We…we don't know them."

"Answer me."

My shaking chin rose higher. "Of course not."

He nodded toward Mom and Jake, that ice not melting at all. "Go. Sit. Let's get started."

There was a time when I'd stand with him, be by his side because he needed me as much as I needed him. Maybe he'd finally given up.

Isn't this what you wanted?

As my heart deflated, the answer finally became clear–and probably too late.

No, it wasn't what I wanted.

Not at all.

"Fine…if that's what you want."

He nodded again, making my face burn.

Fractured Energy

On shaky legs, I walked the few feet to Mom's table, fighting the urge to let her comfort me. Tarek turned his attention to the room as if he'd just dealt with a temperamental subject in his court. Nothing worse than feeling like an annoying gnat who wouldn't shut up.

Tarek cleared his throat a couple times and cracked his neck before giving his attention back to the crowd. "It looks as though we have an issue."

I'm sure everybody in the room caught bits and pieces of what Denzel had told us, seeing as how Farren already knew about Wilma. But no one said a word, their eyes glued to the giant in the front.

"Denzel." Tarek signaled for him to stand. "Why don't you come up here and tell everyone what you told us."

To have the guy explain it again? Waste of time. But I tended to learn from my mistakes and kept my mouth shut.

The Guide stood, his hands trembling as he smoothed hair slick with sweat from his forehead. He didn't look old, maybe thirty-five with a few lines creasing his face, though who knew how old he actually was. But no matter how young he appeared, he couldn't hide how the burden of being here weighted him down. His thin legs moved like bugs in molasses, clothes that Mom must've given him taking away all the dignity his contego suit and rich clothes supplied. Sweatpants and a tank top didn't suit him at all. When he finally found a spot next to Tarek, their extreme height difference almost funny, Denzel's sweating went into overdrive.

"Ah, right, yes." Denzel fidgeted with the edge of his shirt, giving Tarek a quick sidelong glance. "I will have you understand first that Peter and I are with you. All of you." He shot me a pleading stare. "We are not your enemy."

I said nothing, his words meaning little. I believed Peter, an innocent kid caught up in a war he knew nothing about. But I had a feeling Peter would do what Denzel asked, and I didn't trust the older guy at all. Who would trust someone who turned against his own people so quickly? Not me. Apparently Tarek did, though.

Dripping sweat, and with a body that quaked more than a belly dancer's, Denzel let the whole story tumble out. Oren grumbled here and there and Erin gasped, especially during the part about Wilma, but otherwise the room stayed quiet. He finished up with an apology and a positive note. "The satellite feed directed here has been tampered with, destroyed. Rumors circulate Avery deactivated them before turning herself in. They are blind to all of us as of now, something we should use wisely." He went to find his seat, his head down.

Keeping my mouth shut was too hard. "So, she's both helping us and them? What the hell?"

Denzel cleared his throat. "She had no choice with the latter. They hold her Protector captive."

He shared all kinds of fuckery.

Tarek remained quiet for a few minutes, looking around the room, his arms still folded over his chest. We were all used to his bouts of contemplation, no one interrupting the quiet.

Uncurling his arms, he tapped his bottom lip, eyes still sharp and focused. "Plans have now changed."

"What do you mean, brother?" Farren bent forward, resting his elbows on his knees.

"Closing the lines can't be an option right now. We need to concentrate on home, make sure they don't attack our own. Survival's the new objective."

Farren's eye twitched, but he kept his cool. "We have enough people to do both. I mean, if we don't keep pushing them back, always going on the defense, they're going to win."

"I understand, but we all made a promise to those people and their families to keep them safe." When Farren began to speak, Tarek held up a hand. "I'm not saying we abandon the idea. This is for now. And Exemplar is leaving Earth alone. I'd say we're on the right track. We can maybe even gain more ground if we beat them here."

"But..." Farren scrubbed his outgrown hair. "Why don't we open the lines on the bastards, bring Arcus to them like we did Empyrean?"

Yeah, I liked that idea. Liked it a lot.

Winston didn't. "They'll be expecting that and ready. Plus, they got more firepower on their home turf and we had help from Teenesee's army. Going there, it'd be the entire dimension against us. We couldn't beat them. More than likely, they'll knock our asses back a few centuries. Take out the wildlife, too. It'd be suicide."

Belva gasped, shaking her head and tugging on Farren's sleeve. "We can't do that. We won't."

Farren kissed her before hanging his head and nodding. Defeat was never a good color on him. "All right. Any other suggestions?" He brought his eyes back up to Tarek. "How do we keep them away?"

Denzel interrupted, his voice small and shaking. "They won't bleed the lines, either, for fear of losing even an ounce more energy to Arcus. They... Guerrilla warfare would be their best option."

Tarek gave Denzel his attention. "And how would you know this?"

My giant's calm voice helped ease the Guide's tension, his shoulders visibly relaxing. "Because I was once an assistant to Cassondra...before she sent me to Earth. Of course, she has many assistants whom she barely acknowledges." He tilted his head, his eyes lighting. "Which is to our advantage. She spoke of strategy whilst in my presence, giving me the same attention she would a chair."

Tarek smiled, his dimples making him look deceptively innocent. "Well, how careless she was to send her chair to Earth."

Denzel grinned, sweating at a minimum. "Quite careless, yes."

Maybe I jumped the gun on flipping out. If I were treated like an object, I wouldn't be eager to help the asshole guilty of it. Hopefully Tarek wouldn't hold it against me, but who knew? He'd never treated me like just one of the others. Granted, I had never disrespected him as if he were a nobody, dumbass idiot, either.

Tarek scanned the room, his eyes skipping over me. "Farren and Zander, you take charge of creating a recon schedule. I want the woods, castle, and beyond that searched every day. Set up checkpoints, build shelters, whatever it takes to have eyes everywhere, all the time." At Farren's nod, Tarek turned his attention to Winston, Oren, and Erin. "You make sure these people are ready to fight, even the children. Show them how to shoot a gun, throw a knife, anything and everything to give them power. I want no defenseless person in the village."

"Heard." Winston glanced over at Oren and Erin. "We got this."

Oren, always serious, nodded while Erin gave him a thumbs-up.

Tarek targeted Belva. "Make sure your army's ready."

She lifted her chin with a smile. "They will be."

"Good. Shaina and Jacie, you two are responsible for making sure we're ready for any injuries. If you need anything, make a list. I'll send a Protector to Earth. And Jake? You'll be watching our chair, here." Tarek's eyes landed on Denzel. "Make sure he behaves. Maybe ask him a few more questions, get some answers."

"No problem." Jake cracked his knuckles, causing Denzel to squirm.

Swallowing my pride never went down easy, but I had to do it. He hadn't mentioned one part of the plan, the most important part. "Tarek?" When his gaze shifted to mine, the frost returned. But I ignored it. I had to. "What about Wilma?"

He sighed, some heat returning to his eyes. "Help Winston get everyone prepared, Lena." Tarek stormed down the middle of the tables, his boots kicking up dirt from the hard-packed ground. But before I could run after him, pound on his back and forget about respect, he stopped. His huge shoulders heaved as if he adjusted the load of his burden, trying to lighten it. He didn't turn around, but his deep voice carried to my heart. "We never leave one of our own behind." He paused. "Give me time. We'll figure out a way to bring her home."

Lynn Vroman

CHAPTER 11

AVERY

Death

Protectors flanked her, the privilege of roaming freely snatched away. If only that horrid creature had pressed the remote button, she and Nicolette would finally be free of it. All of it. No more worry, no stress, just the release of death. Real death from which there would be no second chances.

She used to fear nonexistence. Now Avery craved it. She had already attempted to end the pain of living–right after Cassondra had her taken from Nicolette's cell. A vertical slice down the center of her wrists and sleep medication to prevent a change of heart.

They brought her back, fixing her mangled body, stuffing her energy back into its shell. Treating her like any other useful tool. Depression weighted her shoulders, the feeling of rebirth too much to bear. Not even Nicolette, with the threat of her losing her mind under the therapy of gallium cuffs, could soothe the near-paralyzing desire to be done.

Her hair hung in ragged knots, her clothes stained. Avery cared for nothing, only the sweet promise of annihilation. The golden nugget Cassondra dangled after they forced another life on her. She should have burned herself alive, destroyed her body so they could not use it again for a new cycle. A body that now felt like acid on her tired soul, forcing it to keep going.

Death. Complete and total death. The promise of it an elixir. She'd do anything to get it.

Even betray every single person who ever trusted her.

All Avery had to do was give Cassondra what she asked for. Information. No more lies or false leads. All truth. Truth that would kill Lena and her people, kill the once desired outcome of freedom–freedom from enslavement, from judgment by those who had no right to judge.

Lena would thank her...right before Cassondra stole away the empty, fruitless hope. To live always fighting was no way to live. Avery had finally accepted that. Perhaps she shouldn't have destroyed the satellites. This end could have come sooner, been less intrusive than what Cassondra had planned.

Cassondra would kill Nicolette, too. Good. Avery's Protector would no longer feel trapped inside a non-functional mind. Nor would she have to face another lifecycle punished by the gallium cuffs, a weapon that destroyed the mind, the very essence of being. Energy forever affected by a simple, heartless tool no matter how many cycles one lived thereafter.

The Protectors halted in front of Cassondra's new wing, across from the room now holding Wilma's energy captive. The room no one could enter. For if a breach were discovered, the guilty would succumb to a similar outcome. An energy caged always the worse fate. To know you were already dead but denied release, not even a forcible recycle back onto Exemplar or devolution to a lesser world. It would create a void deep in the psyche of the strongest energy.

After an eye scan cleared one of the Protectors, the doors swooshed open to reveal a series of smaller rooms. Avery tore her eyes from the raging energy, an opulent blue flame, thrashing against its glass-encased prison. She could not help the Protector now. Avery could only ensure Lena's energy joined Wilma's, perhaps someday when Cassondra stopped displaying her like a trophy. Even though extinction held Lena's future, as likely the rest of those she loved, at least they would no longer live apart. Poetic, really.

Beautiful.

After a prod from one of her escorts, she shuffled into Cassondra's wing, head bent, guilt no longer ripping her heart.

Cassondra's domain sat nestled at the end of the hall, a sentinel overseeing the hive of her minions. Synod elders, so out of touch with reality, let fear dictate their decisions after the failed massacre on Empyrean. They now believed Cassondra could gain back what was lost. Maintain what had been the norm for far too long. Cowards, all of them.

Including her.

The trio strode past the rooms. Exemplians who occupied them were busy staring at maps, old holograms of Arcus, probably wondering how to best attack the imminent threat of Lena and her people.

What happened on Empyrean branded the minds of every man, woman, and rare child in this world. They all worried Lena's army grew enough to do the same here. Exemplians were wrought with fear, stories circulating amongst the taverns and inside homes of lines bleeding and energies stolen. The authority scoured maps, blind to Arcus's progress due to lack of satellite feed, feverishly scrambling to figure out a war plan whilst Avery filled them with empty lies. Cassondra no longer indulged her, the gallium cuffs breaking Nicolette and in turn crushing Avery's will.

They'd have to search no more. Avery planned to end it. End it all.

∞ ∞ ∞

"Can you hear me, Avery? I hope you can. I hope the last words you hear fill you with dread. Consume you with the pain you've given me."

A soft voice invaded her ears, but the gallium cuffs mangled her brain, refusing to let her answer.

Avery held enough of her mind to understand where she lay—in the very laboratory she led for so many years, a place where atrocity happened under the guise of privilege every hour of every day. The cuffs were one last insult before Avery left Cassondra's office. To remember the woman's contented smile as she pushed the button…it mattered no more. Annihilation promised permanent oblivion.

"You've been marked Tainted, sentenced to energy disbandment." The voice shifted to her other ear, hate searing every syllable. "But do not think for a moment I will not make you suffer."

Fear as thick and black as tar slithered through her veins. Avery tried to rise, but the cuffs effectively held her captive.

"You will not disappear. I will not allow it." The voice turned wretched, sobs clogging her executioner's words. "You wanted to play God, turn on those who once trusted you? You are nothing but a weak, heartless woman, and now *I* will be your God."

Last shreds of will helped Avery peel her eyelids open, needing to see. A woman, the Guide who took Avery's position as Creation Lab overseer, drifted above her, eyes filled with unshed tears and loathing. The woman who always stood at Cassondra's side…too close to the authority commander's side.

Lips like elastic, Avery managed to form one word. "Why?"

Fractured Energy

Why wasn't the woman happy? She smiled when Avery confessed her remaining secrets in Cassondra's office. She...smiled.

The woman bent close, her mouth trembling. "Because you are a murderer, nothing more."

Silence answered. Avery could not defend herself, even with the pending threat of more life.

The woman straightened when the sound of footsteps echoed into the room. Avery's eyes closed. Her sapping strength prohibited her from begging the others to save her. Help prevent her from living another life.

Mumbling voices clogged the room. Chaotic, claustrophobic, they suffocated her even as she struggled to cling to them, hoping at least one person would see through the overseer's hate and stop the madness.

A small prick pierced Avery's arm. Poison. In minutes, her body would be dead and the energy released, for the second time in as many days. Most people did not experience the separation of their energy from their corporeal form. But Guides did, every time they took energies from dimensions and dumped them in places they usually did not deserve. Such a place Avery realized her energy would go. A dark place, ancient and vile. A punishment for nameless crimes against a woman she did not know. *A woman who smiled!*

When the shuffling led out the door, the voice quaked against her ear. "You will live in pain and horror and death, over and over. My only regret is that you will not remember who sent you there."

Whatever the woman said after turned to slush as Avery's breathing stopped and her energy pulled away from her body. A shard of dull glass slicing flesh from bone, her essence ripped from her dying form. Pain screamed through her on the inside.

In an instant, the searing torture disappeared. Avery floated near the ceiling, watching as the overseer hunched over her, sobbing before moving to the door to lock it. The woman then lay flat on the hard floor. The image blurred as Avery lost sight, relying on touch and sound. She zinged back and forth, trying to get the woman's attention. *Maybe she'd change her mind.*

Panic didn't allow much logical thought. As Wilma suffered, so too did Avery, locked in her energy form unable to stop thinking, feeling. Knowing.

Before she managed to find the sense to search for a way out of the room, the overseer in energy form, pulsating and magnetic, swooped in and absorbed her light. Warmth calmed the panic, and with a forceful nudge, the Guide took them from the room and out of the world she hated…the world that would now destroy everything that meant anything.

In those final moments before they punched through dimensional lines to a barren world with no discernible proof of human life, Avery found clarity.

What have I done?

CHAPTER 12

LENA

Explosions

For...I don't know how long, probably weeks, closer to a month, we trained, scouted, prepared. The five kids living in the village, the youngest like eight, treated their sessions like a game, their parents encouraging them. Some even made dummies stuffed with twigs and dirt to practice with, dagger slashes decorating the burlap faces. I remember when the threat of Exemplar excited me.

But then Exemplar took everything.

Hopefully these people would never have to experience that.

Time gave core people the feeling Denzel may have exaggerated Arcus's direct threat. Farren grew antsy, believing while we stayed here to train and set up added unnecessary security, Exemplar was doing to another world what they tried on Earth—what they succeeded in doing on Empyrean. He spent a good amount of energy accusing Denzel of lies.

Needless to say, Oren kept Peter far away from Farren while Tarek ordered him to leave Denzel alone. Problem was Ginger's girlfriend happened to control the wildlife. Maybe one day an irate squid might come down from its perch to eat Denzel for a snack.

Yeah, everybody grew edgy, more so as time bled away, maybe taking a few lives on another world with it.

Tarek refused to speak to me, only giving me attention during meetings if I asked a question or gave a suggestion. Not that I didn't try to gain the courage to march to his cabin to plead my case, but the energy it took to explain all the chaos going on in my head wasn't worth the argument expressing it would cause. To think I wanted to close the gap as he became ready to widen it. Bad timing.

But I could deal, as long as there was the promise of finding a way to rescue Wilma from that place. Because even though they treated her like a warning, an object, she was still whole, able to live another life. That information alone for the past few weeks made me stronger, the black hardly ever winning.

One problem: not a single person had a plausible way to bring her back. Farren suggested a covert thing. A clandestine operation, he called it. A few people infiltrate Exemplar, get her, and get out. After Winston stopped laughing and Tarek quit cursing at him, the plan was nixed. Suicide mission, they had said. I thought it the best chance to get her. But no way would I push my luck and demand Tarek come up with something better, and a lot quicker. He might not be talking to me, but I trusted him. He'd find a way. The wait…yeah, waiting sucked.

Life went on, though, as it always unfortunately did.

As soon as we woke up, Erin and I slipped away for our routine morning run. Or an evening run. Who knew? We slept when we were tired, whether that ended up being night or day… stupid purple sky. It changed with Tarek's moods, not like a normal world. Whatever normal meant.

Running cleared away all the stress for a while. Maybe not as efficiently as Cheveyo, but the endorphin rush made carrying the load easier. The symmetry helped, trees or branches never sneaking out to thwack us or get snarled up in our hair. Beat running on an asphalt track any day.

Fractured Energy

Neither one of us spoke as we kept an equal pace. If she sped up, so did I. She couldn't beat me, and I made sure she remembered that. Not at this. This was all me. She might've known how to kill a person a hundred different ways without getting blood on her shirt, but I'd sure as hell whoop her ass in a race. So what if she could sneak into my place and snap my neck before I opened an eyelid.

We sprinted through the trees, squid grumbling, but leaving us alone. Our food source, the snake thingies, dodged our Nikes. We'd hit about ten miles today, meeting the wood's frigid edge near the castle, passing some new checkpoints–small shacks where Protectors volunteered to spend a few days at a time alone with their communicators for company. Winston and Tarek were the only ones with the mind mojo. The rest of us depended on modern technology. We waved at the woman at the nearest checkpoint by the castle, who hid under heavy clothes protecting her from the cold and ice, and kept going.

By the time we closed in on Tarek's place, my resolve weakened. It'd been so long, and the arctic temperature he threw my way gave me frostbite. Wilma was…not alive, but I had the chance to make things right. With everyone. If I let him go on ignoring me, I'd lose him.

I slowed to a jog, letting Erin catch up before switching to a walk. Squid surrounded his cabin, perched in their trees but vigilant. That usually indicated he still hid in there before going out to play ruler for the day. I knew he hated the responsibility, feared it actually. But he did the job, and did it well. Everyone believed in him, not just me.

About twenty feet from the back of Tarek's cabin I stopped, swiping sweaty hair from my cheeks. "Um, hey, I'm gonna… I'll see you back at the village."

Erin laughed, breathing heavy and punching me on the shoulder. "It's like you enjoy torture."

Why did all these Protectors like to punch me? "Shut up. I need to…discuss stuff."

Erin pulled her foot to her butt to stretch her thigh. "The guy's been nothing but frosty since you came back from Earth. He's not going to share a thing."

"He'll share." I kicked at the underbrush. "If I grovel enough."

Her laugh trailed after her as she followed the path to the village. "You grovel? If only I could stay to watch."

After a minute, I stood alone, watching her disappearing back, wanting to throw rocks at it. I could grovel. It had just been a while since I felt the desire to.

While what needed to be said replayed in my head, I trudged the short distance between me and my angry giant.

Good chance he wasn't mine anymore.

Usually when coming here, I'd barge in. Today, I knocked, soft so if he didn't answer, my conscience could say I tried. Talk about losing nerve. Guilt also came to keep me company, singing the song it had repeated for over a year: *You put him before her… You put him before her…*

Was I doing it again? Forgetting her? I–

The door swung open, and when his beautiful, angry face met mine, that guilt grabbed a microphone and blared at my selfishness a thousand decibels louder.

I'd had one other panic attack since Peter caught me in the woods. A record, I'd say. But maybe Shaina was right. Being here, loving him… Guilt created more fear than anything. My lungs constricted, and I gasped and heaved. I reached out, leaning a hand against the cabin wall, trying to get a grip. *No!* Why they came like this, with no warning…

Push out the bad. Pull in the good.

My gaze searched for his through the mist that always came before everything went blurry. If I could get hold of it… "I…"

100

His frown vanished and worry drowned his eyes as he reached for me, his big hands enough, even when I couldn't admit it.

Able to make me feel whole, even when I didn't deserve it.

"Breathe, Lena. Easy..." His words soothed, chasing away the worst of it while a warm palm rubbed circles at the small of my back.

As quick as the threat jumped on my shoulders, the panic dissolved. Embarrassment took its place, along with the guilt. Christ, I swore it laughed at me. Crazy how an emotion became my closest friend over the last year and a half. Pulling in a cleansing breath, I straightened. "Th-thanks. I'm okay now."

Tarek's hand left my back, and he folded his arms over his chest. The frown didn't return, but ice replaced the worry. "Why are you here?"

I swallowed, still dizzy. "Can we talk?"

"There's a meeting in two hours." He didn't move to let me in, but the door didn't slam in my face either.

Baby steps.

"Tarek, please." I moved to touch his cheek.

He dodged my fingers.

Though I expected it, seeing as he hadn't let me near him since I left his cabin a month ago, his aversion cut deep. I'd gotten used to Tarek letting me treat him like shit, taken advantage of it, really.

I dropped my hand, clenching it into a fist at my side. Looked like it was too late for us. Tears blinded me, but I blinked and cursed them away. "People are getting anxious. They... We feel like we should do something...more."

He looked over my shoulder. "What would you have me do? Send people off on a fool's mission and leave the helpless here vulnerable?"

"Well, no, of course not." I shoved a shaky hand through my tangles, sweat making the knots worse. "Maybe have a couple of us go speak with another True Warden, see if Exemplar has messed with them. Maybe even get the bastards focused on something else besides Arcus."

His eyes landed on mine, incredulity widening them. "You still think closing the lines is possible?" Before I could answer, he held up a hand. "That'll never happen. We were naïve to even consider it."

Anger helped erase the guilt and entirely washed away the embarrassment. "How can you believe it isn't possible? We cleaned up Earth. Y-you said so yourself that we were making progress. We–"

"It took an entire year to erase the imminent danger there. And while you and your little army were chasing their bait traps, Exemplar was busy picking off energy elsewhere. They have more resources than a few people who can fight and a bunch of squid."

"*My little army?* You–"

"Is this what you came here to do? Fight with me? Or maybe escape your head for a couple hours in my bed?" He gripped my shoulders so fast, I gasped. "Is this what makes you happy, Lena? Because I'm done with it. Your moods. Your anger." He shook me. "The guilt you carry. The guilt you take out on me. I won't let you do it anymore. I won't."

I wanted to hit him hard enough to erase the truth his words screamed. Yeah, I wanted to break his nose, and I wanted to beg him to forget the last year and a half, know I was getting better. Wilma could live again. I could give her another life–for the life I took from her.

Words froze in my throat, and my fist stayed clenched at my side, even when he let me go.

"I love you, Lena. I love you so much, and I swear it's eating me alive." His voice broke, his eyes shining bright gray. "I–you left for *two months* and when you came home…" He yanked on his hair as the sky darkened.

I stepped closer, careful not to touch him, his tortured face killing me. But all I wanted to do was erase the pain, and touching him was the solution I came up with. Standing on my toes, I kissed him, lacing my fingers through his tangled hair. He groaned, folding me into his arms, his lips demanding–for a moment. Another wounded groan pierced my heart as he pushed me away and stumbled backward.

He punched the cabin door with a loud yell, taking it right off the hinges, and hung his head. The squid cried as his shoulders heaved. "I can't do this, not anymore." His face lifted, those shining eyes meeting mine. "You give me scraps and shove me away after. My head… I can't deal with what you do to me, especially when there's a threat to everyone."

The dark sky and instant pelting rain proved his words.

My fingers touched my swollen lips, my brain refusing to believe I'd lost him. "That's…that's not what I want anymore, Tarek. I…" What did I want?

He waited, his lips curving in a sad smile. "Leave." When he turned away and walked into his cabin, I went to follow, still not ready to give up.

Why can't I say the words?

His next plea stopped me. "Don't come back here. Please."

∞ ∞ ∞

Numb tingling coated my skin while doing its best to stitch a barrier around my heart. I never–ever–expected Tarek to turn away. Selfish not to and now I'd pay for it. His face, so tortured, filled my brain. I finally saw him after all this time. I *finally* looked, and probably too late.

Memories of Wilma's voice circulated around the image of Tarek in my mind. *Dumbass, dumbass, dumbass...*

Yeah, totally and completely, but numbness wasn't gonna win this time. I wouldn't let it. What he said, I deserved. That didn't mean I'd give up. Nope, I'd fight harder. Wilma, if she were here right now, would be slapping me upside the head, demanding I go back there and apologize.

I would, but not right away. He'd never believe me if I did. Actions, the lone believable apology in existence. Saying sorry, as I had in a mechanical, noncommittal tone these past months, would miss the target.

New goals:

Protect Arcus.

Save Wilma.

Show Tarek I was ready to stop being an asshole.

The new agenda, a solid, desired agenda, lightened the ache around my heart and dissolved the numbness. I actually smiled, even laughed a bit. Everything Tarek had said hit home for the first time. Hell, I deserved more, and it woke me up. I'd fix this, all of it. If I had to spend my last breath convincing him I was ready to move on, I would. He was here, alive and with me, and it was about time I appreciated that.

The rain let up, making me feel better knowing his sadness eased. It also scared me some. People usually tended to feel lighter when a cancer was cut from their life, didn't they? No one I knew ever wanted to carry that diseased part again.

No. Not going there. I'd prove myself. He loved me, and I had to remember that as he tossed all his cold and frost my way. We'd been through a few of my deaths, a few of his...a separation of worlds. We'd get through this. We would.

Fractured Energy

By the time I made it to the wood's edge, I had it all figured out. Maybe it was time I let a few more people back in, too. I turned toward Mom and Jake's cabin and ran. Everything looked brighter, if that were possible. The skyline lightened to almost its original purple, and in the distance, silver-gray soared over the tips of the castle the trees didn't hide. The contrast was breathtaking. This place, the place I once thought of as hell, was paradise, and I'd do everything I could to protect it and the people brave enough to live here with us.

Tarek was right. Survival needed to be the main objective. Closing the lines was a romantic idea—and an unrealistic one.

I banged on Mom's door before pushing it open to find her talking with Peter. She smiled while he laughed about something as he ate a bag of barbeque chips. Looked like Zander grew soft on the kid, too.

They both glanced up, Mom's eyes filling with tension as Peter dropped the bag. Smiling shouldn't have been so hard for me, seeing as I'd had an epiphany, but hurt clouded my head. The only time I came to see Mom and Jake lately was when something was wrong.

I smiled, though. Smiled all big and crazy, which caused Mom to hop to her feet, the tension shrouding her turning to fear. "What is it? What's wrong?"

I hugged her. "Nothing's wrong if you don't count me being an asshole for a year. I'm here, Mom. For real, I think."

A soft gasp escaped her lips as she held me tighter. "I missed you, baby."

"Yeah, missed you, too." I held on for a few more minutes, my sweat and grime transferring to her shirt.

She didn't seem to mind, her laugh/cry filling my ears.

I glanced over at Peter, who stared, wide-eyed and confused. One more squeeze and I let Mom go to sit on the middle of the floor beside him. "Don't be a chip hog." I snatched the chips off the floor and nudged his shoulder as I stuffed my face, suddenly ravenous.

"Um…sorry?"

"Forgiven." I offered him the bag, and he dipped his hand in. "Mom? You got any of that pilfered soda?"

She laughed, swiping at a few tears, and went to a chest, pulling out two Cokes. She tossed one to Peter and the other to me. Peter looked at the can and shook it.

"Ah, don't do that, kid." I paused. *Kid.* He was the kid now, not me. "What? Didn't you read those history books?" I remembered when Tarek told me about them on my waterbed–back in the trailer park, so long ago. What I wouldn't give…*no.*

"Y-yes, but this…is it some sort of machine?"

I laughed, reaching over to pop the lid. Brown fizz spurted from the opening, saturating his hand. His eyes opened wider, and he stared at the can in fear.

"Drink it."

"Are you crazy?"

I tipped it to his mouth. "Yeah. Drink."

He gulped what flew out, pleasure replacing any and all apprehension when he drank until the can crunched empty in his hand. "That was the best thing I've ever…" His attention switched to the bag of chips. "And those, too! You ate this food where you're from?"

I slurped my own soda. "All the time."

"Wow, lucky." He snatched my Coke and finished it, a loud burp following. His face reddened. "Sorry. Um…where, exactly, did you live?"

"'Merica." I stuffed a few more chips in my mouth. "Land of the loud mouths and large waists. Hey, you were in Canada. They have this stuff there, too."

"We had our sustenance injections, good for three months." His smile swallowed his whole face. "But…'Merica. I want to go there."

Farren explained once after an earlier mission to Earth how the Exemplian authority was given injections preventing hunger or dehydration. Said it made them efficient killers. This kid, he was no killer.

"Sure, you do. Maybe someday." I stood, tossed him the bag, and went to hug Mom again. "I love you. Just wanted to come by and say it in case you'd forgotten."

"Oh, I never forgot, baby, but I'm glad you're back. Jake will be, too."

"Where is he?"

She pulled away and smoothed hair from my eyes. "In the mess hall, cooking for everyone."

"I'm gonna go there, give him a hand."

"He'd like that. Like it a lot."

I squeezed her shoulder and gave Peter a wave before shutting the door behind me. That felt good, but weird, too, as if my heart sputtered and coughed with the effort to open up again.

After stretching my arms, I headed toward the mess hall, ready to make things right with the man whom I considered a father.

Boom!

The grounded rattled, and I landed on my knees as trees in the distance toppled.

Boom!

Felled trees gave way to towers crumbling in on themselves, the cracking and splintering sound of collapse reaching all the way into the village like a thunderclap. Another loud boom shot through the sky and people piled out of their cabins, frantic and disoriented. Denzel rushed out of his cabin, racing for Mom's. "Peter!"

As Peter and Mom tumbled from her door, Denzel pointed his terrified eyes down to me, holding out a hand. "It's happening."

I clasped his hand and struggled to my feet, the ground quaking. "Find Oren and get everyone to the shelters. Now!"

At his nod, I stumbled toward the woods, focused on the path to the castle. Screams from innocents reverberated through my brain, pushing me faster. Without looking behind, I knew the footsteps pounding closer belonged to Farren as he caught up and ran alongside me, his face set in warrior mode, cold and calculating.

The sound of a motorcycle screamed past us. We dodged its wheels without breaking our stride as Winston flew to the castle, expertly tracking through the woods. In seconds, he disappeared, a couple minutes from being on the frontlines. Farren and I were fast, but it'd take twenty minutes at least. Twenty long minutes before we could help.

We ran hard, our breathing methodical as we pushed ourselves. Years of training together came down to moments like this. Fatigue wouldn't touch us; adrenaline made sure of it. We ran a direct path to the castle, eating up the ground. We knew these woods, how long it took to get from one place to the other by landmarks, and when Tarek's cabin came into view, it told us we were halfway there. *Ten minutes.*

As I knew it would be, when we passed the cabin, it sat empty, the door interrupting our path. We both leapt over it, not skipping a beat.

Tarek already left to face the threat. The man who stressed never to go into an ambush alone did the exact opposite. Hopefully Winston would get to him before–

Fear curled into my legs, pushing them faster.

Exemplar had arrived.

CHAPTER 13

LENA

Buried

We made it to the forest's edge, debris from the four towers skidding far enough into the woods to block us out. The checkpoint, in shambles under heavy stone, had blood staining the broken sticks. We'd lost a Protector. A mental tally ticked inside my head: a woman. The same woman Erin and I passed earlier. She had a husband here.

Explosions still wracked the sky. Dust clogged the air, choking us as we searched for Tarek and Winston. Panic sizzled under my skin, eyes stinging from the ancient stone rolling farther into the woods.

"Tarek!" I tripped over the rock, Farren following, searching under the rubble. Our breath came out in vapors, the debris slick with ice.

Nothing. We found nothing—until the bent metal of Winston's motorcycle smacked into my shins.

No!

I fell to my knees and dug, the frigid temperatures numbing my fingers. "Farren, help me." Desperation colored my voice, pitching it higher.

He bent beside me, throwing off the larger rocks. Wreckage cut my hands, slicing until blood spurted. I kept digging, pain and cold not registering. "Winston!"

Please, please, please…!

"He's not here." Farren stopped, pulling me close, shaking me when I reached to yank more rock off the twisted bike frame. Ice already encased it in a frozen grave. "Lena!"

"No, Farren...please..." Not Winston. No. I couldn't... Oh, God. Shaina.

Farren gripped my shoulders, forcing me to stop. His smile was empty of happiness, but full of relief. "I promise you, he's not here. Look, no blood, nothing but the bike."

Through the sting of grit and tears, I focused on the rubble, the sounds of cracking, thundering stone relentless. Farren was right. "Thank God...Thank God..."

I clutched his shirt as he pulled us both up, searching beyond my shoulder. "They're smart, kid. They're not dead, too stubborn for that, the both of them."

One hand let go of his shirt and pointed to the shack. "She's–"

"Yeah, she is." He laced his fingers through mine and picked through shards of rock, upturned soil, and chunks of broken ice. Squid from fallen trees lay dying or crushed under stone, their cries so human, so devastating. Others grasped their branches, squealing for their family suffering on the forest floor.

Pain skewered Farren's face, but he pressed forward while we navigated around the dead and dying animals. From past incidents, we knew Belva would feel every single death, the loss taking a toll as she sat helpless in one of the underground bunkers near the village.

We made it to the edge of the river, its fluorescent blue running off to the silvery water leading into the gray part of Arcus. A small chasm interrupted the flow, a waterfall frozen and beautiful, dripping at its tips. I unhooked my hand from Farren's and bent to scrub the filth from my eyes and rinse my mouth of dirt, the piercing cold welcomed. Farren did the same, his hands trembling and agony still evident on his face. I knew he wanted nothing more than to go to Belva, ease her ache.

I squeezed his arm, trying to reassure him. "She's strong, Farren."

He washed his face one more time before answering. "I know she is." He didn't elaborate. "We need to scout the area, try to find a way around this mess, closer to the castle."

"Do you think th–"

"Lena!"

My head snapped around and a sob escaped when Tarek charged toward us, Winston beside him. I flew from my spot, slipping on the sleek ground, and flung myself into Tarek's arms, not caring if he wanted to touch me or not. "I thought... There's so much..."

"It's okay." Tarek lifted me up, squeezing me until I couldn't breathe.

Oxygen wasn't important at that moment. He was safe, and that was all I needed to keep on living.

"Why are you here? Why did you come?" He repeated those questions, his voice rough and angry, but he didn't put me down. His fingers reached under my tank top, kneading my side, as if convincing himself I wasn't hurt. They bit and pinched, but I reveled in the warmth of his hand. *Alive.*

"We caught a few portals opening, maybe five or six." Winston began running toward the village. "There ain't nothing we can do here."

Tarek put me down, nodded to Farren, and followed Winston, not letting go of my hand. The contact made it hard to run, but I didn't complain. His touch strengthened me, made me want to fight.

"Son of a bitch!" Farren pointed to the left. Twenty feet ahead of us, a portal opened and two Protectors punched through, taking off before the hole even closed.

Winston waved a hand, slamming one against a tree. The other weaved through the forest, not giving Winston a chance to get him.

Tarek let go of my hand and tackled the guy against the tree as the Protector got up, his gun pointed at us. In seconds, Tarek gripped the Protector's chin and forehead, twisting until the sound of a neck snapping reached above the cries of the squid. A blue flash of light zipped from the dead man's mouth as Tarek held up his hand, the light absorbing into his flesh. He nodded to Winston, his face deadly. "Go get the other one."

Winston tipped his head. A smile that caused the hairs on my neck to stand curled one corner of his mouth. "I won't be long." He took off, not waiting for a reply.

Tarek moved to grab hold of my hand again, dragging me toward the village, the increasing heat of the woods melting the cold running in my veins. "You shouldn't be here," he said.

Before my awakening, I'd have screamed at him, maybe even took a jab at his chin. I yanked my hand from his. "Where else would I be?"

Tarek snatched my hand back, signaling Farren to hurry up, though Ginger was right beside us. "Stupid question, Lena."

"I don't think so." I changed the subject before a brawl erupted. "How many others are here?"

"Ten, maybe." He picked up his speed. "Did everyone make it to the bunkers?"

"I-I told Denzel to find Oren, get everybody to safety."

He laughed, the sound prickling my skin. "So you trusted the 'enemy' to protect our people?"

A low blow, one I deserved. "Maybe I was too quick with the judgment, all right? Happy?"

"Not. At. All."

I tripped, trying to keep up with Tarek's walk. "Tarek! Let go so we can get there faster."

He stopped, pursing his lips and squeezing my hand too tight as he shot a look to the squid, their cries quieting. "If we run, we can't pay attention. Stop talking. Your voice echoes."

Even with the physical contact, he cut himself off from me again. But I wouldn't dwell on that. Not now.

Silence took over the rest of the trek back to the village, all of us scanning the woods, searching for any movement or abnormal cries from the squid. They were dead quiet, as if Tarek gave them the command to stay vigilant.

As soon as the forest broke to reveal the cabins, Tarek let go of my hand and ran down the hill toward the bunkers. Farren and I followed, but still no one spoke. We'd practiced this drill for the past month twice a day, every day. We didn't factor in Exemplar would demolish the castle, but our people adjusted.

We reached the bunkers, about fifty yards behind the mess hall. Thankfully, the sole damage to the village was a dust cloud. None of the Exemplians were around, but this place wasn't exactly hidden. They'd be here soon if we didn't go get them.

Oren and Peter, along with a couple other Protectors, climbed from their perches in tree stands when we stood over one of the three large underground hideouts and gave the all-clear signal. We'd dug out the secured spots the same time we started building the cabins. They weren't exactly four-star accommodations, but they were safe and hidden.

Farren confronted Oren before anyone could speak, his face red and body taut. "Where is she?"

Oren pointed to the first bunker, twenty feet away from our position. Farren stalked to the hatch camouflaged with black soil and deep green shrubs and pulled on the lever, disappearing inside. When the door closed, the bunker vanished under its disguise.

"What happened?" Oren focused on Tarek, his gun tense and ready in his hand.

Peter stood next to him, his weapon drawn, too. The month of training helped, his face not showing how scared he undoubtedly was.

"What do you think happened? The castle came tumbling down!" I didn't want to waste time explaining the obvious. I wanted to run to my cabin, collect my gear, and go hunting.

They ignored my outburst while Tarek explained, mentioning the ten or so authority Exemplians roaming Arcus as we spoke.

"Damn." Oren looked to Peter, who lifted his chin while sweat traced the lines of his face. "You're with me."

Peter nodded once before clearing his throat. "What do we do now?"

"What we've been practicing for, boy. We fight." Oren clapped him on the shoulder, his eyes serious and unblinking. "You shoot to kill, understand?"

"Y-yes."

Tarek grabbed my hand. "We'll split into teams. You and the kid, me and Lena, get Erin and Zander, and a couple more. Winston and Farren will stay here with everyone else." A pause. "Have Jake get weapons and more food into those bunkers. We leave in ten minutes."

Oren nodded, already moving to the middle bunker as Erin hopped from a tree, obviously hearing her part in the plan, running with Oren and Peter.

Tarek stalked to my cabin, my hand tight in his. As soon as we made it to my crooked door, he kicked it open. "Get on your suit and grab your stuff."

Fractured Energy

Even though he was again acting like the Ice King, relief flooded through me. He wouldn't leave me behind. He'd let me fight. Shaking my hand to ease the ache from his grip, I undressed as he turned away, facing the door. My cheeks heated while I rushed, trying to cover up what he'd seen so many times before.

"Um...thank you." I spoke to his heaving back as I laced up my suit and turned it on. Its light flickered before humming to life. *Odd.*

"For what?" Ice chilling his words brought hot tears to my eyes, but I wouldn't let them go. I promised to make things right–after protecting our home.

"For letting me come with you." I whispered it. The tears might be caged in my eyes, but they weren't gonna let me have my voice.

His shoulders slumped, and he turned a fraction before stopping, his eyes still pointed away. "Would you have stayed here if I demanded it?"

I swallowed, going with the truth. "No."

"Thought not. Are you dressed?"

Stupid tears! Stay put. "Yeah."

Tarek turned around, his face impassive. "At my side is the safest place for you. Not one of those intruders wants to be the one to kill me."

Right, because if they did, they'd be stuck here, as the new Warden–and we'd waste no time killing whoever tried. Another backup plan: if one of those bastards got to Tarek, one of us would kill them during their transition. We'd all pledged to take over the responsibility for the safety of the group. The night after we had that conversation, I hid in my cabin sobbing. If he died...I'd never come back from that.

"So you're babysitting me?" As much as I loved him, anger was a hard habit to break.

Tarek smiled, the edge softening in his face. "Something like that. Except my ward knows how to shoot and fight." He brushed a finger across my chin before taking my hand, his grip less crushing this time.

He had a habit of saying the right thing, even when he didn't want to be around me. "Yeah, true. Thank you…again."

He nodded, giving my hand a squeeze. "Let's go. Winston's back."

"So, he killed the guy?" We jogged toward the others as Jake shoved another sack into one of the bunkers.

"He did."

"You're sure?"

He stopped in front of Oren and tilted his head down to me. His brow raised as he let go of my hand to show a blue light in the palm of his. "Yes."

"Oh, right." When would I stop second-guessing him?

Oren and Peter were ready, along with Erin, Zander, and two Protectors whom I never bothered to get to know. I needed to change that, the not-bothering-to-give-a-shit attitude. They fought with us; the least I could do was find out their names. But circumstances forced me to put the meet-and-greet on hold.

Zander smiled at me, holding the sniper rifle we…borrowed from some backwoods house on Earth. Had to love Pennsylvania hunters. Come to find out, Zander could hit a target dead on at 600 yards. We discovered his natural talent a year ago. Since then, he became an asset for hunting and scouting. I smiled back before gauging the mood of everyone else. They all looked excited, ready to go. *Crazy.* But I was excited, too. Those bastards wouldn't win.

Jake rushed over and lifted me off the ground, squeezing me tight. "Thank God you're okay."

I hugged him hard, those tears fighting to break free. "I love you, Jake. I don't think I ever said that…" Why hadn't I ever told him?

"Love you, too. More than anything." He set me down, his cheeks sagging and pale. "Stay safe."

"I will, promise."

Jake looked over my shoulder. "Bring our girl back to us."

Tarek cleared his throat and moved to stand beside me. "Absolutely."

Loud rustling, like bulldozers knocking down trees, filled the air. I gripped Tarek's forearm as I looked up. "What the hell?"

Squid rushed to latch onto the trees surrounding the village, the bright pink barricade at least four rows deep. The sight, both terrifying and exhilarating, swelled my heart, their fishy smell not turning my stomach for a change. I glanced down to find Farren and Belva standing a few feet away. My best friend's tear-stained face held courage and vengeance as she used her arms to guide her army closer. I stumbled to her, never taking my eyes off the cloud of pink tentacles creating a linked barrier around our people. "Belva? They're…amazing."

"They're family." Her hazel eyes found mine, sorrow lancing her pretty face as her bottom lip trembled. "Like you. And they'll protect us, even as they mourn."

Farren pulled Belva in close and kissed the top of her head. His attention shifted to me over the silky brown hair of his love. "Be safe, or I'll kill you."

I nodded, wrapping my arms around them both for a second before going back to Tarek's side. Winston came shooting from the trees, blood staining the front of his white T-shirt. He stopped long enough to say, "Where?"

Oren again pointed to the first bunker, and Winston took off, ripping open the hatch.

Lynn Vroman

Strength seeped into my limbs as realization folded me tight in its arms. That, right there, was what we all fought for. Not revenge, not for hate, but for love, the kind no soul-stealing bullet or threat could erase or diminish. Family.

I'd fight for mine, too–the family here and the family trapped on Exemplar.

CHAPTER 14

LENA

Mistakes

We'd been tracking for the better part of eight hours, stopping long enough to grab a drink from our packs. After a while, Tarek dimmed the light of the sky, darkening it so we'd have the advantage. Like I said, we knew these woods. Exemplians didn't.

First time I'd ever stepped foot on Arcus–well, got yanked through my bed to Arcus–not only the vibrant color stunned me. Noises hypnotized me, too. All the animal calls were backward, snakes walking on land as loud as monkeys and elephants floating in the river as silent as minnows swimming in a brook. Sounds I'd once feared were now sounds I needed to keep me calm.

As soon as the sky blackened, I turned off my suit. Tarek fumbled under my arm to turn it back on.

Shoving his hand away, I reached onto my toes to whisper in his ear. "I'm a beacon with it on."

He cupped my neck, our foreheads touching as his big body tensed. I didn't say anything else as he calmed down enough to realize I was right. After a few minutes, he nodded, letting me go with a hand gesture that said to stay by his side and move forward. He reached under his arm to turn his suit off, too.

That was the extent of our conversation until my radio dinged. Pulling out a set of earbuds from my pack, I stuck one in my ear, plugged them into the receiver, and turned up the volume. "Zander tagged two."

As soon as Erin's words flew across the radio waves, two blue orbs zipped through the woods, heading toward Tarek as if he were a magnet. He closed his eyes as the energy absorbed into his skin, pleasure softening his face. Yes, pleasure. Power had that effect on everyone, no matter how much a person tried to deny it. Tarek never tried, though. He accepted the duty. Once, after we'd…yeah…he said it gave him the confidence to protect us. Selfless to the end. The exact opposite of how I'd been acting.

Shaking the guilt from my mind, I pointed up. We had eight more targets, and if they were smart, they'd be steering clear of the deeper woods while the sky was dark. Best place to spot any movement would be a sky view.

At Tarek's nod, I stuffed my gun into its holster and climbed. As the forest boasted a symmetry, so too did the trees' limbs, being thick and evenly distributed about five feet from the base to tips. Scaling a tree took as much effort as climbing the jungle gym in my elementary school playground. Tarek followed me up, his steps soundless. I hadn't mastered the dead quiet yet, but my footfalls were soft. I cringed thinking about Peter. He'd gotten better, but not by much.

I stopped about ten feet below the squid occupying the tree to let Tarek go ahead of me. Belva made sure to let these guys know who I was a long time ago, but they didn't always listen. Tarek couldn't communicate to them like she could, though they usually did as he commanded.

But what he must've told them terrified me. A squishy tentacle wrapped around his waist, swung him from our perch, and plopped him on the tallest branch before reaching down to do the same to me.

Fractured Energy

I had to bite my bottom lip to keep from crying out as gravity left while I flew out and up, like bungee jumping in reverse. Tarek gripped my flailing arms as the thing let go, and I toppled onto his lap, clutching his shoulders and trying like hell not to hyperventilate. "I don't *ever* want to do that again."

He grunted and moved me in front of him, already yanking binoculars from my pack. I stayed positioned on all fours, my fingers finding no purchase on the sleek, thick limb under us. When I slipped, almost tumbling the hundred feet to ground, Tarek grabbed my backpack and hoisted me up to sitting almost on his outstretched legs. "Don't move."

I heaved in mountains of oxygen. "No problem." Yeah, forgot how much I hated heights.

The squid ten feet under us purred. Tarek closed his eyes for a second, and its long tentacles formed a cocoon around our spot. He gave me a quick glance and shrugged. "Extra security, just in case."

"Good idea." I pulled my pack off and unzipped the first pocket, pulling out two energy bars, tossing one to Tarek. He grabbed it without looking, his other hand holding the binoculars to his eyes.

We ate in silence as he perused the terrain, leaning too far out for my liking to get a view across the silent river. Skidding closer to him, I grabbed a thick knot on the tree trunk while wrapping my free hand around his left calf. When he glanced down with a raised brow, it was my turn to shrug. "Just in case."

Grinning, he peered across the river, still as a statue and saying nothing. While I held his leg and the tree, I searched the forest floor, squinting through the darkness. It didn't take long for cricks to tighten in my neck, my head ready to roll off.

Two hours later, we still searched in quiet, the sound of the forest our company. Ten more minutes of this and my body wouldn't let me fight a water elephant. Leaning up, I stretched muscles in places that shouldn't have muscles, fighting fatigue. No matter how much I wanted to be like Tarek, who only moved to search another area, I needed sleep. Sipping on water, I slouched against the tree, trying to find a nonexistent comfortable spot. As for Tarek's leg, I let go a while back—when he shrugged off my hand to change positions. As I let my mind relax, guilt washed over me. We forgot something at home. Christ, I had to find out names…more than names.

"Hey." He ignored me, and I whispered at him again. "Tarek?"

Dragging the binoculars from his eyes like it was the hardest thing he'd ever done, Tarek's silver darts pointed my way.

"We never told that Protector's husband she—"

"Her name was Katherine, and he was told." He shifted his attention back toward the distance.

"Oh, good. That's good." I should have made an effort to know her name. "Um…why don't you sit down, rest." I held up the radio, earbuds still intact, when he glanced back down. "You can listen in on the others, but it sounds like they're laying low for a couple hours, too." I jiggled it. "No beeps. Radio silence."

He stared holes through me, the war with rest and vigilance written all over his handsome face. After a sigh that wracked his entire body, Tarek tossed me the binoculars and held out his hand until I placed the radio in his palm.

I get pissed, but the silent treatment sucked ass. Nothing annoyed me more than hearing my own voice bounce off closed ears.

My voice, though, stayed low. I was annoyed, not stupid. "You're not even gonna talk to me? Give me a chance?"

He slid down next to me–because there wasn't anywhere else to lean back–and crossed his arms over his wide chest. His head stayed pointed forward, regardless of how hard I drilled his profile with a glare.

"I know you hear me."

After running a hand through his tangled hair, he finally answered. "Do you remember when you accused me of loving someone who didn't love me? Someone who only cared about her own agenda?"

My stomach knotted, butterflies smacking against each other and dying. I remembered. The jealousy I had for my past self almost destroyed the both of us. I accused her of so many things. Apathy and tunnel vision being the big issues. I also accused Tarek of seeing her as this omniscient person who could do no wrong.

Stupid, especially now that I completely understood her, but...

"Tarek–"

"You said she didn't trust me, didn't care as much about me as you did."

Did. No, not past tense. Never. My heart guided my hand to his bicep before my head could warn it might not be a great idea. "I was wrong. So, so wrong."

His eyes closed and his hands resting on his knees clenched. "About some things, yes, but how I loved her...even when she lost sight of herself...that was the truth."

Old jealousies burrowed into my head, but I tamped them down. Being mad at him for loving her was both unfair and ridiculous. His love for her brought him to me. "I know, and I understand, really."

He bowed his head, sighing. "That's not–I'm trying to tell you"–he lifted his gaze to mine–"that you've become her. All the bad you accused her of, everything, you are guilty of now."

Tears spurted from my eyes, down my cheeks. If he had thrown me out of the tree, it would've hurt less. "I-I haven't."

His thumb wiped away a few tears dripping off my chin. "You have. But I love you, even when it hurts." He dropped his thumb and turned away from me again. "Maybe in this lifetime, or possibly the next, you'll finally let us be together."

"I'm ready now." My voice squeaked, despair stopping up my throat. "Please."

"No, you're not." Tarek closed his eyes. "Sleep, Lena. I'll take the first watch."

He gave me nothing else.

Same thing I'd given him for far too long.

∞ ∞ ∞

I slept. My body refused to let my mind and heart stay awake and wallow. But waking up to Tarek's hand covering my mouth, his nose inches from mine, pushed any leftover fatigue away.

I stayed dead still, searching his face for answers. He mouthed *don't talk,* and his palm lifted to guide my attention toward the three Protectors huddled under a tree close to ours.

They sat, backs together and guns drawn. Quiet flooding the woods should've given them a clue, but they didn't seem to notice or pay attention. I knew when the squid and other small creatures lurking around suddenly shut up that I needed to start running.

Fractured Energy

Not them. Silence had the opposite effect, their shoulders relaxed. The dumbasses even began talking in low voices that traveled all the way up to our hideout.

Without a sound, Tarek began climbing down after signaling for me to stay put.

I itched to follow, but as the squid quietly unwove its tentacles to track Tarek's every move, I finally understood the plan. My giant wasn't going to kill them—*his* giant would be doing the job. I slid my gun from its holster, aiming at Exemplian heads anyway. If the squid failed to grab all three, the bullets in my gun would take care of the rest.

The sky lightened a fraction when Tarek balanced on a branch midway down. Not even the burgeoning purple set their alarm bells off. Didn't they read their world histories? Only answer: Cassondra sent a few more unprepared expendables.

What we did for Peter and Denzel, though…having mercy wasn't our best attribute. Exceptions rarely happened, and today not one of us was in the mood to be nice. They demolished our castle and killed one of our own. My gun narrowed in on the person nearest to the tree trunk.

Tarek scratched the bark until I glanced his way. He waved me down, using a gesture to indicate how slow he wanted me to climb. I wanted to argue with a few hand gestures of my own. The shot was clear from where I sat, but yeah, a hundred feet. My aim was nothing like Zander's. I holstered my weapon before strapping on my pack, and picked my way down, slipping some, but otherwise quiet.

Until I was inches from clasping Tarek's outstretched hand.

When I reached the limb above him, a water bottle tumbled from the front pouch of my backpack. Its dull thud echoed as it smacked limbs until it hit the ground. All three Protectors stood. Their surprise lasted seconds before their guns pointed in our direction and bullets started flying, their aim thankfully skewed by the tree.

Tarek yanked me from where I hung and smashed me up against the trunk, shielding me with his body. "Now!"

The squid screeched so loud the sound pierced my eardrums as its arms flew through the air, crashing down on the spot where we'd nested for the past few hours, destroying our perch. Once its tentacles were free of the tree, it snatched up one Protector, and then the other two, squeezing until blood poured over its pink flesh. Two blue lights rushed from the remains of the Protectors and smacked Tarek in the chest. The third scorched through the tree limbs moments later.

Tarek's hands pressed into the small of my back as the light filled him. I said nothing, too busy feeling stupid and careless. Forgetting to zip my pack? Dumb mistake that almost got us killed, and all the noise we made would draw the others over here. Five more to go and now they'd be hunting us. Although better than searching for the village, it put Tarek and me in a bad position.

The radio dinged like crazy in my bag. Tarek breathed in deep before reaching behind me to take it out. Giving one earbud to me, he took the other and held the radio to his mouth. "We got three."

"What was all that noise?" Oren's angry voice screamed into my ear, making the shitty feeling in my gut worse.

My attention landed on our feet as I shook my head. *Stupid, stupid, stupid...*

To my surprise, Tarek tilted my chin until our eyes met. A smile softened his face as he smoothed back sweaty hair plastered on my cheeks. He didn't say anything to me. He didn't need to.

126

Holding the radio close to his mouth again, he said, "Ah…a water bottle."

Even with all the shame building a tent in my gut, I laughed, covering my mouth to keep it from echoing. He chuckled, too, especially when Oren's swearing went pro.

Tarek rolled his eyes and interrupted Oren's rant. "Everyone go back, set up a perimeter around the village. Lena and I will lead the rest farther away."

Once everyone reluctantly agreed, Tarek shut off the radio and tucked it in my pack.

"Screwed up big time, huh?" I tucked hair behind my ear, forcing myself to hold his gaze.

"Not exactly. They'll be coming for us now." He shrugged. "All we have to do is pick them off."

"Silver linings and all that?"

"Exactly." He spun me around to zip up all my compartments. "But let's not push our luck."

Lynn Vroman

CHAPTER 15

LENA

Close Calls

I never liked hide and seek when I was a kid. Hated it, actually. Waiting, without moving or talking, for someone to find me created nothing but panic. I was the dumbass who'd jump up and yell, opting for the seeker to chase me. At least then, we were on an even playing field. But the trailer park kids had nothing on the predators searching for us now. These guys knew how to stay quiet, their stealth as lethal as our silent forest.

Tarek took the lead, veering us off the obvious paths between the trees to the better cover of the dense shrubbery. Every snapping twig or crunching decayed leaf reverberated off the dark tree trunks. Even though Tarek had squid chirping to cover our noise, to me, our feet were too heavy, our breathing too loud. My heartbeat echoed inside my head like a jackhammer. The enemy probably heard that, too.

We'd been steering them away from the village. Our goal was to cross the river, go to the side of Arcus where none of us really ventured, where only Tarek had a vague familiarity. He'd been slowly taking us to the threshold between gray and violet. Purgatory, Belva called it, the in-between, meshing and blending the vibrant forest with the sleek ice. Sweat froze under my clothes, making my teeth chatter so badly I had to clench my jaw until it ached.

Before we set out, Tarek and I donned sweatshirts and loose-fitting pants to hide the glow of our suits. The added layer didn't protect us from the growing cold, temperatures in this spot of the woods dipping so low, dew crystalized on the marbled green and gray bushes.

Cold seeping through my suit was like a lullaby, creating exhaustion as my body fought against it. My eyelids drooped, and my feet grew loud and sloppy while we moved forward, no amount of willpower giving me back some energy. Hours passed, maybe days.

Tarek stopped and turned, anger pursing his lips. When his attention fell on my face, anger softened to concern. He clasped my hand, his eyes growing wide. Looking around for a second, he led us to a hidden spot where brush and leaves piled atop each other in a rainbow of browns, burnt reds, and gold. Tarek pulled me to a tiny hollow created from crumbled rock and leftover castle. The space was big enough for two people, as long as one person sat on the lap of the other.

As soon as my numb body fell onto his, he wrapped me in his arms and began rubbing my hands. The friction sent waves of heat through my frozen fingers, stinging and biting. My chattering teeth sang to us, no matter how tight I held my jaw.

"Your suit's not working right," Tarek said.

No shit.

The warmth of his chest left my back for a second while he wrestled off my pack and his own, pulling a thermal blanket from one. He first draped the blanket across his shoulders before pulling me close to secure us both in the thin fabric. His warm lips smashed against my temple as he pressed a button on the corner of our soft cocoon. Heat instantly radiated from the blanket, transferring to my body. Sleep, all I wanted was to close my eyes forever.

His mouth moved to my ear. "We'll stay here for a while." He squeezed me tighter. "The river...it will be colder, Lena, almost unbearable. I don't know if you–"

"I c-can. G-give me a couple hours." Don't know if he understood a word coming from my numb lips, but he nodded, pulling me even closer.

We sat there, listening, my body too drained to react to foreign sounds. Thankfully, there weren't any.

"Sleep, we're safe for now." Tarek kept his cheek pressed against mine. To give heat, but still, I clung to his nearness. What can I say? He gave me strength.

"What about you?" I snuggled closer, wanting to give him the option to rest, but mind and body weren't cooperating.

"I'll sleep. The squid will let me know if they get too close."

"Do you know where they are?"

"About eight miles south."

I turned, our lips almost touching. "You've known the whole time?"

His eyes closed. He pulled away before opening them again with a nod. "The squid are herding them here. We have about four hours, if the forest does its job and makes it tough for them."

"So, what's the plan?" I faced forward and his cheek returned to mine.

"We force them to follow us to the other side. The river will take care of the rest."

"Oh, um, good idea. Except...why not let the squid handle them?"

"They keep killing squid that outright attack them. We can't afford to lose the animals' protection. The river is the answer. All we have to do is not get shot on the way across."

Right.

Should've known it wouldn't be that easy.

∞ ∞ ∞

As soon as Tarek turned off the blanket, the thing packed up all its heat and left shop. A few hours of sleep nestled in the protection of Tarek's arms brought energy back to my limbs, though not much. I missed how his arms felt–when I actually gave myself permission to love it. Even in this situation... I wished we could erase time and start over. Just forget everything but us.

Unfortunately, my body couldn't adapt here as Tarek's could. I don't think he even felt the cold, other than an annoying chill. With my suit not working properly, I had no defense against it.

He pushed me off his lap to stuff the blanket in his pack. Back to silence, he held a finger to his lips before pointing toward the docile river. At my nod, his quiet footsteps took him from our little haven with me following close behind, yet not as soundless. Every crunch and snap cinched my gut as I searched the symmetrically lined trees for shadows or flying bullets. As much as I disagreed, we left the relative safety of thick, frost-covered foliage to make a direct path toward the river. We transformed to bait. The tactic worked because the foreign sounds I didn't pick up before now played in stereo, moving closer.

When we hit the riverbank, Tarek bent low until his lips touched my ear. "Once you get into the water, make noise. But not enough to–"

I pulled away from his terse whisper, his deep voice right up against my eardrum like a drill, sending rivulets of agony into my skull. "I got it, understood." My voice barely hitched above a breath.

Holding his pack above his head, his chin dipped toward mine. I took my bag from my shoulders, lifting with one hand to copy him while using the other to carry my gun. I ignored the weight of the heavy pack on my left shoulder to sink my foot into the silvery blue water. Shock coursed from my big toe to pelvis, the water burning like palming the inside of a lit oven. Instinct ruled over any command I gave my brain, and I wrenched my foot from what my nervous system considered danger.

Already in the water, Tarek latched onto my forearm, dragging me in. My body rejected the freezing temperature, refusing to acclimate. A scream ripped from my roughened throat, causing the squid to squawk and shake their trees. Hell, I didn't have to force myself to make noise. Animalism taking over rational thought demanded it. I tugged hard, but Tarek's grasp remained firm, his grip so tight, bones crushed together. My suit, flickering on and off before, shut down completely with the cold, its green glow disappearing.

"No, no, no, no…" Tarek's face paled as he picked up speed, driving us farther through the arctic water.

The opposite bank was at least thirty feet away. Each inch traversed through the frigid deathtrap lasted hours, even if it were only minutes. The water level reached my chest, threatening to stop my heart.

Finally finding the ability to get a grip, I shut my mouth. Enough screaming; they heard. My body's pleading shut off long enough to push across to the other side, but Tarek stopped, keeping me close. My teeth chattered, and I'm pretty sure a molar cracked in two. The icy bite of the water was like having a python clamped around my waist.

Thankfully, all my limbs went numb, not affecting me anymore. Well, except for the exhaustion that sagged my eyelids. If Tarek hadn't been holding me up, I'd have let the river take me.

His cold lips moved to my cheek. "They're watching us, to your left. All their guns are aimed at you."

Honestly, I didn't care. Putting me out of my misery would've done me a favor. Unfortunately, Tarek didn't see it my way. After he closed his eyes a moment, the squid screamed and shook their trees with fury, swinging their tentacles toward the five Protectors who were forced from hiding. The squid managed to grapple two, blood spurting red against the silvery bank. As their energy rushed to Tarek, one of the remaining Protectors killed two of the animals before he and the rest rushed into the river, the only path not hindered by raging cephalopods.

Bones again crunched in the arm Tarek gripped. My shooting arm. He wrenched me forward. "Run! Go!"

Run? My legs wouldn't even move. Bullets whizzed by, none near Tarek, all narrowly missing me. I managed to pull my arm from Tarek's grasp and fired off a few shots, a flash of light zinging into Tarek's chest proof I hit one.

My energy drained to an empty tank. "I c-can't m-move." At least I think that came from my mouth. Blackness flirted with me, offering a reprieve from the murderous river.

In seconds, Tarek flung my frozen body over his shoulder and fought the water, our speed more like running through drying cement. If not for my head slamming against his back and my face slipping under the water, I'd have passed out. Bullets, their blue flash like shooting stars, splat and plunked into the calm river as Tarek's legs pumped faster. As soon as his boots hit the slippery rocks of the shallow edge, he threw me over the bank. I landed hard on an unforgiving ground, bones jarring. Too weak to grunt, I curled into a ball and closed my eyes.

I had zero plans to open them again.

Loud rushing water filled my ears, and the wind picked up to freeze the droplets in my hair until icicles scratched my cheeks. With the roaring wind came the pungent smell of fish, strong enough to relieve my stomach of what little it held onto. The chaotic maelstrom of rushing white water was enough to put me over the edge. Warmth from my right shoulder drizzling down to my wrist was the lone comfort my mind registered. I clung to the lazy heat, wishing it'd spread.

Stomping boots with echoes of slurping water landed next to my head. The sound wasn't enough to open my eyes. If the river thing didn't work, and the Protectors made it across, well, then they won. No more fight burned inside. A strong desire for sleep made me smile. I could do it. Sleep. Maybe they'd place the soul-stealer bullet with my energy in it right next to Wilma's. It wouldn't be so bad. We'd at least be together. No bad at all…

"Lena, wake up. Open your eyes."

Not the Protectors. I almost whimpered, disappointment squeezing my heart.

Next thing I knew, I was flying. Arms enveloped me, cradling my body. No, not flying. Floating.

"No. *No!*"

His tortured voice had the effect of a drill sergeant. My lids peeled open to meet gray eyes full of panic. "Tarek?"

His shaking finger traced my cheek. "Stay awake, love. Stay with me."

"W-What?" The black became impatient, demanding I come over to play.

As he lifted his finger, I saw it. Blood. Bright red, exaggerated like everything else on Arcus, stained his hand. "You–they shot you."

I smiled, light-headed, wishing I had the strength to touch his lips. He really was beautiful. "Oh…okay."

After that, the black finally won.

Lynn Vroman

CHAPTER 16

TAREK

Wounded

"Lena!" This time, she didn't open her eyes. Blood poured from her shoulder and saturated her tattered suit.

Please.

Please.

Please.

He ripped the sleeve off. *Please don't be in her shoulder...*

Relief caused him to fall backward, landing on his ass atop frozen, slick rocks. Clean shot, through and through. More of a graze. If it had lodged in her skin—no, he wouldn't let his mind wander there.

Scrambling to his feet, the raging water screaming in his ears, he searched for their packs, both sodden but thankfully not lost to the river. Lena still had a death grip on both her bag and gun. She'd never let go of her gun, even with a bullet hole in her shoulder.

He collected his things and hefted Lena from the hard ground, snatching gear from her now limp hands. Her pale face and blue lips sent rivulets of acidic fear through his veins.

Panic overtook his brain, and he let it. If he carried her like this, while she bled out... *Damn it!*

He set Lena down and tore open his pack. One drenched shirt was the only cloth he had, the bandages they carried soggy and useless. He tore it in two pieces and used one to tie off Lena's wound, yanking the ends so tight she moaned. Blood soaked through, and so he tied the second strip of freezing, wet cloth over the first. The blood continued to seep against any barricade Tarek used. Her energy might still be whole, but if they didn't find a safer, warmer place, that situation would change quickly. But before they could...

He closed his eyes and breathed in deep, going to his calm place, trying to block out Lena's cold, still body.

Right.

Ignoring her pain was as impossible as shutting the door on her, stupid of him to think it possible. But...breathe...

The river raged, but with less intensity. At least the remaining Protectors were floating carcasses. Good enough for him.

Picking her up again, her weight as cumbersome as air, he trudged to the safety of the trees and hit a straight path toward heat. Only three or four miles...might as well have been a thousand. He slogged farther, but every time he glanced at her face, it grew paler, almost translucent. Tarek stopped and looked up. Not many squid spent time in this part of the forest, the frigid temperatures biting and unforgiving, but there were a few. A few would be enough.

If this didn't work, she'd be dead.

Words weren't conveyed to the squid, more like images of what he needed them to do. As soon as the last image left his mind and transmitted to theirs, they hummed. A pink tentacle slithered from the top of the closest tree to wrap around his waist. He held Lena tighter and relaxed his body at the same time. The squid swung them so fast his stomach dipped. Just as it let go after a mad, twenty-yard dash, another clasped onto him, flinging him farther into the woods. Squid after squid carried them closer to the warmth, the tropical heat hinting, and then hammering down on them like rain. His feet stung as they thawed, tiny pinpricks tapping his soles. When sweat poured from his face, he closed his eyes one more time.

The last squid set them gently on the ground, purring as its tentacle slinked higher into its tree. Wasting no time, Tarek set Lena on the ground. The heat did nothing to bring color back to her face. He searched both bags, finding only medicines found on Earth, the last of the Empyrean medicine Teenesee gifted gone long ago. The alcohol would burn, and he hoped to hell it would. *Just give me a whimper, a sign...*

The bloodied makeshift bandage could do nothing else. He delicately untwined it from her wound, hissing when the charred skin already began to pus. Soul-stealers always left a souvenir, even if they didn't stick around to steal the energy. The chemicals in them were foreign to most worlds, even Exemplar. Another stolen resource from another world.

He twisted the cap off the clear bottle. "I'm so sorry, Lena." *For so many things...*

Tarek poured the contents onto her wound.

She barely moved, but she screamed. Screamed so loud, the squid grew nervous in their trees. To him, the sound was better than ambrosia. Better than oxygen filling his lungs.

"That's it, love. Almost done."

She didn't hear him, already passed out again.

The only piece of clothing left was his sweatshirt. He pulled it over his head and dabbed at the wound before pressing his shirt to her shoulder until his fingers whitened. Once the seeping blood turned to a slight drizzle, he slathered on some antibacterial ointment before tying the sleeves tight around her shoulder. That was it. All their resources allowed him to do.

Another search through their bags and he had their blankets, another gift from Teenesee. They were drenched, but as soon as he flicked them on, the heating mechanism instantly dried the fabric. He smoothed one on the ground and carried Lena to rest on it before covering her body with the other.

She never twitched.

Tarek brushed knotted hair from her face, wishing she'd open her eyes. "I'm so, so sorry... I should've never let you come with me." Only, he knew if he had said no, she would've come into the woods with someone else, or worse, alone. Any chance she had to kill an Exemplian, she'd take it. She no longer cared about her life, no matter what she tried to tell him in that tree. So, he had to care enough for her. But look where it got them? Lena shot and almost killed by a soul-stealer.

They were completely damaged. The both of them.

He pulled away from her and built a fire. An unnecessary fire, but he had to do something. Hours later, Winston entered his head: *They're coming from everywhere, attacking the squid. Y'all better be alive.*

Damn it. He closed his eyes. *We're alive. Lena's shot. We're laying low until she can walk.*

Winston: *Where?*

Across the river, about five miles from the village.

Silence wafted between them for a few minutes.

Then Tarek said, *How many?*

Too many. But they ain't even trying to barge in and light a torch. They pick off squid and bounce. Don't know what they're doing. Y'all sit tight; we got this. Just...keep her alive, you heard?

He clenched his fist and nodded as if Winston could see him. *Keep me updated.*

Tarek turned to Lena when Winston said nothing more. He moved beside her and stroked a thumb down her cheek. *No.*

She was burning up.

He grabbed an empty bottle from his pack and went to the river. When he returned, he spent the rest of the night using water to try to cool her down.

He did the same the next day, along with peeling off her clothes, hoping that'd help.

The next day too, only he cleaned her wound with more alcohol. She didn't move.

As tired as he was, he continued to battle her fever on the third day, cleaning her wound, drenching her with water until a sheen of sweat glistened her skin, and drenching her again when the fever returned.

Then a miracle.

"Water."

Day four. He had been cleaning her wound, the skin healing some but still angry and red. Thankfully, no infection set in, the pus from those bullets easily contained if the wound was cleaned right away. As soon as she spoke, he tossed the ointment onto his pack and went for the water bottle. He tipped it to her cracked lips. "Not too much. Take it slow, easy."

Her eyes, delirious and brilliant green, found his. She smiled. "*Him...*"

Then she escaped back into oblivion.

Lynn Vroman

CHAPTER 17

LENA

Thirst

One time, when I was seven or eight, I got crazy sick with meningitis. I swam inside my head for two weeks, underwater and refusing to surface, come back to reality. The first time Tarek jumped into my dreams happened to be when the fever held me captive. He kept me company, promised to find me, bring me home. I believed him. All I had to do was clasp his hand, which was always–always– out of reach. When I finally fought through the muck and opened my eyes, I found myself not with the blond giant, whose smile gave me strength, but in a hospital bed, Mom at my side, crying. She kept repeating, "You're alive! You're alive!" I remember trying to talk to her, squeeze her hand while she clung to me. I wanted to tell her about *Him*. How he saved me.

I also remembered the drought that had attacked my throat, the need for water more important than oxygen.

Thirst like that…hard to forget. Not even those three days trapped on Arcus, what seemed like an eternity ago, could compare. At least there, I had fetid, stale water to ease the ache. No, the thirst after a fever that lasted days…nightmares manifested from that sort of thirst.

The same thirst forced my eyes open, lids scratching my irises. I had no idea where I was, but if I didn't get water soon, I was pretty certain my eyes wouldn't open again.

With a tongue too thick to fit in my mouth, I tried to manipulate it to form one word. "W...water."

I wanted to sit up, search for it myself, but my entire body deflated like a balloon, brittle and thin.

My eyes slammed shut as daggers pierced my skull, thirst gnawing at my brain as much as my mouth and throat. Cramps crippled my body, paralyzing me with an added layer of misery.

Craziness, from somewhere so deep and dark it scared me, bubbled up and spewed on the surface.

Water!

Water!

Water!

Fingers kneaded the back of my neck as my upper body lifted. Cold wetness touched my cracked lips, turning me into an animal. I gulped, the flow choking me. I kept swallowing even as I gagged. Too soon, the life's blood left my mouth. Crazy no longer tamable, I grunted, though in my head it was a scream like a Fury, shattering glass and rock and bone.

"Not too much. Take it slow, easy."

The voice was a melody, maybe an angel. Maybe I was dead and the past three years a dream. The liquid I had managed to consume slithered through my body, bringing parts to life. Still I couldn't move anything except my eyelids.

Above, someone hovered. Worry marred his dirty face. His hair was a tangled golden crown and his eyes shined like uncut diamonds, but he wasn't an angel. No. He was so much more.

He was *Him*, and he found me.

Finally.

Content, I sank back inside myself and drifted.

∞ ∞ ∞

Fractured Energy

Was I swimming? My eyes flew open and I shot up to have gravity push me back down. Sweat emptied from every pore and then some. The heated blanket hummed, slick and clammy against my bare skin. I kicked it off, the humid air of the forest not doing me any favors. Naked and not giving two shits about it, I again tried to sit up, taking it easy this time. Drenched, knotted hair weaved around my arms, searing my scalp while I unwrapped my hands from the mess. I really needed Mom to lop off about ten inches. I–oh.

Everything flooded in, the trek across the river, the Protectors...getting shot. Memories guided my fingertip to my right shoulder, and I hissed when they landed on the bandaged tender spot close to my collarbone.

Soft snoring caught my attention, distracting the panic trying to clog up my judgment. I turned to my left to find Tarek resting on his side, away from me. He'd given me both blankets, leaving him with nothing. Not that a blanket was necessary in Arcus's tropical warmth, but at least it'd protect him from the scuttling, slimy things on the ground.

On shaky hands and knees, I crawled the four-foot gap between us and collapsed behind him. A bottle of water sat above his head, and I snatched it like I'd spent days in the desert, downing it in a few gulps.

Tarek stirred and turned to the crunching sound of plastic as I squeezed the bottle, sucking so hard the thing looked like it breathed. As soon as his eyes were open, he scooped me into his arms and folded me as close and tight to his body as I could get. His chest hiccupped, but otherwise, he made no noise as his big palm smoothed damp hair from my face. His touch soothed, lulling me back to sleep, even though I knew we had to move. But then, I didn't much care for what we *had* to do.

Sometime later, I awoke, nestled in Tarek's arms. Thirst attacked my throat. Again. Squirming from his hold, and trying like crazy to ignore the cramps riding up my legs and massive headache, I searched for my pack, finding it a few feet away. As I moved toward it, an ironclad grip clamped down on my ankle. "You need to rest."

I kicked at his hand, the thirst demanding it, until he let go. As soon as the bag was unzipped, everything flew out until I found liquid gold. All thirty-two ounces slid down my throat– well, all that didn't run down the sides of my face onto my chest. Swallowing the last bit, my tongue was finally a normal enough size to speak. "I'm thirsty."

"I can see that." He stood, stretching his muscles. "How do you feel?"

"Like I got hit by a jet plane." Suddenly aware of my nakedness, I fought between covering up the important parts and ignoring it. He'd seen me naked plenty of times…before he said he was done. Now, it felt awkward. Bringing my knees up to cover my chest, I nodded toward my contego suit hanging on a branch. "Wanna hand that over?"

He smiled before chucking it my way. The torn, mangled fabric landed at my toes. Trying to get the thing on proved impossible, my body as wobbly as gelatin. That didn't stop me, though. I kept shoving and pulling as sweat punched through my skin, slithering into my eyes, stinging them. "Sonofabitch!" I glanced up to find Tarek watching with a raised brow. "Something funny?"

"Yes. Need help?" He stood with his arms over his chest, rocking on his heels.

"Just hand me a blanket."

"Stubborn, even when you're as white as death." He stomped over to my makeshift bed and tossed the soft, humming missile my way. "Hungry?"

146

Without looking up, I hid under the blanket, turning off the heat. "Starving. How long was I out?"

"Almost five days. The bullet grazed your shoulder, but still a nasty wound. You're lucky."

Five days? "No kidding." If the bullet had embedded itself anywhere on my body, I'd be bottled up inside it by now.

Tarek went for his pack, pulling out an energy bar and lobbing it in my direction before sitting back down to eat one of his own. God, I hated these things. Hated them. What I wouldn't give for a greasy cheeseburger and fries right about now. I bit into the powdery, faux chocolate brick of crap anyway, imagining burger juice dribbling down my chin. We ate in silence, my bar gone in thirty seconds flat. Damn thing lied. It didn't give any kind of energy, just sat in my gut like coal. Taking some deep breaths, I swallowed whatever wanted to come back up, my eyes closed and concentrating hard on not being sick.

"You should've eaten slower."

"You're full of wisdom, aren't you?"

"All the time."

Comfortable silence wafted between us while I held onto my gut and he finished his meal. Christ, add the river to a long resume of close calls. Near death didn't even faze me anymore. But as we sat there, the quiet trees finally sank in. That fazed me. A lot. I looked up to see squid, but they barely moved, like bright pink statues frozen in time.

"What's wrong with them?"

Tarek swallowed, stuffing the wrapper into his bag. "Protectors are picking off the squid guarding the village."

My stomach turned to stone. "I thought we killed them all."

"They keep trickling in, a couple at a time. When they found the cabins…it's been nonstop."

Without a word, I found my suit and yanked it on, the energy bar finally holding its end of the deal. The right sleeve gone and the suit not working didn't bother me. I scrambled for my shoes.

"What are you doing?"

I kept looking. "My shoes, where are they?"

"Lena…"

"*Where?*"

"You're not strong enough. We're at least five miles from camp."

"Five miles is nothing." I found my shoes without his help near the base of a tree and shoved them on. When I went to stand, anger and energy bar wasn't enough fuel to keep me on my feet.

Before I could plop down to the ground, Tarek had me in his arms. "Maybe so, but in your condition it might as well be fifty."

"So what's your plan? Hide here until they get through the squid and aim for people? *Our people*?"

His grip on my waist tightened as he bent right next to my ear. "What good are you to them now? They have Winston, Farren, Oren…Zander's been up in a tree, tagging them if they get too close. You go, and all you're going to be to *our people* is a liability."

The stinging slap his words gave my heart and ego took all the rage with it. He was right. I hated that. I also hated how I jumped to anger in the first place. This wasn't how to win his trust back–by not trusting him. "Fine, you're right. It's just…hard to sit here and do nothing."

He let go of my waist after helping me lean against a tree. "One more day for you to rest, two tops, and we'll figure out a way to get back home." He tapped his temple. "Winston's keeping me informed, and no one has been hurt. They… The Protectors are coming, shooting squid. And whomever Zander doesn't pick off opens a portal and leaves. What they're doing is strategic. The ones we killed...they were suicide missions, probably sent to distract me from everyone else."

"Christ." I slumped to the ground. "Are you sure?"

"No, but that's all I have. They knew where the village was the entire time, like someone told them exactly where it was. The castle, those ten...we fell for it."

Hate curdled in my gut, the need for murder causing my mouth to salivate. Someone had to feed them all the information. "Avery."

"Yeah." He threw a few rocks, the hollow sound of the missiles hitting trees following.

"What do you think their objective is, besides wiping us off the planet?"

He gave a soft laugh that held no humor. "Exactly that, though they have some kind of plan I can't figure out...yet."

"What do you think they're afraid of? Why won't they just go into the village and start a war?"

He didn't answer for a while, but moved to sit by me–making sure nothing of his was touching anything of mine. Finally, he said, "They're afraid I'll bleed the lines."

Excitement caused my gut to tingle, like going down the first hill on a roller coaster. "Let's do it, Tarek. Let's open the lines. We can send our people to Cheveyo. He ca–"

"There are innocent people on Exemplar, Lena. Children, those who have no desire to fight, people like Peter. Do we go in blind? Bleed lines and risk the deaths of undeserving people?"

Innocence. What a subjective notion. Nazi sympathizers saw Hitler as righteous. Slave owners, their actions. Murderers, their reasons. My people–ours–hunting...killing those like Peter, Exemplian patsies. "But we need to do something."

149

He laughed, breaking twigs in his big hands. "Well, if you have any ideas, don't be shy."

Oh, ideas played in my head, all sounding as stupid as the next rumbling in. Except one. "We do what they're doing, like Farren suggested in the first place." I said it quiet, almost lower than a breath, wanting him to hear, yet...not. Sending any of our people there would more than likely end in death. Suicide missions. We'd be no better than them.

Tarek kept quiet. His strong fingers crumbling that tiny, delicate twig until it turned to dust, nothingness.

We sat in silence, not the comfortable kind, for what felt like hours. He never looked at me, but my eyes drilled his temple, wishing I could see inside. Fear crept into my heart, not because he didn't answer, but because he *didn't* answer. He heard me; the crushed twig screamed it. What scared me was he might actually be contemplating it. The suicide. One of ours.

Too weak to fight it, my eyes shut. Sleep. We'd sleep on it. Yeah, a few hours would clear all the crazy from our heads. All the impossible. I couldn't kill Peter, and I knew Oren, or even Winston, couldn't, either. To kill a slew of Peters? No, not possible.

"What would they do...once they arrived there?"

His question blared as loud as an angry alarm clock, buzzing, grating, burrowing in my ear like a bug. If I slept, I didn't know.

My eyes opened to find his face, resignation eating his soul. I palmed his cheek, and he clasped my hand like a lifeline. "We don't have to go. We'll find another way."

His shoulders sagged as he nodded.

"Did I sleep?" Fatigue weighting down my bones yelled no. Thirst coming back for another ambush cried yes.

"A couple hours, maybe." Without me having to ask, he reached for water, this time a fluorescent blue in the crinkled bottle, and tipped it to my lips.

I hadn't gotten used to drinking it, even though it tasted fresher than the stale bottled stuff we'd collected and stored over the year. My brain couldn't get past the color, the stuff closer to looking like finger paint than water. But not today. Today I drank as though it were the last puddle in the Sahara. As soon as the cool liquid traveled down my throat, hydrating my insides one vein at a time, exhaustion lifted, my legs not feeling so brittle and useless.

When I emptied the bottle, he went to the river to refill it. I drank that, too. Liquid sloshed and swayed in my stomach, loud, off-key music. He slid the empty bottle in his pack and reached for another energy bar.

I stopped his hand with a weak grin. "Nah, I'm good."

"You need to keep up your strength."

When he shoved it in my face again, I snatched it, giving my rejecting stomach a pep talk. "Fine, but stop acting like my father. I've already had one of those, remember? Didn't work out so well."

He smiled, his dimples peeking out. "Stop being difficult and I will."

I ripped off a big chunk, chewing like a cow gnawing grass. He shook his head, still smiling, as he packed our stuff. I studied him as I chewed, quieter than before. Being Warden put strain on his face. He rarely smiled anymore, not that there was much to smile about. His face, though, still smooth, still beautiful, regardless of the stress he dealt with every day. Some of that stress I caused. *So, so sorry...* Again, the desire to erase the past year ran through my body. I could say sorry a thousand times, but he'd heard that empty apology before.

I swallowed my last bite as he leaned back and closed his eyes. If he caught me staring, he didn't say. He was lost inside his head, lost deep, unreachable.

"How old are you?" The question blurted from my mouth. All this time, I'd never wondered. His face and body were a lie, a defiant snub at aging.

He never opened eyes, his mouth pursed, still in deep thought. I figured he'd ignore me, whatever played in the forefront of his mind more important. But he did answer. "I don't know. This cycle? I think…eighty-three, give or take a few years."

I gasped. Eighty-three? Without thinking it through, I moved to slide a finger down his smooth cheek, a few days' beard soft and scratchy against my fingertips. "My beautiful old man."

He said nothing, motionless as stone.

Not mine anymore.

Not mine, but I'd change that. I would. *If only I knew how…*

His rejection charred my skin. I pulled my fingers away from his face, my attention on his profile. "Ask another question?"

"Do I have a choice?'

"No."

"Well, then…" His eyes remained closed, jaw tight, and dimples a memory.

"When you came looking for me, if I were an eight-three-year-old woman, with wrinkles and a cane, would you have still fallen in love…you know…with *me*?" I pulled the blanket up to my chin, hating the heat, craving the shield.

"I've seen you at eighty-three years old." He opened his eyes and glanced down at his lap. "I've seen you at a hundred fifty years old."

"Yes, but I can almost guarantee that age looks a hell of a lot better on Exemplar, nothing like the old ladies back home." The blanket stayed clenched in my hands, like a grip on a dagger hilt, hoping it'd save me. "But...if you hadn't found me until later, like Oren did Grace, would you have loved me?"

An eternity passed, a lifetime. Finally, he turned to me. His eyes were alive, melting my heart, my blanket dagger useless. He slid closer and pulled the blanket down until his palm pressed against my heart. As he did all those years ago, when I demanded he answer another accusation: *I'm not her.* The thrumming echoed from my chest to his palm, breathing no longer necessary.

Those gray eyes stayed on his hand, the bridge between my body and his. "Your face...to me, the most beautiful creation, whether smooth with youth or lined with wisdom. But...your heart...*you*...both fill and empty me. I'd love you however you are, whoever you are." His warm fingers kneaded my skin, branding me, burning. "Because in here is my life, my everything."

Tears, precious liquid, ran down my cheeks, drowning me. Drowning both of us. I clasped his hand and hoped my plea would somehow transmit through it, showing him the truth. "I'm so sorry, so, so sorry, and I...I'm ready, Tarek. Ready." Ready for what, I didn't know, but I needed him, and not even the guilt could talk me out of it anymore.

He touched his forehead to mine, slipping his hand from my heart, shattering it. "Would you be ready to feel again if we still believed Wilma was gone...forever?"

That stunned me. I backed up, ready to tell him yes, absolutely I would be. But the words wouldn't come out, no matter how hard I argued with my tongue. Would I?

Would I?

153

The light in his eyes turned off before he closed them again. He slumped against the tree. "Thought so. Rest. We're leaving soon."

CHAPTER 18

LENA

His Flaw

Sometimes strength came from purely thinking it existed, even when it didn't want to show up to the party. No, not thinking–swearing and threatening strength to make an appearance sounded more up to my speed.

We moved as slow as snails through the thick shrubs and brush, again staying away from the clear paths between trees. A couple times, when I stumbled, Tarek reached out to catch me. He said nothing, just gave a steel grip on my upper arm until I found my feet again. I'd shrug his hand away every time, which wreaked havoc on my shoulder, but he needed to see me as not helpless. I'm pretty sure, from his scowl, snatching my arm away succeeded in showing him my stubborn ignorance. Christ, I couldn't get anything right when it came to him.

What sucked more, Tarek wasn't kidding about the distance. I could run five miles in my sleep, but we hadn't even walked a half-mile before my body pleaded for me to stop. Who'd have thought a little arctic water and silly bullet wound would put me down for so long? *Hmm, biology, maybe?*

So, yeah, a distance usually a relaxing jaunt for me, took hours, centuries. We stopped every time my body demanded a break, no matter how much I bitched to my inner-self to keep going. Our last pit stop we had a view, though disrupted by trees and distance from across the

155

river, of the squid barricade around our village. It stuck out, like a lighthouse on a cloudy night.

I sipped on fluorescent blue water, handing it back to Tarek, who gulped down the rest, and pointed to the squid. "Probably the worst idea we've had, huh?"

"No. I still believe they knew where to look in the first place. The squid have kept them safe."

I sagged against a tree, sweat blurring my vision. "They would've assumed you'd check out the castle, unless they're stupid–and they proved they aren't. Whom do you think–I mean, they have to be looking for somebody, right?"

"Don't know. It's odd, I agree. Winston, maybe?" He scrubbed at his matted hair, the smell wafting from beneath his arm as unpleasant as the stench leaking from mine. "Maybe Denzel or Peter is more important than we thought?"

Sonofabitch. "Maybe. Guess we need to ask them a few more questions."

"Agreed. But, whoever they want, for whatever reason, it's ensuring they don't wipe the village clean."

Fear, the kind that reeks of self-preservation, hadn't occupied my brain in a while. Fear still existed, but the physiological symptoms, shrinking stomach and tight lungs to name a couple, happened when someone I loved was in danger. Hence, my lovely new affliction, panic attacks. Point being, everyone who meant something to me huddled in the center of that squid fortress–or squatted by my side with concern crinkling his brow.

I stood, my shaking legs complaining. I held onto a branch with one hand and reached for Tarek with the other. "Time to go save the day."

"Do you know how to fly?" He ignored my hand, his butt not moving from the ground.

"What?"

He stayed silent for a minute. "Well…I don't see how you plan to make it across the river and past any Exemplian snipers without getting shot, especially in your condition."

"Let's go. I'm willing to risk it."

"I'm not."

I swallowed some of my frustration, trying not to blow up. "I'll be fine. Don't worry about me."

He bowed his head. "You still don't get it, do you?"

I stomped my foot, and succeeded in sending a dagger of pain to my shoulder from the jolt. "Ouch!" I pressed on my wound, entirely too pissed off to play nice. Blow-ups were cathartic, anyway. "I guess I don't, Tarek. Maybe you should help me out. Tell me what my dumb brain isn't picking up."

Again, silence.

I squatted, and then flopped on my ass, not strong enough to balance. "Well?"

Without looking up, he said, "Everyone has a flaw, that one flaw defining who they are. And despite any of the good inside a person, it means nothing because the flaw is how they define themselves."

Um…what? I put my hand on his shoulder, trying to comfort…whatever irked him. "Listen, I–"

"My flaw is you, Lena." He finally brought his tortured eyes to mine. "You. Putting anyone–anyone–else's life over yours…I'd never risk it. Even at the expense of every single person in that village."

Stunned, my hand froze on his shoulder. Worlds ended and began with flaws like his. His world ended and began anew because of it. As if someone else commanded it, my hand kneaded his tight muscles, wishing to absorb every ounce of pain I'd ever given him. So many pleas whispered in my mind, none I spoke aloud.

Forget me.

Love me.

Hate me.

My hand moved to his cheek, my thumb brushing over his bottom lip. He didn't stiffen and he didn't move away. He didn't come closer, either.

So I moved closer to him.

I slid until our legs touched, my eyes staying glued to his. If I looked away…we'd break. Break apart in millions of pieces scattered on the black soil. I leaned in and touched my lips to his. Both of us kept our eyes open, still connected like two freshly welded pieces of steel. The touch was light, barely existing, exploding.

I pulled back, afraid he'd push me away. "I can't be your flaw, Tarek." I cupped his cheek and repeated words he'd spoken to me, words that burned my heart. *Was* my heart. "Don't you remember? Your energy is the reason mine was created." My voice cracked as tears fell.

His eyes shined as his trembling hand covered mine. "Yes…"

Bridges. They were easy to destroy, tougher to rebuild.

"And not even a few angry, trigger-happy Exemplians can tear us apart." I smiled as I brushed a tear off my cheek with my free hand. "Only I can do that."

He squeezed my hand before pulling it down to his lap, his fingers massaging my palm, bringing back memories of when I first met him. When our troubles, so big then, seemed infinitesimal now. The catalyst to where we ended up.

"No, you can't." His words were soft, his attention on my dirty hand in his lap. He changed the subject before I could pull on those words. Make them true, for both of us. "So, we need to find a way in."

Relief, nerves, and disappointment mingled together, my stomach having trouble knowing what to do. Let the butterflies loose or relax? Tie up in knots? *Hmm, none of the above, stomach.* None of the above.

"Right, yeah." I slipped my hand from his lap, loss rippling from my fingertips up to my shoulder.

For one day, I'd like to be with him without worlds threatening to destroy everything. Maybe a movie? Go to dinner? Laugh like normal people do when they were in love.

He stood and brushed off the dirt coating his contego suit, which still worked. Mine was a dud. He even demanded we switch, but...um...there was a pretty big size gap.

"Do you have any ideas? I'm coming up empty," he said.

Only when we were alone would he ever admit to not having all the answers. Not that he was vain, far from it. But if those innocents who lived in our village, who counted on him to keep everyone safe, found out he was still a human, not Superman, it'd cause panic. The main reason why he had blown up at me in the mess hall all those weeks ago. When he began to push me away.

"I have a few ideas swirling." I leaned against a tree, trying to conserve some energy. Whatever we decided, I'd have to haul ass. Problem was I didn't think my shoulder would let me swim. So, causing the river to rage was out. "The water level needs to stay low and keep calm, or I'm not gonna make it across. But we'll need some kind of cover."

He nodded. "I've taken care of it." The skies already darkened and warm droplets of rain tinkled through the dense canopy of leaves.

The rain felt good against my gritty skin. I lifted my face to it while I thought, letting water cleanse more than surface dirt away. It hit me. "Zander."

"What about him?"

159

I opened my eyes, tilted my head in his direction, and smiled. "More cover."

He folded his arms, staring across the river, silent for a while. Used to his way of hashing out the details, I closed my eyes again and enjoyed the ever-increasing drizzle, relaxing my body. Preparing it.

"We can't afford to take many eyes off the village to help us…"

Did he want me to answer? Because I assumed he'd realized I wasn't an idiot a long time ago.

Guess he didn't expect an answer since he continued, talking more to himself. "But we'd need a couple people. Zander and Winston. There aren't many other options. We'd have to move fast…you don't have an active suit…"

This time I interrupted. "Hey, hey you, over there mumbling stuff." He turned to me, his brow raised. "I'm gonna make it across that river–without another bullet hole. Tell them where we are, have Zander climb a tree and scout our direct path. As soon as we get across, we use the trees for cover until we get home."

He smiled. *Dimples*… "So, that's how it's going to be, then?"

I stood, pushing off the trunk. "Yes. And you can't worry about my suit."

"You broke it."

"How did I…? Whatever." I went to stand beside him, right at the edge of woods where the rocky shore met black soil. "Get inside that head and start making calls. I want to go home."

"You do realize I'm the Warden, right?"

I glanced up at his face, his lips twitching as his dimples gave him away. "Behind every strong man…," I flailed my hands in the air, "yada, yada, yada, and all that."

He nodded, his smile breaking free. "Fine. Stay quiet; you distract me."

"You're welcome."

I zipped my lip, but felt light, even when facing another possible bout of bullets. For the first time in a long time, here in these woods, facing cold, heat, and wounds, I was finally me and he was finally him. For the moment, we were back to us. Even if we were about to go on another suicide mission, I'd lock this memory away. His walls were crumbling down, and I'd do just about anything to make sure he didn't build them back up.

After a few minutes, Tarek's eyes opened and he turned to me. "They're getting into position now. Zander and Winston know where we are. Zander will give the all-clear signal, and then we need to haul ass. Winston is making his way to the edge of the river. He'll get any of the bastards standing outside of Zander's scope."

"All right, chief. Sounds good." I stretched my legs, so ready to get back, see for myself that everyone was okay.

"And, Lena? Your spot is directly behind me. Don't try to get ahead of me or beside me. I *will* knock you out."

Yuck. Having to play the damsel in distress stuck in my craw. "I know how to shoot a gun."

He answered by pressing a finger to my wounded right shoulder, my shooting arm.

"Ouch! What the hell?"

He raised a brow. "Stay. Behind. Me."

"Damn, I get it. God. Be nice."

He hunkered down, tugging on my wrist until I did the same. "That *was* me being nice."

I snorted, trying to get comfortable as we waited. "Where's Zander's perch?"

He pointed to a cluster of trees beyond the wall of squid. I squinted, leaning forward, but not even perfect vision could see that far and make out a body within the burst of bright green leaves.

Zander had sniper down to a science. Even if I were to have had ultra-amazing eyesight, he'd never let me or anyone else see him. Who'd have thought Zander, baby-faced Zander, would turn out to be an excellent killer? Thank God he hadn't discovered that talent when we were in high school. I might have been a memory if he had.

We waited an hour, maybe two, both of us watching that cluster of trees, eating yet another energy bar. I think I even fell asleep for a while. One minute I closed my eyes to rest them, the next I was waking up, slumped against Tarek, my mouth wide open and drool forming a small circle on the sleeve of his contego. I leaned up, not embarrassed in the least. He'd seen me in worse circumstances over the years.

I swiped away the drool struggling to hold onto my chin. "Sorry."

"Forgiven." He kept his eyes on the cluster across the river, but a small smile curved the side of his mouth.

"Thanks. I gotta..." I pointed to some shrubs a few yards away.

"Be quick."

When I came back, pulling up my suit, wincing when I torqued my right shoulder too much, Tarek grabbed my left hand and yanked me down.

"Is it time?"

He nodded and directed my gaze to the tiny silver flash in the trees, a mirror reflecting what little light Tarek left in the sky. As if on cue, it grew completely opaque and the rain, a constant pleasant warm drizzle, turned into a downpour, accompanied by gushing wind. He strapped on his pack before pulling me up to do the same to mine. He slapped my hands away when I struggled to slip it on myself and signaled to move forward. My palms rested flat on his back, the contact my new eyes. Tarek managed to lead us to the bank with barely any sound. One of the perks of being Warden. His eyes worked as well in the light as they did in the dark.

Listening to him, I stayed behind, close enough to crawl onto his shoulders. The water here was thankfully warm like bath water, and the rain, though pelting my face, sent ripples through the usually calm surface and camouflaged our push to the other side.

Tarek moved quickly, the river to about his thighs, my hips. When I stumbled, a few elephants zapped me with their trunks, causing my knees to buckle. Tarek reached behind to plant a hand at my side to steady me, never breaking his pace. We were close to the other side, the smooth riverbed turning rockier, when a quiet ping ripped through the air. Tarek stopped, turning to marble. Another quiet ping followed by a *plink* in the water.

"Get down." Tarek shoved me under the water and silence took over, except for the rain tapping on the surface and dribbling into my skull. He did the same as two more distinctive *plinks* shot through the river's surface, creating a bubbly, white tail as bullets drifted by us.

The peace in the water turned suffocating, my lungs burning. But we stayed down a few seconds longer. An eternity too long. I yanked on Tarek's arm before breaking free, no longer able to hold my breath. Stupid to let the river kill me to avoid bullets. When Tarek surfaced right after, he grabbed my hand and stormed through the water, hair falling into his eyes.

Pings sounded all around us, the thirty feet to the shore a mile. Then there was silence, except the rain and wind. I looked up at Zander's perch, close enough to make out his body–and the body of the dead Protector below him. *Sharpshooter, my ass.* The woman got off at least ten shots before Zander tagged her.

Three more dead Protectors littered the ground farther onto the shore, all their energy slamming into Tarek, who kept pushing on through the euphoria I knew flowed through him. No time to enjoy the high today.

So, maybe definitely Zander was a sharpshooter.

We didn't have one or two to worry about. Protectors polluted our woods. Like cockroaches in a New York City apartment.

As soon as we reached the shore, Winston appeared from nothing, his suit glowing as bright as his eyes. "Y'all need to speed it up. The bastards are everywhere."

Ignoring the screaming in my wounded shoulder, I took off after him, Tarek bringing up the rear. Dead and decaying squid were fading pink mountains we had to hurdle on our way home. No more shots zipped our way, not that they didn't try. Two, really brave or really stupid, Protectors jumped in our path on a direct course toward Winston. Before Tarek could charge or I could draw my gun, Winston flung his hand in the air as if they were gnats. Both simultaneously slammed into trees with so much force, their insides became their outsides.

Christ. Have I mentioned lately how much I loved the guy? But what he did to the Protectors, who now looked more like Jackson Pollak paintings, tightened my gut. That kind of death, no matter the validity of it, wasn't something a person should get used to. Ever.

But I couldn't think about them. I'd wait for later, when the image would replay in my head until my stomach released all the energy bars. We ran and leapt over the pink carcasses littering the forest floor, brave casualties on the battleground. A few quiet pings thumped through the trees at a distance, nowhere near us. My guess, Zander's doing. The three of us kept running, adrenaline injecting speed into my legs.

When we finally hit the protection of squid, all of them, like a chorus, hummed. No squeals, but a hum from baritone to soprano, as though our presence gave them some kind of relief.

To our left, Zander came barreling toward us, not saying a thing, wearing fatigues, not a contego suit. He fell in step beside me, his assault rifle slung across is back.

As if inside a coliseum in ancient Greece, the squid formed a symmetrical arc above our heads that cascaded downward. Their legs interlaced with legs of neighbors, a woven, fleshy shield from the outside. Once we passed the threshold yards from the paths leading down to the village, the arc collapsed to form a solid pink wall. I turned to see one animal from the shield squeal and fall, a bullet spraying its black blood on the squid next to it. The animals drew closer together after, locking legs, as another large squid swung from tree to tree a short distance back, sliding over the still bodies of its comrades to take the place of its dead friend.

The bravery, the sheer courage, these animals displayed pushed me to my knees, tears drenching my cheeks. I loved them, every one.

Zander crouched beside me, hooking his hand under my arm. "A few more feet to go."

"They're killing them, Zander. They're killing us."

"I know." He dragged me to my feet and guided me home.

Lynn Vroman

CHAPTER 19

LENA

Clandestine Operations

No one roamed the dirt paths in our village, a ghost town reverted to the ruins it used to be. I romanticized life here then. Living with Tarek happily ever after, with the only worry bothering me was never having a running toilet. Wilma co-starred in that fantasy, too, bitching about the squid and the heat.

This place went from an imagined Utopia to a warzone, where innocent people hid from Exemplar, the universe's bully–the tiniest world with the largest amount of resources. Hardly seemed right.

Winston never stopped running, giving us a nod as he headed straight for his doorstep. To Shaina. His everything.

I totally understood his need. My first stop was Mom's cabin. I limped to the door, Zander and Tarek flanking me like bodyguards. The door flung wide before I had the chance to push it open. Jake picked me up, crushing me in a hug, torturing my poor shoulder.

"Thank God, thank God, thank God..." He held me tight as Mom cried, clinging to me from behind.

I reached back to grasp Mom with my left hand. We said nothing to each other, Jake's tears soaking my neck. My tears soaking his. We were safe, and maybe we wouldn't be safe the next day, but we were now.

∞ ∞ ∞

"I need to see Belva." My guards followed me. Zander's eyes roamed the barricade and Tarek's palm pressed against the small of my back, his attention darting everywhere.

"She's in her cabin." Zander hesitated. "Lena...she's not okay."

I already knew that, but Zander's warning didn't deserve sarcasm. "Yeah..."

Tarek stopped me a few yards from her door. "I'm going to walk the perimeter, talk to some people." He leaned down and kissed my cheek. "Stay there as long as your body lets you. She needs her friend."

His words seemed to heighten every ache, bruise, and scrape my body suffered. A good five years of comfortable sleep was needed, but to hell with that. My mind and heart were already in Belva's cabin. "Okay. Be safe." I turned to Zander and hugged him. Hugged him like I hadn't seen him in years. Hugged him like I'd never see him again. "Thank you."

He buried his face in my dirty hair for a second before pulling away, his expression stoic—except for his eyes. His eyes glowed with tumultuous dark storms. "Don't ever thank me." Zander lifted his gaze to Tarek. "I'm coming with you."

At Tarek's slight nod, Zander stormed ahead, going straight for Oren's cabin.

"Ah, well, I guess you're going to talk to Oren first."

Tarek smiled. "Well, Peter. Wherever Oren is, Peter isn't far behind."

Zander may have looked like he led, but I was pretty sure that was after Tarek invaded his mind and told him where they were going first.

168

I tucked matted hair behind my ears. "If you find anything...please?"

"I'll let you know, promise." Without another word, he followed Zander, his back straight and head up. No longer the tired man, Tarek lifted a hand to some frightened people who peeked through their windows. He was the Warden, confident and strong. Arcus's God. Its savior...and mine.

I stumbled to Belva's door, demanding my legs to work. My first knock was so light I barely heard it. I knocked again, cringing at the dull thump, like disturbing a funeral already in progress. A soft click and a latch release, and there was my brother, more than my brother. No label was strong enough. Farren. His pale face brightened a fraction.

"Um...hey, Ginger."

He let out a breath and pulled me to him. One thing my bubble was good at? Hugging...and love. The unconditional kind. "You're lucky."

I laughed, the sound muffled by his chest. "Oh, yeah?"

He grunted, rubbing my back. "I almost went out there to kick your ass."

"Well, it was plenty kicked without you."

His arms released me to take stock of my wounds. "Shoulder shot, some bumps and bruises, one hell of an odor...you'll do, kid. You'll do."

I stole a quick glance over his shoulder. "Is she...?"

His face fell as he stepped aside.

Belva, so beautiful, though so frail as if she hadn't eaten in weeks, stared out the glassless window, flinching every time a quiet cry echoed from our pink shield. Squeezing Farren's hand, I went to my best friend, slid an arm around her waist, and mourned with her. We said nothing, her hand clasping mine, her tears silent, haunting.

No words would take her pain away, no promises. But I could share pain with her.

After what seemed like hours, I turned to find us alone. Farren left at some point, but I'd never heard the door open or shut. Sliding my arm from her body, I gently tugged on her shoulders until her eyes escaped the torment outside and focused on mine.

Agony, hot and suffocating, marred her face.

"I'm so sorry, Belva. So, so sorry." I cupped her cheek. "I wish there was something…"

A tortured sound escaped her lips, as if she'd held her breath for years. "I don't know how to stop it. I…I even commanded them to leave."

That terrified me, but I said nothing. If the squid dispersed, our people would be defenseless. Those blue, glowing Exemplian bullets would destroy us all.

"But they wouldn't listen." I had to stifle the relieved sigh as she continued. "They hum to me, coo, telling me no in their gentle song. They're dying for me." She lowered her head. "Maybe…if I were dead, they'd—"

"No, Belva. Stop right there. Your life is just as precious. They die for you because they love you. I'd die for you and anyone else here for the same reason, but not as a sacrifice. No. As a last resort."

She sobbed, crumbling into me, clinging to my back. "I can't bear it. I can't keep standing by…watching."

I held her shaking body, hoping to keep her from falling. Wait, no. We didn't need to stand anymore. I knelt, bringing her with me so we could break, for a moment, together.

∞ ∞ ∞

Crashing, wood creaking…bombs. *They found us!*

170

My gun was out of my bag and in my left hand before I hit my feet.

"Easy, stop right there, killer."

My eyes finally adjusted to the soft light as the memory of where I stood finally plopped into my groggy brain. Belva and Farren's cabin, and at the door, Farren held his arms up, his eyes wide and mouth split in a grin.

"You're getting pretty good with the reflexes. But, please, Belva likes my face the way it is, without any extra holes."

Adrenaline rushed to my fingertips, begging them to pull the trigger. Thankfully, my foggy brain had more control over my actions than the endorphin that had kept me alive for the past three years. I lowered my weapon. "Knock next time."

"I'm not about to start knocking on my own door." His attention shifted to Belva, who lay curled in a tight ball on the dirt floor. Without saying another word, he moved to scoop her up as if she weighed nothing and set her on the bed, brushing away dark pieces of hair from her pale face. He kept his eyes on her when he finally spoke again. "She's barely slept since you left."

I swallowed, not knowing what to say, wishing I did.

Farren looked up at me. "Thank you."

"How does she feel it, their death? Tarek doesn't even…"

Sadness crept into his handsome face. "Don't know, but…they hate when she leaves the cabin. Every time she has to go to the bathroom or…tries to go to them, they squeal so loud it busts the eardrums. It's like they know something we don't."

Oh…damn. Avery was the one who told us what Belva was, an Arcus ancient. And the way she could control the squid here, like they listened for love not duty…some pretty important info to share with the Synod. "Farren,

171

don't let her near the barrier. Don't let her leave the protection."

He raised a brow. "Obviously. No one lea–"

"You don't get it. Tarek and I...we think they're after someone. Someone in our village. Maybe...?"

Instant Protector mode. Instant. "She won't go anywhere without me."

I nodded, knowing Belva was safe. Farren saved my life more than a few times on Empyrean and during our hunting missions on Earth. "I need to find Tarek. Just..."

Farren nodded "I know, kid." He scooped Belva up as if the cocoon of his arms could keep the demons away. If he had anything to do with fate, they would–or he'd die trying to make it so. Belva stirred, curling into his arms, a hand sliding to his neck.

"I'll come by later, check on her."

Farren lay back, never losing his grip on the woman he loved. "Make it later rather than sooner, okay?"

"Yeah, sure, okay." Nothing else needed to be said, not to Farren, anyway.

I ran to Oren's, no longer tired. The powernap with Belva helped give me a boost of energy. Nothing like a good sleep after a heavy cry. Cleansing, really. I shoved his door open after a quick knock. Oren, Zander, Erin, Tarek, and Peter were all crammed in the tiny room with their guns aimed at the door.

Christ, we were a fidgety group. I stormed in, knocking the closest gun, Peter's, away from my face. As everyone else lowered theirs, I found Tarek's eyes and frowned. "They want Belva."

"What're you talking about?"

I ignored Oren and kept my focus on Tarek, whose eyes lighted with understanding. "Of course."

"We need to get her out of here, fast."

"We'll do it now." Tarek was already going for the door.

I put a hand on his arm. "Wait. She's finally asleep. Give her a couple hours."

"Now's better, when she's not up to fight us. We could—"

"All right. What. The hell. Are you talking about?" Oren pushed his way to the front of the crowd, revealing Denzel cowering by the window.

Ignoring the Guide wasn't hard. I still didn't like him. "Tarek tell you his thoughts on why they're coming at us like this?"

Oren nodded, his arms folded over his chest, looking gorgeous and annoying at the same time.

"Well, Farren said the squid get antsy every time Belva leaves her cabin."

Zander snorted. "Antsy? Nice way of saying it. I'm surprised you guys didn't hear them."

I glanced at him and shrugged, before pinning my gaze on Oren. "The Synod has some kind of ulterior motive. That's the reason we're not dust already."

Oren tilted his head to the side, not convinced. "And what…motive…would they have?"

Denzel cleared his throat, timid footsteps bringing him into the spotlight. "If scientists were to get hold of an Arcus ancient, study her, figure out why the animals react to her…they could…ah…find a way to emulate that behavior. If the squid could be controlled on a deeper level, stronger connection, Exemplar could expand, take over this world." He glanced at Tarek, sweat soaking the man's clothes. "With the added power they gained from the attack on Empyrean, they could do it. And…they wouldn't need to replace the Warden. As on Exemplar, a Warden would become obsolete. Energy containments could be constructed, just like there. The terrain here, the animals, it'd be a perfect defense against any threats..." His attention drifted to me.

Sonofabitch.

Tarek spoke when words I tried to push out froze in my throat. "Makes sense."

"I'm speculating. It could very well be something else, but to have control of Arcus...it has been discussed for centuries, after Casimir refused to abide by Exemplian law...when they realized how much raw power dwells in this world."

"We'll from here on out assume this to be their goal," Tarek said.

How could he be so calm? Why was he always so in control?

"Yeah, great, makes loads of sense," I said. "But a month or so ago, the guy told us Exemplar wanted to wipe Arcus off the map. Now he says they want to control it? Not buying it. It's one or the other. Can't be both."

Denzel wrung his hands, nodding. "I understand your skepticism, but I had no clue you harbored an ancient. And if the Synod discovered this..."

Jesus. Avery.

I'd find her.

And I'd kill her. "So what do we do now?"

Peter cleared his throat...and raised his hand.

I rolled my eyes. *This kid.* "Yes, Peter?"

His hand fell to his side, face as red as blood. "Um...sorry. I-I think I have an idea."

Denzel, no longer timid, rushed to the young Protector. "Don't, Peter. Don't you even dare suggest it."

Oren grabbed Denzel by the back of his shirt and threw him on the bed. He pointed at Zander. "Put your gun on him."

Zander smiled–smiled–and nodded, taking up the space between Denzel and the rest of us. When Denzel tried to talk, the tip of Zander's assault rifle slid into the Guide's mouth. "Time to keep quiet." Mewling whines left Denzel's mouth.

Oren gestured to Tarek. "Care to ask the boy a few questions?"

Tarek stepped forward, right by my side. He didn't touch me, but he stayed close. "Explain."

That command, soft and gentle, would have serial killers confessing. It'd also have young, innocent Protectors spilling their guts at his feet. Peter gave his Guide a nervous glance before facing Tarek, his back straightening, pain never leaving his eyes. "My mother…she's a sympathizer…to Lena's cause."

We didn't need him to explain what he meant. Old Lena's cause. Closing the lines, taking away the God status Exemplar stole.

Tarek's shoulders slumped. "As much as I–all of us– understand, I don't quite–"

"She works for the Synod. She's"–Peter shot Denzel, who had tears streaming his cheeks, another worried glance–"the head of the Creation Lab, in charge of coming and going energy. She took over after Avery defected."

Oren whistled through his teeth, the sole sound lingering through the cabin.

We all stayed quiet. Everyone in the room knew Tarek's mind was busy. None of us interrupted the silence, but I drifted to our conversation in the woods: *What would they do once they were on Exemplar?*

Peter gave us the "what." Tarek no doubt wrestled with the consequences. It'd be a sacrifice. A martyrdom he'd have to assign to people in our group.

When Tarek finally spoke, my nerves were shot, and by the strain tightening the faces of everyone else, so were theirs. "We'll need a team, volunteers to take Peter to see his mother."

Oren stepped up. "I'll go."

I thought of Grace. She'd be devastated. So would I.

Then Zander spoke up, and my heart splintered. "Me too."

I wanted to scream, beg them both to let someone else go. Others whom I never took the time to know...like Katherine. Guilt and shame kept my mouth shut.

"We'll hash out the details tomorrow after we get some rest," Tarek said. "We'll need to take the innocents from here, have them sent to Cheveyo until this is over. Belva will go, even if Farren has to tie her up and gag her."

"Erin, you go with Grace, okay?" Oren said. "She trusts you." I didn't miss how his voice cracked.

Erin squeezed his arm, her face softening. "Absolutely."

"All right, then." Tarek took my hand. "Thank you, Peter."

The boy's trembling chin lifted, but he said nothing.

We all filed out, Oren storming over to Grace's with Erin behind him while Zander led Denzel to the cabin by Winston's. He'd fill Winston in on the plan.

Winston would hate it.

Peter walked to his cabin next to Oren's, his head hanging and shoulders shaking. Brave kid. Brave, brave, kid.

Tarek didn't let go of my hand until we stood in front of my doorstep. "Get some sleep."

"Yeah, sure, I'm gonna be able to sleep like a baby. Christ! Avery! She signed our death warrants."

He smiled. "Not necessarily. If we're right, and she told them, it bought us some time. They have a motive besides extermination."

Good way of looking at things. Maybe I'd just maim her. "True. So, before they go, we need to form a plan...that involves getting Wilma back, too."

His silence frayed my nerves, but when he finally answered, I let go of the breath I'd been holding. "We'll do everything we can to get her. But, Lena, you're going to Cheveyo's, too."

Well, there was no way in the universe that was going to happen. "No, I'm not."

"It's too dangerous here."

"Exactly. They'll be coming for you, especially when they realize Belva's gone. I can hel–"

"No, you can't. I can take care of myself, and I'll have Winston. You're leaving. Period." He left, not bothering to listen to me scream at him as he pushed in the door of a cabin twenty yards from mine. He wouldn't stay with me, even if we were still…us. He knew me too well. I'd argue and fight until I got my way–and I usually got my way. But drained and beat down, I didn't follow. I wouldn't listen, though, and I'd need some sleep before I could properly tell him to go fuck himself.

I'd stay with him, no matter what he said.

I'd stay, and I'd die with him.

Lynn Vroman

CHAPTER 20

TAREK

A Thousand Lights

She'd never listen. Even if Winston threw her over his shoulder kicking and screaming, she'd find a way back. What really had shame building in his chest was in the very dark corners of his mind he hoped Lena would figure out how to return. *Damn.*

A fine line existed between the right thing and self-interest.

He had managed to keep the door shut for a month. Why didn't he lock it?

She thought they had a chance to rescue Wilma—the one reason she attempted to heal herself. Maybe they would. Maybe then, Lena would be able to move on. With him. But if they couldn't save Wilma, he wouldn't be able to save Lena.

Tarek understood it, the emptiness. He carried it throughout those seventeen years he'd spent looking for her. His leg began to bounce as he sat on the narrow bunk, options shooting through his head.

Her leaving was the right decision—the only decision. If she returned, he'd tie her up and gag her, put her in a bunker, unless Winston decided to stay. The Protector he counted on could drag her back; maybe get her locked up in a jail cell on Earth for something until this was over.

No time like the present to ask. Tarek closed his eyes and channeled his mind to Winston's. *When everyone leaves...I hate asking...*

I know what you're asking, big man.

Nothing else flowed through his brain. He didn't blame the guy. Staying here was dang–

I'm with you.

His relief stopped his leg from shaking the entire cabin. *Thank you.*

Tarek slid off his shirt and leaned back, folding his hands behind his head. *My flaw...*

She'd be safe, pissed as all hell, but safe. Maybe she'd even be able to resume a normal life, go back to her home. Yeah, and maybe he'd be able to run from this world and go with her. Neither option was plausible. Lena had plans, and none of them revolved around finding a sense of normalcy.

At least she hadn't demanded to go to Exemplar with Oren and Zander–and whoever else volunteered to risk their lives. He hated it, every single part of the plan. Sending their own off on a potential suicide mission turned his stomach to hot tar. While they went to the enemy's frontlines, he'd be stuck here, guarding Arcus from the Exemplians filtering in hoping to find Belva.

She had to be what the bastards wanted, or else they'd all be ash, just like those who burned under sheets on Empyrean–just like the people who used to live on Arcus. This place would've been a desolate ghost town by now if Exemplar had planned to use the same tactics. No, instead they might want to capture Belva, open her up? Study her DNA? Like a lab rat? Civilized monsters were the worst kind.

Their plan had better work.

Peter's mother had better help.

Lena had better keep her ass on Earth.

Fractured Energy

He lifted his hand as his eyelids grew heavy, days without much sleep finally catching up, regardless of the anxiety swimming in his head. He splayed his fingers, making sure to keep the lines from bleeding. Tarek then closed his eyes and did what he always did right before sleep took him.

He wished.

∞ ∞ ∞

A hammer hit his breastbone, one strike after another, sending pain through his body while suffocating him.

Tarek fell off the bed, planting his palms on the ground, his knees digging into the packed dirt. His heart squeezed and cramped. No oxygen, none, made it to his lungs.

This was it. Death. Somehow, they had managed to kill him.

He lifted his head, the veins at his temples straining to break free. They were in the cabin–they had to be. *How did they get past the squid?*

The hammer turned to stings, zapping his organs, even his eyes. He tried to search for his murderer but all he saw was…light. A thousand shards of light attacked his retinas, blinding him, piercing his skull.

"*Ah!*" He tried to call for help, tried to focus his brain long enough to contact Winston, but the light stole his voice and pain banished reason from his mind.

Lena. She'd open his door and find him dead, another Warden in his place. An Exemplian who would kill them all. No one would be going anywhere, their energy trapped in bullets and paraded in front of Exemplian civilians as warnings, right alongside Wilma's.

Failure. He failed everyone.

He curled into a ball, not able to do anything as the light relentlessly barraged him with blade after blade. Whatever the weapon, it worked, torturing him until all he could do was drool and froth at the mouth, as if his body purged his soul. Maybe they found a way to trap his energy? He'd be the first Warden to ever live past the first life–his energy in a tank on Exemplar. Another science experiment right beside Belva. They'd bleed lines with Arcus and make Exemplar bigger, invincible. Worlds wouldn't have a chance.

His own failure jumped in to assist his killer. *Stop...stop...stop...*

Then the pain receded, slow at first. But with each breath, the stinging became less potent. Light retreated to the darkness, and clarity came back to bring him a miracle.

One other time, just once, he had experienced this kind of torture.

When he became Arcus's Warden.

His body was no longer heavy, but light as if he'd been drowning since that day. The weights finally slid from his chest so he could swim for the surface.

Tarek rolled to his back and stared at the ceiling. He counted the cracks as he did every night in his own cabin.

This can't be happening.

He lifted his arm to the splintered wood.

Not possible.

He splayed his fingers, letting his mind open.

No...

Tarek closed his eyes and wished.

CHAPTER 21

LENA

Miracles

I didn't remember stripping off my clothes in exchange for Wilma's T-shirt. I couldn't recollect folding Tarek's shirt-pillow into my arms, and I wouldn't be able to gauge the exact time my brain shut off and my eyes closed.

But I had no trouble feeling the oxygen escape my lungs when a large palm pressed against my mouth and the pain searing my bum shoulder when an even larger body fit on top of mine. I screamed. The sound muffled as I scrambled to punch at the kidneys of my attacker, brain now alert and in survival mode.

Grunting filled the room, fueling my fear, my fists slamming down on flesh.

"Shh, stop. It's me, just me." Tarek's whisper tingled in my ear, fear now replaced with rage.

I switched from beating the crap out of him to shoving at his chest when his palm released my mouth. "*What're you doing*?"

His eyes shined with something crazy, insane...almost unnatural as he put a finger to my lips. A smile widened his mouth, and I had the distinct notion he'd lost his mind during the space between his walk to the vacant cabin.

"Tarek?" I pushed at his chest again, and this time he got up, taking me with him. He held me on his lap and laughed. At least I think he laughed. I didn't know. The one thought going through my mind was finding a way to get to Winston so he could help me with our broken Warden.

He brushed hair from my eyes and kissed me. Kissed me until I couldn't breathe.

As much as I loved it, I didn't love the way he acted, his usual calm a memory. I pulled away and cupped his cheeks, forcing him to focus. "What's wrong with you?"

His face was so bright, so young. "Nothing is wrong. Everything...finally...is right."

"I don't understand."

He kissed me again, this time softly, reverently. His lips rose a fraction above mine. "It's gone."

Sometimes, when loving someone completely, little faults needed to be overlooked. Up until that moment on my bed, with Tarek making absolutely no sense, I thought my giant's fault was putting up with me over the past year and a half. Easy enough to ignore due to its benefits. But...I remembered Casimir, how this place affected his mind. If Tarek were slipping, his mind melting into an abyss I couldn't reach, well, there wasn't a doubt in my mind about what I'd do.

I'd slip with him, gladly. Mad hatters, the both of us.

But I wouldn't skip down crazy lane without a fight.

"Tarek?" His name left my lips as a gentle plea. "Please...it's gonna be okay. Everything will work out. We–"

He laughed, pushing me back on the bed, covering my body with his again.

Oh, no. Maybe it was too late.

His eyes shined with delusion–the best way to describe it. "No, Lena, don't give me that hollow pep talk. I don't need it because it's not going to be okay. It's going to be perfect. *I'm free.*"

Fractured Energy

I brushed tangled blond hair from his eyes, patience hugging my words. "Yes, you are. Let's try to sleep, okay? I'll go to Shaina. She'll have something to help you–"

"I don't want to sleep. Ever. I want to live. Now. *Right now*."

I palmed his cheek, my heart breaking. "Of course you do."

He laughed again, his dimples... Like the first time I met him, his face not as stressed then, with no responsibility except keeping me alive.

God.

My life had taken his away.

Tarek captured my fingers from his face, kissing each tip. "Come on, I want to show you something." He jumped up, dragging me off the bed.

We went to the edge of the barricade, the squid uncommonly hissing. I wished I had telepathy, the power to contact Winston, have him come to help me calm Tarek down. But–the hissing. Never had the squid hissed when Tarek was near.

We stopped, and Tarek, smiling like a beautiful maniac, slung an arm around my waist, yanking me close until our chests crushed together. He held his free hand in the air. Never taking his eyes off mine, he said, "Look up, love."

Fighting tears, I did as he asked, my mind already working out a plan to help him, keep this new development from everyone but Winston. But when my eyes found his fingertips, I couldn't hold the tears at bay. They came down my cheeks in droves.

Above his hand, the sky split and crackled, and a thin line opened to reveal a hole. A portal. Currents of energy tugged on Tarek, lifting us a few inches from the ground as wind kicked our hair around, tying it in even more knots. The slice in the atmosphere, a wound in the sky, the most perfect imperfection I'd ever seen, and the lines–they didn't bleed.

His hand closed into a fist, the tear disappearing, leaving a faint scar. He pulled back when our feet touched the ground, his eyes searching mine, hope turning the gray to bright, combustible silver. "See?"

That face, the face I loved more than anything, the face I believed a month ago I loved too much, like him, my flaw. Tears blurred that face. As much as the tears frustrated me, distorting my vision, they cleansed my heart, my soul. I stood on my toes, touching my lips to his, convincing myself this wasn't a dream, a terrible, flawless trick. His lips softened under my kiss, exploring, feeding my heart, filling any residual emptiness.

When I pulled away, I nodded, my own laugh bubbling to the surface, causing the squid to howl. You know what? I howled with them, letting everything go. Tarek picked me up, swinging us around, hooting right along with me. The squid climbed lower. Tarek, smiling so bright I swore he stole the sun, put me on the ground, clasped my hand, and ran a safer distance away. I think...I don't know...I laughed, cried, thanked the purple sky.

Chuckling, a much quieter sound, Tarek stopped at my cabin, putting a finger to my lips. "Shh, you'll wake everyone."

I dragged his finger away, my own smile hurting my cheeks, bliss chasing away doubt, making me light enough to float to the treetops. *Who was the crazy one now?* "I don't care, I don't care, I don't care!"

He leaned his head back and hooted again, as if we weren't in the middle of a barricade, trying to figure out a way to save the lives of everyone here. One minute we were outside, the next, we were in my cabin, him picking me up and spinning me in circles.

Fractured Energy

I grew dizzy, because of the spinning or euphoria I didn't know, or care. "Tarek?"

He stopped twirling, letting me slide to my feet, his arms cemented on my waist, belonging there. "Yeah?"

"You're right." I kissed each dimple, my salty tears coating my lips. "You're free."

∞ ∞ ∞

Everything had a consequence. Sometimes the consequences weren't so bad, but empirical evidence over the past few years proved those I loved got hit with the bad mojo whenever things looked like they might be improving.

Tarek's freedom was no exception.

Reality, the spiteful bitch, rolled under the door like fog. As if we both realized the implications together, Tarek's smile faded and worry dulled the gray of his eyes.

I moved away to think clearer and asked his silent question. "How is it possible?"

I didn't want the answer–I didn't want to ask the question. Neither of us did.

He ran a hand through his tangled hair, his face still dirty. I didn't bother cleaning up once we made it back from the woods, either. Hygiene unfortunately hadn't been a concern for a while. The squid probably smelled better than we did. But you get used to things.

"I honestly don't know. The only way..." He didn't finish; he didn't need to.

I knew the answer.

Death.

"Well, looks like that's not the only out anymore." My voice leaked from my mouth in a whisper, afraid if I said it too loud, a reaper would leap from the shadows and collect what he had forgotten.

"Yes…" Tarek moved to the window.

"Does this mean you're not Warden anymore?" I stayed in the middle of the room, worried that if I touched him I'd wake up, and he'd disappear.

He looked at the darkened sky, shaking his head. "I don't know." He turned to me. "But I do know I didn't turn the sky this black."

"Oh, shit."

He nodded. "Sounds about right."

"So…we need to–what do we need to do?"

"I still have energy–ah, the collection–inside. I can feel it, but I'm fighting to hold onto it. It wants to leave." He shrugged. "Whatever's going on, I haven't lost complete control."

The relief that loosened my knees because one chain still cuffed his ankle didn't surprise me. Tarek being free of this place would be great for us. Only us. "Okay, so we don't tell anyone yet. Maybe just Winston."

As I said so many times before, in my eyes Winston was the man with all the answers. I held out a hand and after a slight hesitation, he took it, and said, "Well, then let's go talk to him."

Christ, all that hissing, like the cephalopod barricade was pissed at Tarek, as if he willingly abdicated his throne. The loud sound, like a horde of cicadas on a warm night, woke a few people. Grace came out from her cabin, worry on her aged face. She wrapped a thin blanket tighter around her shoulders. "Is everything all right? Should I get Oren?"

Tarek stopped at her door, his back straight and confidence hiding any concern underneath. "No worries, Gracie. They're just a bit agitated."

"Are they close?" She didn't have to specify. Exemplians had been *They* as far as everyone here was concerned after the massacre on Empyrean. Ghosts.

188

Nameless, faceless apparitions who had turned all our lives upside down.

Tarek squeezed her arm with a soft smile. "No. They–"

"Grace?"

Tarek's shoulders slumped.

Should've known Oren would hear Grace's voice, like his eardrums were trained to pick up the soft, lilting sound of it. A goddamn Grace bloodhound.

Oren stomped over, though his footsteps were quiet as if he walked on cotton. "What's going on, Tarek?"

Another thing I admired, and hated, about Oren was his annoyingly fine-tuned bullshit meter. Lying to him never worked. Believe me. I'd tried more than a few times.

Tarek, who never felt the need to lie to anyone, didn't change his mind then, either. He gave Grace one more of his smiles, complete with dimples, and she smiled back. He then gathered her hands in his, and said, "Everything's fine, but there have been some...developments. I'm going to talk with Winston–and now apparently Oren, too. I'll let everyone know after, okay?"

Oren didn't fall for the dimples. "Let everyone know what?"

I nudged him and shook my head. For once, Oren listened, giving Grace a hug after taking her hands from Tarek. He whispered in her ear, and she smiled at him as she did Tarek, but this time, it lit up her entire face. I'd love to know their past. The past Oren knew and Grace probably heard a few times over the years. Someday, maybe he'd tell me. Doubted it, but maybe.

After Grace went back inside, the three of us made a path to Winston's, Oren's ridiculously gorgeous face set with grim lines, his smile a memory. Tarek stayed close to me, but his hands remained at his sides and his attention pointed forward. As soon as we reached Winston's door it creaked open in that familiar laidback way. He met us in boxers, all of his tattoos out for public consumption. "Y'all are as loud as a commercial airstrip. What're you doing here?"

No, we weren't loud. As I said, Oren walked on cotton most of time and Tarek was quieter. I wasn't so bad at stealth, either. Supersonic hearing was another talent in Winston's arsenal.

"We need to talk." Tarek stepped forward, barging past Winston. Oren and I had enough sense to wait until he invited us in. If Tarek were changing back to his former self, he'd better adjust the way he acted around the guy.

Shaina lay in their bed, still sound asleep. Even though Winston refused to use persuasion on her in the past, I had a feeling he made sure she stayed unconscious now.

But her being able to sleep with all of us there might have something to do with comfort, too. Their cabin was double the size of everyone else's, and their bed a luxury. A queen-sized mattress sat on a wooden frame–a real mattress with expensive sheets. Canvases were set up everywhere on easels with Winston's creations brushed across the surfaces, some finished, some not, all breathtaking. Despite the darkness outside, soft light glowed in the room, powered by Winston's extra...abilities.

A half-finished painting in the corner caused a tiny gasp to escape. My mind went blank, filled with the subject on the canvas: me holding my hand out to Wilma as her body lifted into a portal. Tears made the muted color blurry as I stumbled to it, touching Wilma's face as worshipfully as a priest caressed his rosary. The room was silent, or maybe I just couldn't hear anything, my focus on the missing piece of my heart.

Hands massaged my shoulders and warm breath touched my ear. "We'll get her back. *I'll* get her back. I promise."

Fractured Energy

Tarek's whisper caused hope to flutter, battering the threatening despair. The blackness that had been my life, lifting with Denzel's revelation, tried to have another go, but Tarek drove it away with his words.

We'd get her together. I turned to him, swiping at the tears and swallowing the sorrow. "Wherever you go, I go."

He tilted his head, concern coloring his face. "It's too dangerous." Still he whispered, our conversation ours.

I squeezed his forearm and looked straight into his eyes, needing him to see whatever warning or excuse he gave meant nothing. "I'm going."

"How 'bout one of you include the rest of us?" Winston's voice was as calm as ever. "If y'all wanted a private conversation, there are better places than mine."

Tarek ignored him, his eyes still begging me to change my mind.

They wouldn't. The only way I'd stay behind was if someone held me down and forced me to.

I dared any one of these people to try.

Clearing my throat, wiping away any evidence of weakness still on my face, I moved from Tarek's silent plea to face Winston. "The painting...it's beautiful."

His eyes softened, and he gave a subtle nod. "It was a surprise, for your twentieth. Shaina said we needed to do something special."

Oh, right. I had a birthday coming up in a few months. Things like that never really mattered even before my life changed. Now that it had, they were completely forgotten. "I...thank you."

"Any time, Tainted." Winston cracked his neck, all soft and sweetness replaced with his normal lazy irritation. "One of y'all need to start talking, though. Wait." He held up a hand when Tarek opened his mouth. "Lemme start by saying how stupid the idea of going to Exemplar is. Thought we quashed that when Farren brought it up."

After a deep breath in, I said, "Well, there've been some changes."

"Like that kid's mother? You going to infiltrate the most advanced world because somebody's mommy had a soft spot for your old self?"

"Uh...yeah?"

"She's in charge of the Creation Lab." Oren's smooth voice floated through the air.

"What? You going for this, too?" Winston lowered his voice when Shaina stirred. "Man, y'all are crazy."

Tarek moved to stand beside me, his attention on the two Protectors. "Crazy, I agree, but...something else has happened. Something that makes the decision to go to them more sensible."

Winston folded his arms across his bare chest. "And what's that, big man?"

Tarek hesitated before holding his arm in the air. The blur and sway of the atmosphere gave way to a tiny tear, wind whistling through the crack. He let the portal stay open for seconds, but seconds were all he needed to make both men's jaws drop. His hand searched for mine without looking at me, and I obliged, sending him all my strength through our linked fingers.

No one said a word, Winston and Oren uncommonly speechless. Christ, if someone didn't say something, I was gonna scream to fill the void.

About the same time I decided to give my lungs a stretch, Winston spoke. "Well, this ain't good."

Oh, I beg to differ. "I think it's pretty *great*." Tarek squeezed my hand, and I looked at him in time to see a small smile flitter across his face.

Oren agreed with Winston. "This has to be Exemplar's doing. *Has to be*. If there's no Warden here, they're going to–what are they going to do?"

"I don't think it's Exemplar. All the energy we've collected, I still have it. It's a struggle to hold, but it's still there. Why would they let me keep it, plus be able to go through the lines? That'd be dumb. Besides, no nests have been set up anywhere that I can feel." He turned to me. "Have you?"

I shook my head with a smile; he already knew the answer. I hadn't felt one Guide besides our own since authority Protectors blew up the castle, never mind a whole nest. If they really had figured out how to take power away from a Warden, they'd be all in, coming at us hard.

Tarek shrugged, acting calm, though I knew he was anything but. "Then I'd say they're not planning a full-on attack yet."

Yeah, exactly.

"You have all the energy still? Impossible. You wouldn't be able to open a line without bleeding them." Winston came over and palmed Tarek's heart as if nothing Tarek might say to the contrary would be believable. After a minute, he backed up wide-eyed. "I'll be damned. I feel it, all of it. How's that possible?"

Definitely the question of the hour.

Tarek shook his head. "I have no idea, but I'm not about to waste the opportunity to use it against the bastards."

"So now what?" Oren's familiar scowl returned, though worry clouded his blue eyes.

Tarek looked to Shaina, who sighed in her sleep, her lips curving up. "We get everyone out of here, let the squid rest. Those remaining Exemplians outside the barricade will think we've found another hiding spot and begin to search for us. Least it will do is buy some time while we go play in their backyard."

Panic set in, my head shaking before the words could leap out. "So, we leave Arcus with no one? Unprotected?

They'll destroy it." Huh, a few years ago, I'd have loved the idea.

Tarek grabbed my shoulders and bent until we were eye to eye. "They won't know right away. They'll stop picking off the squid, give them a break if the things stay in their trees and keep quiet."

"Yeah? Because by the way the squid are hissing, I don't think they'll listen to you."

He stayed silent for a moment, a soft sigh escaping his lips. "They listen to Belva."

Dread kept flooding in. "Belva won't leave them. She won't go."

Winston laughed. "That girl won't have a choice. I'm sure Red can manage to sling her over a shoulder and open a line at the same time."

I worried my bottom lip, really hating the idea of stealing Belva's choice, but… "Yeah, okay. You're right." I looked from Oren to Tarek. "So, when do we leave?"

Oren raised a brow. "What do you mean by 'we,' exactly?"

"Uh…pretty self-explanatory." I stared at Tarek, daring him to side with Oren. In reality, I could do nothing. But going to Exemplar, there was a good chance some wouldn't come back. If Tarek didn't come back…

Wherever he went, I'd be right behind him–even if it were into oblivion.

As Tarek and I had a silent argument with our eyes, something we'd perfected over the years, Winston butted in. "I think I can handle you and opening a portal, too."

No way would I be able to get away from him. No. Way. I ignored Winston and pleaded with my giant. "Tarek? Please."

His lips pursed as if in physical pain. If he refused, I wouldn't be tagging along–unless I could convince one of the Protectors in our village to dump me on Exemplar.

Like I said, let them try to keep me away. Options were everywhere.

Tarek closed his eyes. "She comes with me." His voice barely rose above a whisper.

But it was loud enough to piss off Winston. "No." He no longer spoke quietly, but raged loud enough to make the squid even more nervous than they already were, their heightening tempers singing through the window. "Absolutely not. You wanting to kill her, man? Is that it?"

Pissed Winston rarely showed up. The one time I'd ever witnessed him lose it was on Empyrean, right before he helped Tarek bleed the lines.

Shaina stirred, sitting up. "What's going on, *mi vida*?" We all turned to stare at her. "And what are all of you doing in my house?"

Yeah, Winston said he'd never use persuasion on her. Guess he meant it. He flung an arm in Tarek's direction. "This idiot wants to take Lena to Exemplar, sweetie. How you feel about that?" The pleasant tone didn't fool any of us.

"Winston…" Tarek's voice was full of warning, hot as volcanic ash. If somebody didn't say something to diffuse the situation, this cabin wouldn't be so pretty anymore.

Leave it to Shaina to do exactly that. Her dark eyes found mine and she tilted her head as she spoke to Winston. "Lena has been fighting for as long as I've known her. What makes you think she'd sit on the sidelines now?"

Ah, I loved her.

Winston threw his arms in the air. His loss of control was so shocking I laughed—and shut up when he glared at me. "You got a death wish, Tainted. One someone needs to save you from." He pointed to Tarek. "Someone who thinks with more than his heart." He stormed out, still in boxers.

Shaina sighed and slid from the bed, her tiny body as graceful as a ballerina's. She hugged me. "Let him cool off, deal with it in his own way."

"Why? I never thought..." Really, Winston cared about Shaina–and Winston. Or so I believed.

"Well, I don't think he realized it, either." She pulled away, eyeing the three of us. "Now, get out of my house. I've an angry man to calm down, and I'm not into audiences."

Ugh, she had to go there.

Oren's face burned red, his feet taking him out into the humid air. "Ah, yeah, right. I'm going to talk to the kid and his Guide, get some details."

Tarek nodded, lacing his fingers with mine as he headed for the door, not the least bit embarrassed by Shaina's words. "Get Zander, too. We'll meet you at your place in a while."

We walked in silence. Heat radiated off Tarek's body, transferring to mine through our joined hands. The squid again hissed louder as we neared our destination. Without him having to say a word, I knew what we were going to do. Let Belva know she'd be leaving her army. Since Farren brought her here, she'd left Arcus three or four other times. Those incidents were short trips for supplies. Trips she dreaded. What Tarek was about to demand of her wouldn't sit well. But she needed to be safe...

Oh.

Right.

Gotcha, Winston. His worry finally had sank in.

Was it selfish I insisted on going to Exemplar? Stupid? Probably both. But I could fight and I could shoot. Belva staying here, even if she controlled her squid army, was killing her. Watching them die ate at her like cancer. Not to mention, if Exemplians managed to break through the barrier, which they would eventually, she had no fighting skills. Farren would have to stay, and–no, losing them was off the table.

Before we made it to their door, I stopped. Tarek turned to me, his face a calm mask except for his eyes. He could never hide the storms in his eyes. "What's wrong?" he said.

I snorted, couldn't help it. "Um…everything?"

"Besides that."

Was I making a mistake? God, I hoped not. "Why are you letting me go?"

He palmed my cheek, saying nothing.

His pauses…I'd grown patient over the years–on the outside. On the inside, I screamed.

Finally, he said, "If we fail, if they find us, they'll come looking for you. The universe isn't big enough. They *will* find you. And when they do…" He bit his lower lip for a second while he snuck a glance toward the sky. "I need you beside me, Lena. I *need* you. As much as I hate that, as much as I didn't want it anymore, I can't change that fact. I haven't been able to for lifetimes."

The torture on his face would undo me. But his weakness…it mirrored mine. The cause of my panic attacks, needing those I loved, fearing they'd die because of me–like Wilma. I got it. I hated it as much as he did, but I understood. I covered the hand he kept on my face. "We're going to be the end of each other one day." I squeezed his hand. "Or each other's savior."

He took his hand from my cheek and went to knock on the door. "I guess we'll have to wait to see what the outcome will be."

Quiet rustling came from the other side of the door, but I couldn't leave us like this. I nudged his arm, trying for a smile. "Personally, whatever the outcome, I'll be right beside you the entire time."

He gave me one last look, his gaze daring me to lie. Daring me to tell the truth. "Even if we can't save Wilma?"

I so wanted to say yes, as I wanted to in the woods, but–nothing. Again. "I…"

His eyes left mine to focus on the door, and under his breath, he mumbled, his words camouflaged by all the hissing.

But I heard what he'd said.

My flaw.

CHAPTER 22

LENA

The New Warden

"For the love of–could you please put on some clothes? My retinas are burning."

Leave it to Farren to answer the door with a gun in his hand and a blanket tucked around his hips. A small, threadbare blanket. God, I could never un-see that.

He didn't bother listening.

"What the hell's going on out there?" Farren looked beyond our shoulders to the squid, concern wrinkling his otherwise smooth brow.

"Put some clothes on and we'll tell you." I crossed my arms, not budging from the doorstep, and slammed my eyes shut.

Tarek chuckled, acting completely himself, as if we hadn't just admitted we were both totally screwed up. "I'll have to agree with her."

I opened one eye and peeked at Farren, who planted his hands on his narrow hips, gun dangling on his pointer finger, not at all worried about his near-nakedness. "You guys are–"

"Farren?" Belva's soft voice wiped the smirk off Ginger's face.

He sighed and turned toward her, opening the door wider. "We have visitors." She was as naked, but thankfully covered in a bigger, less revealing blanket. Farren turned back to Tarek and me. "Give us a second."

The door slammed in our face.

While we waited, both of us quiet, a revelation smacked into my brain. *I'm ready.* I grabbed his hand. "Tarek?"

"Yes?"

He refused to look at me, so I moved to stand in front of him, my heart thumping like a marching band in my chest. "I'm ready. *I am.*"

I was, plain and simple.

First step: telling him.

The next: making him believe me.

Hope simmered when he raised our joined hands to his lips and kissed my fingers. He didn't say anything, or acknowledge what I'd said, but his touch was enough. It had to be.

After what felt like days, the door finally reopened, Farren and Belva both up and covered with shorts and tank tops.

"Better?" Farren gestured for us to come in—with a bow and dramatic sweep of his arm.

"Not much." I shuffled past him and went right to Belva. I wrapped her into my arms, my right shoulder protesting. Fortunately, I'd grown used to ignoring physical pain a long time ago. "Hey, pal."

She seemed stronger, but I'm sure the rest she'd gotten, along with the explanation behind her and Ginger's former state of undress, had a lot to do with it.

"What're you guys doing here?" She squeezed me before pulling away. Worry colored her face as she found Farren's arms.

I tilted my head. "Can't you hear your buddies?"

"They're pissed, so what? Wouldn't you be, too?"

"Well, yeah, but–"

"Deal with it." She stood taller, even as her body moved closer to Farren's, who didn't seem to mind at all. "They're dying for us."

"Hey, no, calm down. I'm not here to complain about them." I held up my hands. "We came because…" No way did I want to tell her. I looked at Tarek, who stood by the door.

Another silent conversation.

He nodded and turned his attention to Farren. "We've decided your plan wasn't such garbage, after all."

Farren's eyes went blank and his brow scrunched up. "Ah…great. What plan?"

Tarek's big body heaved with a sigh as he moved closer to me. "Going to Exemplar."

Farren actually jumped up and hooted, as if we'd told him Santa pushed Christmas up to tomorrow. Definitely some wires not plugged into the right outlets in that ginger brain. "When do we leave?"

"You won't be going on this one." Tarek spoke with quiet authority.

Just like that, he'd taken Christmas morning away from Farren, his smile disappearing and replaced with a frown. "Why not?"

"I need you in other places." Tarek rubbed at the hair on his cheeks. "We need you *both* somewhere else. Earth. Cheveyo's, to be exact."

When I first met Belva, I hated her. I mean, really hated her. Not only was she a bitch, but she had this way of looking at me, with her nose in the air and her back ramrod straight, that said she thought she was better than me. That look hit Tarek now. "I'm not going anywhere."

But unlike me, who didn't stop backing down to her until I hit the eleventh grade, Tarek's lips curved up, loving the challenge. "Yes, you are. My world, my rules. You can tell them to stay hidden in their trees before you go." He focused on Farren. "Get her to see reason or she's going to have to leave bound and gagged over your shoulder."

Farren's face burned with the same fire that colored his hair. He was pissed, disappointed, and if I knew him as well as I thought I did, resigned to what Tarek said. Farren understood when a Warden spoke people listened, especially in wartime. "Fine. But who's going?"

Tarek already headed for the door. "Zander and Oren...among others. Everyone else is leaving. Tonight."

Farren's eyes brightened before a deeper frown formed on his lips. He tagged me with his dark stare. "Don't tell me you're going."

I lifted my chin, trying not to feel like my big brother threatened to beat up my boyfriend. "I–"

"We'll let everyone in on the plan in an hour. Mess hall, be there." Tarek grabbed my hand. "You can yell at her then."

Belva rushed behind us. "So we leave them alone? Let those bastards kill them off while we run and hide?" Her plea found its mark on my conscience, and Tarek's, too.

Tarek stopped and closed his eyes. "I'll be here. My company was all they had for months before everyone arrived. They'll be safe–and stay hidden, especially if you ask it of them. I promise." With that, he let go of my hand and shoved his way out, stomping toward Oren's place.

Huh. Would you look at that?.

Tarek told his first lie ever. Well, the first outright lie I'd ever heard him tell.

I ran to catch up to him. "Hey. *Hey!* You lied."

He grinned. "Thank you for telling me."

"But why? Why did you lie to her? To Farren?" I grabbed his forearm and tugged until he stopped. "Why not tell them about you?"

He shrugged. "Don't you think she'd be more comfortable leaving knowing I'd still be here to protect them?"

"Yeah, but–"

"Well, there you go." He opened Oren's door to a full house, not offering anything else.

As I studied the excited looks on Zander's and Peter's faces, the dread on Denzel's, and the determination on Oren's, I sighed, shaking my head.

We all had issues.

∞ ∞ ∞

I recognized his face even though I never took the time to learn his name. The emptiness filling his eyes, the blank stare, not caring at all about the commotion in the room, I knew it. Too well. My face was his face up until a month ago. His pain, I carried it inside, too, dulled by renewed hope. People around him asked Tarek and Winston hundreds of questions, the cacophony of mingling demands and ideas melding into a blur. He didn't look up, just stared straight ahead at me. Through me.

Katherine's husband.

I doubted the fact Katherine's energy still flowed here– flowed within Tarek–meant much to him. He was from Earth, somewhere in America, I think, where there was a heaven and a hell, a place where life had no do-overs.

He'd never see her again, not the wife he knew.

No do-overs.

As if my heart led my legs, I floated from my seat next to Mom and went to his lonely table, his mourning almost tangible, like a shield he'd built to keep the rest of us out.

When I sat next to him, he didn't acknowledge me as he kept staring at nothing. Or maybe staring into the past when ignorance of what his wife really was protected him.

203

So much I could've said, things that wouldn't have made a difference, things that would funnel into the swampy noise polluting the humid air. He didn't need words. He needed his ignorance. I knew that even more than I understood the trance from which he refused to wake. I wished I could give it back to him.

My hand covered his resting on the tabletop.

He never looked my way.

∞ ∞ ∞

Everyone left, anxious to get out of there.

Most everyone.

Not those I considered family. They argued. To stay.

They lost, all of them.

Grace gave the least amount of heat, simply asking Oren to return without any extra holes. He'd handed her his quilt, the one she'd made, and kissed her cheek before Erin took her away, promising nothing.

I didn't miss the looks between Zander and Erin, either, before she left. Worry clouded her light eyes as she stared in Zander's direction while he gave her a small grin and a nod. That grin and nod: *No worries. I'll come back.* Those of us who hunted the past year perfected that grin and nod when loved ones were afraid.

Well, sonofabitch. How'd I miss that? Christ, I'd missed a lot of things.

Mom and Jake hitched a ride with Winston, who then came back five minutes after he left to get Shaina. Before my mom–and yeah, dad–left though, they smothered me with arms and soft pleas. They knew better than to try to change my mind–it had never worked before. They also

204

demanded a promise from me. A promise that I'd stay safe, come home.

The grin and nod.

I had no qualms about lying to them. I wasn't Oren, honorable to the last grumpy breath.

Then there were only four left not going to Exemplar. Winston, Shaina, Farren, and Belva were all frowning at the rest us, the hunting party leaving for Exemplar as soon as they were safe. Farren tried to convince Tarek to make me stay. Smart move, I guess. He knew better than to try to convince me. Winston stayed quiet, until Farren yelled, even threatening to beat the shit out of Tarek, who grinned, letting his dimples flare. He wasn't happy. Nope, pissed. Ready for a fight.

Zander, Oren, Peter, and Denzel quietly went to the weapons cache after Zander made some lame excuse when the yelling got serious, none obviously willing to get involved between the two largest men there.

Winston had no problem getting into the fight. He froze Farren's fist before Tarek even had a chance to duck. "She ain't going to listen, Red, and neither is he. Get over it."

Winston didn't mention he'd already tried. He didn't mention Tarek would be coming with me, either.

"Fine, goddamnit! Fine." Farren stopped struggling, his face flaming. After Winston released him, he stalked over to me. To my surprise, he lifted me off the ground by my T-shirt, careful to leave the bullet hole in my right shoulder alone. He raised me until we were eye level, his gaze intense, searching.

Shock chained my tongue, no words allowed to escape.

After a straight minute of him drilling me with all his worry, frustration, anger, and finally grief, every emotion that saturated his brown eyes transmitting to me, he said, "If you do anything stupid…"

The tears hiding behind my lids surprised me. Maybe emotion could be transferred because anxiety and fear crept into my brain, what I knew swam in Farren's. "I won't."

Again, his despair stabbed me right in the heart to where I almost changed my mind.

Almost.

He set me down without another word, without anything. Belva was in his arms a second later. She gave me a sad smile and mouthed *Love you* as Farren held his hand in the air. The wind kicked as the tear screeched open. Squid surrounding us, our organic barricade, screamed as if they were being turned inside out. Belva slammed her hands over her ears and screamed with them.

But as the portal yanked Farren off his feet, Belva's stayed planted on the ground, causing Farren to gasp as the arm holding her jerked violently.

The squid grew louder, bringing me to my knees as I tried to block out the sound. I turned to my right to find Tarek in the same position, but he wasn't covering his ears.

He was arched, bent backward as blue light, a bursting comet of energy, rushed from his chest and slammed into Belva's. Farren lost his grip on her, and he plummeted from the tear, crashing onto his back. When the portal closed, the screaming animals purred and hummed. The trees shook as squid doubled and tripled on branches, the limbs bending until some of those long tentacles were close enough to soothe Belva as she heaved, curled onto her side.

Torn, I glanced from Tarek to Belva, both struggling. The choice was simple.

I went to my heart. "Tarek!"

Two fingers to his neck.

A strong pulse thumped against them. Relief turned my body to liquid.

Fractured Energy

His eyes opened.

Before I could say anything, I kissed him, needing to feel his warmth, prove to myself that life flowed through him. I lifted my lips just enough to say, "Are you...free? Completely now?"

He nodded, a smile hinting at the edges of his mouth. "Yes."

That smile. I'd do anything if he just kept giving it to me. I cupped his cheek, sliding my thumb across his bottom lip. "Finally."

He grunted as I helped him from the ground. His legs were a little wobbly, but otherwise he seemed fine. Then both of us glanced in Belva and Farren's direction.

"Holy shit." The curse ricocheted inside my brain, scraping and loud. On the outside, the squids' purrs swallowed it.

As Farren helped Belva to her feet, she opened her eyes.

They were no longer hazel.

Gold. Bright, beautiful gold. She turned to me and smiled. The atmosphere glowed around her as she offered me her hand.

A strange, almost hypnotic feeling washed through my body. I wanted to bow, revere her as if she were a god.

Maybe she was.

By its own volition, my hand slid into hers. Her radiant smile melted my shock enough to speak. "How?"

"I belong here." She left me to again stand by Farren, whose awe turned his face into the sun.

The new ruler of Arcus.

Winston sighed, always ready to state the obvious. "Looks like some of us will be staying here a while."

Shaina moved beside him. "I'm staying, too."

Winston shook his head. "I–"

"No, *mi vida*. I'm staying."

"Well, damn." Winston pulled her into his arms. "All right."

CHAPTER 23

TAREK

Welcome Home

Areas to open a portal without getting their asses shot off were slim. But he knew where they needed to go. The last place he'd been before giving his life to Arcus.

Wilma's house.

They'd decided on it before coming. Not a solid plan, but the one available. The Synod never bothered with this sector, already counting those who lived here dead. No more resources wasted on people who weren't willing to accept them anyway.

The Abrogation sector. This place was the last stop until death, a release from Exemplar, where tired people who served the government in one form or another held the promise, and nightmare, of forgetting past lives and starting anew.

Furniture still lay in shambles, strewn over the cloud-like floor. The way Wilma left it–after she found out about the beginning of the rest of their lives.

Good.

If the place were occupied, they would've had to take care of it, something he didn't relish, but had no trouble doing.

Tarek signaled everyone to stay quiet before pointing to rooms in the dark house for each person to check. As everyone moved forward, he dragged Lena behind him. She tugged at his hold, silent except for the curses radiating from her eyes. She didn't have to scream the accusations he knew were echoing in her head. Those green eyes shot enough fire for him to get the gist. Shaking his head, he let go and signaled to a room farther down the narrow hall. With a nod, she moved ahead, gun drawn and keeping to the wall.

She was smart, good at this hunting game. Too good. He'd have to remember that.

Everyone met up in the main room, where Denzel stood wringing his hands, after the all clear from each searcher. Zander dropped his pack in the middle of the room, Peter doing the same before slumping on the sofa. The kid looked like he needed a year's worth of sleep. Hell, they all did, right after they scraped an inch of crud off their skin. The clean air circulating clashed with the stench coming from six unwashed bodies. Showers, definitely. Or the neighbors might think something died in here when the acrid smell of sweat and filth filtered through the outdoor ventilation system. They'd have company then, one of the few times the governing body came into the sector, the body-collecting branch of the Synod.

Oren took up a spot near a window, his gun lifted and ready as his attention stayed on the happenings outside. The guy never relaxed, a trait Tarek depended on. He set his own pack next to the others and went to Oren.

Before discussing the next step, he gave Lena a quick glance. She sat next to Peter, offering him one of those disgusting energy bars. His love always worried about everyone else, carrying the guilt of death and loss for anyone who landed in her path, whether they asked her to or not. She carried it while it ate at her, inch by inch.

Enough.

Tarek tore his eyes from her to focus on Oren. "We need to find the kid's mother, sooner rather than later."

From there? Who knew. Information she would hopefully share would lead them in the right direction.

Oren nodded, never taking his attention off the window. "We can't leave in the daylight–or at night, right now." His gaze shifted to the group huddled around the sofa. "We all look like those paintings on Winston's cabin." Oren gestured to Tarek's face. "Especially you, man. You glow like a filthy, reeking angel."

Tarek laughed. Yes, he'd agree. The smell made his eyes water. It blended with the environment on Arcus. Here…not so much. "So, we shower, wait out the color. For what? A few days, maybe? It should fade by then. In the meantime, we're going to have to get our hands on a communicator, an untraceable one. Best to keep surprise on our side for as long as possible." He paused. "Maybe one of the neighbors will have one. We'll send Denzel, the least intimidating."

Oren turned back to the window. "No, I don't trust that guy, but I know someone." His hand tightened on his gun, one he'd picked up somewhere on Earth. One he never went without. "I'll share details later after everyone gets cleaned up and rests, including you. I'll take first watch."

There would be no point in arguing. From the past year and a half of knowing him, Tarek found Oren to be straight-up Protector–all the time. No relaxing, no rest, always on. "Thanks, man." He went to the couch and held out his hand. "Showers. You first."

Lena's startled gaze shot to his hand and moved toward his face before she patted Peter's leg, recovering like a pro. When she stood, she gave the kid a smile. "Get some sleep. I'll wake you up when it's time to clean your ass."

The kid grinned. "Yes, ma'am." His eyes closed and he was snoring before the smile even disappeared from his face.

Zander worked to pick up the mess, everyone ignoring Denzel, who shuffled to a back room. The quiet swoosh of a door echoed down the short hall.

Tarek tilted his head, giving Zander a smirk and making a mental note to keep an eye on the Guide hiding in the back. Avery's betrayal left a sour enough taste to remind him not to trust too easily. "What're you doing?"

Zander shrugged, shoving all the broken pieces of chairs and table into a far corner. "If we have to stay here, might as well make it comfortable. Ah, by the way, congratulations? Never thought it was possible, but damn. Lucky you."

"Thanks." He rocked on his heels. "Now what are you doing?"

Zander went to the kitchenette, grabbed a cloth, and dumped some water on it from the tap to swab the dust off every surface. "I got allergies."

The guy was a walking anomaly, a sniper rifle slung across his back and a dust rag in his hand. Good thing Tarek didn't kill him all those years ago. It would've been a waste of a good shot.

Tarek folded his arms over his chest, getting an unwelcomed whiff of the rot living under his arms. "You know, it's fitting, you cleaning up the mess."

Zander stopped wiping the kitchen counter and glanced up. "Huh?"

He grabbed Lena's hand with a smile, remembering Wilma's tantrum. Zander lucked out being in a locked room on Arcus when Wilma found out about his involvement to get her to Casimir. "You're the reason it looks like this."

He left Zander there, a dumb look contorting his dark face, and led Lena to the bathroom. Once inside, he shut the door behind him and let go of her hand. "Lights."

Fractured Energy

A faint cast flooded the space, the room clean except for a thin layer of dust the magnetic ventilators didn't catch and dispose of, like in the rest of the house. Had to love modern technology–at least people tried to convince him. He already missed his cabin in the woods.

Lena reached to touch his cheek, but he jerked back, her fingers never making contact. Disappointment shadowed her face for a moment before she recovered.

A person could handle so much unfulfilled hope before the pain inside calcified. She said she was ready, but it'd kill him if he let her in only to find out she wasn't. To soften his action, he smiled. "What do you think?"

"Your eyes, you look like a vampire…or an angel. They're so bright, like swirling, melted silver."

Heat burned his cheeks, and old anger at her and the situation surfaced, forcing him to tamp it down. When she let her guard down like this, as she had in the past couple weeks, it almost convinced him. Almost. Another forced smile. "Definitely not an angel and I meant about the bathroom."

She snorted and turned in a circle, wide-eyed, her dirty face and matted hair an insult to the stainless metal walls and marble shower system. "Holy shit is what I think. Wilma lived like a queen here."

He searched the cabinets, some of the tension in his body loosening when he found what he was looking for. "Not exactly."

"Agree to disagree, I guess." She walked over to the shower, hiking her bag higher on her left shoulder. "Hey, how do you even turn this on?" Her hands waved over the area where knobs would've been in showers she was used to.

"In a minute. First things first." He held the plain white tube out, wiggling it. "Take off your clothes."

"Um…"

"Relax. Your shoulder…let me fix you." Without waiting for her permission, he pulled her T-shirt low until the angry welt on her shoulder appeared. Keeping his eyes on hers, he squeezed some gel from the tube and slathered it over her wound. In seconds, discomfort left her face, replaced with euphoria.

Everything inside screamed to touch her droopy lips with his, taste the sweet smile on her face. He wouldn't, though. Barriers he'd built around himself crumbled when they shot her, and shattered when he felt the weight of Arcus lift, barriers he worked to build for a month–when she walked out of his cabin. But he wouldn't give in completely, not until he knew for sure she was ready to come back to him.

Pulling his fingers away, her skin scorching him, he stood back and snapped the lid on the tube. "Better?"

She smiled as though she were intoxicated–or returning from a trip to Cheveyo's. She hid her physical pain so well most of the time, always tucking it underneath the emotional aches.

"Better…mmm…that word's too small. Perfect fits." She rotated her shoulder, smiling so wide it became infectious, and his lips curved even when he told them not to. She turned toward the mirror, inspecting her wound. A slight pink, puffy scar remained. "It's gone! Now I'll be able to shoot."

The things she had to get used to slayed him every time he thought about it. "Good to hear. Shower."

"My pleasure."

He hit the sensors right outside the unit, adjusting the temperatures when the water sprayed. "The water's anti-bacterial already, so soap isn't necessary. Do what you can with your hair. There are things in the cabinet that might help with tangles, but–" He turned to find tears, the green of her eyes jeweled liquid. "What's wrong?" Her body was in his arms before he had the chance to talk himself out of it.

He loved her.

That simple.

That complicated.

His flaw.

"The water...it smells like vanilla." Her tears saturated the front of his T-shirt, no contego suit protecting his skin from the warm liquid.

"It's the anti-bacterial component. I can change it if you–"

"No, don't change it." She pulled away from him. "It smells like her, like Wilma. I remember–no." A pause. More tears. "Please. Leave it."

"Okay." He used his thumb to wipe away a stray tear.

She nodded, her shaky hands slapping at her cheeks to rid herself of what she considered a weakness. "Yeah, okay...okay."

"The drying unit is here." He went to the sidewall, moving away from her so she could compose herself. Any time he had tried to comfort her in her moments of "weakness," she pushed him away with poisonous words. He turned on the unit, and said, "Just tap this button," before turning it off again.

"Thanks, really. Thank you."

Still, he didn't look at her. Couldn't. "I'll take your clothes. They'll be clean before you're even done." He reached behind him. Swishing sounds of clothes plopped to the floor. Then her things were in his hands.

So damn hard not to look at her.

"Clean clothes? Now that's a novelty. We stay here too long, I might get spoiled." A bag unzipped and more clothes rustled. "Here, um, could you super-wash this, too?"

He smiled when Wilma's big T-shirt landed in his hands but kept his face to the wall on the way to the door. "Anything else?"

"No. Ah, Tarek?"

His finger floated over the sensor as his eyes slammed shut. If she asked him to stay...

Please don't ask. He wasn't that strong. "Yes?"

"Belva... How do you think it happened? I mean, like all of a sudden...?"

"I don't know." He wished he did. But, maybe a little relieved he didn't. If what happened could un-happen, he'd be locked to that world again. No, on second thought, he didn't care to know at all, wanting to be completely oblivious. Science and logic were overrated sometimes.

"You think she'll be okay?"

"She's exactly where she wants to be."

"And you? Will you be okay?"

Silence. Then, "I'm exactly where I want to be, too."

"Good."

He heard the smile in her voice and almost spun around. If he could just believe her...

If she could believe herself.

He opened the door.

"One more thing."

Leaving the room was getting harder and harder. Pretty soon, he'd be running away–or staying to let hope have another chance to win the war. "Yeah?"

"Make sure we don't stay too long."

Relief flooded through him, even as he stepped from the room and away from temptation. Even as doubt hung a black cloud between them.

Exemplar, with all its comforts and barren tranquility, wasn't a place where people who desired to live wanted to stay.

Maybe there *was* hope, after all.

CHAPTER 24

TAREK

Arratoi

Stuck in a tiny house with six normally active, always irritated, people wasn't exactly pleasant. They hashed out plans, but any action was a no-go until they stopped resembling caricatures of themselves.

Peter didn't help the wait. The kid had more questions than an interrogator. Oren seemed responsive enough, trying to convince the boy his mother would be fine, though he eventually started deflecting everything to Lena. Tarek stopped counting how many times she told the kid to "Shut the hell up."

He smiled after every time she said it. A few minutes later, she'd always apologize, offering up some empty "we'll figure it out" promise. Her go-to line when life became sticky.

Peter would stay silent for an hour, maybe two, and gradually start mouth vomiting again. On the fourth day of the same walls, disgusting power bars, and no action, Zander had even snapped. He dropped one of Wilma's books he'd spent the wait reading and put his faithful rifle up to Peter's head. "Stop talking."

That worked.

Until the fifth day.

Luckily, the color had faded from all their faces enough, putting Zander and everyone else in a better mood. Truth was, no one wanted to admit the reality of the situation. If Peter's mother helped, she'd be in danger. Real danger. The Synod had eyes everywhere, and helping the number one threat to Exemplian way of life? She'd be lucky if all they did was mark her *Tainted* and disburse her energy. They could make her suffer–especially if they got their hands on Peter. It wouldn't be the first time the Synod's authority punished traitors by example. A well-known motto: *You take from us; we take from you.* Exactly what Cassondra did to Lena. The bitch could've killed her on Empyrean, but no. Lena needed to suffer, and she had in spades.

He'd kill Cassondra for it, as he killed her brother.

Lena came out of the bathroom still clean after five days, which was a new development, her long hair now tangle-free and in a braid down her back. She had only taken Wilma's shirt off to shower every night, spending hours in the vanilla-scented room and always coming out with red-rimmed eyes. With her hair soft and clean and body swimming in that shirt, she looked so vulnerable.

But she never sounded it. "Tonight's the night, fellas. No more waiting around, or I'm gonna shoot one of you." She slapped Peter with a glare, but he shrugged, obviously more than used to the recent threats on his life.

Thoughts, guilty thoughts, raced in his head as he glanced away from her. If his honor would've let him, he'd have stolen her away in the middle of the night, taken her, willing or not, to a world far away from here. From everything, just as he had fantasized during those long nights when he lifted a futile hand to the ceiling. She could hate him all she wanted as long as she was alive doing it.

It was the guilt from that selfishness, that irrational desire, keeping him exactly where he was: fighting a war he had no more desire left to fight.

"Well? Anyone gonna answer, or are you all just okay with staring at me for another night with those stupid-ass expressions?"

Lena's voice brought him out if his head. Time to fight, even if he didn't want to. He stood, already on his way to the back bedroom. He'd dwell on his weakness later. "As much as I enjoy staring at you, I agree, but we can't blend looking like we do now."

Lena snorted, walking right behind him. "When have you ever blended?"

Biting back a smile, he rummaged through built-in compartments on the polished white wall. The green glow of the track lighting in the drawers helped some, but there was no guarantee what they put on would match, the lights in the bedroom dim. It didn't matter. Where they were going, mismatched attire was the least of their worries.

Oren knew somebody, all right, somebody who lived where most Exemplians considered Hell. Not everyone on Exemplar enjoyed a peaceful existence–too boring, especially for some newer energies. What they did enjoy were the benefits of being Exemplians. Tarek shook his head, his shoulders tensing as he pulled out some clothes, tossing them to Lena. He'd take Arcus's wildlife over Exemplian chaos any day.

"What the hell am I supposed to do with these?"

He yanked out some more clothes before answering her. "Wear them."

"You're serious?"

His lips twitched when she held the too large pants to her small waist. "Yes."

To the chorus of her swearing, he trudged past her, arms full of attire for everyone else. Thankfully, Wilma never had an interest in high fashion. If so, they all would have ended up looking like giant women.

He unloaded the pile in the middle of the living room. Everyone grabbed something and undressed without any discussion, even Peter, thankfully.

Lena, who barged in not caring in the least there were five almost-naked men in front of her, had a lot to say. "Now what, huh? Maybe there's a blanket somewhere that'd fit better, 'cause this isn't gonna fly."

Tarek gathered his clothes, managing to pull on pants before she stormed in, and led her back to Wilma's bedroom. "This might come as a surprise, but I doubt they want to put on a show for you."

The clothes hung on her, the pants held up with her hands clutching fistfuls of fabric, her shirt revealing her collarbone, lower. "Well, excuse the hell out of me, but they'll be getting a show, too, if I let go of these pants. And...how do they fit you?" She released her hold on the pants with one hand to grab at his. "These should be up to your thighs. Christ, Wilma was at least a foot and a half shorter than you."

He grinned as he dodged her fingers and got an earful of even more colorful words. Wilma taught her a lot, one thing being how to curse like a gutter rat.

"Hold still!" She kept grappling at his pants, laughing while getting a little close to–yeah–getting a little too close.

"*You* hold still." He finally captured her busy hand with one of his and reached for her thin waist with the other. Pulling her close effectively shut her mouth as her breath hitched. Possessive, almost feral need bubbled to the surface, his attention automatically going to her parted lips. All joking and laughter escaped the room, replaced with something more potent. This part of their relationship...they never had issues. The electricity never went away, shocking even with the rippling undercurrent of the familiar, maybe more so because of it. He was hers.

Always.

"Um…" That soft sound, like life support, left her lips to skate across his.

Swallowing, he found the mechanism he was searching for on her pants and slid his finger across it. In seconds, the fabric hugged her body perfectly. Without releasing his hold, his hand moved up the lithe arc of her back to take care of the shirt, his mouth going dry. When her top fitted against her soft curves, he still didn't let go, the feeling of her body against his skin…he missed it.

"See? Trust me." His words were a whisper, a promise.

She nodded. "I do." Before he had the good sense to pull back, she reached on her toes and kissed the corner of his mouth, undoing him. "Trust *me*."

∞ ∞ ∞

Stealing shuttles from Abrogation citizens wasn't exactly one of the prouder moments in his life, but choices were limited. Where they were going, the added protection of a couple tons of metal would come in handy.

Algae-fueled, non-hovering models didn't require eye scans to start, just some quick fingers and an elementary understanding of circuit boards. Come to find out Zander wasn't only a crack shot, but an expert car thief, too. Two shuttles were out of their driveways in less than five minutes without one person coming to investigate. The guy was a genius.

Lena and Zander rode with him, while Oren and the other two led the way in a sleek black shuttle Lena likened to a Lamborghini, whatever that was. Zander spent the twenty-minute ride giving Lena the rundown: *no eye contact; keep your head down; if you see a fight, even if blood is involved, ignore it; biggest thing to remember, always shoot first.*

None of it fazed her, not one ounce of fear coloring her face. She nodded and checked the safety on her soul-stealer. Then Zander snatched it from her hands.

One thing he'd learned: don't get in between Lena and her gun.

"Hey!" She reached behind to grab it back, but Zander tossed it out the window after yanking the clip from its home.

Stupid guy earned himself a throat punch.

But Zander did a good job dodging her quick fist and handed her a pistol instead.

"Those are authority-issue. You tag someone with one and we'll have the bastards closed in on us in seconds." He shoved the Glock in her hand when she refused to take it. "People won't think twice about this. Weapons are pilfered from other worlds all the time, seeing as regulars aren't allowed to carry guns."

"Still, won't this make us look suspicious, too, Einstein?"

Zander sat back. The sound of his rifle engaging filled the small cab. "Nope."

"Really, huh? And our faces, that not gonna give us away faster than an illegal gun?"

"Probably. That's why you shoot first."

She glared at Zander before turning to drill the side of Tarek's head with her green daggers. Him? He kept his eyes pointed on the road and concentrated on the flow of traffic, laughing.

"What're you laughing about?" She whirled back to Zander. "And when did you get to be an expert on everything?"

Tarek caught Zander's shrug in the dash monitor. "I read. You should try it sometime."

Fractured Energy

"What? I read! *My* history books don't cover as much, asshole." She turned around front…and punched him in the arm. "Stop laughing!"

Once they hit Heterodox, all humor left the shuttle as tension found his shoulders again. The sector wasn't one he'd spent too much time in, not in the six hundred or so years and five lifetimes he'd lived in this world. Situated beyond the outskirts of the capital, this place was what mentors used to scare their young wards beginning at the age of six.

If one were to die here unlawfully, their energy went directly to the Creation Lab, but too many deaths–actually, too many rebirths into the Exemplian population–drove a person insane. The zombie-like, empty faces of those shuffling with the crowd on the sidewalks were proof. Those carcasses roamed around others living in this sector until exhaustion ordered them to sleep. Death, especially when another life followed shortly after, did damage to the brain.

Worse, if not active, if a person never volunteered to collect energy or work for the Exemplian cause, the Synod wouldn't give them a chance to retire, forget. They recycled those energies like metal, until the energy finally had enough, too weak to fill a corporeal form. They were invisible here, but strong somewhere else where their energy would help a world's evolution. No sense giving another place the throwaways, right? Everyone had a use, human energy more productive when occupying a body. And when the energy couldn't handle another go at life? Simple. Their energy would then charge a coffee dispenser or water filtration system.

Yes, everyone had a use.

Civilized monsters.

"This place is like New York City on crack. And shit…static overload." Lena's attention stayed on the happenings outside her window. One hand pressed against the glass, as if that would get her closer to the action, while the other pressed to her head. She'd get used to the fuzz; he'd gotten used to it already. Yet his easy acclimation probably had something to do with lives remembered here.

But whatever place she compared the sector to must be crazy because *this place* was nothing short of chaos. Addicting for some, a nightmare for others. Lights, like lasers jutting across the sky in rainbows, flickered into the shuttle with enough frequency and change to cause seizures. Shops opened here all hours, along with brothels and taverns. Storefronts screamed with color and detailed holograms of exactly what each establishment offered. Places that fed that part of the brain always in search of a thrill—or a spark that proved life, no matter how many times lived, was worth the effort.

At every stop, people pounded on the windows, causing Lena to jump—at first. When it became obvious no one could see in, and the windows wouldn't shatter, she relaxed—after she engaged her gun, keeping it close to her side, finger on the trigger.

Oren's ride wasn't fairing much better, some tweaked-out groups even rocking it when crowds would prevent the traffic to flow. Oren lucked out, though. His shuttle was loaded, newer. An electric shock lighted the shuttle's body, zapping the lunatics on their asses.

"*Holy...* Can we do that?"

He took a second to glance in Lena's direction. Her eyes shined with either excitement or tension, he couldn't tell which. He looked again.

Excitement.

Epiphanies hit at the most inconvenient times, but her lack of fear—lack of self-preservation—had realization slamming deep into his head. She needed to get on with living, re-learn to thrive amongst normality. Hers. What she knew before he jumped back into her life. He wouldn't take her to some other foreign world where she'd have to figure out how to survive. No, he'd take her to Earth, where she knew how to survive without killing, hiding, or starving.

"Tarek?"

He gripped the lever tighter, so as not to let the flash of common sense run them into the throngs of people. "Ah, looks like Oren got the nicer stolen shuttle."

She leaned back, returning her attention to the window. "Well, damn, too bad."

He shook his head. Yes, after this was over, he'd give her back what she deserved.

A few minutes later, Oren led them into a dark underground hanger, the sudden loss of whipping light as shocking as the lights themselves. Total darkness? Here, he thought Oren had brains. But when the guy said they'd be going in the back way, Tarek assumed a back door, not a place every single Exemplian with an ounce of intelligence avoided.

Once they parked, Tarek punched off the silent engine and grabbed Lena's shoulder as she reached for the door latch. "Not so fast, love."

"If you wanna open my door, trust me, the chivalry's not necessary."

He grinned, not loosening his hold on her. "Understood, but if you open that door without proper light and a few simple crash courses, you might need me to carry you. It'd be a bit difficult to walk without feet."

Her face paled and her hand slipped from the latch. "You have my attention."

"It's about time." He ignored her huff and let go of her to reach for his bag. Zander plopped it in his hand, the guy's pack already open and taser light out. Tarek found two in his and handed Lena one. "You see this button?" He flicked his on before reaching over to do the same to hers. When she nodded, he continued, "As soon as you open the door, *arratoi*, ah, rats will be at your feet. And I'm not talking about the cute little rats you're probably used to."

She laughed, but...yes. Some nerves. "I lived in a trailer park my whole life, Tarek. A few rats aren't gonna make me girl-out. Don't worry."

Hide behind the bravado, love. She seemed to forget he knew her better than he knew himself. He liked the nerves underneath, liked she could still feel fear. For herself. He cupped her chin. "I'm not worried. But you should be."

Better. An even paler face and a bottom lip tremble. "You're not very good at giving the it's-gonna-be-okay pep talk."

His thumb slid over her shaking lip. She could have her words. He knew her heart, and her heart said, "*Get me out of here.*"

"Disagree," he said. "I think I'm finally getting past that thick skull."

She yanked her chin from his grip. Even better. Fear masqueraded as anger. Maybe she'd actually listen and not go storming outside, gun blazing. "So, what now? Educate me so I can get out."

Zander snorted, and mumbled, "Read a book."

Lena tagged him in the jaw, her fist lightning-quick. She missed the throat.

"Ouch!"

"Shut. Up."

"Goddamnit! Cheap shot! And Wilma had a library! You could've–"

"Enough." Tarek lifted his door a fraction. "Lena, come out my way. Zander, you crawl up and do the same." He shot her one more warning glance. "Press that button and shoot at anything that moves. Anything. I mean it."

She nodded, the sweat on her forehead glowing green with the light. "Gotcha."

Tarek gave Oren's ride one quick glance. They were all jumping out, green lights flashing. Squealing reached through the crack of the open shuttle door. Deep breath.

Latch click.

He leapt from safety, already shooting. "*Go! Go! Go!*"

Lena and Zander whipped out, and Tarek brought up the rear as they raced toward Oren and a set of stairs. Six bouncing green lights were their guide. They all pressed buttons into the sea of vermin, animals that were three feet long with canines as sharp as steel needles and glowing red eyes as soulless as stones. No one spoke. No one screamed. Everyone ran. The *tink* and *clank* of metal meeting boots screamed loud enough for them.

Oren hit the door first. His shoulder slammed against rusted metal and slime until the decrepit thing squeaked open wide enough for them to squeeze through one at a time. Tarek shoved Lena and Zander in after Peter and Denzel.

A rat latched to Tarek's shin before he followed, its teeth grazing him through his pants and slicing his flesh. He gritted his teeth to keep from yelling and crushed its skull with his boot once the thing broke free.

When Tarek made it on the other side of the door, he and Oren slammed the thing home, blocking out the rats and darkness. Razor-like nails scratched at flaked metal, the rats not happy to lose a rare chance at some fresh meat.

Slumping to the ground, Tarek grappled for his pack and searched until he found the same ointment he'd used on Lena's shoulder. Without saying a word to anyone, he smoothed the medicine over the two-inch gash on his shin, biting the inside of his cheek. Flesh mended while spitting out the poison from the rat's saliva.

Sweat stung his eyes, and he slammed them shut as metallic blood filled his mouth. He had to relax. *Relax.* His teeth slowly unhinged from his cheek, and he leaned to the side, spitting out the blood.

The few seconds the poison was allowed free rein caused a small portion of skin to blacken and rot, falling with a *splat* onto the dirty ground.

"Jesus Christ!" Lena hunched down beside him, holding his leg between her hands. "Your leg!"

"It's okay. Just give me a minute." More deep breaths. The pain ebbed, but the residual ache gnawing at his leg thumped like a toothache. One thing about the rodents' poison: it liked to throw wild parties with skin cells.

Familiar panic settled on Lena's face and her breathing quickened as her throat bobbed. Her grip on his leg tightened.

No, love, don't lose it. Don't...

"Your leg has a h-hole in it. You're n-not okay."

"It'll heal." Plus leave an indented scar, but she didn't have to know the details. "Calm down. It's fine. Promise."

Her eyes closed as she inhaled deep and exhaled slow. Sweat trailed down from her hairline even as she shivered. But she grabbed control after a minute while he smoothed hair from her face, her breathing normalizing. When she opened her eyes, they targeted Oren with a sneer.

Tarek grinned, dropping his fingers from her hair. "Keep your hands to yourself, Lena. Not his fault."

She ignored him, except for the gentle pressure she put around his wound, to give Oren an earful. At least she didn't reach up to hit the guy, probably because her hands shook too much. She'd want to keep her narrow escape from losing it a secret. "Was this necessary? Bringing us here to be rodent food?"

Oren shrugged, still heaving like the rest of them, luckily disguising Lena's minor episode with the same

228

exhaustion and adrenaline rush everyone felt. "Yes." He tilted his head toward Tarek. "Are you able to walk?"

"He has a hole in his leg and his skin is hissing on the ground next to you. What do you think?"

Through the pain, Tarek smiled and pressed the waistline of his pants. The torn fabric surrounding the bite mended, hiding it from her inspection. Out of sight, out of mind, right? "I'll make it."

Lena stood, offering him an unsteady hand. "Well, then let's see it, tough guy."

He palmed her hand and pulled himself up, wincing when he put too much pressure on his leg. The ointment kept working, though, its tingling warring with the thrumming burn. Sweat poured from his face like a broken water main, and as much as he hated to admit it, he needed Lena's shoulder in order to stay off his ass. "Please tell me this is the building we need to be in, man. No more *arratoi*."

Oren smiled as he wiped his dirty hands on the front of his pants. "It is. Sorry about that, but this was better than having your face out on the streets. People thinking Arcus's Warden has come to visit would create a riot, not to mention gain some unwanted attention by the higher-ups."

Smart move. He nodded. "Good thinking. Lead the way."

Oren scanned the dank stairwell and scrunched his nose, the lingering smell of rat feces and stringent piss obviously doing the same to his stomach as it did to Tarek's. "All right. Time to go up." With that, Oren climbed, everyone following.

Tarek, trying hard not to put too much weight on Lena's thin shoulder, took the stairs slowly until the pain was bearable. One had to love Exemplar medicine. Actually, Empyrean medicine this world stole, but as his leg began to feel normal, he couldn't drum up righteous indignation toward Exemplian thievery. At that moment, he was glad for it.

When he let go of Lena and gestured for her to move faster to catch up, she stopped and raised a brow. Fear–for him–still danced in her eyes. "You're sure?"

He stomped the foot of his injured leg on the slippery metal with a grin. "Good as new."

"Hmm, except for that little hole-in-the-leg issue?"

Bigger grin. "Except for that."

She trudged forward, mumbling, "I thought this world was advanced. This place looks about advanced as my old waterbed."

"Every world has a dump. This sector happens to be Exemplar's." He kept climbing, recognition of the symbols decorating the doors on each landing sinking in. Oren had told him what his contact did, but the news was hard to believe until it actually tapped him in the face. The guy always acted so stiff, a steel pole permanently shoved up his ass. A building like this was the last place Tarek would've associated with him.

"Arcus doesn't have a dump. Neither does Empyrean." She slogged onward, bitching under her breath as if it were her duty to defend the worlds she loved.

"Arcus hasn't been disturbed by human consumption in centuries, and yes, Empyrean has a shithole. You just didn't see it."

More grumbling, and then, "Whatever. Stop getting bit."

"I'll do my best."

His eyes watered as they clambered the rest of the way in silence. Rat piss was strong, and no amount of distance from the abandoned hanger, even with the buffer of being in a stairwell, lessened the stench, like it followed them. Chances were the stairwell probably had nests on some levels. Peter gagged a few times and had to lean over the railing to let the contents of his stomach free. The boy's vomit had a more pleasant odor.

To the rest of the group's credit, everyone else was able to keep it together, though Tarek's stomach wanted to come out and play with Peter's. Finally, Oren stopped at a door.

Surprise made Tarek laugh when Oren's retina scan gave them access. "Been here a couple times, have you?"

Zander, and even Denzel, snickered while Lena's and Peter's faces went blank. Peter was too young to know where they were, and Lena, well, she'd catch on soon enough.

The door scraped open, leading to a long corridor filled with apartments. Then Oren, red-faced, threw a grin behind him. "Once or twice."

Lynn Vroman

CHAPTER 25

LENA

Blue Light Warning

We stopped at a door in the middle of the hallway when Oren turned to me. "Refrain from your usual pleasant demeanor, will you? Bitchiness might get one of us killed." His smirk almost succeeded in me losing the control I'd been fighting for since leaving the shuttle.

"Don't worry about me, jackass. Just knock on the door so we can get this over with." Even the sweat and grime from the hanger didn't turn down the volume on his looks. Jerkoff. The rest of us could be poster children for the homeless. At least he smelled like a toilet, like everyone else. Good looks couldn't deflect the clinging stench of rat feces.

"That's exactly what I'm talking about." He rapped his knuckles on the door. After a subtle rustling from the other side, his finger jammed into my chest. "Behave."

"Like I said, don't worry. I'll be too busy standing in the corner and contemplating the idiocy of every decision you make. Rats, for Christ's sake."

He actually smiled. "Good girl."

The last thing I imagined when traipsing into the magical world of advanced technology were rats the size of full-grown Labradors. I mean really, didn't they have some sort of high-powered pesticide available? A nuclear bomb, maybe?

Tarek's flesh dying off and sizzling on the metal floor like a frying egg–yeah…not good. My hands still shook. Even though he seemed fine, his limp less noticeable, I had to hold his hand. Contact with his skin was necessary if I wanted to keep the threatening panic attack away. Weakness. I hated it.

As we gathered around the door, I had to rely even more on Tarek and his warm palm against mine. Funny how being near him, hearing his voice, kept the coward inside at bay. Unfortunately, Tarek didn't fit in my pocket so I could take him everywhere. I would have if he'd let me, except the ice he'd built around us had only started to melt. No, that wasn't true. It wasn't his ice; it was mine. He finally came to his senses and insulated himself against it.

I squeezed his hand tighter. I'd never let go again.

Locks clicked.

The door creaked.

Oren smoothed his hair and cleared his throat.

And fuzz slammed into my brain with enough force to knock me to my knees.

Tarek pulled me up by our joined hands, his grip tight and palm now slick with sweat. I glanced up to find the same magnetic pull slackening his face that I knew sagged mine. Licking my suddenly dry lips, I said, "You feel it, too. The static. How?"

He shook his head, as confused as I was.

Tearing my eyes from his, the static as euphoric as it was painful, I gauged the reactions of everyone else.

Holy hell.

We all felt it, whether Protector or Guide.

"Oren? Who's behind that door?"

Before he could answer, a woman with a glittering silver tattoo along the entire left side of her face appeared at the door. That tattoo, ivy and flowers, mesmerized me. Even if I wanted to say something about her scant clothing and piercings that trailed the length of her arms and across her collarbone, I couldn't. My focus remained completely on the left side of her face, the ivy turning from silver to red to green so fast I thought I imagined it. Add that to the magnetic pull, I was pretty sure it was close to what an acid trip felt like.

When she spoke, her words were like music. Not addicting like Cheveyo's, but whatever she said sounded like a symphony. I barely noticed when she switched to Desis. "...when your ID came through I thought it a cruel mistake. Yet here you are, as handsome as ever. A bit dirty, but you know I always enjoyed you more all mussed up."

Was she talking? Or casting a spell? We all took a step toward her.

Oren's face burned red under the coating of dirt, his eyes closing to half-moons. "Celeste, I..."

Well, sonofabitch. Exotic tattoo lady made Oren speechless. Wonder if she'd be interested in coming home with us?

Her purple eyes, the same color as Arcus's sky on a good day, traveled around the semi-circle of our dirty six before stopping on Tarek. "Why don't you bring your friends in, hmm?" Those odd-colored eyes shifted to the far corner of the hall, toward a blinking green light. "Then maybe you can explain why I'm owed the pleasure of your returning company."

Oren fidgeted–seriously. He acted like a tween at his first dance. Didn't blame him, though. She was a drug. "Thank you." He waved us all to go in ahead of him, giving me a warning frown as I passed by.

My mouth was the least of his worries.

As soon as Oren shut the door, the woman's palm met his cheek. The loud smack reverberated through an apartment that didn't match the poor conditions of the building. "That is for leaving without telling me." She struck him again. "And that is for making me miss you."

If the static would quiet down for a second so I could concentrate enough to enjoy Oren getting smacked around...

Oren grabbed Celeste's wrist when it came up for a third time. "Please, forgive me." He moved closer to her, his hips brushing hers. To be honest, this was the first time I'd ever witnessed Oren use his looks to get his way. I had always figured he was clueless or didn't care. "If I would've come here before, I'd have never left."

Yuck.

I kept my mouth shut, though, even if my gag reflexes started working overtime.

Celeste didn't seem too convinced, either. "Your lies are as pretty as your face." She snatched her wrist from his hand and backed away, standing tall with her chin up as if she were the rat queen. "You've perhaps thirty seconds before I bring the authority down upon all of you."

Well, that made me nervous enough to speak, despite the fuzz clanking around in my head and Oren's stupid warning. "No, wait, don't do that." Desperation made my voice hitch. "Look, I know he's a dick, but he swore you could help us."

She crossed her arms and sat in a chair without legs. It floated, like the beds on Empyrean. "I know who you are. And I see Oren decided not to kill you." Her attention drifted toward Oren. "Wasn't that the plan?"

His smooth chuckle irritated the hell out of me. "Plan backfired."

"Yeah, great. Perfect. Everybody knows who I am. That's the problem, obviously." I scooted closer to her chair, trying hard to shove some calm rationale into my voice. "But all I want is to get this world off my ass so I can move forward. I don't have any plans to start any wars. I just want my life back."

In that moment, revenge stopped being the motive. Or maybe I finally realized it no longer existed. Either way, it made me feel lighter.

Tarek came up from behind and grabbed my hand. I glanced up to see…yeah. I saw it. Hope.

Celeste cleared her throat, effectively pulling my attention from his. "Lovely words." She crossed her legs and leaned back. "So, closing the lines to stop the big bad ugly from ruling the universe and saving the day…not work out as you expected?"

How did she know that? "No."

She stared at me, as if her gaze alone was some sort of high-tech lie detector. For all I knew, maybe it was. "I believe you." She shifted her lie detector to Tarek. "But you, Warden, how is it possible that you've come to this world?"

Tarek said nothing, but his grinding back teeth scraped against my eardrum.

"It is true, then." She sat up, excitement deepening the violet and turning the tattoo to a rainbow. "You've discovered an ancient."

No lie I could think of would explain Tarek's appearance without revealing Belva, so I stayed as silent as everyone else.

"None of you need to admit what I know is truth. Arcus is such a fertile place, plenty of resources to utilize. Your ancient will be hard-pressed to keep Exemplar's very long arm out of it. And her mate…he's a natural-born, yes?"

Seriously? How in the hell…?

"Um…" I turned to Tarek, and whispered, "What does that mean?"

He shrugged, and mouthed, *I don't know.*

237

"It means Empyrean is not the only place to collect power, especially if the world can be controlled by the...gifts of an ancient. And perhaps this young man's mother will enlighten you on how Exemplians are born." Celeste found Peter with her smile. "Come here, boy."

Peter shuffled over, his boots leaving a dark trail behind him on the clean, what looked like Formica floors. We dirtied up this place. It was all beige and cream with random splashes of color on the walls that changed like her tattoo. Her chair even swiveled from blue to purple, and if the rotten smells we carried in here from the hanger were bad in the hallway, they were exponentially more obvious in the apartment that otherwise smelled like cinnamon.

As soon as Peter stood in front of her, Celeste smiled brighter, seemingly not the least bit concerned he reeked like a sewer. "Your mother is worried about you, young one. She fears you are dead."

"How do you know my mother?" Fear stain Peter's cracking voice.

Celeste tilted her head to look behind him. "People trust me with secrets."

My gaze whipped around to find Oren grinning, rocking on his heels. "You have a trusting face."

What the...? Was he actually flirting?

"Among other things." Her response was almost a purr. She returned her attention to Peter. "Is this the...help...you seek from me? Communication?" Her eyes slid to me. "You want me to contact his mother, let her know he's alive and well, maybe ask her to commit treason?"

Zander grabbed Peter's arm when the boy's lip trembled and yanked him away from the woman. "I'm done with this." Zander's rifle rose, aiming at Celeste's heart.

She smiled. "You could try, Guide. Many have in the past. Perhaps your bullet will finally put me out of my misery."

I tagged her with a scowl. Yeah, forget the static, and forget watching my mouth. We didn't come this far for a– who knew what she was–to screw with our plan. "Look, help us or not, but don't sit there and try to scare him. He understands the danger."

"Does he?" She stood. "Do you?"

A cluster of monitors clicked on behind her. In seconds, a bright blue light filled each screen, a comet zinging back and forth, slamming against a glass encasement.

She's a warning to all who might be thinking of treason...

Wilma.

I backed up, as if a few feet of distance would make the image go away, make it unreal. My back slammed against something solid and hands folded over my shoulders. A voice whispered in my ear. "We'll get her back."

Tarek.

Guilt, hate...blackness, everything I had believed was on the mend inside came unstitched, the wound ripping open. Revenge fought for a chance to sit at the head table again. "No..."

"Your Protector is suffering." Celeste paused. "She is trapped in the middle of life and death, a nightmare that cannot be fixed with a simple rescue. Her energy is damaged. Is that what you want for yourself? For this boy? His mother?"

My head moved side to side–maybe up and down?–but I didn't know why or how. At that moment, my body wasn't my own.

Tarek's voice rang behind me, anger saturating every syllable. "Let's go. She can't help us."

"Oh, but that is where you are wrong, Warden. I can help. People's secrets...I am paid handsomely to hear them. Everyone needs confession, even when in the arms of a whore. Isn't that right, Oren?"

"You are no whore, Celeste." His words were quiet, but they reached through my haze.

I couldn't say anything. My eyes remained on the screens. On Wilma.

"But I am, and I am quite good at it. Cassondra thinks so, too."

The authority commander's name snapped me from my misery, rage now combustible in my chest. Thankfully, the only revenge that won was the desire to end Cassondra. The smaller dose of the cancerous emotion was still an improvement. But the need to release Wilma from her prison soared with renewed vigor that ate at the common sense I tried so hard to regain. I turned toward Celeste. "I'm gonna kill her."

"I hope that you do, Guide, no matter how well she has paid to occupy my bed in the past." A single tear slid from her eye, gliding over that tattoo. "But if you do not succeed, it will be you or another you care about flailing around in a glass prison. Coming to Exemplar was a foolhardy risk."

"We *all* understand the risks, even the boy," Tarek said as he squeezed my hand.

Celeste nodded, not looking at him but at Oren as if his face were an anchor. "Very well." She closed her eyes and went silent, still, as if in a trance. When she opened them, she smiled at Peter, who turned pale. "It is done. Your mother has given you clearance to the place beyond the falls. She will see you there."

How did she do that? No Guide could–but Tarek felt the static, too. Was she a Guide or a Protector? And from what Peter had said, his mother was a Guide. How was she able to respond to Celeste?

Oren had a lot of explaining to do.

Peter sagged against the arm of a chair, relief finally filling his light eyes. "Th-thank you."

Celeste acknowledged him with another nod and focused on Denzel when he placed a hand on Peter's shoulder. "And, Denzel, is it?"

He took his hand from Peter and lifted his chin. Regardless of the regal act, he couldn't hide his trembling. "It is."

"Drea trusts you will bring her son to her safely, but...I do not trust you like she does."

Denzel shook his head so quick, that thick skull of his looked in danger of falling off. "I–"

"Why?" My fists clenched. If the son of a bitch tried to betray us, I'd gut him.

Her violet gaze finally returned to mine, but she didn't address me. Her warning was for one person. Denzel. "Cassondra made sure Avery and her Protector suffered for their treason, even when they decided to cooperate. And now they are no longer, Denzel. Remember that."

Lynn Vroman

CHAPTER 26

TAREK

Reality Check

"What is she?" Tarek caught up with Oren as they rushed to the stairwell, asking the question they all wanted an answer to. The static still lingered in his head, more potent than any Exemplian he'd ever experienced.

But Oren didn't answer until they were through the door and on the stairs. Tarek remained patient, understanding the guy's silence. Stairwells didn't have active cameras in the corners. "Sometimes science isn't black and white. There's still some gray left, even on Exemplar."

"You know what?" Lena stopped at a landing, her hands on her hips and fire shooting from her eyes. "Now's not the time for being vague. Black, white, gray, who gives a shit? We need straight answers, and I'm not moving until you give them."

They all stopped their descent, everyone staring up at her, including Oren, whose grip on the railing turned his knuckles white. "What would you like me to say? That I know what she is? I don't, and neither does she. All she knows—*all she suffers*—is that she doesn't age, she doesn't require medical help, she can't die, and she's lived once." He checked off each point with a finger. "And that life? For her, it's lasted as long as time. Centuries of having to survive, always hiding, *always* at the mercy of those we asked her to betray. So, you can stop being self-righteous, and you can stop acting like you know what you're doing, because you don't. None of us do. She just committed treason for us, so how about a little gratitude."

Lena, with her eyes wide and mouth agape, stood there looking lost and scared. Instinct begged him to smack Oren in the jaw. The guy breached Lena's wall and showed her vulnerability with a few sentences.

But the bastard was right.

Lena wasn't the only one who wanted this to end. The exhausted looks on the four other faces in the stairwell showed that. Even Oren didn't steam with anger, but frustration, as if his lashing out were a plea.

Tarek cleared his throat and nodded for everyone to head down. "Go on. We'll catch up."

Zander gave Lena a sympathetic smile before leading the rest of the group downstairs. Oren stayed at the railing for a moment longer. "I'm not your enemy, Lena, so stop acting like I am."

Her mouth closed, along with her eyes, but she gave a subtle nod.

Oren shot him a frown before following everyone else, but Tarek ignored him. His eyes never left the torture scarring Lena's face.

When the sound of their footsteps disappeared, he took the stairs two at a time to reach her. Tarek put tentative hands on her shoulders, refraining from bringing her closer. He didn't speak, either. Once she locked her emotions back up, she'd talk.

"Did you see her, Tarek?"

"Yes." His fingers kneaded the tight muscles bunched under her shirt, wishing the contact could suck out the venom the screens injected into her heart.

"And is Celeste right? Is Wilma—is her energy damaged?"

Fingers pressed tighter. "Yes."

Tears escaped her closed eyelids.

"But whatever we do, whatever happens, I can promise you before we leave this place, Wilma will no longer suffer."

Her eyes opened, showing pools of bright green. "I want to go home." A sob. "I want to go home with her."

He hugged her then, stroking her hair while she cried. "Okay." He repeated that one word, forcing every ounce of conviction he had into it.

Minutes later, or maybe it was hours, Lena's sobs quieted. She wiped her eyes and nose on his shirt before pointing her swollen, puffy gaze at his face. "Sorry."

He smiled, relieved. After Wilma died, she'd become empty, like those Exemplians roaming the streets of Heterodox. The ones who died too often, killing their energy's will. Emotion flitted in those puffy eyes, sadness. He'd take it over the nothingness any day. "It's fine, washable in under twenty seconds."

"Good to know." She pulled away and wiped her eyes, taking a deep breath. "I'm gonna lose it, Tarek. I can feel it. Just when I think I got a handle on things, I'm reminded–"

"I know." What else could he say? Convince her she's wrong? He could see her trying. He could see her slipping at times, too. To lie and say they'd figure it out... That was her line, not his.

"Maybe I should apologize to him, stop being a bitch all the time."

With a grin, he clasped her hand and started walking down the stairs. "Don't do that. They'll think you're sick."

She snorted. "Ha. You're *sooooo* funny. Like a real goddamn comedian." Her voice sounded nasally and congested, but at least the tinge of grief wasn't there.

"Happy to help." He kept grinning. More and more, as time passed, his Lena dug her way to the surface. Not the past Lena who couldn't find her way, lost in apathy, but the Lena he'd met and fell in love with over three years ago.

They trundled down the stairs in silence for a while.

Then her voice snuck through the quiet. "Do you believe her, about Denzel?"

Another landing, stronger rat piss. "Honestly? I don't know, but I'm not going to forget about it. We'll have to watch. Anything suspicious, I'll take him to Arcus, let the squid have him."

"If he betrays us—"

"He won't be given the chance."

When they reached the door leading to the hanger, everyone stood there staring at them. Either shirt collars or hands covered their noses. Lena let go of his hand to confront Oren, arms folded over her chest.

Oren looked down at her and shrugged. "Yes?" He had his hand cupped over his nose, making his voice sound like he'd sucked in helium.

Tarek bit the inside of his cheek to keep from laughing, saying nothing to interrupt.

"I'm…sorry." Lena stuck out her hand. "Still friends?"

Shock widened Oren's eyes as his hand slowly left his nose to clasp hers. He smirked, the guy never one to let bygones be bygones. "When were we ever friends?"

Lena grinned, taking back her hand so she could punch Oren in the shoulder. "Good point."

"All right, now that everyone's kissed and made up, what next?" Zander reached in his pack for his taser light. "I mean, what's next if we manage to prevent the very good possibility of becoming rat food."

Tarek grabbed his and Lena's tasers, the others doing the same. "Where to, kid?"

Peter gagged when he had to remove his shirt from his nose to hold his taser. "A safe house, off the grid. It has to be what Celeste meant. She said my mother gave me clearance, so..."

"Well, where's that?"

The boy took a deep breath, then proceeded to gag some more, choking on what sounded like the rest of his last meal–the part that didn't escape earlier. "Um...ah...sorry." Peter's watery eyes found his. "N-near Shalen Cliff. At the tree line meeting the river below. Do you know wh–"

"I know exactly where that is."

∞ ∞ ∞

As they headed toward one of the last remaining natural habitats left on Exemplar, all surviving another trek through the hungry rats and Heterodox, Tarek's mind refused to stop searching the past. Shalen Cliff. He hadn't been there since the night he left to find Lena. These cliffs, the meadow only miles away, it was their place from the past, where they first fell in love. Bringing Lena here...surreal.

"How much farther?" Lena's voice, soft and tired, pulled him out of his head to check the distance remaining on the dash monitor.

"Not far, about eighty miles or so."

"Eighty miles? So, like an hour and a half? Damn."

Zander's laughter snuck out from the back seat. "Impatient to leave civilization again, are you?"

"No. I like civilization, as long as that civilization isn't trying to kill me."

"When's the last time you were in a civilized place where someone wasn't trying to kill you?"

She shrugged, actually contemplating the question. "Hmm, you're right."

Despite himself, Tarek grinned as he unlocked the turbo.

Zander leaned up, putting an elbow on each of their seats. "That's just sad."

Lena shrugged again, pushing his elbow away from her face. "Well, I seem to recall you helped get the killing ball rolling. And you need a shower."

Zander sat back, laughing some more. That they could joke about their past always fascinated him. The guy went from being her best friend to enemy and straight back to someone she trusted with her life. Granted, Zander deserved the trust, proving himself on Empyrean and over the past year.

"All right, if you're both done, strap on your harnesses." Tarek shot Lena a wink as he switched to autopilot after punching in the coordinates and engaging the turbo. They were finally free of buildings, people, and heavy Synod observation. "We'll be there in five minutes."

As soon as the shuttle came to a stop in front of a tiny cabin that blended in with the forest, Lena unstrapped her harness, pulled on her latch, and crawled out of the shuttle. She fell on all fours and decorated a patch of bright flowers with regurgitated energy bars.

He sighed, unstrapping to go hold back her hair. Rat piss didn't make her lose it, but a little speed did. He swiped the hair from her face with one hand and rubbed her back with the other. "Are you going to make it?"

More vomit.

"Easy."

Finally, her heaves settled. "Don't...ever. Never again."

He smiled, really trying to be sympathetic. "Understood. No more fast cars."

She looked up, all pale and pissed off. "You think this is funny? And that's not a car; it's a rocket ship."

Laughing now, he helped her to her feet, keeping a hand at the small of her back when she wobbled. "Agree to disagree."

"Oh, this is so not an agree-to-disagree subject. That thing could shoot us into space."

"Well, that one can't, but hovercrafts can. There's actually a vacation spot right–"

"Nope. Don't wanna hear it." She palmed her stomach after a few more dry heaves. "I believe you."

Zander came up beside them, all three of their packs in his hands. "You going to live?"

She glanced up at him, licking her dry lips. "I sure as hell hope so."

"So, I guess there aren't many roller coasters in our future."

"Ugh, don't even say it."

"Too soon?" Zander grinned and moved ahead with the others, missing her weak attempt at punching his arm.

Tarek, on the other hand, was smart enough to keep his mouth shut, never one to poke a bear. His grin faded when Peter ran up the porch steps, yelling for his mom as soon as his eye scan opened the door. The mixture of fear and anticipation in the boy's voice pulled on his conscience. How many other innocent Exemplians did they send to Earth under the guise Lena was their enemy?

Yet, he already knew the answer to that question by how many pure energies Zander had brought to Arcus. Truth was they *were* Exemplar's enemy, and they killed quite a few innocent people like Peter to prove it.

They ended up being no better than the Synod, no better than Cassondra. But Belva carried all that energy now. Maybe...maybe an ancient had the knowledge and power to give those innocents another life because he didn't have a clue. If not, maybe she'd agree to set them free, something he refused to do for fear it'd weaken the world they all hoped to strengthen, their new home.

Everyone followed Peter into the cabin that was large enough to house a small army, even though it looked more like a one-bedroom shack from the outside. Whoever Peter's mother was, she was smart. Building something like this was a perfect cover. A fortress hidden behind a tiny shack-like exterior. Inside carried all the advanced technology Exemplar provided, a war-house like he'd never seen. Peter's mother wasn't just a sympathizer. Maybe they'd all come out of this alive, after all.

The boy kept yelling for his mother, his voice carrying from the second floor. The sound of doors swooshing open met Tarek's ears. When Peter came back down to the main level on the hydro-lift, looking lost and confused, Denzel rushed to him, a gentle smile on his face as he reached up to clasp the boy's shoulder. "She'll be here, son. Give her time."

"B-but she said to meet her here. This has to be where she meant. Home…she wouldn't want me to go to the capital, would she?"

More gentle words from the Guide. "She meant here. All will be well. Your mother is quite intelligent. She knows what she's doing."

Tarek let go of Lena and headed toward the lift when it looked like Peter might lose it. "You can't crack, kid. You're not, are you?"

"I…" When Peter's eyes filled, Tarek yanked him off the lift. The boy didn't need gentle words. He needed someone to remind him of what he was. A fighter.

"You will not crack, do you hear me? We need to hide the shuttles and come up with a plan. There's no time to coddle you."

Peter's eyes dried and his shoulders straightened. "Y-yes, Warden."

Tarek let go of the boy. "I'm not the Warden. I'm Tarek, or sir, and you will button it up and get yourself in order. You know this place. We don't. And those shuttles need to be invisible to the authority's recon branch, understand? If they get suspicious, we die. That simple."

Peter nodded, already moving for the front door. "Yes, s-sir. There's an underground hatch around back."

"Good. Take another person with you, and get them there."

Zander dumped the bags in the middle of the floor and followed Peter. "I got one, you got the other."

Tarek eyed up Denzel when the front door closed behind the two. The Guide turned a shade whiter. "He doesn't need you pampering him."

"He's just a boy." Denzel held out his hands. "He shouldn't have to–"

"It doesn't matter now, does it? He's not a boy anymore; he's not allowed to be." Tarek moved closer to the smaller man. "And if you do anything–anything–to jeopardize the lives of my people to try to 'save' that kid? I'll end you." He turned. "And I'll end him, too."

Lynn Vroman

CHAPTER 27

TAREK

Truth

Amazing what a shower and some real food could do. If one considered freeze-dried, vacuum-sealed powder food. All it took was a rotation or two in the nifty little food processor on the counter, and they had a feast of ham, potatoes, and blueberry crisp in seconds. All things Lena chose from the huge supply of food, weapons, contego suits, and more stored in the basement rooms. They sat around a large oval table, concentrating on inane conversation. For the first time in a while, a hint of normality teased them all.

Tarek had refused to live like most Exemplians. Their way of technology turned them into robots, and he needed to experience life. Hunting, building his own fire, going hungry when the day's hunt didn't go well, anything he could find to help keep his humanity for as long as possible. Otherwise, he'd have turned into an android, a functioning shell. Like Lena had before she died–before she rediscovered the will to live during this cycle.

But tonight he relished the convenience, loved the texture of meat and berries as the food hit his tongue, food that took seconds to prepare. This was exactly why he stayed away from it in the first place. A person could get used to just existing, having things handed to them instead of going out and finding it.

But normal ended with the meal. After dinner, while they all stood around a hologram of the capital, Peter asked the million-dollar question. "So, now what?"

Oren answered. "We wait for your mother."

Their whole plan was to find Peter's mother and have her give direction to what they actually *could* do. Flimsy plan, but it was better than being trapped on Arcus, waiting for Protectors to pick everyone off until they got to Belva. This was it, though. The last hurrah. If they failed, Exemplar won. They couldn't go on just surviving anymore.

"All right, and what part will she play? They scan recent brain activity every time she goes into the lab. If they read any treason, she–"

Oren held out his hand. "Zander, take Denzel upstairs. Keep an eye on him, will you? Find a room and lock him in it." He glanced at Peter. "We don't talk strategy around your Guide."

Peter glanced at Denzel, and Tarek could see the boy warring with indecision: Should he trust him? Would Denzel betray them?

When Peter finally nodded, looking away from his Guide, Denzel lifted his chin, tears shimmering in his aged eyes. "I would never do anything to hurt you or your mother, Peter. But if this is what you want, if my not being here will make you feel safer, then so be it." Without waiting for Zander, Denzel went to the lift.

"Nice speech." Zander picked up his rifle. "Fill me in later."

After Denzel was safely out of earshot, they all kept staring at the hologram, clueless. Lena stared in awe at the sleek silver buildings that shined like mirrors reflecting the sun, all of them uniform and symmetrical, like Arcus's forest. The hologram was real-time, and people in the typical muted robes walked around in the cabin's main rooms that now looked as though it sat in the middle of the city square.

Lena reached out to touch the face of a woman who stopped to look in a shop window. No emotion flitted over the woman's face as she analyzed the newest kitchen gadget. "They're all like zombies."

"Pretty close." Oren moved beside her and pointed at a building situated in the middle of the organized chaos of the capital. People drummed along the white stone walkways like ants. "This is the authority building, the Creation Lab is underground, a lab that expands the entire length of Cynosure."

"Cynosure?"

Oren sneered with a grand wave of his hand. "The capital, otherwise known as the hub of the universe."

Lena tilted her head, giving him a smile. "Not for long."

Oren's tight laugh, like a dud firecracker, described Tarek's thoughts exactly. "Wish I had your optimism," Oren said.

"Well, get with the program because I'm planning on going home." She turned to Peter. "Your mom, does she have access to where Wilma is?"

Peter moved closer to her, fidgeting as he squinted at the authority building. A gate surrounded it, an electric barrier heavily guarded and impossible to infiltrate. "Yes, I believe so. She cried when she first saw the image on the screens." A pause. "She wished to free your Protector."

"Looks like her wish is about to come true."

Peter shook his head, his face white with panic. "How will she be able…? No one knows. I don't–"

Polite electronic bells dinged.

Tarek knew that sound all too well.

Warning bells.

He rushed to deactivate the hologram, the city blinking out in an instant, the cabin going dark. No one had to be told what to do. They understood his urgency.

Lena grabbed her gun, and Oren did the same. He then shoved Peter behind him, the position the boy had since Oren took over his training. Peter didn't hesitate, either, his gun drawn and fear in his eyes.

Tarek looked toward the second floor to find Zander already in position, his rifle pointed to the door, the single entrance they'd found into the house besides a small window in the front bedroom upstairs. To outsiders, this place resembled a tiny shack. Hopefully whoever tripped the alarm would pass on by.

In moments, the alarms stopped dinging and relief filled his gut.

Until the door to the below storage compartments opened.

Tarek whipped around, signaling everyone to do the same, his finger already on the trigger. A woman in a contego suit and holding a gun of her own, shot up the stairs, eyeballing everyone until her gaze fell on the boy.

"Peter!" Her gun landed on the floor with a thump as she ran toward him, practically pushing Oren on his ass.

Muffled cries ripped from everyone, especially Lena, who had to holster her gun to wipe tears off her face. Relaxing, he holstered his, too, and signaled for Zander to do the same. Just as Zander's safety clicked, the door behind him swooshed open.

Denzel came rushing to the lift, jumping off it before the thing even touched the bottom floor. He said nothing as he ran to Peter and his mother, capturing both in his arms. The three, so obviously a family, held each other while everyone else tried to give them privacy. Oren awkwardly scooted from the trio to stand by Lena. Her tiny hiccups beckoned Tarek as Oren patted her shoulder. Tarek folded her in his arms, waiting for…Drea, he believed Celeste called her, to acknowledge them.

Funny that no one thought to ask the kid his mother's name. "Peter's Mother" fit fine enough not to worry about it. And he thought she was a Guide. The woman looked nothing like the insipid Synod Guides he'd had the misfortune to run across, Avery being one of them. No, this woman had a strong fighter build, as if she could take out a couple Protectors on her own, and her gun hand hadn't trembled with fear or nerves. Instead, it pointed directly at his heart when she had run up the stairs, the one part of the house not advanced. Stairs were only in Heterodox, not even in Abrogation.

His heart skipped with a little of that optimism Oren mentioned. Maybe she wouldn't crack under the pressure. Hell, she'd had this place built.

When the three broke apart, Drea cupped her son's face, tears glistening in light eyes the same as his. "Are you well?"

Peter nodded, reaching his palms up to cover her hands.

"I thought…I thought for sure they killed you."

Tarek cringed inwardly. *They*, meaning his people.

Drea gave her son one last kiss and reached over to squeeze Denzel's hand. "Thank you, my friend."

"I promised you, Drea," Denzel said. "I promised."

"You did, yes, and please forgive me for doubting you." Drea turned to Tarek. Her eyes widened as if it were the first time she actually saw him in the room. "It's true."

Here we go. He let go of Lena and stood in front of the woman with his hands behind his back. "I assume you're talking about our ancient." He made sure she knew Belva was one of them, a warning, really.

"Oh, yes, but…I'm speaking rather of her mate. He's a natural-born."

257

There it was again. Natural-born. What did Farren have to do with anything?

"So, that's the second time we've heard that term. You're talking about Farren, who I should mention is my closest friend, so tread lightly." The need to threaten came out of nowhere, forcing its way past the need to be polite in order to beg for help.

The left corner of her mouth curved up and all traces of tears and fuzzy-warm homecoming disappeared. "I've no designs on your friend…though *I should mention* you might want to thank him for your release."

Lena stepped forward, her fuzzy-happy gone too. "The fuck are you talking about?"

Exactly.

Drea shot Peter a reassuring smile before heading toward a side table where a good amount of silver canisters lined its surface. She took her time pouring a drink, the amber liquid splashing in a crystal glass, reflecting back at them in rainbows. After pouring another when she drained the first, Drea came back to their small circle and tilted her head. "Your friend…he is able to create children."

"I'm not in the mood for riddles." Tarek fought to keep his voice even, at the same time curling his fists. If she thought to waste his time by spewing needless information, his disgust of Synod politics wasn't as popular as he'd thought. No problem. He'd show her.

Drea kept her cool, sipping her drink before setting it on the table. But her eyes didn't match the calm façade. She stole a quick glance at her son and the equally nervous Denzel, who subtly shook his head, before facing Tarek head on. "Come, all of you. I'd like to show you something." Without waiting for a reply, Drea headed back toward the stairs.

Tarek stopped Oren and Zander as they went to follow. "No." He nodded toward Denzel and Peter. "You two first."

Oren tilted his head toward Peter after he shrugged off Tarek's hold, clearly not in the mood to listen to him. "It's okay, kid. I'm right behind you."

"What's down there? I mean, all we found was food and weapons. What the hell's going on?" Peter, stubborn and holding onto the back of a chair like a lifeline, didn't budge. Tarek smiled despite the situation. The kid's language...Lena did have quite the influence.

"Your mother is about to reveal some truth, secrets no Synod member wants its citizens to hear." Denzel glanced at all of them. "I hope you're all prepared."

Peter still refused to move.

Tarek sighed, clasping Lena's hand, needing her near, and headed down the stairs, not bothering to respond. Better to rip the bandage off instead of tugging a little at a time. As soon as his boot hit the first step, Zander and Oren were behind them. He pulled out his gun, everyone else doing the same. If this were a trap, at least they'd take a few with them. But when they reached the bottom, no Protectors came out from the darkness. Always a good sign.

When he moved forward, Denzel came up from the rear. "This way." He veered left, to an open door that led to another set of stairs. As they descended, the hall became brighter, almost blinding, and when they reached the end of the stairs, Tarek's gun almost slipped from his numb fingers.

A stark white, stainless steel lab three times the size of his cabin on Arcus was decked out with tools and machines he'd never seen. Everything was polished and pristine, even the metal table in the middle of the room big enough for a body maybe the size of his. True, he had no idea what any of the machines were, but he did know one thing. The woman headed the Creation Lab, after all, and this had to be a smaller version of that.

Any doubts about his conclusion disappeared when his gaze darted to the back of the room. An incubation tank held a human that had no discernible facial features. The body had tubes hooked to its head, heart, and wrists as it lay peacefully, its chest moving up and down in a steady rhythm. But there was one thing recognizable.

The body had the exact build as Peter, lanky and too tall for a fourteen-year-old kid.

"What...what have you done?" Lena's grip tightened on his hand, and her attention fell on Drea, who stood in front of the tank like a guard, defiance clear on her face.

Drea opened her mouth to answer, but Peter's cry broke the tense silence. "Mom?"

"Peter, please, I–" She moved to pull him in her arms, but he backed away, his eyes wide and head shaking. Drea dropped her arms and tears filled her eyes. "I didn't want you to find out this way."

"Find out what?" Tarek asked the question when Peter, or anyone else, said nothing.

A tear escaped the woman's eye. "The truth." She wrung her hands, probably to keep from reaching out to her son, who found his way next to Oren.

Oren stood closer to the kid, rage staining his face. "Whatever the 'truth' is, maybe you should spill it before there's a brawl in your pretty lab."

Drea swiped at her cheeks, her neat bun coming undone around her face. "Exemplians have figured out a way to...create a human without depending on chance." She walked over to the table and brushed a shaky hand over the shining surface. "For centuries upon centuries, most Exemplians have been created on a table like this one." Tears splashed down, forming silvery pools on the table. "Including my own son."

Her admission garnered a room full of silence. What could he even say to that? They weren't...human? No, the notion refused to sink in. Zander opened and closed his mouth at least a hundred times, while Oren's rage transformed to shock.

Drea continued, seemingly lost inside her head. "They found ways to produce the perfect human, give them skills no human should possess. We are–most of us–the epitome of mastered biotechnology. We can create life with machines, true life...never making another genetic mistake again."

She grew quiet, tears sliding down her cheeks while she stared off into another time.

Her silence gave Tarek's mind permission to wander. *Not real?*

As if realizing she wasn't alone, Drea's eyes focused, landing on her son. "Somewhere along the way, they figured out how to construct people who could procreate. And when the first child was born of these...creations...it was a miracle." She paused, swallowing a few times before bowing her head. "I wanted to bear a child, feel it grow inside my womb." Her eyes then shifted back to Peter, who sobbed quietly next to Oren. "But there are other ways. You are my son, made from my DNA and Denzel's."

"No..." The boy backed up until he bumped into the sterile wall, shock on his face. "It can't be real."

"I'm so very sorry. But *you are my son*, in every way." She held her hand to her stomach, as if she wished.

"I can't be here." Peter stepped from the wall. "I...can't be around you." He turned and ran from the room, ignoring Drea's pleas for him to stay.

261

Drea went to run after him, but Oren stopped her. "I'll go. The boy doesn't need you right now." He nodded to everyone else. "Explain it to them and come up with a plan so we can all leave this place."

Once Oren stormed out, the only sounds were Drea's quiet cries.

Sweat pooled under Tarek's arms and his whole face went numb. None of it made sense. He was a manufactured product? A flesh and bone manmade machine? No...

His gaze found Lena, who had concern all over her face as she looked up at him. She was the singular "real" human in the room. At least in her present life. She was born. A true infant who grew into the woman she now was. But he was a...thing.

A shaking hand wiped the corners of his mouth, trying to force it to work. "So... But...I remember being a child in my first life, a toddler. My mother...I remember her before she left, before I was fostered out to train."

The misery on Drea's face was so acute, as if the emotion swarmed around her, alive and screaming. "Memory implants. Most bodies are grown to the age of five their first cycle before the energy is inserted. Only natural-born are true infants. Cassondra and her brother were twins and some of the rare natural-born Exemplians, like your friend."

"Farren's lived for four cycles."

"Yes, but in his first, he was natural-born. The lab has always had his original form for subsequent recycling."

Lena's hand squeezed his tighter. He looked down to see her holding Zander's arm with her other. Zander's dark face reflected the same misery as Drea's. As his. Tarek wanted to slay the woman. Rip out her manmade heart. But this wasn't her doing. Killing the messenger never worked to solve the problem. He wished it did. "So, when we come back here, after death...?"

Drea cleared her throat, pressing her hands on the metal table. "It's easier if we have the original body, again, as your friend. Repair what made it stop working, give it a chance to heal, erase a few years from the face, make the body strong again. Then it's a simple matter of installing the soul back in. After all, the energy is attracted to it still."

Soul... She said soul.

Lena's hands shook, but she stayed silent, as did Zander, obviously both just as shocked.

Drea continued as if she hadn't destroyed his world. "When the body isn't available, things take longer, become more complicated." She turned and moved to the chamber, caressing the encasement as if it were her son. "We must pull the DNA on file, grow another body. Sometimes it takes months." A sob escaped. "That is why Denzel and I created two bodies, just in case. This body has grown right along with my son. If Peter were to die and his body destroyed, Denzel was to bring his energy here. Once his energy—his soul—was implanted, he would have a second chance."

Tarek raised a brow, his stomach churning. "The Synod let you do this?"

"They do not know I have a son. I implanted his energy into an infant form, kept him safe, hidden here. It was easy, once he reached five, to place him into the Protector program, due to the abilities we spliced into his DNA."

"Celeste knew you had a son," Tarek said.

She bowed her head. "Celeste knows many things."

Tarek's knees gave. Thankfully, two chairs lined the wall and he was close enough to stumble over before falling to the floor. He remembered. The first time Lena died, when some wild animal in Andor mangled her body, a world no one sent or collected energy from anymore. He had to plead with the Warden to release her energy, give it to the Synod Guide he dragged from bed to go collect it. While he begged Wilma to take over Protector duties, he also hounded Avery because it was taking too long for Lena to come back. She lied to him, straight to his face with a smile, telling him nothing but that it'd be soon. He never asked why. Never cared to know how. He just wanted her back. But what Drea said now made everything so clear.

He shook his head, his leg bouncing overtime. "This is madness."

Lena rushed over to sit next to him, leaving Zander to stare at the other two, his finger on the trigger and rifle moving to the center of Drea's chest.

"Don't, Zander," Tarek said. "Stand down."

"This bitch is telling us we're all a bunch of machines!" Zander raised his gun higher until the sights centered between her eyes.

Denzel rushed to stand in front of her, even as the woman lifted her chin in defiance. "This is not her fault! She's telling you what they've done to *all* of us. For centuries. She wants it to end, like the rest of you. We all want a chance to live another life oblivious of this travesty."

Zander's gun still didn't move, and Tarek didn't have the energy to stop him. A part of him wanted Zander to take them out. But Lena stood, pressing on the barrel of Zander's gun until it lowered. "We will end this. And they'll help." She nodded toward Drea. "Right?"

"Yes. Absolutely. I've wanted to destroy this craziness as long as I've worked for the Synod lab–for seven of my lives. We *will* end it…on one condition."

"You're not in the position to give conditions." Lena's attention stayed on Zander's tortured face as she spoke.

"Then I will not help you."

Tarek squeezed his eyes shut for a moment, a fresh shot of adrenaline shooting through his body. "What do you want?"

"I want Peter away from here–and Denzel. I want them safe. I…I want them to have a chance to live a normal life." She swallowed. "And a true next life."

"No, Drea."

Tarek ignored Denzel and nodded. "Done."

Lena piped in. "Wait." She turned to Drea. "Are you telling us you have a plan, something less destructive and stupid than Avery's? Or are you giving us a line of shit to save your family?"

"I do have a plan, yes. And I will not fail as Avery did. She was weak, afraid to do what must be done."

Lena nodded. "And Farren? Why do you and Celeste keep mentioning him?"

Tarek watched Drea's reaction closely, waiting for any tell, any indication of lies.

"Avery told them you harbored an ancient." Hate dripped from her words. "She also told them about the ancient's Exemplian lover. They searched the name she gave and found Farren to be a natural-born. They want to kill him and collect her before…" Drea's attention turned to him, wonderment in her sad eyes.

"Before what, goddamn it?" Lena never did have the patience for drawn-out explanations.

Drea's eyes found hers, a tiny smile shadowing her lips. "The reason Tarek has been released is because your ancient is with child."

"What?" Lena's eyes widened, tears forming at the corners.

"She is carrying the future Warden of Arcus in her womb." Drea turned to him. "You, Tarek, are our wild card. As long as they do not know it has happened yet, they will not destroy your world. They will continue to tread carefully in order to ensure the survival of the ancient in hopes of bringing her here to dissect her, try to emulate her DNA."

Tarek stood, fear prickling his skin. "Show me your screens."

CHAPTER 28

TAREK

A Small Reprieve

He hoped she was lying.

An army of thumping boots followed close behind him as he bee-lined it for the back wall in the main room.

Panic took over.

Home.

Home.

He had to see…had to know…

He ripped the cover off the screens' control panel and found it security coded.

No surprise.

Tarek turned to search the sea of faces until his eyes landed on Peter. "Turn these on."

Peter jumped to do what Tarek demanded, even as Drea commanded they stop.

Tarek pointed at her, all his rage shooting from his finger. If it were possible, if he had the ability, that one finger would've sent her across the room. "Shut. Up."

The screens exploded on, no sound, just the blaring continual feed of Wilma's prison, her energy jutting against the glass encasement. Lena let a small cry escape, but bit her bottom lip and closed her eyes. Tarek didn't dare go to her. If he showed her any sympathy, revealed her weakness in front of these people, she'd crumble.

Instead, he shoved Peter away and moved to punch in Arcus's coordinates.

"If you try to tap into Arcus's feed, the authority will be on our heads in minutes."

His finger froze over the first digit, Drea's warning finally hitting home. "They have it monitored, don't they?"

Drea nodded once, her body tense as she kept focus on him.

He forgot how the Synod worked already. Funny what three years of freedom could erase. His hand lowered along with his head. Arcus could have already fallen and they'd not know it.

"Damn it." He whispered the curse as it screamed inside his head. He jabbed the deactivation button, the blinding light of Wilma's prison burning his retinas and magnifying his rage. Three steps took him to Lena, who still had her eyes shut. He bent low, his mouth right next to her ear. "It's over, love. Open your eyes."

When she did, there were no tears, just complete and utter misery, emptiness he'd become too familiar with. Still, he didn't touch her. People in the room depended on her to keep it together, and she would. On the outside. Her strength was hers, no matter how contrived.

Drea spoke, making it easier to concentrate on something besides Lena's torment. "You would have discovered static, anyway. There are no more satellite feeds from Arcus, which is why they monitor screen activity for anyone who tries its coordinates. Everyone living on Exemplar knows this. Only someone who didn't would try."

"They shut down the feed?"

"No." Drea's lip curled. "Avery and her Protector managed to destroy the feed before they turned themselves in."

That's right! Denzel had told them already.

Tarek punched the wall. He almost blew their cover because he couldn't keep it together enough to remember.

Lena squeezed his forearm, using more pressure when he balled his fist to take a jab at the wood again. She turned to Drea. "So…she *did* help us?"

Drea nodded. "Right before she plunged the dagger in your back. But she was weak, her plan to close the lines cowardly. A plan that would have never gotten her hands dirty, only those foolish enough to believe it feasible."

"We are those *foolish people*," Lena said. "And we've all sacrificed because of it." She looked toward the black screens. "Some more than others."

"Your sacrifice is no greater than my own–than so many who suffer here."

Tarek had to hold onto Lena when she went for the Guide's throat. "You bit–" She slammed her mouth shut then took a deep breath. "Why should we trust you?"

Drea went to stand in front of Lena and looked her straight in the eye. "Like I said, I've done what needed to be done. I will not fail."

Tarek let go of Lena to lean against the edge of a table, his legs betraying him. "I…I don't know what to say."

"If it helps, when they sent the traitor to me for annihilation, I refused to give her the peace of nothingness." Drea's gaze landed on Peter, her eyes filling. "She put my son in danger with her silly notions and inability to see them through."

"*We* put your son in danger. Christ, we could've killed him!" Lena stood taller, her fists clenched, and all traces of misery again protected behind her wall. She skirted around Drea and went to Peter, as if she were trying to shield him from a what-could've-been past. "I was the one who held a gun to his head."

Peter glanced down at her as he groped for her hand. His eyes said, *It's okay*, while a smile teased his lips. "I'd have taken you."

His voice, so young. *Damn it.* This war needed to end before they all turned into savages.

Lena smiled. "Yeah, sure you would have." She turned to Drea, her smile gone. "What makes you think we wouldn't have killed him? Or Denzel for that matter? Because, trust me, I wanted to."

Drea moved in the direction of her son, but Peter stiffened, holding out a hand. Her shoulders sagged, and she inhaled deeply, before saying, "Because I trusted you before, and I had to trust you again. I had faith you'd see his innocence, and Denzel promised to compromise with you if caught. When they chose him to go, to be sacrificed..." A tear slipped down her cheek. "I died inside. Thank you, all of you, for bringing my son back to me, regardless of your reasons."

Enough.

Tarek shot Oren a look. "Take the kid and Denzel to Earth. Ask Cheveyo if he has room for two more. Before you come back, check on Arcus—and get Winston. We're going to need him."

"Wait, no! No way. I'm not going anywhere." Peter shrugged from Lena's grip and confronted Tarek, the boy's face red as his voice dipped and cracked. "Don't send me away, please. I can help. *I can help.*"

Tarek pulled his hands behind his back to prevent himself from comforting the kid. Peter had to go. He had to get a chance at life. If they failed here, Cheveyo would protect him. The Synod would never know he existed or tried to help. He'd be free. "Not this time, kid."

Peter turned to glare at his mother. "This is because of you, isn't it?"

"Peter, please. I–"

He held up his hand. "None of you trust Denzel. I get it; trust me. Send him, but I want to fight. I-I want to make them pay for...for–"

"We'll make them pay." Tarek kept his voice calm, understanding the boy's thirst. His hands tingled with the desire to feel blood and bones crunching under his fingers as he ripped out throats.

Lena cupped Peter's face, forcing him to look at her. "You deserve blood, I know. But you deserve a chance to be a kid more. A kid who drinks soda until his stomach hurts and eats chips until he vomits. You deserve better than this." She gave Peter the same smile that melted Tarek every time she took it out of her arsenal. "Go. We'll be right behind you. And together we'll finally get to be normal people."

Peter's tears soaked Lena's fingers. "But...I'm not even human, am I?"

"*Yes*, you are." She found Tarek's eyes. "We *all* are."

"What did my moth–what did she tell you?"

"It's not important. All that's important right now is surviving. And I, for one, can't concentrate on surviving if I know you're in danger. Congratulations, you've made me like you. A lot. The prize is freedom, from all of this."

She kissed his cheek and backed away, nodding to Oren. "Go. Get them out of here."

Oren raked a hand through his hair, clearly on the fence, but he'd go. The kid meant more to him than any person in the room. "I'll be back soon, but I won't guarantee Winston will be with me. The guy has no desire to come back here."

Tarek pursed his lips. "No, he'll come. He'll bitch about it, but he'll be here, especially after you fill him in."

Oren gestured for Denzel to come to his side and hooked Peter's arm. "Guess we'll see."

The tear ripped open, and Drea rushed forward before it sucked them through. She clung to Peter. "I love you, son. Please...forgive me."

Peter said nothing, only held his mother for a second longer before the three left this world for a safer one.

"Now," Tarek said, rubbing his face, "time to get down to business. What's the plan?"

Drea's tears stained her cheeks, but to her credit, she bounced back, unzipping her contego to reveal a tank top and some impressive biceps. "Simple. We destroy them from the inside."

Lena snorted, nudging Zander, who looked defeated. "Christ. She don't have a clue." Zander strapped his rifle on his back. "We might as well waltz into the front doors and ask them to stop being mean."

The guy had a point. Tarek had enough of grandiose plans, too. Closing the lines? Look how well that turned out and the only individual who could pull off a miracle might decide not to come play with them.

Drea smiled, too, slinking out of the rest of her suit. Her tank top and cotton pants showed the body of a fighter. Maybe…maybe she wasn't another Avery. "I wouldn't suggest it, but if that's your style, be my guest." She stalked toward the far wall and pressed on a panel. A sleek computer system folded down and the monitor came to life. She cracked her knuckles and began typing. "I plan to get started in the comfort of my home."

Curious, Tarek sauntered over after shooting Lena a raised brow, who shrugged and followed. He sat in the chair beside Drea. "What do you have going on over here?"

Drea squinted at the screen and typed some more until a bunch of important-looking files streamed on the monitor. "This and that." A hologram of a lab ballooned above them. "But I thought we'd start with the absolute destruction of Exemplar's creation practices."

∞ ∞ ∞

Not real.
Not real.
Not real.

Nothing was more frustrating than that little mantra stuck on replay and racketing through his skull. Sleep was out. Every time his eyes closed, images of machines splicing together humans on a manufacturing belt mocked him.

Not. Real.

Lena tried to talk about it, make him open up, but...no. Not really a conversation to have with the love of your life: *Hey, I was made in a factory. You know, not born. Made with tools and machines. You?*

Definitely not a topic he wanted to beat with a talking stick.

Nothing would change the fact, and no amount of hashing out the details or hearing the "it's not important" speeches would help. Sweeping it out of his head was the best answer he came up with, and that required a whole lot of nonverbal communication. They all knew it was there, so why bring it up? Zander and Oren felt the same, giving Lena the no-go, which was the underlying topic of every argument he had to suffer through these past few days.

But, really, all of it was...disturbing, to say the least.

At least Winston came back with Oren, and Arcus held up against the guerrilla warfare tactics Exemplians were still implementing there. Belva managed to control the weather in a way he never could. Winston said the entire forest was now a winter wonderland–except for their squid-protected village. She didn't even have to be pissed or upset.

The animals seemed to fare well enough in the temperatures, too. The Protectors funneling in weren't, though. Winston and Farren would go out to collect bodies occasionally when an influx of energy would slam into Belva's chest.

Silver linings.

For three days, they sat around that house, a prison full of good food and gadgets that made life as sloth-like as possible. Lena and Zander spent a good part of that time arguing about the not-real topic, and when they weren't arguing with each other, they'd tag team Oren, who usually shrugged them off. None of them handled inactivity well. They functioned better when a bit of violence threatened the horizon.

Winston and Drea spent the time planning, hunched around her console, saying little to each other outside of grunts and hand gestures. Well, Drea spent time planning when she didn't go to work. Had to keep up appearances, not miss a day of manufacturing more clueless biobots. Tarek couldn't help but respect her, though. She'd go in, always in danger of being found out. One blip in the brain scan, and her ass would be in a cell for an energy reading. She'd told them after years of practice, she had the brain activity of a sociopath. He didn't know what to think of that.

He slogged to the lift, half tempted to leap to the ground floor for the excitement of not knowing if he'd make it down there without a broken ankle. Certainly some nifty tool or machine was somewhere in the house able to fix him up, good as new.

When the lift stopped, Tarek nodded to Lena, who scowled at him. "I gotta get out of here. Soon."

He hesitated halfway between where she stood by the kitchen counter and where Winston sat, plugging away at the keyboard. With a sigh, he went with the choice he'd always make.

She'd win every time.

Should he hug her? Anger, exacerbated with boredom, radiating off her body said probably not. He did anyway, kissing the top of her head. "It's not safe."

She stiffened and shoved at his chest. "Well, it's not safe for any of you if I don't get the hell out of here for a while. I don't care where we go as long as it's not…here."

Another sigh.

"Tarek? Come on, please? You have to know a place we can go. Someplace where there isn't a bunch of computerized crap and blinking lights."

"That's the problem. Blinking lights are everywhere. Static-inducing blinking lights."

Her anger dissolved into something else. Desperation. "Please."

He searched her face, wishing her irritation would come back, so much easier to say no to. "Give me five minutes."

"Okay." When she smiled, those green eyes filling with liquid, he'd give her the world if he could.

As she moved to go upstairs, he grabbed her elbow. "You will put on a contego, make sure your gun–and your backup gun–are loaded and functional, and inject a sustenance booster. If we get caught out there, I don't want to have to worry about food and water."

She saluted him, that smile stopping his heart. "Yes, sir."

He grinned. "Now, I like the sound of that."

Her laughter followed him to Winston. "Yeah, well don't get used to it."

"Wouldn't dream of it." Tension already lifted off his shoulders. A little danger eased the feeling of helplessness.

"Wouldn't dream of what?" Winston kept his back to Tarek, not breaking his typing rhythm.

The guy had tattoos from his neck to the tops of his feet, and the sleeveless T-shirt and cutoff shorts displayed a bunch of them. So, Winston wasn't only a badass with every heightened power manufactured by what Tarek knew now to be their makers, but a genius computer hacker, too. Tarek ignored the question. He knew Winston's supersonic hearing heard the entire conversation. "How close are we?"

Winston and Drea weren't playing games, and as much as it annoyed everyone in the house to have to sit and wait, they were making a failsafe plan, one with as little confrontation as possible.

Winston stopped typing and swiveled in his chair until he faced Tarek. "Things are coming along. We should be outta here and back home in time to listen to Red panic about fatherhood. You should've seen his face when Oren spread the good news. White as death, he got."

Relief. Such a good feeling. "He'll be a great father."

Winston grinned, a chuckle rumbling his chest. "Sure, after he's done being afraid of it." He tapped a finger to his lips. "You think it's such a good idea to leave? Recon's everywhere."

"There are places..." Excitement made Tarek's stomach flip, though he kept it straight on the outside. Last thing he wanted was to look like an overeager boy about to cop his first feel. But he needed this as much as Lena did.

"No, there ain't. Just places they don't watch as much."

"I'll keep her safe. You do whatever computer thing you're doing and we'll be back soon."

"It's not her I'm worried about." Winston always appeared calm, except there was no hiding the way his fingers clenched the chair's armrests. "They find out you're here, they're gonna napalm Arcus–where my girl is, you feel me?" Winston didn't bother to hide the edge cutting into his words.

"It'll be fine." He wouldn't explain himself to anyone, not even Winston. Risk didn't escape him. He got it, and the last thing he'd do is jeopardize anyone, but...

His flaw.

"Imma hold you to it, man. But if you're spotted, if shit goes down, I'm outta here and ya'll are on your own."

"Fair enough."

Winston twirled back toward the computer and began punching away at the keyboard. "I'd say so."

Not much more to say to that, but when Lena jumped on the lift and breezed down, a bright smile animating her face, the apprehension Winston's logic planted in his brain disappeared. Any risk they were about to take was worth it. She rushed over as Zander shuffled out of an upstairs room. He leaned over the upper-floor railing, and once he took in her contego and guns, excitement replaced all traces of sleep. "Is it time? Where're we going?"

Lena snarled as she whipped her head toward the upper level. "It's not time, and *you're* not going anywhere."

"Wait, why do you get to go?" Zander's yelling echoed off the walls in the cavernous room.

Lena turned. With that smile in place, she almost glided to Tarek and slipped her arms around his neck. "I have a date."

Every time. Every. Single. Time. His heart thumped against his rib cage, as if it were the first she'd ever touched him.

"Hey! I wanna go!" Zander didn't like to give up often.

Neither did he.

Tarek tore his gaze from Lena's to acknowledge Zander. "Not invited." He reached for Lena's hand behind his neck, keeping it clasped tight. "Come on."

"Where're we going?" She skipped along beside him toward the door leading to the underground hanger.

He brought their joined hands to his lips and kissed her fingers. "A surprise."

"I don't like surprises."

"You'll like this one."

Lynn Vroman

CHAPTER 29

LENA

Home

His scent had triggered ghosts when I first met him. Apples and lilacs. The day he became Warden, I had started to carry those smells in my heart, clinging to his memory. Home. Apples and lilacs were home.

When Tarek landed Drea's shuttle in an orchard, with apples littering the ground in patches of lilacs, tears burned my eyes. Those ghosts from three years ago, those hints of something more, funneled into my brain with as much force as rushing water collapsing a dam. The doors hadn't even opened yet, but I smelled everything already–I didn't need the actual scent. It lay nestled in my soul for years.

But as soon as the door swung up, that fragrance, it punched me right in the heart. I stumbled out of the shuttle and fell to my knees.

Home.

The reality of it, this place I'd heard about through stories Tarek would tell, I wanted to collect the sensations, physically hold them in my hands, and keep them locked inside my arms.

"Lena?"

I couldn't... I just... *Home.*

Tarek gently lifted me from the ground. "Come on. There's more I want to show you."

As we stood there in the middle of our meadow, something...happened. Residual jealousy of my past self, the jealousy that still snuck up on me from time to time, broke free from my soul and dissipated into a cloud, forgotten. At that moment, I loved her, understood her, and even mourned her.

Tarek guided me with a hand at the small of my back as we left a thick grove of apple trees to the more open field. *That smell!* I wanted it to meld with my skin, become a part of me. We walked in silence, neither of us willing to break the spell. His hand quaked on my back, and heat and moisture from his sweating palm seeped through my contego, searing my skin. He was afraid of my reaction, and he didn't need to say it for me to know it.

A year and a half ago, I would've hated him for bringing me here. Envy of his past with another woman he loved was more than I could carry on my shoulders. So stupid. I understood that now, especially after losing Wilma, experiencing what real pain felt like, absolute misery.

I intended to allay his fears until we reached a blackened circle of ash about the size of my old apartment on Earth. The burnt char insulting the apples and lilacs was subtle, almost indistinct, but it existed, like an infection under unblemished skin. I glanced up to search Tarek's pale face; his cheeks so white, I worried he might pass out. That hand against my back shook harder, its tremors feeding my anxiety. He hurt. Hurt in a way I didn't but could fully comprehend. Our home, the one he'd built, the one he'd used as a model for the cabins on Arcus, was reduced to a singed memory.

"Hey." I cupped his cheeks, forcing him to look away from the remains to meet my gaze. "*Hey*."

His eyes closed as he covered my hands with his. "Wilma... She had to burn it to the ground."

"I know." This story had been told more times than I could count, but he needed to tell it again. Purge himself of the reality of it.

He opened his eyes, his heated palms still clinging to my hands. "I built it for you, all of it. Everything I do is always for you. *You*. I wanted to bring you here… I wanted to show you…"

My heart broke in a million pieces. I had so much to make up for. My rock, my reason for breathing, he never gave up, even when he swore he couldn't fight anymore, even when it killed him on the inside. No words would convince him, and as I stared into those gray depths, I finally saw what had been there the whole time. I finally woke up. Completely. Horror clogged my throat, filled my eyes. I had almost lost him. "I… I'm–" No words. He didn't need any more of them.

I reached on my toes and touched my lips to his, afraid he'd pull back, not believe I was ready.

But I was, more now than ever. With him by my side, I could do anything.

He didn't pull away.

His kiss deepened.

The fire that always simmered for him flamed.

He healed me, and I healed him.

One minute, I was standing on my toes, struggling to get closer, to crawl inside if I could. The next, I was off my feet, my legs wrapped around his waist. The birds in the trees chirped louder. *All* sounds around us switched to full blast. Everything became more vivid as the synapses in my brain went into overdrive.

Dizzy and aware all at the same time, I cupped his neck, bringing him in closer. Tarek pulled the ponytail holder from my hair, lacing his hands in the tangles, tugging as he brought my lips harder against his. God, his lips were soft, skilled. I missed them, missed them more than I'd miss breathing.

When we toppled to the ground, he rolled so that I lay on top of him, his body cushioning mine from rocks. Even during the fall, he continued to assault my mouth without breaking the rhythm. His scent, all apples and lilacs, even though the smell had become a phantom scent over the past couple years.

Home.

The scruff on his face tickled my cheeks and neck when he buried his face at my throat before coming back to my lips. The one hand I didn't have balled in his shirt found jagged rocks hidden under the soft, verdant grass. The sharp edges bit into my palm, forcing me to come up for air. Every nerve vibrated, screaming for us to keep going, but there was always that reminder, and the sharp sting from the rocks brought it to the forefront of my mind. Blinking lights, some so advanced I wouldn't see or feel them until it was too late.

"We can't, not here." I whispered above his open mouth, my hips grinding against his as if they argued with my words, fighting them.

A ragged breath escaped his lips. "You need to stop doing that with your hips, or it's going to have to be here."

I laughed, despite the growl he released into my mouth that sent my body into overdrive. "Where... We need to find a place..." I showered his face with light kisses, loving the feel of his chest pressed against mine. "Please. Find a goddamn place."

He kissed me before answering, branding me, scorching my heart, reclaiming his spot. So fast, I moaned from the shock, he rolled and jumped up before yanking me off the ground. "There's a place, about ten miles from here, close to Drea's, actually."

Ten miles?

Fractured Energy

Ten miles?

"That shuttle have turbo?" I took off running toward the shuttle as he laughed, sprinting to catch up.

By the time we made it to the door, both of us were panting–and not from the run. We both felt it, the wall disappearing. We were back. We were us.

I tried to flip the door latch, anticipation heightening the irritation. "The door won't open!"

His grin melted my insides, and those dimples I used to see all the time, but only caught glimpses of lately, came out of hiding. God, I loved him.

"Allow me." He tapped an invisible button on the door and it flew up. Before I could move, he trapped my body against the side of the shuttle as his lips came down again, devouring me, making me whole. Bringing his mouth up enough to talk, he asked, "Anxious, love?"

I smiled and bunched all that silky hair in my fists, needing him to see. I needed him to know. I was here. Really here. "I love you, Tarek. *I love you.*"

His smile softened as he slid a finger down my cheek. "Welcome back."

∞ ∞ ∞

I would've thought the hidden cocoon behind a waterfall something special. The smooth, wet stone underneath my back probably would've garnered some appreciation, too. Tarek said I used to leap off the cliff right beside these falls and into the pool below. For once, a past story of me produced a smile. I doubted if I could ever jump of the cliff because, hey, I wasn't crazy, but it must have felt nice for... her. The freedom–even if it were just an idea in a world where freedom was an illusion.

But where we were didn't matter. What mattered was Tarek's body against mine, his lips trailing heated paths down my skin. Our contego suits now a pillow that protected my head from the cave's hard surface.

This.

Perfection.

Bliss.

Tarek moved to sit up, but my arms tightened around his waist. "No. Please. Stay, right here. Forever."

He smoothed sweaty hair from my face and leaned in to touch my lips. "I've never left this spot." He kissed the corner of my mouth. "And I never will. Even when I tried, I couldn't. I belong here; I always have."

Tears. Again. But happy ones, the best kind. "I'm so sor–"

His kiss shut me up. A kiss that savored, explored, made the tears come faster. His skin was sleek with perspiration, and everywhere our bodies connected tingled with heat.

Why? Why had I pulled away?

Right.

I remembered.

Guilt.

Wilma.

I tugged on his hair and bit his lip until he pulled away. "Could you please let me apologize? Pretty sure it's the first step toward not feeling like shit."

A soft smile tilted up the right side of his mouth. "You don't have to say it. You have nothing to be–" His face grew serious and he cupped my cheek, his callused thumb wiping away a tear. "We *will* get her back."

"Drea said we could crash their system from here, without even going into Cynosure. How can I put us all in danger for–" I couldn't finish. What the hell was I trying to say? We shouldn't get Wilma?

Was I really saying that?

"We don't leave one of our own behind." His hand captured my chin when I tried to look away. "You're not the only one who lost her. We all–*all of us*–want her out of there. Her energy…she might be damaged, but leaving her in the state she's in? No. Annihilation would be better."

Panic sizzled in my gut. "I-I don't think I can–"

"And we won't, at least not right away. That will be our last resort." He released my chin to glide a finger over my jawline. "We'll take her to Teenesee, see what she can do."

My rock. My everything. "Tell me if you get tired of hearing it, but…" I leaned up to kiss his cheek, trailing my lips across the soft hair he hadn't shaved off in weeks until I reached his ear. "I love you, Tarek Montigue, my heart, my soulmate."

He tensed. "Even after what Drea told us? Even after that?"

This was the first time he brought it up. I tried at least a hundred times with him and Zander, and they both shut me down.

I put my hand on his heart, same thing he always did to me, the action that always made me complete. "What she said changes nothing because I fell in love with what's in here, something no man made, could *ever* make. *You*, Tarek, were made for me, and I for you. It doesn't matter how."

For the first time, after everything we'd been through, tears slid from those beautiful gray eyes, filling me and tearing me apart. "Love… It's such a small word, not big enough, not strong enough."

My tears matched his, but I smiled, lacing my fingers through his hair. "Does this mean you'll quit sleeping in a separate bedroom? I mean, that's just pissing me off."

He kissed me, his laugh reverberating off my lips. Whole. We were whole again. "Well, I wouldn't want you

285

to be pissed off." He winked. "No one's happy when you're bitching."

"Yeah, that's the point, ace."

He rolled to the side and pulled me close until my back jutted up against his chest. "I guess I can deal with you hogging the covers again."

"Hey, I have to listen to you snore." I snuggled closer. "But I'm willing to sacrifice."

His chest rumbled against my ribs. "Fair trade, then."

"I don't know about fair, but..." I yawned, my eyelids drooping.

"It's fair, and sleep. Let's finally sleep, okay?"

Yeah, finally. Maybe we'd finally rest, at least for a while. "Okay."

We slept. For hours or days, I had no clue. But for the first time in a long time, nightmares and guilt didn't interrupt me. What *did* interrupt the best sleep I'd had in a while was the fuzz.

No!

Zander's pull was like comfort under a heavy quilt on a cold day. This fugue gave no such warm and cozy. It burned in my brain as powerful as Drea's but magnified by a hundred. The last time a heavy dose flooded my body, I turned into a drooling idiot, a zombie attracted to brain matter.

Not this time.

A year of practice with having Zander zip around me in his energy form until I stopped passing out from the euphoria helped ease the desire to find the source.

The gushing water sounded exactly like the static in my brain, as if the waterfall were now in stereo. I had to bite down on my lower lip to keep from moaning in both ecstasy and pain. Just because I could fight the urge to chase after the magnet, didn't mean it still couldn't cripple me. Naked and now shivering, gooseflesh riddling my arms and legs, I nudged Tarek who shot awake and was alert in an instant, a talent he shared with Farren. As soon as his eyes found mind, I put a finger to my lips before pressing on my forehead. He nodded, completely understanding.

We dressed in silence, lacing up our suits in a matter of seconds. Tarek grabbed his gun and signaled for me to do the same. Not necessary. I already had a gun in both hands, cocked and ready to go.

We inched to the slick opening of the cave, careful to avoid any slippery, moss-covered rocks while keeping to the shadows. Neither one of us spotted any orbs, but that didn't mean they weren't there. Experience with the assholes reminded me that some Synod Guides were pretty advanced. Like when they found me and Farren at Cara's on Empyrean. Fuzz emanating from me would blend into the environment, be as unnoticeable as a hundred-year-old tree.

Pain stabbed my heart and all that anger came boiling to the surface. Cara and her baby died because of us, and no matter how much Farren tried to tell me otherwise, that wound still festered. Magnetism didn't make it hard not go out there, guns blazing. Revenge did.

I swallowed it down and slammed my eyes shut with a few deep breaths. Going out there would be our deaths. I'd heard what Winston said to Tarek, too. If they found out Tarek was no longer Warden, our strongest person was gone. I didn't blame him. I'd do the same thing in his position.

I opened my eyes when Tarek gripped my elbow. He pointed to the tiny speck in a clump of thick trees about a hundred yards away, to the shuttle we borrowed from Drea. Three bright blue orbs with orange-fired tails zipped around the vehicle like gnats. After what felt like hours, the three blinking bastards took off, comets rushing through the sky. The fuzz in my head disappeared like mist after the sunrise.

Tarek holstered his gun, all traces of our time together washed from his face. "We have to go."

CHAPTER 30

LENA

The Rebel

Prison was easier now that I had my giant sleeping beside me. Drea's shuttle, registered to a fake scientist she'd made up, didn't lead anyone back to the house. The recon Guides' interest was protocol. Wasn't illegal to land a shuttle in the woods and go for a hike, especially if that hiker happened to work in the Creation Lab–another little tidbit Drea added to her fake scientist's MO. Anymore outings would be too risky, though.

At least, Drea and Winston saw it that way. Oren didn't care. He wanted to blow up Cynosure and go in shooting. Oren began talking anarchy, an uprising, a campaign of truth spreading among the innocents, starting in Heterodox.

I agreed with him. "Maybe we should cause a stir, create suspicion. Give those people a reason to fight against the bastards."

Tarek and I lay in bed, what we did most of the time since coming back from Shalen four days ago. He didn't answer at first, his finger busy tracing a pattern on my back. Then, "Aren't you tired, Lena? Tired of fighting?"

"I…" Seriously, wasn't I? "I don't know."

He rolled until he lay on top of me. His scarred hands cupped my cheeks as he bent to kiss my nose, my chin, and a soft touch to my lips. "We need to stop. We need to live. What Winston and Drea are doing will cripple the Synod, and Cassondra won't have the resources to come after us.

There *will* be chaos here." He stroked my hair as he searched my eyes. Silence slithered between us before he whispered, "I want you to promise me something."

I reached up to play with his beard, loving how the coarse hair felt against my fingertips. "What?"

"After this, if we succeed, I want to go back to Earth, live the rest of our lives there."

Shock, blinding white shock, froze my fingers on his cheek. "But...Arcus. That's our home. We–"

"I want to live on Earth, with you. Live where our struggle will be to pay bills on time, not worrying about any of this. Just you and me. Please, Lena."

Paying bills...I liked that. I smiled, feeling lighter than I had in forever. "All right. We get Wilma, take her to Teenesee, and we go home. To Earth."

"Yeah?"

I smoothed hair from his eyes. *Everything I needed...* "Yeah."

He jumped off the bed, dragging me up with him, and swung me around while he hooted so loud, Zander came running. Our door ripped open and we met the end of Zander's gun.

Completely naked.

"Oh, shit. Sorry I...um...sorry." Zander's eyes opened wide as he lowered his gun. He didn't bother to leave, either, freezing as if our nudity scared him.

Hell, it probably did.

"Zander! Christ!" I slammed my body up against Tarek's chest, but Zander got an eyeful. Tarek's chest was wide, but it couldn't wrap around to cover my ass.

Tarek rushed me back to bed, throwing blankets over my body before turning toward Zander. My giant didn't share my love for decency, stomping in Zander's direction not looking to cover up. "Get. Out." He yanked Zander by his collar and shoved him out before slamming the door in his face.

Another muffled apology sailed through the closed door, followed by, "But why the yelling? You never yell. And why are you yelling naked? Wait, don't answer that."

Tarek smiled as he leaned against the door, not an ounce of embarrassment coloring his cheeks, while we listened to Zander ramble on. Finally, my giant let him off the hook. "We'll be out in a minute. Go find something to do until then."

As Zander's footsteps took him away from the door, I laughed and tossed the covers off to reclaim my spot in Tarek's arms. I didn't want to waste any more chances, and if my man stood naked in my presence while all I did was lounge in bed, I would call that a wasted moment.

I got about two feet from him before he moved to scoop me up again. He took us both to the bed, obviously not intending to go anywhere. His lips skimmed my collarbone, and I could feel the smile he still held onto. I did that. I finally made him smile again. Christ, he could demand anything from me as long as he made my body tingle with that smile.

When he moved to kiss my earlobe, his whisper sent waves of heat rushing to my toes. "Hey, I need to ask you something else."

"Hmm...?" He could've asked me to fly, and I'd have started gluing feathers together with a smile on my face.

"When we go in to get Wilma...I want you to stay here."

Cold buckets of ice tamped down the growing heat. I shoved against his shoulders until he pulled up to look me in the eye, not moving from his spot on top of me.

"Ah, no. No deal. I want to go, Tarek. I *need* to go."

"If you go....I can't..." Pause. "If I'm worried about you–if Winston has to worry about you–we won't be focused. We need to get in and out, silent and quick."

"I can't be silent and quick?"

"Please."

The thought of sitting there, helpless and wondering, while everyone else went to risk their lives caused my breath to quicken and stars to appear before my eyes. If something happened...

If they died...

If Tarek died...

Bad stuff out, good stuff in...

"Look at me, Lena." He captured my face in his hands as I wheezed. "Everything will be fine. We go in once the system crashes; no one will be paying attention in the chaos. We know where she is. An in-and-out operation, I swear."

"But...what if? W-what if you don't come back to me?" The room swirled and his weight crushed me. I pushed until he moved to the side. He kept a palm on my stomach, kneading the tightening abdominal muscles.

"I will, and if something happens, Zander will be there to collect my energy, and Winston can...he can bring my body back here. All you'll have to do is wait for Drea to perform some of her magic and I'm....good as new." He stumbled over the last few words, his voice faltering.

"What if Winston dies? Then what?"

Tarek raised a brow. "Really?"

"It's possible."

"The odds are pretty good he'll be fine." He tried to smile, but it slipped as I struggled for breath. "Lena, please, calm down."

"What if Zander...?" God, if I lost any of them...I couldn't. I'd break and nothing in this universe would be strong enough to piece me back together.

"How many times do I have to say it? Trust me." His warm palm relaxed my muscles and my breathing eased while he held me with his eyes.

Sincerity and confidence swimming in the gray managed to dive into my green until the panic subsided. I trusted him. Logically I knew he was right, but logic had nothing to do with how fragile my grasp on keeping it together was.

Bad stuff out, good stuff in... "And Oren?" When Tarek pursed his lips and stilled his massaging hand, I knew exactly what Oren's job would be. "He's to get me out of here if the plan goes bad, right?"

Tarek nodded. "He wanted to take you away now, make you go to Cheveyo's with everyone else."

"No! I–"

"Easy, love. I said no, but to everything else, I agreed with them. You'll go back with me...after we take Wilma home. "

"So everyone was in on the plan but me, that it?"

His cheeks burned red.

"When? When did you all have this little conversation *without me*?"

"Lena–"

"When?"

"Last night, while you slept."

I shoved him away and went to get dressed, skipping the contego for a tank top and shorts. "Got it. Loud and clear. Poor, broken Lena too unstable to make decisions for herself." I snatched my shoes from under the bed. "I need to get out of here."

"I don–"

I held up my hand and sighed. When he stared at me, pleading with me, really, I shook my head and went to the window. "I understand. I hate it, but I understand. I'd be in the way, maybe too emotional, but...why do you have to go?"

"Winston's afraid Oren will start an uprising. He thinks Oren will crack. Oren actually agreed, so..."

Oren and I were the two who could never go into a situation without our emotions getting in the way. My revenge and penchant for panic attacks when someone I loved was in danger and his need to save every wronged, downtrodden innocent who suffered because of the Synod became our burdens. *Would you look at us?* We were a pair. "So, you all thought to include Oren, but not me?" I turned to face him. "You don't think I can be rational?" *I couldn't, but...*

"Of course you can't." He grinned. "But neither can I when you're around. So you stay because, let's be honest, I have bigger muscles than you."

Stunned, I stared at him—and proceeded to laugh my ass off. I laughed until tears streamed from my eyes. He slid off the bed and wrapped me in his arms. We stood in the middle of the room, a perfectly comfortable, perfectly advanced room. Suffocating.

He leaned down to nuzzle the sensitive spot right beneath my ear. "Still want to get out of here?"

Heat simmered again, even though I was somewhere in the middle of pissed and resigned. "They won't let us."

"*They* don't have a choice." He gave me a soft kiss. "Let's go back to Shalen, one last time. Maybe try jumping off the cliff?"

I liked that idea a whole lot, even the cliff-jumping part. So much, it almost brought tears to my eyes. Maybe I was a little crazy, after all. No, a lot crazy. "Yeah, okay. Um...maybe we should bring Zander, get him out of here for a while before Winston beats the crap out of him."

He groaned, but his dimples popped out. "That means we'll have to wear clothes."

"The sacrifices we make..." I tapped his cheek. "Get dressed. I'll go get him."

∞ ∞ ∞

They might not have a choice, but Drea and Winston sure as hell had a few things to say about it. Tarek handled them, though. The three huddled near the computer setup thing, not-so-subtly arguing while Cynosure highlighted the entire room. They fought while holograms of people went about their daily life, shopping, working, staring up at the community screens shining on the face of buildings. Wilma's light. The only time I'd ever caught glimpses of emotion on the stony faces of capital dwellers was when they stopped to watch Wilma fight against her prison. Fear, the slightest twinge of it, darkened their eyes and turned their lips downward.

Their fear made me happy. I wanted them to be afraid. I wanted them to worry. We'd destroy all the comfort they enjoyed, the comfort gained from pilfering other worlds. I was all right with that.

But I couldn't watch Wilma with them. Not without wanting to storm the capital, which was impossible, and that impossibility ate at my gut. So, while those three argued, I went to Oren, who sat at the kitchen counter studying his hands, the usual serious scowl twisting up his pretty face.

"Hey." I punched him in the shoulder when he didn't acknowledge me. "Um...*hey*."

He turned that lovely scowl on me. "What?"

"Well...nothing, really. Just looked like you could use some company." Why did I bother? Oh, right, because I worried about the asshole.

"Look harder." His focus went back to his hands.

If he thought that'd push me away, he needed to pay more attention. Beneath the scowl, sadness lingered. And son of a bitch, I wanted to make him feel better.

"Wouldn't hurt you to be nice every once in a while, you know."

That earned a snort. "Says the pot."

What...? Oh! Another punch to the shoulder. "Haha, funny. Seriously, what is it, besides all the obvious?"

He sighed and lowered his gaze to find his shoes. The way his shoulders slumped...Christ, I almost hugged him.

"What's going on, Oren?"

Silence, except for the stressed whispers coming from Tarek's corner, wafted between us. I'd wait him out. As stubborn as he was, I could outmatch him any day.

Finally, "The virus Winston and Drea are shoving into the system–*the system*–it's going to make it even harder on these people."

Tread carefully, Lena. Don't say something ignorant. "Yeah...yeah, I guess it is." So hard not to place Exemplar's sins on the heads of everyone who lived here, something Old Lena did, which was why Oren hated me the first time we met.

"I..." He brought his eyes up to mine, misery swarming in those blue pools hitting me right in the heart. "We'll leave here, finally free from the Synod. But...people like Celeste, lost and forgotten, they'll pay for it."

"What can we do about it?" When his vulnerability turned into his usual shield, I squeezed his arm. "No, really, Oren. What *can* we do?"

His face softened, and he clasped my hand. *Wow...* "I don't know. Wish I did."

"Me too."

As if he realized he showed a smidge of tenderness, he released my hand like it burned him. "Ah...right...well." A smile. A real, honest-to-goodness smile. "Still find you irritating."

"So do a lot of people." I rubbed my hand. "Hey, um, tell me about you and Grace."

He raised a brow. "What do you want to know?"

"Did you two…were you ever…?"

"Not every Protector sleeps with their Guide, Lena."

My face burned. "Well, obviously!" I swallowed down the scathing words he usually brought out of me. "Why did you wait so long, you know, to find her?"

The grin left his face, a faraway, contemplative look replacing it. "I had things to do here, things your prior self didn't like very much."

"Sorry. Did I ever say that to you? Sorry?" I shrugged. "But who knows if I would've done things different, knowing what I know."

"Doesn't matter now, does it? Anyway, when Grace–" His smile returned. "Her name used to be Bellerose."

"Beautiful, both names."

"Yes, well, when she decided to retire, it killed me. A part wanted to follow her lead, forget everything, but…then I met Celeste. She showed me the pain behind those empty faces in Heterodox, just as she has done for Drea, by the way."

"What're you talking about?"

"Celeste gave Drea an advantage, a way in, so to speak. Drea took it. She's brave, Lena, not like Avery. We're lucky."

I did trust her, mostly. But that trust came from having no other options. Oren believing in her helped ease any nagging doubts. I bumped his shoulder with mine. "If you say so. Now, finish your story."

"Right, so, Grace went to Abrogation to live out the rest of her cycle, and I naively believed I was starting a rebellion. Long story short, years after Grace left, right after your execution, I found out I was on your radar. All it would've taken was one person fishing around for info and everything Celeste and I accomplished would have been destroyed."

A tear slipped down my cheek. Why? I didn't really know. Residual guilt for a life I didn't remember, maybe? "So you found Avery?"

He shook his head. "She found me, told me she knew of my actions, and promised to keep quiet if I left." His eyes found his hands again. "And I demanded she tell me where to find Grace in exchange for not finding you." He laughed with no humor. "Imagine my surprise to learn we all squatted in the same world. So many of us, Winston, too. Sometimes…I think about what if. What if the Synod found out about Avery and her dumping ground for traitor Exemplians earlier? Earth would've been destroyed, no matter how large the dimension."

I squeezed his hand. "So sorry."

"No, stop. My issues are mine. We'll leave here after they get Wilma, but…maybe someday I'll come back."

That was the last thing I wanted him to do, put his life at risk for people I didn't know. But Oren…he had always been honorable, unlike me. Regardless of which life I lived. He didn't need to hear me beg him not to come back to Exemplar, though. His decision, not mine.

I cleared my throat to get rid of all the pleading words. "Hey, we're going to Shalen, one last trip before never coming back here again. It's kinda nice in some places, peaceful. Wanna tag along?"

"That what they're fighting about?" He pointed toward Tarek, who had his hands up and shaking his head before stalking over in my direction at the same time Winston stormed down the storage level's stairs.

Not good.

"Yup."

"Drea might beat your man." He gestured toward the Guide's red face and balled fists.

I looked over with a shrug. "Why don't you go smooth things over, use that pretty face for something beneficial."

He smirked. "Ah, yeah, I doubt *I* could make her happy. Maybe you, not me."

Huh? Oh. Oh, right. Interesting. "Whatever. You coming?"

Oren nodded. "Yeah, why not?"

Tarek squeezed my side, the tension riding in his fingertips hard to ignore.

What the hell were we doing? The risk, no matter how small, wasn't worth it. "Maybe we shouldn't go."

"We're going," Tarek said. "Drea told me there's a gap in the recon's routine in three hours while hydro-blimps do their thing. We'll go then."

"You're sure?"

Oren got up and went to the lift. "I'm going, whether you decide to stay or not. Unlike most of you, I happen to love my world and want to spend the last few moments in it not figuring out how to destroy everything."

I watched him walk away, still unsure. "I—"

"We're going." Tarek tilted my chin for a kiss. "Get Zander. Tell him to be ready."

Lynn Vroman

CHAPTER 31

LENA

Choices

Jagged rocks dug into the soles of my feet. I climbed higher, avoiding both the pain and my inner voice telling me to get down. My grip slipped on the wet stone as the roar of the waterfall followed me with every shaky step upward. Adrenaline flooded my legs, making them tingle. Mist sprayed my cheeks. Most people with a healthy dose of acrophobia usually avoided high places. Probably because they believed we had one shot at the whole life thing.

One shot…yeah, unfortunately, I knew better.

I glanced up to find hydro-powered blimps, the precipitation predictors. Thunder and flashes of lightning followed the vehicles while they sprayed a nearby field.

I missed nature, real nature.

I missed Arcus.

Once I reached the top, I scooted closer to the edge, my heart doing backflips. After a deep breath, I closed my eyes and held out my arms, fingers splayed, reveling in the briny scent of the air. If I wussed-out, there'd be an audience who'd never let me live it down. But as I stood there, feeling the water spraying my cheeks, no old fears of heights surfaced.

Freedom.

Ah, now I understood her, Old Lena. This endorphin rush, this maelstrom taking over my body, no amount of money could replicate it.

One thing I figured out while being in this hole was the temperatures never changed. A constant *just right* warm and sunny always showed up every morning. But right here, at this spot, I could imagine dark storms and angry gusts, the perfection of imperfection. *Home.*

To the chorus of screaming water, I leaned forward and let myself fly. Wind smacked my face and teased the edges of my shirt while I fell the hundred feet to the warm, calm waters below. I didn't open my eyes when Tarek yelled for me to straighten my arms; the warning in his voice added to the excitement.

I kept my arms wide a few seconds longer and adjusted to dive, immersing with a soft splash. My body sank deep. The stifled symphony of the falls crashing against the boulders had a hypnotizing effect, inviting.

Dying didn't scare me anymore. Living did sometimes, though.

I kicked to the surface, my lungs ready to burst. Water as clear and clean as a mountain spring sluiced against my eyes, and the bright sun reflected off its surface. Everything blurred into a postmodern painting, colors and shapes meshing. But Tarek was my beacon, my gaze attracted to him without needing perfect eyesight.

There he was, waiting for me.

Tarek swam closer and pulled me in as I pushed all my hair from my face. His hands roamed across my rib cage, tickling me, heightening the rush that still had me giddy. "Stop! What're doing?"

He smiled, his busy hands switching from my ribs to wrap my legs around his hips. "I'm just checking for broken bones. Ah…old habit."

When I smiled, the relieved expression on his face melted my heart. His tentative delve into our past lives together didn't cause a twinge of jealousy. Maybe I had actually grown up? "You find anything broken?"

"No. At least, I don't think so."

I tugged on his wet hair until our foreheads met. "Nope. Everything's whole. Finally."

Thunderclaps made me jump, and I clung tighter to Tarek's neck. Above us, those three hydro-blimps hovered, pelting the docile waters with stinging rain. "What the hell are they doing? Watering the water?"

Concern wiped the smile off Tarek's face. "I–"

"Hey! Move it!"

We looked up to find Zander ready to leap off the cliff. Oren swam over to us, a smile on his handsome face. "You might want to go over there."

We swam out of the way, the warm water like a bath. Zander, with absolutely no grace, leapt from the edge and smacked the surface of the water. Forever passed before he popped to the surface, his face pinched. "Ouch."

I laughed. "Well, you dumbass! Why'd you jump like that?"

Zander doggy paddled to us, groaning with every stroke. "Not like I meant to."

"Not too grace–"

Loud, screeching sirens blared from the blimps as they floated lower, still pummeling the water with what looked like hailstones.

"What are they doing now?" I grabbed Tarek's wrist and glanced over his shoulder to find Oren holding his head. "Oh, no."

Tarek scanned the bank on either side of the falls as the sirens continued. He stopped and pressed a hand to his head with a grimace. The sirens weren't bothering him or Oren.

Static.

I panicked. "Let's go, okay? Time to go."

Tarek nodded. "Good idea. Follow me, get our things, and get in the shuttle."

"Those hydro-blimps…why are they blaring alarms?"

Oren was all warrior, like Tarek. "Looks like they're more than rainmakers."

Sudden silence ringing in the atmosphere scared me. We all looked up to find the blimps gone. One thing I had learned while living on Arcus: silence was never a good thing.

Tarek and Oren were calm, where Zander gulped in air as his eyes widened. Exactly like me.

We all swam toward the shore, fear making my legs thick and clumsy. None of us made a sound, our strokes through the calm water not disrupting the surface.

Tarek was the first to hit the rocky edge. He bent to slide on his shirt before slipping his gun from its holster, leaving everything else behind. Oren pushed up onto the bank next, his face a stone mask as he copied Tarek's moves. When Zander and I reached our stuff, we were as quiet, but Zander's tense face matched the storm thundering in my chest. No Guides were around, which was good, but Tarek and Oren still had that look–the one that said the fuzz hadn't dissipated.

We should've stayed at the cabin!

Guns drawn but nothing to aim at, we were like easy targets in a children's carnival game. Either the Protectors had no idea we were there or they were waiting for the right moment to smoke us. Cowards. It'd be so much easier if they came out shooting. At least we'd have a chance.

Or maybe not.

The trees to our right came to life with about ten black-suited Protectors holding tasers. The Synod's authority. Only plus, their weapons weren't soul-stealers.

"Tarek!" I ran to him, but regardless of how hard I tried, my movements were like swimming in quicksand. Terror, raw and painful, made my body numb as glowing contego suits crowded the bank, all of their weapons pointed at us, their faces shocked. Probably because it sunk into their skulls exactly who they had surrounded.

Tarek heaved me toward the water and pointed to the opposite shore. "Go. Run. I'll find you."

"But–"

"*Run.*"

It was too late for me to go anywhere, and we both knew it. His eyes became swirling, wild pools of gray as his cheeks sagged, causing my heart to fold. We would die here, on this bank.

His anguish didn't stick around, and once we both realized the lone option we had was to fight, fire burst from the end of his gun. We didn't mess around with tasers. Our bullets sprayed their blood all over the trees and rocks. Zander hit five; we took care of the rest.

Hope.

Glowing orbs punched through the chests of the dead Protectors as we high-tailed it to the shuttle. Just a few more feet.

Just a few more…

Oren flipped the latch on the driver's side and leapt in as the passenger side door lifted. "Move! Move! Move!"

One foot slid into the shuttle. I turned to Tarek and smiled. We made it. We–

A knife zinging through the air with deadly grace arced over the bushes, the rocks… and found its target.

"*No!*"

Tarek's eyes widened as blood spurted from his mouth. The tip of the blade glared at me from his heart as he slumped to his knees.

Gurgling…

So much blood…

I tried. I couldn't hold onto him. He slipped away.

"*Please! No! No! No!*" I found Zander yards away, his face a mask of shock. "*Please!*"

Zander's body flopped to the ground as his blue energy burst from his mouth, intercepting the gray bright light flowing from Tarek.

This isn't happening

Not happening.

No. Not again.

Oren came from somewhere as the trees exploded with more black suits. "Lena, move, please. Let me get his body in the shuttle. *Move.*" He threw me when I refused, my palms pressing on Tarek's chest, even though his light had already escaped his shell.

My hands, covered in blood. Tarek's blood. I held them out. "I…"

Zander's body lay below, but his light shimmered above, meshed with my love's soul. Screaming and yelling, soggy and blended in my ears, grew louder. Oren lifted Tarek's body. His lifeless body. Zander awoke and tugged for me to get up.

"*No!*"

Fire rained down on us, the shuttle getting pummeled with hit after hit. Protectors moved closer. One grabbed Zander, yanking him away from us.

I ran to him, my gun drawn and firing. Echoes of Oren's voice chased me, yelling to come back. More shooting. The shuttle lifted off the ground.

Tarek's body…gone.

His energy, right in front of me. I chose.

I chose.

I clung to Zander, clung to Tarek, as Protectors took us to the ground. They wrenched my hands from Zander, yanked them behind my back. More slush filled my ears. Ringing, all of it, every sound ringing. *No...*

Zander reached for me, but feet kicked at his hands, stomping them into the ground, crushing them. He didn't cry out. He stared at me, his eyes welling.

But he gave what I needed: "I have him, Lena. I have him."

Lynn Vroman

CHAPTER 32

LENA

Nightmares

Nightmares were funny things. They created a toxic potion of horror and relief. They also trapped the mind and attacked deep-seeded fears, ate at tender insecurities. Relief jumped into the unconscious prison when the sleep cycle wound down to the end of its course. That relief, a soothing hand on a forehead, whispering, "It's not real."

It's not real.

It's never real.

My eyes opened. I reached to my left. Nothing. Just air. "Tarek?"

I turned.

Nothing.

Real, all of it. "No."

Gagging, sobbing tears filled the room. "No!"

The bed was soft and comfortable, opposite of the burn eating my insides.

Real.

"Tarek..." His name, maybe if I said it loud enough, he'd find me. I'd wake up, and he'd... *he'd find me.*

Panic seized my heart. Maybe it'd finally kill me.

Please kill me!

Doors swooshed open. Blurred images charged the bed.

A needle pricked my skin.

The nightmares attacked again.

∞ ∞ ∞

"Wake her. Now."

That voice. I'd heard it once before. But it gnawed its way into my memory, tucked up nice and tight with the revenge that covered me again like a familiar blanket.

Cassondra.

Without opening my eyes, I batted at the hands groping at me. "Get away from me."

The air cleared and my lids popped open. Misery, deep and black, threatened to take over, but I couldn't let it, not now. Hope. I still had it. Zander carried my love with him. Oren had his body.

Hope.

I'd cling to it until I stopped breathing.

"So, you caught me. Now what?" I did my best to keep any inflections from my voice. She wouldn't see my weakness. I wouldn't let her.

"Sit up and face me, Tainted. I'd have you looking at me while I plunged a stake in your heart."

Her calm voice sparked ugly, feral hatred inside my gut. If she did anything to Zander–to Tarek's energy–there wasn't a strong enough Protector in the room to save her. I sat up and stared at her colorless face, my head swimming with whatever drugs they pumped into my bloodstream. I had control of my arms and legs, though. That would be all I needed.

She waved a hand, and a chair floated to her side, the same kind of hovering chair as Celeste's. She took the time to adjust her robes when she sat, a pleasant smile on her lips that didn't mask the hatred in her eyes.

Seemed we had something in common.

"So, would you like to tell me who my people killed in the woods? Your friend wasn't very forthcoming during his interrogation."

She didn't know!

Christ, she had no clue.

Hope simmered brighter.

"Um… They killed somebody?"

Her smile turned into a smirk. "You don't want to play dumb with me."

That was where she was mistaken. "I think his name was Go Fuck Yourself."

"Cute." She stood and moved to a single screen on the wall. With a delicate flick of her wrist, the monitor flashed on. Zander, on his own comfortable cloud bed staring at the ceiling, his bandaged hands folded on his chest–and cinched with gallium cuffs.

I wanted to fall to my knees and beg. Relief and horror, the cocktail didn't only linger in nightmares. I stayed on the bed, forcing my attention away from the screen, keeping it on her profile.

"Now, all I have to do is push a button and your dear friend will no longer be able to hold his bladder. Is that what you want?"

Silence was all she got from me. I had a hard enough time keeping my knees off the floor.

But she wasn't looking for silence. She whipped around. "*Is it?*" Spit flew from her mouth. No more calm, the psychotic rage underneath the veneer rearing up.

"N-no. Of course not."

"Tell me who they killed."

I swallowed and closed my eyes. "Oren. They killed my friend, Oren."

"And who took his energy? His body?"

No hysteria or mistrust laced her voice. She believed me.

Thank God.

"S-some Guide we found on Earth. Denzel."

"Has anyone else come with you? A small army, perhaps? Maybe you found traitors on my own soil?"

I bowed my head, tears dripping from my eyes to the floor. "No. No one else would come."

Silence.

Christ! Did I say something wrong? Did I blow it?

"Good girl."

I opened my eyes to find her signaling to one of the Protectors in the room. "Go. Take his cuffs off. I need him whole."

Air gushed from my lungs and I sagged. *Keep it together.*

"Does that make you happy, Tainted?"

Before I could stop myself, I nodded.

"Maybe I should reconsider, no?"

I glanced up, my pleading no act. "Please. Don't."

"Will you help me, then?"

"Help?"

She smiled and sat back down, her calm in place. "Do you think Arcus's Warden will bargain for your lives?"

I stared, shocked. *She doesn't know...anything.*

"Suppose I do not really need an answer. I expect he will." Her colorless eyes turned to stone. "He killed my brother for you, after all."

"H-he'll bargain." Everything inside wanted to crack and split. Tarek...dead.

No. Not for long. He'd live again, soon. I had to believe it or the misery would kill me.

"I'm glad you think so." She tilted her head, scrutinizing my face. "You've caused so many problems, Tainted. But... you've also uncovered so much treachery within my own ranks. So, thank you. Perhaps all this turmoil was worth the struggle." She stood and signaled one of her dogs to open the door. Without looking at me, she said, "It will all be over shortly."

As soon as she and her entourage of assholes left, I ran to the monitor, tapping on it, wishing he could hear. "I'm coming, Tarek."

Zander disappeared from the screen, replaced with a bursting blue light, pulsating in the middle of a glass prison. Tears escaped and I palmed the glowing orb, wishing it'd leap into my hand. "I'm coming for you, too."

∞ ∞ ∞

Every cell in my body pleaded to allow it to decay in misery. Give up. Die with them because living without them would never work. But buried deep inside my dulled brain a single fighting cell screamed above the despair. *Fight! Get up and do something about it!*

So for five days…

I showered when they told me to.

I dressed in the clothes they threw inside my room.

I took the sustenance injection after they demanded I hold out my arm.

I got up and tried to figure out a way to do something about it.

The next time the doors slid open, I sat on the floating chair, legs crossed and face disguised behind a mask of fear. They wanted me afraid, and I made sure they got what they wanted. If they found my revenge, Tarek and Wilma wouldn't stand a chance. For some reason, all this cooperation kept the panic attacks away, as if my body finally decided to listen, trust that I'd get back what belonged to me.

"Get up."

"Wh-Where're we going?" My legs shook as I stood, which wasn't hard to fake. They did quiver with adrenaline.

Desire to kick out kneecaps and break necks created elation and forced me to suppress a smile. Killing them.... Jesus, what had I become?

The two Protectors didn't bother answering, their faces showing no anger, showing no emotion, really. These people were already dead inside.

They each grabbed an elbow and led me from my comfortable prison. When the doors slid closed, the monitor still showcasing Wilma's light disappeared. Panic squeezed through my tight control. Her light, fighting in a glass prison, didn't send me spiraling anymore. It gave me strength. If she could fight, so would I.

Push out the bad.

Bring in the good.

We passed face after expressionless face, no one shocked or enraged Lena Tulman–ah, Montigue–intruded their sanctuary. None cared. Not one.

A lift took us to an underground floor. Temperatures remained neutral, air clean and fresh, the lift like traveling on cotton.

Another hallway.

More zombies.

A door.

Another prison.

"Um... What...?" *What to ask them?* They weren't gonna answer me.

One of the Protectors leaned in and a scanner shot out a red beam, reading the guy's retina. When the door glided open, they shoved me in, not following. The shutting door stole any light, leaving me in pitch black. Not at all what I had expected. What was this, some kind of torture tactic?

After a few swallows to tamp down any crazy thoughts, like man-eating rats or Protectors using me as target practice, I slid along the smooth wall. The sleekness of the cool wall made me think of pearls–and my mind drifted to oysters. Big oysters like our squid that would think I was a grain of sand and push me back into its throat to form calcified layers of beautiful shell, trapping me. The ground squished, too. Way softer than the floor in my other prison.

Crazy assh–

"Hello?"

Zander...

Tarek.

"Zander!" I rushed into the darkness, no longer caring about angry giant oysters. "Where are you?"

Zander's static filled me up, saving me. A sob escaped as his arms wrapped around my waist from behind. I turned into his chest, pressing as close as I could to his warmth, palming his heart, kneading his skin. Tarek was in there, right under my fingers.

Hope.

"Are you...is he...?"

"Shh, don't say anything." He nuzzled my cheek, touching my earlobe with his whisper. "They want us to talk. We say nothing, okay?"

I nodded next to his smooth skin, wishing I could crawl inside of him, blend with whom he carried in there. "I'm so scared."

"Me too." He pulled me to the ground and bunched me up into his arms. "Whatever happens in this room, don't break. None of it will be real. Be strong."

"What're you talking about?" I honestly didn't care. I had him; that was enough.

Every time I closed my eyes, Tarek's pale face pierced my soul, blood funneling from his mouth, his big body slumping to the ground. My worst fear already became a reality. Nothing else would have any effect.

"They'll try to get inside your head, make you crack. Don't."

"I won't." I pressed my body closer. *Please bring me inside!* "Are you...okay?"

His arms squeezed tighter. "Everything's okay, Lena. *Everything.*"

Tears leaked from eyes. "Thank you."

"Lena...?"

I swiped my eyes and nose on the front of his shirt. "Yeah?"

"Nothing like history repeating itself, huh?"

"What?"

His hand pressed harder, bringing me even closer. Not close enough. "None of this feels familiar? You, me, trapped in a room by the big bad enemy? At least it's more comfortable."

God, yes. So long ago, like it was a dream. In Casimir's manse, cold and starving with my father, fighting to stay alive while waiting for the Cavalry. Only, "No one is coming to save us this time." More than likely, Winston already left to get Shaina. I hated him for it now. I got it, but I hated him nonetheless.

"Guess we'll have to save ourselves, then."

"Piece of cake."

His chest rumbled. "Yeah, sure, darlin'."

We had a few moments of peace, my hand sinking into his skin while he massaged my back. The pressure I put on his ribcage had to hurt, but he didn't tell me to stop or heave me off him. All he said was, "He loves you."

More tears, only they weren't from despair. They cleansed my mind, erased my doubts. We'd get out of here, and I'd have Tarek back.

Lights flared, blinding us. I slammed my eyes shut, the pain of adjusting from the darkness too much.

"Remember. Don't let them get to you."

As soon as his frantic words registered, sounds of a battle, its explosions and cries from the wounded and dying, rendered the air. I peeled my eyes open. Empyrean. The cobblestone under us swayed and bounced as I tried to stand. Zander tugged on my hand, and I glanced down to find him shaking his head, worry in his dark eyes. "It's not real."

I wanted it to be, even if we were in the middle of a war with Protectors and Empyreans fighting and killing each other, energy bursting in the air. People ran past us, guns drawn and firing. So many people...

"Maybe, maybe they found us."

"No, Lena. Don't. Say. A. Word."

"May–"

"No."

I wrenched my hand away from his to run through the streets until I reached the municipal building where the Guide nests hid. Just as I climbed the steps, the marble and stone exploded and crumbled to the ground. Charred rock and burning flesh scorched the inside of my nose, making me gag. I remembered this. I remembered exactly this.

Wilma...

I turned from the rubble. She came toward me, her arms outstretched. I stumbled to her as the bullet lodged in her chest. "Wilma!"

Hands grabbed me from behind, reaching up to cover my eyes as I screamed. "No, Lena. Not real, not real, not real..."

They took her away from me, all over again. Cassondra...I'd kill her. My eyes slammed shut under Zander's hand as I breathed. *Not real!* Losing her, though, that was real. As I calmed, the noises and smells of that day drifted from the room–and changed to biting cold and the stench of sewers.

Zander's chest heaved. I pulled his hand from my eyes and gasped.

Arcus.

We stood in our past prison, the door wide open, inviting us to leave. I gripped Zander's hand and ran toward the stairs.

"No, Lena." Zander stopped on the third stair, jerking my arm almost from its socket. His voice...so far away, like an echo.

I glared at him, forgetting whom he held inside because I knew who was standing in the room below. "I'm going. *I'm going!*" I took off. He groaned and followed right behind me.

We hit the landing as soon as the steel poker embedded into Casimir's skull. Tarek looked at me–*right at me*–and fell to the floor as shards of light attacked him. *No!*

"Tarek!" I ran. Not this time. This time, I wouldn't let him go.

I felt him, his body as solid and tangible as mine. He was in that oyster with us. He was there...

I glanced up, reaching for Zander. "His body... His body is here. Hurry... *Hurry!*"

Zander gathered me in his arms and slid away from Tarek. "No, no he isn't. Stop talking. Don't talk anymore."

I struggled against him, needing to get back to Tarek. "But he's here..."

It's not real...

Everything evaporated from the room except for Tarek's body, still and quiet. Peaceful. Fear jutted through my veins, turning all my joints to dust. I groped at Zander until we were facing each other. His eyes widened and his mouth opened, a silent *no* escaping his lips.

I didn't listen. "They know, don't they?"

Zander gripped my shoulders, pulling me up until his mouth touched my ear. "Please, Lena. Shut up. Please, shut up."

Why didn't I listen? I whipped around to find Tarek's body still there. Maybe they found Oren. Maybe they discovered Drea's shack. They took his body. They took it, and now it was here, right in front of us. Zander could release his energy, make Tarek whole again, bring him back to me. Right now, he could be alive. *Right now.*

"Please, Lena…"

I ignored him. *Why did I ignore him?* I crawled to Tarek, cradled his head in my lap, and ran my fingers through his knotted hair. "They know." I bent to kiss his cheek, my tears drenching his face. "They know…"

Tarek disappeared, his body vanishing from my arms like vapor. Darkness again took over the room as I sat with my legs under me, holding out my empty hands. Gone, just like that. Again.

From somewhere inside my misery, I felt Zander's hands scoop me close, his face tucked against my neck. "I'm sorry, Lena. So, so sorry."

At least, I think he said that. I couldn't hear anything over my own sobs. For what felt like hours, we sat there, Zander rocking me, repeating sorry until my sobs quieted. They broke me.

They destroyed me.

Silence wafted between us, the steady movement of Zander swaying us back and forth helping. *Stupid, stupid, stupid!* Why didn't I ever listen? The only good thing coming from the sorrow was they still had no clue about anything. Maybe, *maybe* we'd figure a way out before they discovered our secrets.

Then again, maybe not.

Her voice, that toneless voice that blended with the darkness, clicked into the room on a set of tinny speakers. She did this. She watched her own brother die again to make me talk. And she succeeded, didn't she? "What, exactly, do we know, Tainted?"

Zander's body froze "Oh, no."

Lynn Vroman

CHAPTER 33

LENA

A Plan

Soft light flickered through the oyster, and machines from somewhere out of sight clicked and hummed. In the middle of the room, which was all white, from the cushioned floor to the ceiling, Zander and I sat clinging to each other. Waiting.

Too afraid to say anything, afraid I'd let something else slip past my lips and give all our secrets away, I held onto Zander, wishing we could disappear. Wishing the air itself would suck us in and banish this place into the deep recesses of our minds, hide it away in nightmares where it belonged.

Zander moved, and I hugged tighter, terrified he'd leave me too.

Again, he found my ear, his hot breath hitting my lobe. "We have a plan, a plan I gotta speed up now." Pause. "Don't talk. Do you hear me? A plan, Lena, stay quiet." His desperate words broke me from my misery, allowing the fight to barge back in.

"How?"

He stood and offered me his hand as he mouthed a word. His lips barely moved, but I caught what he said.

Winston.

He stayed.

He stayed...

Doors rushed open, and Cassondra walked in ahead of five Protectors, their guns drawn and pointed. Soul-stealers.

She sauntered over to us, her hands folded behind her back and no emotion on her face. But her eyes... They couldn't hide anything. Excitement sizzled there. She wanted us dead. Wanted all of us gone.

Cassondra said nothing for a minute, just tilted her head to scrutinize us. Zander or I, I couldn't tell whom, trembled. But when Zander's arms tightened around me, and the jarring continued until my teeth rattled, I realized exactly who shook. I glanced up at him to see defiance all over his face, his body stock-still. He was no longer a Guide. He was a warrior.

And it was about time I joined him.

I straightened and stood on my own. With every ounce of strength I could muster, I stared the bitch in the eyes and lifted my chin. We always had a plan. Always. Some things I should never forget. But if this elusive plan didn't involve gutting her, I'd have to tweak it.

A slight smile shadowed her face. "It appears we are having a problem contacting Arcus's Warden."

Don't panic, don't panic, don't panic. The plan...

I matched her smile. "Yeah? Maybe he doesn't like me so much anymore."

"I wouldn't blame him." A pause. "But I find that improbable."

No retort from me. Nothing. If I kept talking, she'd find what she fished for. She knew something. After watching me lose it, she at least had a clue. No way would I validate any suspicions.

"You've had help here." Not a question. "Tell me who."

I had no problem playing the quiet game.

Zander had other intentions. "If I tell you, will you let us go?"

What the hell...?

I whipped around to face him. "Zander? No..."

He'd never betray me. Ever. *God, please let this be part of the plan.*

Zander acted as though I hadn't spoken and sang for his audience. "Take us to the Creation Lab. I'll show you what I know. I'll prove it to you, and you'll let us go."

"Why the Creation Lab?" The bitch's face turned an even paler shade of white.

"You want your traitor?"

Cassondra backed up as if he'd slapped her. "You're lying."

"I'm not. The head of your Creation Lab's been screwing you over. You'll know it's true as soon as she sees us."

"No!" I struggled against the expressionless Protectors, their hold on me like glue. If this were part of the plan, I had to go with it, but the anger churning inside my gut was real, no matter how much I trusted Zander.

"Quiet, Tainted. Your friend wishes to speak." Cassondra held a set of gallium cuffs, dangling them in front of me. Tears brightened her eyes. "Perhaps you need some help?"

"Stop, wait. There's more. Just...leave her alone. She's in mourning."

Zander...please.

"More?" Cassondra kept her attention on me while she spoke to Zander, her bottom lip shaking as a tear slipped down her cheek. "Please, share with me."

"T-Tarek. He's dead."

Nooo! Why did he have to share that?

My knees gave and I sagged in the clutches of those hands. Screams, anguish, misery, all of it escaped my lips, refilling as fast as it left. Black. I wanted the black. I wanted it permanently.

Cassondra smiled through her own tears. She watched me and smiled.

Before I met the black, I'd make sure she found it first.

"When did he die, Guide?"

"Right before we came here. One of your men...they shot him. W-Winston Candell killed the Protector before the light left Tarek's body."

What?

I looked up, still sobbing. *Please, please, please!*

We *did* have a plan. *I love you, Zander!*

Cassondra no longer smiled. Nope. And she couldn't hide the fear mixing with the odd sorrow behind her usual indifference. Winston Candell, the new Warden of Arcus. Wouldn't that make it harder to get to Belva and Farren, to get our ancient and kill the natural-born?

Her throat bobbed. "Interesting." Her face paled even more. Didn't think it was possible, but yeah. All the blue veins tracing her forehead magnified by a thousand. "And he would not be interested in a trade?"

Zander laughed—a bark too loud and disjointed to fit in our tranquil white oyster. "He doesn't give a damn about either one of us. All he cares about is killing you, like your people who helped us get here."

Not even her lips held any more color. "The Creation Lab?"

"That's what I said, isn't it?" Zander moved to snatch me away from the now lax hands.

I struggled for show, but what I really wanted to do was hug him and sob my gratefulness.

"You want the truth, take us there. If not, kill us now because I'm done. I'm over it."

"If you are wrong, I will make sure your death is not easy." Cassondra stumbled on the way to the door. "Follow me."

Not so calm now, are you?

I sure as hell wouldn't want to be on Winston's bad side. From how the five Protectors finally cracked a frown, they got it, too. Maybe they witnessed what Winston could do on Empyrean? *Yeah, keep thinking it, assholes.* If he could do that as a Protector, think what he could do as a Warden. The thought even scared me.

Lift after lift transported us through a myriad of wings, the capital's hive busy at work ruling the universe. They'd be surprised in a few minutes. We were about to shut it down. All of it.

Hallways blended into more hallways until we found ourselves in one that almost stole the courage from my bones. Blazing blue light smeared the iridescent glow that illuminated the rest of the compound. My heart filled and bled at the same time, my footsteps steering toward the glass-walled room until my hands pressed against the barricade. No one tried to stop me. I'd have killed anyone who dared.

Wilma crashed against the walls, her light angry and swirling–until I stood in front of the room. That zinging fire stopped its rampage, smashing up against my palms. So close. So close, I could imagine her scent. Vanilla. Feel her strong arms, soft and comforting. Hear her raspy voice.

Lena...

I opened eyes I hadn't remembered closing and lifted the cheek I hadn't remembered pressing against the glass. I heard my name again. She knew. She saw me, too.

Lena... Help me.

Strength, hot and searing, flooded my entire being. I bit my lip to keep from crying out, to prevent myself from screaming until someone listened, and nodded. *I'll save you, Wilma.*

Her light glowed brighter, and she moved away from her prison wall. No more crashing and swirling. Instead, she floated and pulsed in the middle of the room. Waiting for me.

I swiped at the tears on my cheeks and turned to Cassondra. "You'll let her go, too."

Pale and almost fragile-looking, she shook her head. "She is payment for your sins, Tainted. She goes nowhere."

Before I killed her, I'd make sure she suffered. "I guess we'll see, won't we?"

CHAPTER 34

LENA

Welcomed Betrayal

Security in the lab was tight. Scan upon scan met with Cassondra's retina as machines swarmed above our heads, bleeping and ticking. One stopped in front of Zander, bouncing off his chest with loud screeches. His hand cinched tighter around mine.

Cassondra moved to his side. "You hold energy, Guide."

Zander shrugged even as sweat beaded at his hairline. "A few rowdy people in Heterodox we had to take care of. Planned to give it to Winston after we were done killing you."

"Your plans have changed." Her anger and misery couldn't hide, no matter how pleasant her demeanor. She wasn't as skilled as her late brother. "Our people will be sure to dispel you of your burden."

"Makes no difference to me." Zander stabbed her with hate. "But he'll still come after you."

She swallowed, her throat dancing. The doors in front of us opened after the machines zipped away. Zander tugged on my hand and moved forward, his palm sweaty.

The lab, a bigger, more wretched version of Drea's lab, stung our eyes. Chambers, resembling where Peter's body-double lay, were more like holding tanks with human carapaces piled on top of each other. Faceless, hairless bodies treated like wrenches or hammers, tools used to control the universe. Tubes from floor to ceiling ignited with thousands of pulsating orbs, globs of souls waiting in an assembly line for bodies. Madness, all of it screamed of complete and utter madness.

I forced my stunned attention away from the tubes to the far left corner of the room—where Drea sat with her back to us, punching at a keyboard, seemingly oblivious to our invasion into her madhouse. She wore a contego suit, its green glow matching some of the orbs battering against the tube's walls.

Zander took his hand from mine and waved toward Drea. "There you go. Now get us the hell out of here."

Cassondra's eyes filled with tears and her mouth fell open. "Impossible."

Shock sprung through my anger.

Drea tapped the keyboard a few more seconds before standing to meet us. She pressed a finger to her wrist and smiled. "You seem surprised, my love."

Cassondra backed up against the wall. "No... You... Drea?"

What?

Then everything became clear. *Avery was not willing to do what needed to be done—I was.* No wonder Drea never got caught, and no surprise she was able to build a state-of-the-art home in the middle of nowhere without any unwanted attention. How Peter existed without questions from Synod members.

She did what needed to be done.

Drea rushed to palm Cassondra under her nose, knocking the grieving woman to the ground. She then snatched a gun from her holster faster than my eyes could track the movement while tossing another in Zander's direction. In seconds, fire lit up the room. I ducked behind a nearby table, the same kind of morbid creation table in Drea's house, trying to find some sort of weapon.

Anything. Medical instruments, shining and lethal, glinted on a connected side table. I snatched up a scalpel-looking thing.

After one last deep breath and a silent *Holy fuck!*, I shot out from behind the table and headed straight for Zander, who blasted at the Protectors from the center of the room, totally exposed. He brought down two quick, his aim as sharp as ever. Drea managed to hit one before Cassondra jumped up enraged, tackling Drea to the floor.

The other two Protectors kept right on firing while talking into their wrists, bringing more people down here. I made it a foot away from Zander, and one of the Protectors aimed at him from behind the shield of a holding tank.

"Zander, look out!"

Too late. Just as the bullet left the guy's barrel, the knife flung from my hand, catching the Protector in the neck. His blood spurted everywhere, smearing the round window of the tank, masking the bodies inside. But his dying didn't interest me. Zander's living did.

I held onto him as he stumbled to the ground, his gun still firing, finally hitting the last Protector. As soon as I made sure his head wouldn't bounce off the hard floor, I examined his wound.

Soul-stealer, soul-stealer... A little object lodged in his leg that would steal Zander and Tarek away from me.

"Stay with me, Zander. *Please stay with me.*" I ripped his pant leg, my fingers not getting at the bullet fast enough. I'd dig it out if I had to.

"Lena...I'm good. *Everything* is good."

Relief gushed through my veins. Flesh wound. A scratch.

I crawled up to gather him in my arms, dragging him behind another holding tank, hiding him as best I could. "You're alive...*You're alive...*" I smacked his shoulder. "Why the hell didn't you find cover?" Tears and spit landed on his face when I stopped hitting him to press my lips against his temple, squeezing the skin on his chest, above his heart. *They're alive.*

"Go. I'm good. Kill that bitch. Kill her." His fist clenched my shirt, his eyes seeing right into my soul.

Yeah.

A boom reverberated outside of the room, shaking the floor. Distant cries leaked into the lab.

I smiled. Our Cavalry was here.

My kiss moved to his mouth, my lips lingering for a moment. Alive. "Stay here."

"I got nowhere else to be." He shoved his gun in my hands. "One shot, through the back of the head."

I checked the clip, three bullets left. Two more than I needed. Perfect. Torturing her wouldn't be a luxury I had now, but I'd take this.

Time to end at least one part of the nightmare.

I snuck out from behind the tank, keeping low to the ground. When I found Drea pinned to the wall and Cassondra's hand up, holding her there, I slowed down. As much as I wanted Cassondra dead, I had to remember she was pretty hard to kill. I slipped closer to another metal table and grabbed a knife.

"Why...? I gave you *everything*." Cassondra moved closer, her hand shaking and voice quavering as she kept her hold on Drea. Telekinetic power didn't last forever and it took heavy concentration–a lesson learned being around Winston and Wilma. Drea wouldn't be on that wall forever, and I couldn't waste the opportunity to end it while Cassondra mourned her lover's betrayal.

A smile played on Drea's lips. She told us her brainwaves read like a sociopath. I believed her. Not one tremor. Not one tell. While Cassondra crumbled into a heartbroken mess, Drea didn't struggle against the wall. She had either no fear of dying or a huge fear of living.

Fractured Energy

I moved in closer.

Another boom rocked the lab, debris as fine as dust swaying from the ceiling to the ground. Drea slipped a fraction, and her eyes darted in my direction. That one mistake cost me the advantage.

I flung the knife, putting all my strength behind it. Drea fell to the ground and the knife stopped midair.

I raised my gun.

Cassondra swung her hand, knocking it from my grip. "You think you can kill me?" Tears stained her face. The put-together woman in my nightmares, the one who shot Wilma with no effort, was close to breaking. But she would make sure I paid first.

From the corner of my eye, I noticed Drea rushing back to the computer, smacking the keyboard, talking into a device on her wrist. The plan needed more time.

I'd have to give it to them.

I tested my fingers, my toes. Everything worked, nothing frozen. Cassondra was strong, but not as strong as Winston, or even Wilma. I cleared my throat. "We can end this, right now. No one else has to get hurt." I tamped down the air, my voice as soothing as I could get it.

She produced a gun from the folds of her robe. "I don't care about anyone else." The barrel of her soul-stealer whipped around toward Drea.

I leapt.

Another boom, followed by louder screams.

I landed on Cassondra's back, tackling her to the ground, and slammed her head against the unforgiving floor. Boom after boom pummeled the compound like the grand finale on the Fourth of July. We all flopped and struggled, but Drea was alive, Cassondra's bullet embedded in the wall behind her–and the monitors crowding the walls went black.

Drea ran to me, the smile shining on her face a cross between psychotic and effervescent. "It's over, Lena. It's all gone. All of it."

As she spoke, the tubes holding all those souls burst, releasing thousands, blinding us as they shot through the crumbling rubble and chaos.

Free.

All of them.

We both tore our gazes away from the light when the doors to the lab blew off. And there stood my freedom. Farren, Oren, Erin, and Winston. My warriors. Drea stumbled to them, crying as a smile shined on her lips.

Without even thinking about it, I pushed off Cassondra's unconscious body and staggered toward them, screaming or laughing, I had no idea. I cried when Zander limped out from behind the tank with bodies now disintegrated. No more biobots. No more. Erin rushed to him, moving to lodge her shoulder under his arm, holding him up. Her eyes shined with tears, too.

Seriously, how did I miss that?

Farren picked me up and swung me around. "Why are you always getting yourself into trouble, kid?" He smoothed my hair with a shaky hand, kissing the top of my head.

I laughed, not having a thing to say to that. Finally, we'd leave here, bring Tarek back, get Wil–

Oh, no.

Oh, no!

I heaved Farren away and did a frantic search of the lab. She wasn't unconscious. "Where did she go?"

Drea met my eyes, her smile disappearing as terror leaked into her face. She turned to the gaping exit door by the containment units.

I swallowed the panic and found Winston in the crowd. I pointed at Zander and Erin. "Take them and Drea to the cabin." My voice broke. "Bring Tarek back."

"We got about ten minutes before this place is ash. Time to leave–for all of us."

No. I wouldn't leave. No until I had everyone. "Ten minutes is enough."

"She ain't going nowhere, Tainted. Oren has the place rigged tight. It'll be smoke soon. *You won.*"

I leaned to the side to eyeball Oren. He shrugged with his gun up and ready for a fight. "Looks like they were right not to want me to come along."

"Well, I'm glad you did." I turned back to Winston. "Please, take them and go. Winston...*please.* It's not Cassondra I'm after."

He drilled me with a death stare for about five seconds before nodding. His hand came up and waved toward Drea. She flew into his arms as booms and screaming still polluted the air. "You know where Wilma's at?"

I was already out of the room, Farren and Oren on my heels. "Yeah, I know exactly where she is."

Everywhere we turned, shots fired at us, even those who worked the computers before had guns drawn, shooting at–my God.

Heterodox invaded their evil tower. Oren started his rebellion, after all.

Those emotionless Synod zombies no longer existed. Everyone who gave us no thought when coming down here with Cassondra now fought for their lives. Funny how true death could wake someone from a stupor.

People who didn't match the robed Synod Guides or the contego-wearing Protectors flooded the halls, war cries tripping from their pierced lips as tattooed arms strained under the kick of their weapons. Every screen that filled the walls was now showing static. No more helpless worlds monitored under callous scrutiny.

No more Wilma flashing warnings to potential traitors.

I ran harder.

To my left, Farren kept shooting, no chaos swarming his face. Oren, on the other hand, shot with a bright, crazed smile on his, killing any and all Synod members–even the ones cowering behind desks, terrified with hands up in surrender.

I'd worry about his bloodlust later. Someone else needed me more, and we had about eight minutes left.

As soon as we hit the right hallway, much of the screaming and shooting remained in the distance. I stopped at the beginning of the hall, my flanks following suit. "You two stay here. Cover me."

"Don't think so, kid."

I pointed to Wilma's prison, and repeated his motto, "In and out. Easy peasy."

His full lips curved in a slight grin. "Is that right?"

I nodded. "Seven minutes."

Oren came from behind after popping some woman running from her office.

Not one ounce of mercy.

"Hurry." Oren shoved me forward. "Six minutes."

Right.

I grabbed his extra gun from his waist holster. "You and I are gonna talk later."

He grinned. Even crazy he was gorgeous. "Looking forward to it. Now, go."

No more time needed wasted. I slid against the glass wall to the left that encased offices. All the same, all simple and efficient, except for one. My focus on that room, I pushed forward. Cassondra would be in there. She would. God, I hoped she would. If she didn't die, this…this way of life would never end. Revenge didn't want her dead. Nope, just the strong desire for relief.

Thunderclaps moved the floors as another succession of explosions erupted.

Five more minutes.

I cocked my gun, a soul-stealer, and inched closer to the room. No sounds of people or computers interrupted the silence. I'd take screaming and shooting over this quiet any day. I didn't trust it at all.

Speeding up, I barged into the prison, Oren and Farren shielding me with their firing guns from a surprise attack. Getting in the room was easy, all security in the compound crumbling with the system.

My stomach fell.

Empty.

No.

I whipped around searching every corner, every small nook. Nothing. She was gone. Cassondra beat me.

"Did you think I'd let you have her?"

Fear rode up my spine. I stood and turned to the doorway. Wilma's light, again stuck inside a bullet, small and cramped, burned blue between Cassondra's pointer finger and thumb. Her face, a chaotic mess of tears and pain, with blood dripping from her forehead, ripped at my conscience. *So, she could feel.*

I straightened, my conscience clearing when I focused on Wilma. I lifted my gun, aiming for Cassondra's head. Four minutes.

"If you kill me, I will press the release and her energy will disintegrate. You took my brother, threatened our entire universe, and stole my..." Her voice cracked, and she swallowed. "Drea."

I had nothing to say to her except, "Bullshit."

I pulled the trigger.

Her brain blew out the back of her head and smeared the glass wall. The soul-stealer bullet lodged in her splayed skull went from dull silver to flaming white. Her energy, trapped there forever.

I caught Wilma's bullet as it slipped from Cassondra's dead fingers. Instantly, warmth filled my chest and my soul mended. Love poured through me as the bullet glowed in my palm.

Lena...

Booms broke the trance, the whole room falling apart. The ceiling cracked and the floor split.

Time was up.

I fell to the ground, cradling Wilma's energy against me as I crawled into the hallway. Farren ran toward me, panic on his face as he lifted me up, grabbing under my arm. "*Run.*"

All the lifts between the levels were in shambles, but that didn't stop us. Oren leapt down to a platform of tumbling stone and glass and reached for me. I didn't have to jump to meet him. Farren shoved me off the now-cliff of offices and defunct computer systems. That was as far as the three of us got. There was no way out.

Except one.

Like so many other Protectors around us, Farren lifted his hand in the air, as did Oren. Without hesitation, I jumped into Farren's hands, falling dust and spraying water from fire systems coating our bodies, screams from the dying following us.

"See you soon." Oren was gone in a matter of seconds, pulled through to some other world.

I didn't want to leave Exemplar. Not yet. Not without Tarek.

But...choices. I pulled on Farren's neck until his ear touched my lips. Amid the screeching and death, I whispered, "Take us to Empyrean."

He pulled back and searched my face with his dark eyes.

I held up Wilma's light. "Please."

He nodded, bringing me closer. His fist opened and wind rushed down on our heads. One more explosion rendered the air, piercing my ears. After the blast, high-pitched screeching erupted in my eardrums. Office shrapnel crashed down on our perch and sent us flying. Warm blood trickled down my temple.

Farren's tear ripped wider as the debris beneath us gave way.

Then we were sailing.

Lynn Vroman

CHAPTER 35

LENA

Wilma

Silence shrouded me except for the pinging attacking my eardrums. All around us, pandemonium erupted. Blood and sweat invading my eyes blurred everything, but the direness of the situation was all too clear: defectors.

Portal after portal released terrified Exemplians into the field beyond Teenesee's manse. Some had guns, others clutched people. Some even clung to children in Synod robes, all the young faces at least five years old. I looked up, holding Wilma's energy tight to my heart.

Oh my God...

Calm skies stretching across the very last floating village in eyeshot ripped open with flashes of light. So many people...

They were right to be afraid. Empyrean's army stormed the field, coming from the drawbridge and the forest behind. Horses leapt from the edges of the floating villages, not breaking speed as they landed on the solid ground beneath, their riders' weapons drawn and firing. They wouldn't stop to wonder after what happened last year. They would kill. Exemplians weren't welcomed here.

Farren yanked me from the ground. He spoke, but...the pinging...

I got the gist when he tugged on my hand, his feet already carrying him toward Teenesee's manse. He didn't raise his gun at any Empyreans, nor did he take out the shell-shocked refugees. We just ran in a zigzag motion, trying not to get shot.

Ping, ping, ping.

Everything played in slow motion, my ears screaming with that incessant ringing. I held Wilma's light so tight my nails broke the skin on my palm. I wouldn't lose her. Not after all of this, she wouldn't end up trapped in the bullet, buried in a field.

I slammed into Farren's back, and we both fell to the ground when a horse reared up in front of us the moment we touched the smooth surface of the bridge. Farren heaved my body out of the way before two iron-shoed hooves crushed my skull. Still I heard nothing. But I didn't need my ears.

Pit, commander of Teenesee's army.

I scrambled farther away from Pit's angry horse as Farren pleaded with him, grabbing the horses bridle with one hand, and pointing at me with the other. Farren waved a hand at all the dying Exemplians, some children now standing alone in the field sobbing.

Jesus, this had to end. All the killing…it needed to stop.

Finally, it did.

Pit yelled across the field, touched his ear and spoke, and almost instantly, all around us no more bullets punctured the air. Empyrean soldiers corralled those they didn't kill, some even jumping from their horses to comfort the crying children.

I fell to my knees, bringing Wilma's light to my cheek. *It's over, Wilma. It's finally over.*

∞ ∞ ∞

Fractured Energy

Everything changed inside Teenesee's home. The main rooms used to be bright and airy while the ground swayed underneath.

Now, windows were latched tight, candles the only light source. Ghosts of the past–paintings of Teenesee's daughters cloaked in darkness on the walls–haunted every room.

No, not different. Not since the last time I'd been here. Everything was the same. Even without the threat of war, she mourned still. I should've come sooner.

Pit led us into the room where I first met Oren and the others Winston scrounged up to help fight. So much fear then, so much hope, too. Now...Now only exhaustion. I wanted to go home.

I wanted Tarek.

Pit spoke, and I watched his lips: *She'll be here soon.*

Farren nodded and clapped the commander on the back, smiling. Of course, he smiled. We managed to make it out of a battle–all of us. My fingers tightened around the glowing bullet.

Pit nodded to me, and I hugged him. "Thank you."

He cringed and pulled away. After a slight bow, he left.

Farren turned to me and nudged my shoulder. His lips read, *Why you yelling?*

I pointed to my ears and shook my head.

His lips: *Well, shit.*

I shrugged with a grin. If the ringing would've shut up, the not hearing thing might've been all right.

All smiles disappeared when Teenesee walked into the room. Her face, still beautiful, was drawn and tired. But everything about her screamed power even as the misery shadowed her dark face. She went straight for me, taking me into her arms. Her body trembled, and a patch of wetness seeped through my tangled hair where her face rested on top of my head.

I should've come sooner...

Her chest hummed and vibrated, and her lips moved in my hair. Farren's hand landed on my shoulder and squeezed. Whatever they talked about, the conversation lasted for seconds before Teenesee's palms covered my ears. Heat radiated from her skin, soothing the pinging until the room came to life. A fire crackled, floorboards creaked with the sway, and Teenesee's soft crying broke my heart.

I looked up to find her smiling through her sadness, the topaz of her eyes shining brighter. Her palms slid from my ears to my shoulders. "Hello, my dear friend. I've missed you."

"I'm so sorry. I-I should've..."

She pressed a finger to my lips. "You are here now. That is all that matters." Her attention went to my clenched fist, and she gasped. "You've brought her here."

I opened my hand, and Wilma's blue light glowed in the room. "I thought...maybe... She's so broken, and..."

"Give her to me."

Never thought it'd be hard to hand Wilma over to Teenesee. My plan–Tarek's plan–was to save her, bring her here. But I wanted to cling to her light, absorb it, afraid if I let her go, the hole would empty again, leave me broken and incapable of moving on.

Wilma, no matter what, could always read my heart, though, even when I didn't know what it said.

Let me go...

A cry broke free from my throat, but I did as she asked. "Okay."

I love you. I'll always love you.

Tears, so many tears these past couple years. "I love you, too."

Fractured Energy

As soon as the bullet touched Teenesee's hand, Wilma's light escaped its prison–and absorbed into the Warden's chest. I touched Teenesee's heart. Its strong beat reassured me, my hole never returning. Complete. Finally.

Teenesee placed her hand over mine. "I will heal her, and I will make sure her next life is a happy one. I promise you."

Damn tears. Damn them. "I can never repay you."

"But you have. You've ended Exemplar's control, have you not?" She tilted my chin until our eyes met. "Your fight, your struggle, it will have an end, but not now. Those who still dwell in that world, who have known such power, will not bow down so easily. You must prepare yourself."

"I'm so tired."

"I have faith in you and yours, my friend."

I stepped back until I hit Farren's chest. His strong arms came around me. "You got me, kid. You always got me."

Yeah, I had faith in mine, too. But…"What about all those people? Children, the scared?"

"Refugees will be welcomed in this world, and many others, I assume. They are innocents. We will not harm them." Teenesee moved to the window and pressed a button. The shutters rose and a fresh breeze rushed into the room. She signaled for me. "Look."

Soldiers carried children, bandaged the wounded. Empyrean citizens ran off the bridges leading to the fields, carrying supplies.

Peace.

"Now go, Lena. Go to your people. Tell them what you see here, and plead they do the same. If my people can look past grief to see innocence, so can yours. If we are unified, if we show mercy, we will be an unbreakable front to those on Exemplar who are not yet ready to relinquish their power."

I gripped Farren's hand, his strength flooding into me. "We will, Teenesee…we will."

Not an hour later, Farren had an arm in the air and the other around my waist.

"We need to go back to Exemplar. Tarek." *Please be alive. Please…*

Farren raised his hand higher, splaying his fingers, the tear slicing an inch of atmosphere. "He's home, along with everyone else."

Hope burned inside my heart, causing my fingers to shake around the grip on Farren's suit. "He's alive?"

"Yeah, kid."

"You're sure?"

He lowered his hand and tapped his temple. "That's what my lady's telling me."

I buried my face in his chest, so, so tired. So relieved. "Thank you."

"Ah, you should know. Tarek…he…"

I looked up to meet his worried gaze. "What? What is it?" Panic teased the hope.

He sighed, deep, but his face softened. "Nothing. I…I'm just here for you. Remember that, okay?"

"Yeah, sure, okay. Me too, Ginger."

He straightened, his hand shooting back up. "All right. Ready?"

"Absolutely." I smiled up at him as the tear opened. "So…Daddy, huh?"

A huge grin lit up his handsome face, all the tension from a few seconds ago gone. "Crazy, right?"

I leaned my cheek against his pounding heart. "The craziest."

CHAPTER 36

TAREK

One Last Promise

Cold metal pierced his skin, but he couldn't move to escape it. Nothing worked. Nothing would listen.

Move!

Muddled voices bled into his ears like fog, thick and incoherent. What were they saying? Who was saying it?

The cold, like razors scratching his flesh.

Then pain.

Not the cold–not physical. Pain so acute, so potent, it convinced him moving wasn't what he wanted anymore.

Death. Complete and permanent death.

Memories flooded in, waging war with his will.

He should've never taken her there. Lena was dead because he couldn't–*I should've never taken her.* They killed her, took her energy while he managed to get recycled. In a fake body made with machines.

His life should have never touched hers.

Hot moisture leaked from his eyes and agony ripped from his throat.

Why? Why had he ever searched for her? A man who wasn't…real. A man who could never give her anything but pain and sadness and disappointment. A man who took everything away from her and had nothing to give back.

Hands clamped on his shoulders when despair gave his limbs enough strength to move. "Easy, big man. You're all right. Stay calm…"

Winston. Another fake human, given enough power to control everyone and everything around him. False power. Manufactured.

Tarek curled into a ball, no energy left in his body to fight against the black.

Why did I take her there?

Dead.

Dead.

Dead.

Because he could never say no.

"Listen, Tarek...we gotta get out of here. They're gonna find us..."

He curled tighter, wishing the air would swallow him up and end it. Maybe if he didn't open his eyes. Maybe he'd still be dead if he just kept his eyes closed. "Don't care."

"Well, I do. I don't wanna have to, but if you make me force you off that table, I ain't got a problem with it."

Maybe if he could find the knife that killed him, plunge it back into his heart. "Leave me."

Silence. Empty silence.

A blanket fell over him. Someone tucked the edges around his waist. "Goddamnit. You're gonna make me do it, aren't you?"

Wherever he went, this life wouldn't last much longer. He couldn't live again knowing she wasn't.

Another hand squeezed his shoulder. "You know this is a side effect of...recycling. It'll pass. Just fight through it."

Zander.

Tarek opened his eyes to meet the dark, worried face of the Guide. "How many times have you died?"

Zander shook his head. "Never."

"Then how would you know?" He closed his eyes, done with all of it. Done. "Leave."

Not real. He wasn't real and Lena…dead. Why did they bring him back?

The air crackled and wind kicked up. His body lifted, but he didn't struggle. Even if he had the energy, he wouldn't try to fight against Winston's power. It'd be pointless. Tarek would end it soon enough.

But then Winston spoke. "Lena's alive, and she's waiting for you. Just thought you should know."

A sliver of light erased some of the despair. Alive. *Alive.*

He'd hold onto life, just so his death wouldn't destroy her.

But as the portal pulled him away from that cold, metal table, he made one last vow.

Lena could no longer be his flaw.

He loved her too much.

Lynn Vroman

CHAPTER 37

LENA

Forever

He wasn't there. Everyone else waited for us, but...Tarek didn't stand in the middle of our village when the portal spit us out. All the vivid trees, the squid, the familiar scents, all of it dulled compared to the ache growing in my chest.

He wasn't there.

Maybe Belva lied. Maybe Drea couldn't bring him back.

Maybe...

As soon as Farren let me go, I fell to my knees. Tired. My body too tired to fight the panic bubbling in my gut and squeezing my lungs.

Please...please...please.

Gentle hands rubbed my back. "Bad stuff out, good stuff in, *chica*. You can do it. Breathe."

I wheezed, wanting–I wanted Tarek. That was all. Nothing else.

Winston squatted in front of me and tilted his head. He tipped my chin when my attention went to the ground. "Oh, no you don't, Tainted. Not after everything you been through. You ain't allowed to check out, you heard?"

People crowded me: Zander, Erin, Mom, Jake, Oren, Grace, Belva, Farren, Peter...everyone, including Katherine's husband and those who had lived here for over a year. Everyone but *Him*.

349

"She–Belva lied. She lied." So close to losing it...so close.

"She didn't lie. He lives."

Numb lips barely let me speak. "Wh-what?"

"You done with this? Wanna start breathing now?"

He lived. I turned into Shaina's arms, her soothing voice calming the storm. *Deep breath in, bad stuff out.*

One more deep breath and I pushed away from her with shaky hands as I looked around the circle crowding me. "Where is he?"

Mom's eyes filled as she reached for me. "Oh, baby."

I smacked her away. No. Somebody was gonna talk. I stood on trembling legs, scanning my bubble until my attention fell on Winston. "*Where is he?*"

He moved from behind Shaina and headed for the woods. "Walk with me, Tainted."

Stumbling from the crowd, ignoring everyone, I followed.

Winston didn't say a word until we were deep into the woods. Squid still guarded the village, but it wasn't necessary. Not one refugee slipped from a portal as far as I could see. Doubt Arcus was high on any escape options list. Right then, I didn't care.

"He's alive."

"You said that. That's all you said." My voice sounded like a choking seal, my lungs not in the mood to cooperate yet.

He sighed and stopped to lean against a tree trunk. "When Drea dropped the how-Exemplians-are-created bomb on y'all, she ever explain how screwed up coming back to life is?"

"No?" Rage settled in, better than the panic, easier to handle than fear. "Drea has more explaining to do, huh? Well, let's go get some answers." I headed for the village.

"Where you going?"

"Where do you think?"

I froze, and against my will, my body swooshed back to Winston. "You need to control that temper."

"Let me go."

"She ain't here, Tainted. She stayed behind, all set on rebellion."

That took the fight right out of me. "What?"

He released his hold, and I landed on wobbly legs. "Oren's on his way there, too, but he wanted to say goodbye first, to Grace…and you."

"What?"

"You gotta stop saying that. I know you can hear me." He pushed off the tree and walked over to me, sliding a finger down my cheek. "Things change, Tainted. People change. Especially after they're thrown back into life. And what he's been through in the past three years? That's gonna eat at him." He backed up and held out his hands. "I mean, damn! The man just found out he was created in a lab. He's…broken."

"Where is he, Winston?" I grabbed his hand and squeezed. "Please."

"Go back to Earth. Take the kid. Zander and Erin want to go with you, too. Give Tarek time. Trust me on this one."

I lurched backward. No, this wasn't how things were supposed to end. Tarek…he'd never… "Where?"

He hung his head. "It could take months–years–before he can handle living again." His gaze lifted to mine. "You sure this is what you want?"

I stared right at him, not answering. The answer should've been obvious.

"His cabin."

I ran.

His door opened, and my hand stayed on the wood until my eyes adjusted to the dark. The one window had a thick blanket covering it, but I never needed light to guide me to him. "Tarek?"

His bed creaked and his big body turned so that he faced the wall. He said nothing.

Not good enough.

I rushed to the bunk and lay beside him, feeling his chest move up and down, reveling in the life flowing through him. He lived. Whatever else going on we'd handle, nothing else mattered beyond the warmth of his body, his beating heart. I pressed my face into his back, breathing in his scent.

"We never should have gone to Shalen."

His voice jumped out in the dark, causing tears to gush down my cheeks. *He lives.* "It doesn't matter now. None of it matters. We're finally free."

His breath hitched and his chest heaved.

I'd guide him through the pain, as he did for me. I held tighter as sobs wracked his body.

"I...I should've stayed away...three years ago...I should have left you alone."

"No."

"You deserve better than me. You deserve someone...real."

"Tarek—"

"Leave, Lena. You have to go."

This isn't happening! My hands kneaded his stomach as if somehow I could steal all the hurt and sorrow and guilt. What was this? *What the hell was this?*

"I'm not going anywhere." I didn't recognize my voice. It shouldn't sound desperate and ragged. He lived! What about happily ever after? Why couldn't we ever have that?

He shoved my hands away and pushed me from the bed without even looking at me. "Go."

Too stunned to move, I kept my ass on the floor, shaking my head.

This isn't happening...

Finally, he turned. His eyes shined with tears I could see even with the stingy light sneaking in from the open door. So much misery scarred his beautiful face, so much...

"Get. Out."

Didn't he see it? Couldn't he feel it? We were made for each other. His face, though...all that pain, as if death still lingered in his soul.

"No. No, I won't. I can't." *Stop it, stop it!*

He shook his head. "I...don't want to see you again."

His words bit into my chest, stabbing my heart. "You don't mean that. You—"

"*Please.*"

I stared at his face, searching for something—anything—that denied his plea.

Nothing.

Give him time...

Yes. He lived, and whatever it took to make him whole again, I'd do it–even if it killed me.

So, I stood and went to him.

I kissed his unresponsive lips.

And I walked away.

But one more thing, one thing he had to know as he fought what sorrow ate him, what I couldn't help with. The same thing he promised me when I couldn't escape the black. "I'll wait for you, Tarek. I'll wait for you forever."

ENERGY REBORN

COMING SOON

Book 4 of the Energy Series

Lynn Vroman

GLOSSARY

Arcus- A world deplete of humans, with an evolution that falls behind many others. This world's highest evolved species is giant tree squid. Also, the vivid color permeating the world is "contagious" and transmits to those humans who happen to go there.

Contego suit- An Exemplian uniform that protects from dangers found in all the worlds.

Cycle- Each life a person lives is considered a cycle.

Desis- A common language spoken in many worlds, including Earth.

Dimensions/Worlds- Dimensions are worlds connected to each other with dimension lines. Each dimension is in a different stage of evolution, with some more advanced than others.

Dimension lines- Intangible lines, akin to electrical currents, separating each world. Only Protectors have the ability to open these lines to other worlds. In some cases, when a Warden is strong enough, the lines can be bled between worlds, or erased, for short periods of time.

Empyrean- A world more evolved than Earth but not as advanced as Exemplar. The villages float over lush fields and streams. This world is as close to utopian as possible.

Energy- The soul

Exemplar- A world that is more evolved than any other world known. Humans from this world are more advanced, as well. Exemplar is responsible for manipulating the energy circulation throughout the entire universe. Only the most "privileged" energy is brought to Exemplar to live a cycle.

Guide- An advanced person from Exemplar who has the ability to read energies and transport them to other worlds. Also, their energies are able to leave their corporeal form and travel to other dimensions. Some are more advanced than others, depending on how many cycles they have lived in Exemplar.

Pairing- The act of one Guide and one Protector being matched together in Exemplar. The Pairing helps Protectors know if their Guides are in danger.

Protector- An advanced person from Exemplar who has the telekinetic ability to open lines between worlds. They are able to travel across world lines in their corporeal form, unlike Guides. Their duty is to protect Guides as they collect energy from other worlds. As with Guides, some Protectors are more advanced than others, depending on how many cycles they have lived in Exemplar.

Synod- Exemplar's governing branch

Synod authority- Exemplar's army

Tainted- 1. (n) An Exemplian traitor
         2. (v) To be treacherous

ABOUT THE AUTHOR

Lynn Vroman

Born in Pennsylvania, Lynn spent most of her childhood, especially during math class, daydreaming. The main result that came from honing her imagination skills was brilliantly failing algebra. Today, she still spends an obscene amount of time in her head, only now she writes down all the cool stuff.

With a degree in English Literature, Lynn used college as an excuse to read for four years straight. She lives in the Pocono Mountains with her husband, raising the four most incredible human beings on the planet. She writes young adult novels, both fantasy and contemporary.

OTHER WORKS

BY LYNN VROMAN

Young Adult Contemporary Romance

Macy Diaz has managed childhood friend Jeb Porter's crush for years. However, his infatuation turns to obsession, even putting a kid in the hospital just for hitting on her. In the past, Macy brushed it off, explained his bizarre acts away. But now she harbors a secret. She's in love...with Jeb's sister, Rachel.

By some miracle, Rachel loves Macy back, and despite the small minds polluting their sleepy southern town, they're sticking together. Unfortunately, making sure Jeb never grows suspicious proves harder every day—until everything falls apart.

As a sick, unstable Jeb starts to threaten all Macy values, she is reminded of what has always been perfectly clear. Macy belongs to him, only him, and he won't let her go. Ever.

If only Macy could've loved Jeb, she wouldn't have to worry about surviving him now.